THE TWILIGHT WATCH

In Russia, the three volumes of the *Night Watch* trilogy have sold over two million hardcovers between them. *The Night Watch* has been adapted into an internationally successful film, which has been distributed round the world. Sergei Lukyanenko lives in Moscow.

Also by Sergei Lukyanenko

The Night Watch
The Day Watch

THE TWILIGHT WATCH

SERGEI LUKYANENKO

Translated from the Russian by Andrew Bromfield

WILLIAM HEINEMANN: LONDON

Published by William Heinemann, 2007

4 6 8 10 9 7 5 3

First published in Russian under the title Дневой Дозор
by Издателъство ACT, 2004

William Heinemann
Random House, 20 Vauxhall Bridge Road,
London SW1V 2SA

www.randomhouse.co.uk

Addresses for companies within The Random House Group Limited can be found at: www.randomhouse.co.uk

The Random House Group Limited Reg. No. 954009

A CIP catalogue record for this book
is available from the British Library

ISBN TPB: 9780434014446
HB: 9780434016105

Typeset by Palimpsest Book Production Ltd,
Grangemouth, Stirlingshire
Printed and bound in Great Britain by
CPI Mackays, Chatham ME5 8TD

This text is of no relevance to the cause of the Light.

The Night Watch

This text is of no relevance to the cause of the Dark.

The Day Watch

Story One

NOBODY'S TIME

PROLOGUE

THE GENUINE OLD communal courtyards in Moscow's apartment blocks disappeared sometime between the eras of the two popular bards Vysotsky and Okudzhava.

It's a strange business. Even after the revolution, when for purposes of the struggle against 'the slavery of the kitchen', they actually did away with kitchens in housing blocks, nobody tried to get rid of the courtyards. Every proud Stalinist block that displayed its Potemkin façade to the broad avenue beside it had to have a courtyard – large and green, with tables and benches, with a yard-keeper scraping the asphalt clean every morning. Then the age of five-storey sectional housing arrived – and the courtyards shrivelled and became bare, the yard-keepers who had been so grave and staid were replaced by yard women, who regarded it as their duty to give little boys who got up to mischief a clip round the ear and upbraid residents who came home drunk. But even so, the courtyards still hung on.

And then, as if in response to the increased tempo of life, the houses stretched upwards. From nine storeys to sixteen, or even twenty-four. And as if each building was allocated the right only to a certain volume of space, rather than an area of ground, the courtyards withered right back to the entrances and the entrances opened their doors straight onto the public streets, while the male and female yard-keepers disappeared and were replaced by communal services functionaries.

Okay, so the courtyards came back later, but by no means to all the buildings, as if they'd taken offence at being treated so scornfully before. The new courtyards were bounded by high walls, with fit, well-groomed young men sitting in the gate lodges, and car parks concealed under the English lawns. The children in these courtyards played under the supervision of nannies, the drunken residents were helped from their Mercedes and BMWs by bodyguards accustomed to dealing with anything, and the new yard-keepers tidied up the English lawns with German mowers.

This courtyard was one of the new ones.

The multistorey towers on the bank of the River Moscow were known throughout Russia. They were the capital's new symbol – replacing the faded Kremlin and the TsUM department store, which had become just an ordinary shop. The granite embankment with its own quayside, the entrances finished with Venetian plasterwork, the cafés and restaurants, the beauty salons and supermarkets and also, of course, the apartments with two or three hundred square metres of floor space. The new Russia probably needed a symbol like this – pompous and kitschy, like the thick gold chains that men wore round their necks during the period of initial accumulation of capital. And it didn't matter that most of the apartments that had been bought long ago were still standing empty, the cafés and restaurants were closed, waiting for better times to come, and the waves lapping against the concrete quayside were dirty.

The man strolling along the embankment on this warm summer evening had never worn a gold chain. He possessed a keen intuition that was more than adequate as a substitute for good taste.

He had switched his Chinese-made Adidas tracksuit in good time for a crimson club jacket and then been the first to ditch the crimson jacket in favour of a Versace suit. He was ahead of the game even in the sports that he played, having abandoned his tennis racket for mountain skis a whole month before all the Kremlin officials . . . even though at his age the pleasure he could get from skis was limited to standing on them.

He preferred to live in his mansion house in the Gorki-9 district, only visiting the apartment with the windows overlooking the river when he was with his lover.

But then, he was planning to get rid of his full-time lover – after all, no Viagra can conquer age, and conjugal fidelity was coming back into fashion.

His driver and bodyguards weren't standing near enough to hear what their employer was saying. But even if the wind did carry snatches of his words to their ears, what was so strange? Why shouldn't a man make conversation with himself as the working day was drawing to a close, standing all alone above the dancing waves? Where could you ever find a more sympathetic listener than your own self?

'Even so, I repeat my proposal . . .' the man said. 'I repeat it yet again.'

The stars were shining dimly through the city smog. On the far bank of the river, tiny lights were coming on in the tower blocks that had no courtyards. Only one in five of the beautiful lamps stretching along the quayside was lit – and that was only to humour the whim of the important man who had decided to take a stroll by the river.

'I repeat it yet again,' the man said in a quiet voice.

The water splashed against the embankment – and with it came the answer.

'It's impossible. Absolutely impossible.'

The man on the quayside was not surprised by the voice that came out of empty space. He nodded and asked:

'But what about vampires?'

'Yes, that's one possibility,' his invisible companion agreed. 'Vampires could initiate you. If you would be happy to exist as non-life . . . I won't lie, they don't like sunlight, but it's not fatal to them, and you wouldn't have to give up risotto with garlic . . .'

'Then what's the problem?' the man asked, involuntarily raising his hands to his chest. 'The soul? The need to drink blood?'

The void laughed quietly.

'Just the hunger. Eternal hunger. And the emptiness inside. You wouldn't like it, I'm sure.'

'What else is there?' asked the man.

'Werewolves,' the voice replied almost jocularly. 'They can initiate a man too. But werewolves are also one of the lower forms of Dark Others. Most of the time everything's fine . . . but when the frenzy comes over you, you won't be able to control yourself. Three or four nights each month. Sometimes more, sometimes less.'

'The new moon,' the man said with an understanding nod.

The void laughed again:

'No. Werewolves' frenzies aren't linked to the lunar cycle. You'd be able to sense the onset of the madness ten or twelve hours before the moment of transformation. But no one can draw up a precise timetable for you.'

'That won't do,' the man said frostily. 'I repeat my . . . request. I wish to become an Other. Not one of the lower Others who are overwhelmed by fits of bestial insanity. Not a Great Magician, involved in great affairs. A perfectly ordinary, rank-and-file Other . . . how does that classification of yours go? Seventh-grade?'

'It's impossible,' the night replied. 'You don't have the abilities of an Other. Not even the slightest trace. If you have no musical talent, you can be taught to play the violin. You can become a sportsman, even if you don't have any natural aptitude for it. But you can't become an Other. You're simply a different species. I'm very sorry.'

The man on the embankment laughed:

'Nothing is ever impossible. If the lowest form of Other is able to initiate human beings, then there must be some way a man can be turned into a magician.'

The dark night said nothing.

'In any case, I didn't say I wanted to be a Dark Other. I don't have the slightest desire to drink innocent people's blood and go chasing virgins through the fields, or laugh ghoulishly as I lay a curse on someone,' the man said testily. 'I would much rather do good deeds . . . and in general, your internal squabbles mean absolutely nothing to me.'

'That . . .' the night began wearily.

'It's your problem,' the man replied. 'I'm giving you one week. And then I want an answer to my request.'

'Request?' the night queried.

The man on the embankment smiled:

'Yes. So far I'm only asking.'

He turned and walked towards his car – a Russian Volga, the model that would be back in fashion again in about six months.

CHAPTER 1

EVEN IF YOU love your job, the last day of holiday always makes you feel depressed. Just one week earlier I'd been sunning myself on a nice clean Spanish beach, eating paella (to be quite honest, Uzbeki pilaff is better), drinking cold sangria in a little Chinese restaurant (how come the Chinese make the Spanish national drink better than the natives do?) and buying all sorts of rubbishy resort souvenirs in the shops.

But now it was summer in Moscow again – not exactly hot, but stifling and oppressive. And it was that final day of holiday, when you can't get your mind to relax any more, but it flatly refuses to function properly.

Maybe that was why I was glad when I got the call from Gesar.

'Good morning, Anton,' the boss began, without introducing himself. 'Welcome back. Did you know it was me?'

I'd been able to sense Gesar's calls for some time already. It was as if the ringing of the phone changed subtly, becoming more demanding and authoritative.

But I was in no rush to let the boss know that.

'Yes, Boris Ignatievich.'

'Are you alone?'

An unnecessary question. I was certain Gesar knew perfectly well where Svetlana was just then.

'Yes. The girls are at the dacha.'

'Good for them,' the boss sighed at the other end of the line, and an entirely human note appeared in his voice. 'Olga flew off on holiday this morning too . . . half the Watch staff are relaxing in southern climes . . . Do you think you could call round to the office straight away?'

Before I had time to answer, Gesar went on cheerily.

'Well, that's excellent! See you in forty minutes then.'

I really felt like calling Gesar a cheap poser – after I hung up, of course. But I kept my mouth shut. In the first place, the boss could hear what I said without any need of a telephone. And in the second – whatever else he might be, he was no cheap poser. He just didn't like wasting time. If I was about to say I'd be there in forty minutes, what was the point in listening to me say it?

And anyway, I was really glad I'd got the call. The day was already shot to hell in any case. It was still too early to tidy up the apartment – like any self-respecting man whose family is away, I only do that once, on the final day of bachelor life. And I definitely didn't feel like going round to see anyone or inviting anyone back to my place. So by far the most useful thing would be to go back to work a day early – that way, I could ask for time off with a clear conscience when I needed to.

Even though it wasn't the done thing for us to ask for time off.

'Thanks, boss,' I said with real feeling. I detached myself from the armchair, put down the book I hadn't finished, and stretched.

And then the phone rang again.

Of course, it would have been just like Gesar to ring and say: 'You're welcome!' But that definitely would have been cheap clowning.

'Hello!' I said in a very businesslike tone.

'Anton, it's me.'

'Sveta,' I said, sitting back down again. And suddenly I tensed up – Svetlana's voice sounded uneasy. Anxious. 'Sveta, has something happened to Nadya?'

'Everything's fine,' she replied quickly. 'Don't worry. Why don't you tell me how you've been getting on?'

I thought for a few seconds. I hadn't had any drinking parties, I hadn't brought any women back home, I wasn't drowning in refuse, I'd even been washing the dishes . . .

And then I realised.

'Gesar called. Just a moment ago.'

'What does he want?' Svetlana asked quickly.

'Nothing special. He asked me to turn up for work today.'

'Anton, I sensed something. Something bad. Did you agree? Are you going to work?'

'Why not? I've got nothing else to do.'

Svetlana was silent. Then she said reluctantly:

'You know, I felt a sort of pricking in my heart. Do you believe I can sense trouble?'

I laughed:

'Yes, Great One.'

'Anton, be serious, will you!' Svetlana was instantly uptight, the way she always got when I called her Great One. 'Listen to me . . . if Gesar asks you to do something, say no.'

'Sveta, if Gesar called me in, it means he wants to ask me to do something. It means he needs help. He says everyone's on holiday . . .'

'He needs more cannon fodder,' Svetlana snapped. 'Anton . . . never mind, you won't listen to me anyway. Just be careful.'

'Sveta, you don't seriously think that Gesar's going to put me in any danger, do you?' I said cautiously. 'I understand the way you feel about him . . .'

'Be careful,' said Svetlana. 'For our sake. All right?'

'All right,' I promised. 'I'm always very careful.'

'I'll call if I sense anything else,' said Svetlana. She seemed to have calmed down a bit. 'And you call, all right? If anything at all unusual happens, call. Okay?'

'Okay, I'll call.'

Svetlana paused for a few seconds, then before she hung up, she said:

'You ought to leave the Watch, third-grade Light Magician . . .'

It all ended on a suspiciously cheerful note, with a cheap jibe . . . Although we had agreed a long time ago not to discuss that subject – three years earlier, when Svetlana left the Night Watch. And we hadn't broken our promise once. Of course. I used to tell my wife about my work . . . at least, about the jobs that I wanted to remember. And she always listened with interest. But now she had come right out with it.

Could she really have sensed something bad?

Anyway, I got ready to go slowly and reluctantly. I put on a suit, then changed into jeans and a checked shirt, then thought 'to hell with it!' and got into my shorts and a black T-shirt with an inscription that said: 'My friend was clinically dead, but all he brought me from the next world was this T-shirt!' I might look like a German tourist, but at least I would retain the semblance of a holiday mood in front of Gesar.

Eventually I left the building with just twenty minutes to spare. I had to flag down a car and feel out the probability lines – and then tell the driver which streets to take so we wouldn't hit any traffic jams.

The driver accepted my instructions hesitantly, he obviously had serious doubts.

But we got there on time.

* * *

The lifts weren't working – there were guys in blue overalls loading them with paper sacks of cement. I set off up the stairs on foot, and discovered that the second floor of our office was being refurbished. There were workmen lining the walls with sheets of plasterboard, and plasterers bustling about beside them, filling in the seams. At the same time they were installing a false ceiling, which already covered the air-conditioning pipes.

So our office manager Vitaly Markovich had got his own way after all. He'd managed to get the boss to shell out for a full-scale refurbishment, and even worked out where to get the money from.

I stopped for a moment to look at the workmen through the Twilight. Ordinary people, not Others. Just as I ought to have expected. There was just one plasterer, not much to look at, whose aura seemed suspicious. But after a second I realised he was simply in love. With his own wife! Well, would you believe it, there were still a few good people left in the world.

The third and fourth floors had already been refurbished and that really put me in a good mood. At long last it would be cool in the IT department too. Not that I was in there every day now, but even so . . . As I dashed past I greeted the security guards who had clearly been posted here for the duration of the refurbishment. Just as I got to Gesar's office, I ran into Semyon. He was impressing something on Yulia in a serious, didactic voice.

How time flew . . . Three years earlier Yulia had been just a little girl. Now she was a beautiful young woman. And a very promising enchantress – she had already been invited to join the European Office of the Night Watch. They like to skim off the young talent – to a multilingual chorus of protests about the great common cause.

But this time they hadn't got away with it. Gesar had held on to Yulia, and into the bargain let them know that he could recruit young European talent if he felt like it.

I wondered what Yulia herself had wanted to happen.

'Been called back in?' Semyon enquired sympathetically, breaking off his conversation the moment he spotted me. 'Or is your time up already?'

'My time's up, and I've been called in,' I said. 'Has something happened? Hi, Yulia.'

For some reason Semyon and I never bothered to say hello. As if we'd only just seen each other. And anyway, he always looked exactly the same – simply dressed, carelessly shaved, with the crumpled face of a peasant who's moved to the big city.

That day, in fact, Semyon was looking more homely than ever.

'Hi, Anton,' Yulia replied. Her expression was glum. It looked as though Semyon had been lecturing her again – he was always doing that sort of thing.

'Nothing's happened,' Semyon said, shaking his head. 'Everything's perfectly calm. Last week we only picked up two witches, and that was for petty offences.'

'Well, that's great,' I said, trying not to notice Yulia's imploring glance. 'I'll go and see the boss.'

Semyon nodded and turned back towards the girl. As I walked into the boss's reception room, I heard him saying:

'So listen, Yulia, I've been doing the same job for sixty years now, but this kind of irresponsible behaviour . . .'

He's strict all right. But he never gives anyone a hard time without good reason, so I wasn't about to rescue Yulia from the conversation.

In the reception area the new air conditioner was humming away quietly and the ceiling was dotted with tiny halogen bulbs for accent lighting. Larissa was sitting there – evidently Gesar's secretary, Galochka, was on holiday, and our field work co-ordinators really didn't have much work of their own to do.

'Hello, Anton,' Larissa said. 'You're looking good.'

'Two weeks on the beach,' I replied proudly.

Larissa squinted at the clock:

'I was told to show you straight through. But the boss still has visitors. Will you go in?'

'Yes,' I decided. 'Seems like I needn't have bothered hurrying.'

'Gorodetsky's here to see you, Boris Ignatievich,' Larissa said into the intercom. She nodded to me: 'Go on in . . . oh, it's hot in there . . .'

It really was hot in Gesar's office. There were two middle-aged men I didn't know languishing in the armchairs in front of his desk – I mentally christened them Thin Man and Fat Man, after Chekhov's short story. But both of them were sweating.

'And what do we observe?' Gesar asked them reproachfully. He cast a sideways glance at me. 'Come in, Anton. Sit down, I'll be finished in a moment . . .'

Thin Man and Fat Man perked up a bit at that.

'Some mediocre housewife . . . distorting all the facts . . . vulgarising and simplifying everything . . . running rings round you! On a global scale!'

'She can do that precisely because she vulgarises and simplifies,' Fat Man retorted morosely.

'You told us to tell everything like it is,' Thin Man said in support. 'And this is the result, Most Lucent Gesar.'

I took a look at Gesar's visitors through the Twilight. Well, well! More human beings! And yet they knew the boss's name and title. And they even pronounced them with candid sarcasm. Of course, there are always special circumstances, but for Gesar to reveal himself to ordinary people . . .

'All right,' Gesar said with a nod. 'I'll let you have one more try. This time work separately.'

Thin Man and Fat Man exchanged glances.

'We'll do our best,' Fat Man said with a good-natured smile. 'You understand, though – we've already had a certain degree of success . . .'

Gesar snorted. As if they'd been given some invisible signal that the conversation was over, the visitors rose, shook the boss's hand in farewell and walked out. In the reception area Thin Man made some flirtatious remark to Larissa, and she laughed.

'Ordinary people?' I asked cautiously.

Gesar nodded, gazing at the door with a hostile expression. He sighed:

'People, people . . . All right, Gorodetsky. Sit down.'

I sat down, but Gesar still didn't say anything. He fiddled with his papers and fingered some bright-coloured, smoothly polished glass beads heaped up in a coarse earthenware bowl. I really wanted to look closer and see if they were amulets or just glass beads, but I couldn't risk taking any liberties in front of Gesar.

'How was your holiday?' Gesar asked, as if he'd exhausted all his excuses for delaying the conversation.

'Good,' I answered. 'I missed Sveta, of course. But I couldn't drag little Nadya out into that scorching Spanish sun. That's no good . . .'

'No,' Gesar agreed, 'it isn't.' I didn't know if the Great Magician had any children – even close associates weren't trusted with information like that. He probably did. He was almost certainly capable of experiencing something like paternal feelings. 'Anton, did you phone Svetlana?'

'No,' I said and shook my head. 'Has she contacted you?'

Gesar nodded. Then suddenly he couldn't contain himself any longer – he slammed his fist down on the desk and burst out:

'Just what did she think she was doing? First she deserts from the Watch . . .'

'Gesar, every one of us has the right to resign,' I objected. But Gesar had no intention of apologising.

'Deserts! An enchantress of her level doesn't belong to herself! She has no right to belong to herself! If, that is, she calls herself a Light One . . . And then – she's raising her daughter as a human being!'

'Nadya *is* a human being,' I said, feeling myself starting to get angry. 'Whether or not she becomes an Other is for her to decide . . . Most Lucent Gesar.'

Gesar realised that I was all set to blow too. And he changed his tone.

'Okay. That's your right. Pull out of the fight, ruin the little girl's life . . . Anything you like! But where does this hate come from?'

'What did Sveta say?' I asked.

Gesar sighed:

'Your wife phoned me. On a number that she has no right to know . . .'

'Then she doesn't know it,' I put in.

'And she told me I intended to have you killed! That I was hatching a highly complicated plot for your physical elimination!'

I looked into Gesar's eyes for a second. Then I laughed.

'You think it's funny?' Gesar asked in a pained voice. 'You really think so?'

'Gesar . . .' I said, struggling to suppress my laughter. 'I'm sorry. May I speak frankly?'

'By all means . . .'

'You are the greatest schemer I know. Worse than Zabulon. Compared to you, Machiavelli was a mere pup . . .'

'Don't be so quick to underestimate Machiavelli,' Gesar growled. 'I get the idea, I'm a schemer. And?'

'And I'm sure you have no intention of having me killed. In a crisis, perhaps, you might sacrifice me. In order to save a commensurately greater number of people or Light Others. But not that way . . . by planning . . . and intriguing . . . I don't believe it.'

'Thanks, I'm glad to hear it,' Gesar said with a nod. I couldn't tell if I'd nettled him or not. 'Then what on earth has Svetlana got into her head? I'm sorry, Anton . . .' Gesar suddenly hesitated and even looked away. But he finished what he was saying: 'Are you expecting a child? Another one?'

I choked and shook my head:

'No . . . at least, I don't think so . . . no, she would have told me!'

'Women sometimes go a bit crazy when they're expecting a child,' Gesar growled and started fingering his glass beads again. 'They start seeing danger everywhere – for the child, for their husband, for themselves . . . Or maybe now she has . . .' But then the Great Magician got really embarrassed and stopped himself short 'That's rubbish . . . forget it. Why don't you pay your wife a visit in the country, play with your daughter, drink some milk fresh from the cow . . .'

'My holiday ends tomorrow,' I reminded him. There was something not right here. 'And I thought the idea was that I was going to work today.'

Gesar stared hard at me:

'Anton, forget about work. Svetlana shouted at me for fifteen minutes. If she was a Dark One, there'd be an Inferno vortex hanging over my head right now! That's it, work's cancelled. I'm extending your holiday for a week – go to the country to see your wife.'

In the Moscow department of the Watch we have a saying: 'There are three things a Light Other can't do: organise his own personal life, achieve worldwide peace and happiness, and get time off from Gesar'.

To be honest, I was quite happy with my personal life, and now I'd been given an extra week of holiday.

So maybe worldwide peace and happiness were only just around the corner?

'Aren't you pleased?' Gesar asked.

'Yes,' I admitted. No, I wasn't inspired by the prospect of weeding the vegetable beds under the watchful eye of my mother-in-law. But Sveta and Nadya would be there. Nadya, Nadyenka, Nadiushka. My little two-year-old miracle. A lovely little human being . . . Potentially an Other of immense power. An enchantress so very Great that Gesar himself couldn't hold a candle to her. I imagined the Great Light Magician Gesar standing there holding a candle, so that little Nadya could play with her toys, and grinned.

'Call into the accounts office, they'll issue you a bonus . . .' Gesar continued, not suspecting the humiliation I was subjecting him to in my mind. 'Think up the citation for yourself. Something like . . . for many years of conscientious service . . .'

'Gesar, what kind of job was it?' I asked.

He stopped talking and tried to drill right through me with his gaze. When he got nowhere, he said:

'When I tell you everything, you will phone Svetlana. From here. And you'll ask her if you should agree or not. Okay? And you tell her about the extra holiday too.'

'What's happened?'

Instead of replying, Gesar pulled open the drawer of his desk, took out a black leather folder and held it out to me. The folder had a distinct aura of magic – powerful, dangerous battle magic.

'Don't worry, open it, you've been granted access,' Gesar murmured.

I opened the folder – at that point any unauthorised Other or human being would have been reduced to a handful of ash. Inside the folder was a letter. Just one single envelope.

The address of our office was written in newsprint, carefully cut out and stuck onto the envelope.

And naturally there was no return address.

'The letters have been cut out of three newspapers,' said Gesar. '*Pravda, Kommersant* and *Arguments and Facts*.'

'Ingenious,' I remarked. 'Can I open it?'

'Yes, do. The forensic experts have already done everything they can with the envelope – there aren't any fingerprints. The glue was made in China and it's on sale in every newspaper kiosk.'

'And it's written on toilet paper!' I exclaimed in delight as I took the letter out of the envelope. 'Is it clean at least?'

'Unfortunately,' said Gesar. 'Not the slightest trace of organic matter. Standard cheap pulp. "Fifty-four metres", they call it.'

The sheet of toilet paper had been carelessly torn off along the perforation and the text was glued onto it in different-sized letters. Or rather, in entire words, with a few endings added separately, and with no regard for the typeface:

'The NIGHT WATCH should BE INTERESTED to know that a CERTAIN Other has REVEALed to a CERTAIN human being the entire truth about oTHErs and now inTENDs to turn this human beING into an OTHER. A wellWISHer.'

I would have laughed, but somehow I didn't feel like it. Instead, I remarked perspicaciously:

'"Night Watch" is written in complete words . . .'

'There was an article in *Arguments and Facts*,' Gesar explained. 'About a fire at the TV Tower. It was called "NIGHT WATCH ON THE OSTANKINO TOWER".'

'Clever,' I agreed. The mention of the tower gave me a slight twinge. That hadn't exactly been the best time of my life . . . I would be haunted forever by the face of the Dark Other I threw off the TV Tower in the Twilight . . .*

'Don't get moody, Anton, You didn't do anything wrong,' said Gesar. 'Let's get down to business.'

'Let's do that, Boris Ignatievich,' I said, calling the boss by his old 'civilian' name.

'Is this for real then?'

Gesar shrugged.

'There's not even a whiff of magic from the letter. It was either composed by a human being, or by a competent Other who can cover his tracks. If it's a human being, then there has to be a leak somewhere. If it's an Other, then it's a totally irresponsible act of provocation.'

'No traces at all?' I asked again to make sure.

'None. The only clue is the postmark.' Gesar frowned. 'But that looks very much like a red herring.'

'Was the letter sent from the Kremlin then?' I quipped.

'Almost. The postbox the letter was left in is located on the grounds of the Assol complex.'

Great tall buildings with red roofs – the kind that Comrade Stalin would have approved of. I'd seen them. But only from a distance.

'You can't just go walking in there!'

'No, you can't,' Gesar said with a nod. 'So, in sending the letter from the Assol residences after all this subterfuge with the paper, the glue and the letters, our unknown correspondent either committed a crude error . . .'

I shook my head.

'Or he's leading us onto a false trail . . .' At this point Gesar paused, observing my reaction closely.

* See *The Night Watch*, Story Two

I thought for a moment. And then shook my head again:

'That's very naïve. No.'

'Or the "wellwisher",' Gesar pronounced the final word with frank sarcasm, 'really does want to give us a clue.'

'What for?' I asked.

'He sent the letter for some reason,' Gesar reminded me. 'As you well understand, Anton, we have to react to this letter somehow. Let's assume the worst – there's a traitor among the Others who can reveal the secret of our existence to the human race.'

'But who's going to believe him?'

'They won't believe a human being. But they will believe an Other who can demonstrate his abilities.'

Gesar was right, of course. But I couldn't make sense of why anyone would do such a thing. Even the most stupid and malicious Dark One had to understand what would happen after the truth was revealed.

A new witch hunt.

And people would gladly cast both the Dark Ones and the Light Ones in the role of witches. Everyone who possessed the abilities of an Other . . .

Including Sveta. Including little Nadya.

'How is it possible "to turn this human being into an Other"?' I asked. 'Vampirism?'

'Vampires, werewolves . . .' Gesar shrugged. 'That's it, I suppose. Initiation is possible at the very crudest, most primitive levels of Dark power, but it would have to be paid for by sacrificing the human essence. It's impossible to make a human being into a magician by initiation.'

'Nadiushka . . .' I whispered. 'You rewrote Svetlana's Book of Destiny, didn't you?'

Gesar shook his head:

'No, Anton. Your daughter was destined to be born a Great

One. All we did was make the sign more precise. We eliminated the element of chance.'

'Egor,' I reminded him. 'The boy had already become a Dark Other . . .'

'But we erased the specific quality of his initiation. Gave him a chance to choose again,' Gesar replied. 'Anton, all the interventions that we are capable of have to do only with the choice of "Dark" or "Light". But there's no way we can make the choice between "human" or "Other". No one in this world can do that.'

'Then that means we're talking about vampires,' I said. 'Supposing the Dark Ones have another vampire who's fallen in love . . .'

Gesar spread his hands helplessly:

'Could be. Then everything's more or less simple. The Dark Ones will check their riff-raff, it's in their interest as much as ours . . . And yes, by the way, they received a letter too. Exactly the same. And sent from Assol too.'

'How about the Inquisition, did they get one?'

'You get shrewder and shrewder all the time,' Gesar laughed. 'They also got one. By post. From Assol.'

Gesar was clearly hinting at something. I thought for a moment and drew yet another shrewd conclusion.

'Then the investigation is being conducted by both Watches and the Inquisition?'

There was a brief flicker of dissatisfaction in Gesar's glance.

'Yes, that's the way it is. When it's absolutely necessary, in a private capacity, it is permissible to reveal yourself as an Other to human beings. You've seen yourself . . .' he nodded towards the door through which his visitors had left. 'But that's a private matter. And the appropriate magical limitations are imposed. This situation is far worse than that. It looks as if one of the Others intends to trade in initiations.'

I imagined a vampire offering his services to rich New Russians and smiled. 'How would you like to drink the people's blood for real, my dear sir?' But then, it wasn't all about blood. Even the very weakest vampire or werewolf possesses power. They have no fear of disease. They live for a very, very long time. And their physical strength shouldn't be forgotten either – any werewolf would beat Karelin and give Tyson a good whipping. And then there was their 'animal magnetism', the 'call' that they had such complete control over. Any woman was yours for the taking, just summon her.

Of course, in reality, both vampires and werewolves were bound by numerous restrictions. Even more so than magicians – their instability required it. But did a newly initiated vampire really understand that?

'What are you smiling at?' Gesar asked.

'I just imagined an announcement in a newspaper. "I will turn you into a vampire. Safe, reliable, a hundred years' guarantee. Price by arrangement".'

Gesar nodded.

'Good thinking. I'll have the newspapers and internet noticeboards checked.'

I looked at Gesar, but I couldn't tell whether he was joking.

'I don't think there's any real danger,' I said. 'Most likely some crackpot vampire has decided to earn a bit of money. Showed some rich man a few tricks and offered to . . . er . . . bite him.'

'One bite, and all your troubles are over,' Gesar said.

Encouraged, I continued:

'Someone . . . for instance, this man's wife, found out about the terrible offer. While her husband hesitates, she decides to write to us, hoping that we'll eliminate the vampire and that her husband will remain a human being. Hence the combination of letters cut out of newspapers and the post office in Assol. A cry for help. She can't tell us openly, but she's literally begging us: Save my husband!'

'You hopeless romantic,' Gesar said disapprovingly. 'So then she takes a pair of nail scissors, and snippety-snips the letters out of the latest *Pravda* . . . Did she get the addresses out of the newspapers too?'

'The address of the Inquisition!' I exclaimed, suddenly realising the problem.

'Now you're thinking. Could you send a letter to the Inquisition?'

I didn't answer. I'd been put firmly in my place. Gesar had told me straight out about the letter to the Inquisition!

'In our watch I'm the only person who knows their address. In the Day Watch, I presume Zabulon is the only one. So where does that leave us, Gorodetsky?'

'You sent the letter. Or Zabulon did.'

Gesar only snorted.

'And is the Inquisition really uptight about this?' I asked.

'Uptight is putting it mildly. In itself, the attempt to trade in initiations doesn't bother them. That's standard business for the Watches – identify the perpetrator, punish him, and seal the leak. Especially since we and the Dark Ones are both equally outraged by what has happened . . . But a letter to the Inquisition – that's something really exceptional. There aren't very many Inquisitors, so you can see . . . If one side violates the Treaty, the Inquisition takes the other side, maintaining equilibrium. That gives all of us discipline. But let's just say somewhere in the depths of one of the Watches a plan is being hatched for ultimate victory. A group of battle magicians who have come together and are capable of killing all the Inquisitors in a single night – that is, of course, if they happen to know all about the Inquisition – who serves in it, where they live, where they keep their documents . . .'

'Did the letter arrive at their head office?' I asked.

'Yes. And judging from the fact that six hours later the office was empty, and there was a fire in the building, that must have been where the Inquisition kept all its files. Even I didn't know that for sure. Anyway, by sending the letter to the Inquisition, this person . . . or Other . . . has thrown down the gauntlet. Now the Inquisition will be after them. The official reason will be that security has been breached and an attempt is being made to initiate a human being. But in reality, what's driving them is concern for their own skin.'

'I wouldn't have thought it was like them to feel afraid for themselves,' I said.

'Oh yes, and how, Anton! Here's a little something for you to think about . . . Why aren't there any traitors in the Inquisition? Dark Ones and Light Ones join them. They go through their training. And then the Dark Ones punish Dark Ones severely, and the Light Ones punish Light Ones, the very moment they violate the Treaty.'

'A special character type,' I suggested. 'They select Others who are like that.'

'And they never make a mistake?' Gesar asked sceptically. 'That couldn't happen. Yet in the whole of history, there has never been a single case of an Inquisitor violating the Treaty.'

'They obviously understand too clearly what violating the Treaty leads to. There was one Inquisitor in Prague who told me: "We are constrained by fear".'

Gesar frowned:

'Witiezslav – he's fond of fine phrases . . . All right, don't bother your head about that. The situation's simple: there's an Other who is either in violation of the Treaty or taunting the Watches and the Inquisition. The Inquisition will conduct their investigation, the Dark Ones will conduct theirs. And we are required to send a staff member too.'

'May I ask why me in particular?'

Gesar spread his hands expressively again:

'For a number of reasons. The first is that in the course of the investigation you'll probably come up against vampires. And you're our top specialist on the lower Dark Ones.'

He didn't seem to be making fun of me.

'The second reason,' Gesar went on, opening the fingers of his fist as he counted, 'is that the investigators officially appointed by the Inquisition are old friends of yours. Witiezslav and Edgar.'

'Edgar's in Moscow?' I asked, surprised. I couldn't say that I actually liked this Dark Magician who had transferred to the Inquisition three years earlier. But I could say that I didn't really dislike him.

'Yes, he is. He completed his training course four months ago and flew back here. Since this job means you'll be in contact with Inquisitors, any previous personal acquaintance is useful.'

'My acquaintance with them wasn't all that enjoyable,' I reminded him.

'What do you think I'm offering you here, Thai massage during working hours?' Gesar asked cantankerously. 'The third reason why I particularly wanted to give this assignment to you is . . .' He stopped.

I waited.

'The Dark Ones' investigation is also being conducted by an old acquaintance of yours.'

Gesar didn't need to mention the name. But he did anyway.

'Konstantin. The young vampire . . . your former neighbour. I recall that you used to be on good terms.'

'Yes, of course,' I said bitterly. 'When he was still a child, only drank pig's blood and dreamed of escaping from the "curse" . . . Until he realised that his friend the Light Magician burns his kind to ashes.'

'That's life,' said Gesar.

'He's already drunk human blood,' I said. 'He must have! If he's in favour in the Day Watch.'

'He has become a Higher Vampire,' Gesar declared. 'The youngest Higher Vampire in Europe. If you translate that into our terms, that means . . .'

'Third or fourth level of power,' I whispered. 'Five or six lives destroyed.'

Kostya, Kostya . . . I was a young, inexperienced Light Magician back then. I just couldn't make any friends in the Watch, and all my old friendships were rapidly falling apart . . . Others and people can't be friends . . . and suddenly I discovered that my neighbours were Dark Others. A family of vampires. The mother and father were vampires, and they'd initiated their child too. There was nothing really sinister about them, though. No nocturnal hunting, no applications for licences, they respected the law and drank pig's blood and donors' blood. And so, like a fool, I let my defences down and became friends with them. I used to go round to see them and even invited them to my apartment. They ate the food I'd cooked, and praised it . . . and, idiot that I was, I didn't realise that human food is tasteless to them, that they are tormented by an ancient, eternal hunger. The little vampire kid even decided that he was going to be a biologist and discover a cure for vampirism . . .

Then I killed my first vampire.

And after that Kostya joined the Day Watch. I didn't know if he'd ever graduated from his biology faculty, but he'd certainly shed his childish illusions.

And he'd started receiving licences to kill. Rise to the level of a Higher Vampire in three years? He must have had help. All the resources of the Day Watch must have been brought to bear so that the nice young lad Kostya could sink his fangs into human necks over and over again . . .

And I had a pretty good idea who had helped him.

'What do you think, Anton?' said Gesar. 'In the given situation, who should we appoint as the investigator from our side?'

I took my mobile out of my pocket and dialled Svetlana's number.

CHAPTER 2

IN OUR LINE of business you don't often get to work undercover.

In the first place, you have to completely disguise your nature as an Other, so that nothing gives you away, not your aura, or any streams of power, or any disturbances in the Twilight. And the situation is quite simple – if you're a fifth-grade magician, then you won't be discovered by magicians weaker than you, those who are sixth- and seventh-grade. If you're a first-grade magician, then you're concealed from the second grade and below. If you're a magician beyond classification . . . well, then you can hope that no one will recognise you.

I was disguised by Gesar himself, immediately after speaking to Svetlana. The conversation was brief, but painful. We didn't quarrel. She was just very upset.

And in the second place, you need a cover story. The simplest way to provide a cover story is by magical means – people you don't know will gladly believe you're their brother, their son-in-law's father or the army buddy they drank home brew with when they went absent without leave. But a magical cover story will leave traces that any reasonably powerful Other can spot.

So there was no magic involved in my cover story. Gesar handed me the keys to an apartment in the Assol complex – a hundred and fifty square metres of floor space on the eighth floor. It was registered in my name and had been bought six months earlier. When I opened my eyes wide at that, Gesar explained that the documents had been signed that morning, but backdated. For big money. And the apartment would have to be handed back afterwards.

I got the keys to a BMW just to add substance to my story. It wasn't a new car, or the most luxurious model, but then my apartment was a small one.

Then a tailor came into the office, a mournful little old Jewish man, a seventh-grade Other. He took my measurements, promised the suit would be ready by the evening, when, he assured us, 'this boy will start to look like a man'. Gesar was extremely polite to the tailor, opening the door for him and seeing him out into the reception. As he said goodbye, he asked timidly how his 'little coat' was coming on. The tailor told him there was no need to worry. A coat worthy of the Most Lucent Gesar would be ready before the cold weather set in.

After hearing that, I wasn't as delighted as I had been at first with the decision that I could keep my suit. The tailor clearly didn't make genuine, top-quality garments in half a day.

Gesar himself provided me with ties. He even taught me a particularly fashionable knot. Then he gave me a wad of banknotes and the address of a shop and ordered me to buy everything else to match, including underwear, handkerchiefs and socks. I was offered the services of Ignat as a consultant, one of our magicians who would have been called an incubus in the Day Watch. Or a succubus – he didn't really care much either way.

The expedition to the boutiques – where Ignat felt right at home – was amusing. But the visit to the hairdresser's, or rather the 'Beauty Salon', left me completely wrecked. Two women and a young man who tried to make out he was gay, although he wasn't, took turns inspecting me. They sighed and made uncomplimentary remarks about my hairdresser. If their wishes had come true, the hairdresser would have been condemned to shearing mangy sheep for the rest of his life. And, for some reason, in Tajikistan. This was clearly the most terrible curse for hairdressers. I even decided that after my mission I'd drop into the second-class hairdresser's where I'd been getting my hair cut for the last year, just to make sure they hadn't left an Inferno vortex hanging over the man's head.

The collective wisdom of the beauty specialists was that my only hope of salvation was a short comb-cut, to make me look like one of those small-time hoods who fleece traders at the market. In consolation they told me that the forecast was for a hot summer and I'd feel more comfortable with short hair.

After the haircut, which took more than an hour, I was subjected to a manicure and a pedicure. When Ignat was satisfied, he took me to a dentist, who removed the scale from my teeth with a special fitting on his drill and advised me to have the procedure repeated every six months. Afterwards my teeth felt somehow naked, and it was unpleasant to touch them with my tongue. I couldn't think of what to say in reply to Ignat's ambivalent comment: 'Anton, you look good enough to fall in love with!' and just mumbled something incomprehensible. All the way back to the office I served as a defenceless target for his unsubtle wit.

The suit was waiting for me. And the tailor too, muttering discontentedly that sewing a suit without a second fitting was like getting married on impulse.

I don't know. If every marriage made on impulse was as successful as that suit, divorce rates would be reduced to zero.

Gesar spoke to the tailor about his coat again. They had a long, heated argument about the buttons, until the Most Lucent Magician finally capitulated. I stood by the window, looking out at the evening street and the small blinking light of the alarm system in 'my' car.

I hoped no one would steal it . . . I couldn't set up any magical defences to frighten away petty thieves. That would give me away more surely than the parachute trailing behind the Russian spy Stirlitz in the old joke.

That night I was due to sleep in the new apartment. And I had to pretend it wasn't the first time I'd been there. At least there was no one waiting for me back at home. No wife or daughter or dog or cat . . . I didn't even have fish in an aquarium. And it was a good job I didn't.

'Do you understand your mission, Gorodetsky?' Gesar asked. The tailor had left while I was daydreaming at the window. My new suit was amazingly comfortable. Despite the new haircut, I didn't feel like a thug who terrorised market traders, but someone a bit more serious. Maybe a collector of protection money from small shops.

'Move into Assol. Meet with my neighbours. Look for any signs of the renegade Other and his potential client. When I find them, report back. In dealings with the other investigators behave civilly, exchange information, be co-operative.'

Gesar stood beside me at the window. He nodded.

'All correct, Anton, all correct . . . Only you've missed out the most important thing.'

'Oh yes?'

'You mustn't cling to any theories. Not even the most likely ones . . . especially the most likely ones! The Other might be a vampire or a werewolf . . . or he might not.'

I nodded.

'He might be a Dark One,' said Gesar. 'Or he might turn out to be a Light One.'

I didn't say anything. I'd been thinking the same thing.

'And most important of all,' Gesar added, 'remember – "He intends to turn this human being into an Other" could be a bluff.'

'And maybe not?' I asked. 'Gesar, is it really possible to turn a human being into an Other?'

'Do you honestly think I would have hidden something like that?' Gesar replied. 'So many Others with broken lives, so many fine people condemned to live only their short, human lives . . . Nothing of the kind has ever happened before. But there's a first time for everything.'

'Then I'll assume it is possible,' I said.

'I can't give you any amulets,' Gesar advised me. 'You understand why. And you'd better not use magic. The only thing that is permissible is to look through the Twilight. But if the need arises, we'll be there quickly. Just call.'

He paused and then added:

'I'm not expecting any violent confrontations. But you must be prepared for them.'

I'd never parked in an underground car park before. It was just as well that there weren't many cars, the concrete ramps were flooded with bright light and the security man sitting there watching the monitors politely pointed out where my parking spaces were.

Apparently it was assumed that I had at least two cars.

After parking, I took my bag out of the boot, set the car alarm and walked towards the exit. The security man was amazed, and he asked me if the lifts were out of order. I had to wrinkle up my forehead, wave my hand around and say I hadn't been there for about a year.

The security man asked which floor I lived on, and in which block. Then he showed me the way to the lift.

Surrounded by chrome, mirrors and conditioned air, I rode up to the eighth floor. I actually felt rather insulted that I lived so low down. I hadn't been expecting the penthouse exactly, but even so.

On the landing – if you can a hall with thirty square metres of floor space a landing – I wandered from one door to another for a while. The fairy tale had come to an abrupt end. One door was completely missing, and behind the blank aperture there was a gigantic, dark, empty room – concrete walls, a concrete floor, no internal divisions. I could hear the faint sound of water dripping.

It took me a long time to choose between the three doors that were in place – none of these had numbers. Eventually I found a number someone had scratched on one door with a sharp object, and the remains of some figures in chalk on another. It looked like my door was the third one. The most unprepossessing of them all. It would have been just like Gesar to put me in the apartment that didn't even have a door, but then the cover story would have been shot to pieces.

I took out a bunch of keys and opened the door fairly easily. I looked for a light switch and found an entire array of them.

I started switching them on one at a time.

Once the apartment was flooded with light I closed the door behind me and looked around thoughtfully.

Maybe there was something to this after all. Maybe.

The previous owner of the apartment . . . okay, okay, according to the cover story, that was me. Anyway, when I started the finishing work, I'd obviously been full of truly Napoleonic plans. How else could I explain the custom-made patterned parquet, the oak window frames, the Daikin air conditioners and other distinctive features of a truly sumptuous residence?

But after that I must have run out of money. Because the immense studio apartment – with no internal dividing walls – was untouched, virginal. In the corner where the kitchen was supposed to be there was a lopsided old Brest gas cooker, which could well have been used for cooking semolina in the days of my infancy. Nestling on its burners, as if to say 'Do not use!', was a basic microwave oven. But then there was a luxurious extractor hood hanging above the appalling cooker. Huddling pitifully alongside it were two stools and a low serving table.

From sheer force of habit I took my shoes off and walked over into the kitchen corner. There was no refrigerator and no furniture, but there was a big cardboard box standing on the floor, full of supplies – bottles of mineral water and vodka, cans of food, packets of dry soup, boxes of crispbreads. Thanks, Gesar. If only you'd thought of getting me a saucepan as well . . .

From the 'kitchen' I walked towards the bathroom. Apparently I'd been clever enough not to display the toilet and the jacuzzi for everyone to see . . .

I opened the door and looked round the bathroom. Not bad, ten or twelve square metres. Nice-looking turquoise tiles. A futuristic-looking shower cubicle – it was frightening to think how much it would have cost and what fancy bits of technology it was stuffed with.

But there wasn't a jacuzzi. There wasn't any kind of bath at all – just the blocked-off water pipes sticking up in the corner. And in addition . . .

I looked frantically round the bathroom and confirmed my terrible suspicion.

There was no toilet there either!

Just the exit pipe to the drains blocked off with a wooden plug.

Great, thanks, Gesar!

Stop, no need to panic. They didn't put just one bathroom in apartments like these. There had to be another one – for guests, for children, for servants . . .

I darted back out into the studio space and found another door in the corner, right beside the entrance. My premonition had not deceived me – it was the bathroom for guests. There wasn't supposed to be a bath here, and the shower was simpler.

But instead of a toilet, there was just another plugged pipe.

Disaster.

Now I was really screwed!

Of course, I knew the genuine professionals didn't take any

notice of such petty details. If James Bond ever went to the bathroom, it was only to eavesdrop on someone else's conversation or waste the villain hiding in the flush tank.

But I had to live here!

For a few seconds I was on the point of calling Gesar and demanding a plumber. And then I imagined what his reply would be.

For some reason in my imagination Gesar smiled. Then he heaved a sigh and gave the order – after which someone like the head plumber of all Moscow came and fitted the toilet in person. And Gesar smiled again and shook his head.

Magicians of his level didn't make mistakes in the detail. Their mistakes were cities in flames, bloody wars and the impeachment of presidents. But not overlooked sanitary conveniences.

If there was no toilet in my apartment, then that was the way it was meant to be.

I explored my living space once again. I found a rolled-up mattress and a pack of bed linen with a cheerful design. I laid out the mattress and unpacked the things from my bag. I changed into my jeans and the T-shirt with the optimistic message about clinical death – I couldn't wear a tie in my own home, could I? I took out my laptop . . . Oh yes, was I supposed to get onto the internet via my mobile phone?

I had to make yet another search of the apartment. I found a mains connection in the wall of the large bathroom on the 'studio' room side. I decided that couldn't be accidental and glanced into the bathroom. I was right – there was another mains socket beside the non-existent toilet.

I'd had some odd ideas when I was working on this place . . .

The power was on. That was good at least, but it wasn't the reason I'd come here.

I opened the windows to dispel the oppressive silence. The warm evening air came rushing into the room. On the far side of the river, lights were twinkling in the windows of the buildings – the ordinary, human buildings. But the silence was just as intense. No wonder, it was after midnight.

I took out my minidisc player, rummaged through my discs and chose The White Guard, a group that was never going to top the charts on MTV or fill sports stadiums. I stuck the earphones in my ears and stretched out on the mattress.

When this battle is over,
If you survive until the dawn,
You'll realise the scent of victory
Is as bitter as the smoke of defeat.
And you're alone on the cold battlefield,
With no enemies from now on,
But the sky presses down on your shoulders,
What can you do in this empty desert?
But you will wait
For what time
Will bring,
You will wait . . .
And honey will taste more bitter than salt,
Your tears more bitter than the wormwood in the steppes,
And I know of no pain worse than this,
To be alive among so many who are sleeping.
But you will wait
For what time
Will bring,
You will wait . . .

Catching myself trying to sing along out of tune with the quiet female voice, I tugged out the earphones and switched the player off. No. I hadn't come here to lounge around doing nothing.

What would James Bond have done in my place? Immediately found the mysterious renegade Other, his human client and the author of the provocative letters.

And what was I going to do?

I was going to look for what I needed desperately. If it really came to it, there had to be toilet facilities downstairs, at the security point.

Somewhere outside the window – it seemed very close – a bass guitar began growling ponderously. I jumped to my feet, but couldn't see anyone in the apartment.

'Hi there, you mob' said a voice outside the windows. I leaned out over the windowsill and surveyed the wall of the Assol building. I spotted some windows open two floors up – that was where those unusually arranged, aggressive chords on the bass guitar were coming from.

> I haven't squeezed my guts out for a long time,
> It's a long time since I've squeezed out my guts,
> And just recently I happened to notice
> How long it is since I squeezed out my guts.
> But I used to squeeze them out so fine!
> No one else could squeeze them out so far!
> I squeezed them right out there for everyone,
> I was the only one squeezing them out!

It was impossible to imagine a greater contrast with the quiet voice of Zoya Yashchenko, the female singer with The White Guard, than this extraordinary song. But there was something about it I liked. The singer ran through a three-chord bridge and continued with his lament:

> Sometimes now I still squeeze them out,
> But now it's not the way it used to be.

They just don't squeeze out the same way at all
I'll never squeeze them out again the way I used to . . .

I started laughing. It had all the distinctive features of Russian 'gangster' songs – a lyric hero recalling his former splendour, describing his present fallen state and lamenting that he will never recover the glory of former days.

And I had a strong suspicion that if this song were played on Radio Chanson, ninety per cent of the listeners wouldn't even suspect it was a send-up.

The guitar gave a few sighs. And then the voice launched into a new song:

I've never been in the loony bin,
So stop asking me about that . . .

The music broke off. I rummaged in the cardboard box, found a bottle of vodka and a stick of smoked salami. I skipped out onto the landing, pulled the door shut and set off up the stairs.

Finding the midnight bard's apartment was about as hard as finding a working pneumatic drill in the bushes.

The birds have stopped their singing,
The sun no longer shines
There are no vicious kids frolicking
Round the rubbish tip outside . . .

I rang the bell, certain that no one would hear it. But the music stopped, and about thirty seconds later the door opened.

Standing there in the doorway with an amiable smile on his face was a short, stocky man about thirty years old, holding a bass guitar. With a certain morose satisfaction, I observed that he had a 'bandit' haircut like me. The bard was wearing threadbare jeans and an amusing T-shirt – a paratrooper in Russian uniform slitting the throat of an American soldier with a huge knife. Below the picture was the defiant slogan 'Let us remind you who really won the Second World War!'

'That's not bad, either,' the guitarist said, looking at my T-shirt. 'Come on in.'

He took the vodka and the salami and moved back inside.

I took a look at him through the Twilight.

A human being.

And such a confused jumble of an aura that I decided there and then not to try to understand his character. Grey, pink, red and blue tones . . . a really impressive cocktail.

I followed him inside.

His apartment turned out to be twice as big as mine. Oho, he didn't earn the money for that by playing the guitar . . . But then, that was none of my business. What was really funny was that, apart from its size, the apartment looked like an exact copy of mine. The initial phase of a magnificent finishing job hastily wound up and left incomplete.

Standing in the middle of this monstrously huge living space – at least fifteen square metres – there was a chair, and in front of the chair a microphone on a stand, a good quality professional amplifier and two enormous speakers.

Over by the wall there were three immense Bosch fridges. The guitarist opened the biggest one – it was empty – and put the bottle of vodka in the freezer. He explained:

'It's warm.'

'I haven't got a fridge yet,' I said.

'It happens,' the bard sympathised. 'Las.'

'What do you mean, "las",' I asked, puzzled.

'That's my name, Las. Not the one in my passport.'

'Anton,' I said, introducing myself. 'That is the name in my passport.'

'It happens,' Las sympathised again. 'Come far?'

'I live on the eighth,' I explained.

Las scratched the back of his head thoughtfully. He looked at the open windows and explained:

'I opened them so it wouldn't be so loud. Otherwise my ears can't take it. I was going to put in soundproofing, but I ran out of money.'

'That seems to be a common problem,' I said cautiously. 'I haven't even got a toilet.'

Las smiled triumphantly.

'I have. I've had it for a week! That door over there.'

When I got back, Las was melancholically slicing the salami. Unable to resist, I asked him:

'Why is your toilet so huge and English-looking?'

'Did you see the company label on it?' Las asked me. '"We invented the first toilet". Just had to buy it, didn't I, with that written on it? I keep meaning to scan the label and change it a little bit, write: "We were the first to guess that people need . . ."'

'I get the idea,' I said. 'I do have a shower installed, though.'

'Really?' Las said, standing up. 'I've been dreaming about having a shower for three days . . .'

I held out my keys.

'Meanwhile you organise the hors d'oeuvres,' Las said happily. 'The vodka has to cool for another ten minutes anyway. And I'll be quick.'

The door slammed shut, and I was left in a stranger's apartment – alone with an amplifier that was switched on, a half-sliced stick of salami and three huge, empty fridges.

Well, how about that! I would never have expected the easy-going social relations of a friendly communal apartment – or a student hostel – to exist inside buildings like this.

You use my toilet, and I'll get washed in your jacuzzi . . . And Pyotr Petrovich has a fridge, and Ivan Ivanovich promised to bring some vodka – he trades in the stuff – and Semyon Semyon cuts the sausage for the snacks very neatly, with loving care . . .

Probably the majority of the people with apartments there had bought them 'for posterity'. Using every last bit of money they could earn – and beg, steal or borrow. And it was only afterwards that the happy owners had realised that an apartment that size also required major finishing work. And that any construction firm wouldn't think twice about ripping off someone who had bought a home here. And that they still had to pay every month for the massive grounds, the underground car parks, the embankments and the park.

So the huge building was standing there half-empty, very nearly deserted. Of course, it was no tragedy if someone was a bit short of cash. But for the first time I could see with my own eyes that it was at least a tragicomedy.

How many people really lived in the Assol complex? Was I the only one who had noticed the bass guitar in the middle of the night and before that had the strange musician made his racket entirely unchallenged?

One person on each floor? It was probably even less than that . . .

But then who had sent the letter?

I tried to imagine Las cutting letters out of *Pravda* with nail scissors. I couldn't. Someone like him would have come up with something a bit more imaginative.

I closed my eyes, picturing the grey shadow of my eyelids falling across my pupils. Then I opened my eyes and looked round the apartment through the Twilight.

Not the slightest trace of any magic. Not even on the guitar, although a good instrument that has been in the hands of an

Other or a potential Other remembers that touch for years.

And there was no trace anywhere of blue moss, that parasite of the Twilight that feasts on negative emotions. If the owner of the apartment ever fell into a depression, then he didn't do it here. Or else he had such a genuinely good time that it burned away all the blue moss.

I sat down and started carving the rest of the salami. To be on the safe side, I checked through the Twilight to see if it was really a good idea to eat it.

The salami turned out to be all right. Gesar didn't want his agent to go down with food poisoning.

'Now that's the right temperature,' said Las, removing the wine thermometer from the open bottle. 'We didn't leave it in for too long. Some people cool vodka to the consistency of glycerine, so that drinking it's like swallowing liquid nitrogen. Here's to our meeting!'

We drank a glass and followed it with salami and crispbreads, which Las had brought from my apartment – he explained that he hadn't bothered to get any food in that day.

'The entire building lives like this,' he explained. 'Well, of course there are some people who had enough money to finish their places and furnish them as well. Only just imagine how wonderful it is living in an empty building. There they are, waiting for the petty riff-raff like you and me to finish our places off and move in. The cafés aren't working, the casino's empty, the security men are freaking out from sheer boredom . . . two of them were sacked yesterday – they started shooting at the bushes in the yard. Said they'd seen something horrible. They probably did too – they were as high as kites.'

And so saying, Las took a pack of Belomor cigarettes out of his jacket pocket and gave me a cunning look:

'Want one?'

I hadn't been expecting a man who poured vodka in such good style to fool around with marijuana.

I shook my head and asked:

'Do you smoke many?'

'This is the second pack today,' Las sighed. And then he suddenly realised. 'Hey, come on, Anton! These are Belomor! Not dope! I used to smoke Gitânes before, until I realised they were no different from our very own Belomor.'

'Original,' I said.

'What's that got to do with anything?' Las said, offended. 'I'm not trying to be original. You only have to be a bit different, not like the rest, and straight away they say you're putting on airs. But I like smoking Belomor. If I lose interest a week from now, I'll give up.'

'There's nothing wrong with being different,' I said, putting out a feeler.

'But really being different is hard,' Las replied. 'Just a couple of days ago I had this idea . . .'

I pricked my ears up again. The letter had been sent two days earlier. Could everything really have come together so neatly?

'I was in this hospital, and while I was waiting to be seen, I read all the price lists,' Las went on, not suspecting a trap. 'And what they do there is serious stuff, they make artificial body parts out of titanium to replace what people have lost. Shinbones, knee joints and hip joints, jawbones . . . Patches for the skull, teeth and other small bits and pieces . . . I got my calculator out and figured out how much it would cost to have all your bones totally replaced. It came out at about one million seven hundred thousand bucks. But I reckon on a bulk order like that you could get a good discount. Twenty to thirty per cent. And if you could convince the doctors it was good publicity, you could probably get away with half a million!'

'What for?' I asked. Thanks to my hairdresser, my hair wasn't able to stand up on end.

'It's just a fascinating idea,' Las explained. 'Imagine you want to hammer in a nail. You just raise your fist and smash it down, and the nail sinks into concrete. Those bones are titanium. Or say someone tries to punch you . . . nah, of course, there are drawbacks. And artificial organs aren't coming on too well yet. But the general trend of progress looks good to me.'

He poured us another glass.

'It seems to me the trend of progress is in a different direction,' I went on, sticking to my guns. 'We need to make greater use of the potential abilities of our organisms. All those amazing things that lie hidden inside us. Telekinesis, telepathy . . .'

Las looked a bit put out by that. I was getting depressed too, trying to play the idiot.

'Can you read my thoughts?' he asked.

'Not right now,' I confessed.

'I don't think we ought to invent any extra dimensions of reality,' Las explained. 'We've already known for a long time what man is capable of. If people could read thoughts, levitate and do all that other nonsense, there'd be some proof.'

'If someone suddenly acquired abilities like that, they'd hide them from everybody else,' I said, and took a look at Las through the Twilight. 'A really different, Other kind of being would provoke the envy and fear of people around him.'

Las didn't betray the slightest sign of excitement. Just scepticism.

'Well, surely this miracle worker would want to give the woman he loves and his children the same kind of abilities? They'd gradually take over from us as a biological species.'

'But what if the special abilities couldn't be inherited?' I asked. 'Or they weren't necessarily inherited? And you couldn't transmit them to anyone else either? Then you'd have the normal people and these Others existing independently. And if there weren't many of the Others, then they'd hide their abilities from everybody else . . .'

'Seems to me like you're talking about a random mutation that produces extrasensory abilities,' Las said, thinking out loud. 'Only if that mutation is random and recessive, it's absolutely no use to us. But you can actually have titanium bones installed right now!'

'Not a good idea,' I muttered.

We both had a drink.

'You know, this is a pretty weird situation we're in here,' Las mused. 'A huge empty building, hundreds of apartments – and only nine people living in them . . . that's if we include you. The things you could get up to. It takes your breath away. And what a video you could shoot! Just imagine it – the luxurious interiors, empty restaurants, dead laundries, rusting exercise machines and cold saunas, empty swimming pools and casino tables wrapped in plastic sheeting. And a young girl wandering through it all. Wandering around and singing. It doesn't even matter what.'

'Do you shoot videos?' I asked cautiously.

'Nah . . .' Las frowned. 'Well . . . just the once I helped this punk band I know shoot one. They showed it on MTV, but then it was banned.'

'What was so terrible about it?'

'Nothing really,' said Las. 'It was just a song, nothing offensive about it, in fact it was about love. The visuals were unusual. We shot them in a hospital for patients with motor function disorders. We set up strobe lights in a hall, put on the song "Captain, captain, why have you left the horse?" and invited the patients to dance. So they danced to the strobes. Or they tried to. And then we laid the new sound sequence over the visuals. The result was really stylish. But you really can't show it. It has a bad feel somehow.'

I imagined the visuals and squirmed.

'I'm no good as a video producer,' Las admitted. 'Or as a musician . . . they played a song of mine on the radio once, in the middle of the night, in a programme for all sorts of hardcore weirdos. And what do you think happened? This well-known songwriter immediately called the radio station and said all his life in his songs he'd been teaching people about good, and about eternal values, but this had cancelled out his entire life's work . . . You heard one of my songs, I think – did you think it was encouraging people to do bad things?'

'I think it made fun of bad attitudes,' I said.

'Thank you,' Las said sadly. 'But that's exactly the problem – there are too many people who won't understand that. They'll think it's all for real.'

'That's what the fools will think,' I said, trying to console the unacknowledged bard.

'But there are more of them,' Las exclaimed. 'And they haven't perfected head replacements yet . . .'

He reached for the bottle, poured the vodka and said:

'You drop in any time you need to, don't be shy. And later I'll get you a key for an apartment on the fifteenth floor. It's empty, but it has toilets.'

'Won't the owner object?' I asked with a laugh.

'It's all the same to him now. And his heirs can't agree on how to share out the space.'

CHAPTER 3

I GOT BACK to my place at four in the morning. Slightly drunk, but remarkably relaxed. After all, you don't often come across people who are so different. Working in the Watch encourages you to be too categorical. This guy doesn't smoke or drink, he's a good boy. This one swears like a trooper, he's a bad boy. And there's nothing to be done about it, those are precisely the ones we're most interested in – the good ones as our support, the bad ones as potential Dark Ones.

But somehow we tend to forget that there are all different sorts of people . . .

The singer with the bass guitar didn't know anything about Others. I was sure of that. If only I could have sat up half the night with every one of Assol's inhabitants, then I could have formed an accurate opinion of all of them.

But I wasn't entertaining any such illusions. Not everybody will ask you to come in, not everybody will start talking to you about obscure, abstract subjects. And then, apart from the ten or so residents, there were hundreds of service personnel – security guards, plumbers, labourers, bookkeepers. There was no way I could possibly check all of them in a reasonable amount of time.

I managed to get washed in the shower – I'd discovered a strange sort of hose that I could get a jet of water out of – and then walked out into my one and only room. I needed to get some sleep . . . and the next morning I'd try to come up with a new plan.

'Hi, Anton,' a voice said from the open window.

I recognised it. And immediately felt sick at heart.

'Good morning, Kostya,' I said. The words of greeting sounded inappropriate somehow. But not to greet the vampire at all would have been even more stupid.

'Can I come in?' Kostya asked.

I walked over to the window. Kostya was sitting on the outside sill with his back to me, dangling his legs. He was completely naked. As if to demonstrate straight away that he hadn't climbed up the wall, but had flown to the window in the form of a gigantic bat.

A Higher Vampire. At not much more than twenty years old.

A talented boy . . .

'I think not,' I said.

Kostya nodded and didn't try to argue:

'As I understand it, we're working on the same job?'

'Yes.'

'That's good.' He turned round and flashed his teeth in a gleaming white smile. 'I like the idea of working with you. But are you really afraid of me?'

'No.'

'I've learned a lot,' Kostya boasted. Just like when he was a kid and he used to declare: 'I'm a terrible vampire! I'm going to learn how to turn into a bat! I'm going to learn how to fly!'

'You haven't learned anything,' I corrected him. 'You've stolen a lot.'

Kostya frowned:

'Words. The usual Light word game. Your people allowed me to take it, so I did. What's the problem?'

'Are we just going to carry on sparring like this?' I asked. And I raised my hand, folding the fingers into the sign of Aton, the negation of non-life. For a long time I'd wanted to find out if the ancient North African spells worked on modern Russian creatures of the Dark.

Kostya glanced warily at the incomplete sign. Either he knew what it was, or he'd caught a whiff of power. He asked:

'Are you allowed to breach your disguise?'

I lowered my hand in annoyance.

'No. But I might just risk it.'

'No need. If you say so, I'll leave. But right now we're doing the same job . . . we have to talk.'

'So talk,' I said, dragging a stool over to the window.

'You won't let me in then?'

'I don't want to be all alone in the middle of the night with a naked man,' I laughed. 'Who knows what people might think? Let's hear it.'

'What do you make of the T-shirt collector?'

I looked at Kostya quizzically.

'The guy on the tenth floor. He collects funny T-shirts.'

'He doesn't know anything,' I said.

Kostya nodded:

'That's what I think too. Eight of the apartments here are occupied. The owners of another six show up from time to time, but all the rest are very rarely here. I've already checked out all the permanent residents.'

'And?'

'Nothing. They don't know anything about us.'

I didn't ask how Kostya could be so sure. After all, he was a Higher Vampire. They can enter another person's mind as easily as an experienced magician.

'I'll deal with the other six in the morning,' said Kostya. 'But I'm not hopeful.'

'And do you have any suggestions?' I asked.

Kostya shrugged:

'Anyone living here has enough money and influence to interest a vampire or a werewolf. A weak, hungry one . . . newly initiated. So the list of suspects is pretty long.'

'How many newly initiated lower Dark Ones are there in Moscow?' I asked. I was amazed at how easily the phrase 'lower Dark Ones' slipped off my tongue.

I never used to call them that.

I used to feel sorry for them.

Kostya reacted calmly to the phrase. He really was a Higher Vampire. In control, confident.

'Not many,' he said evasively. 'They're being checked, don't worry. Everybody's being checked. All the lower Others, and even the magicians.'

'Is Zabulon really concerned?' I asked.

'Well, Gesar isn't exactly a model of composure,' Kostya responded. 'Everyone's concerned. You're the only one taking the situation so lightly.'

'I don't see it as a great disaster,' I said. 'There are human beings who know we exist. Not many, but there are some. Onemore person doesn't change the situation. If he makes a sensation out of this, we'll soon locate him and make him look like some kind of psycho. That sort of thing has already . . .'

'And what if he becomes an Other?' Kostya asked curtly.

'Then there'll be one more Other,' I said and shrugged.

'What if he doesn't become a vampire or a werewolf, but a genuine Other?' Kostya bared his teeth in a smile. 'A genuine Other? Light or Dark . . . that doesn't matter.'

'Then there'll be one more magician,' I said.

Kostya shook his head:

'Listen, Anton, I'm quite fond of you. Even now. But sometimes I'm amazed at how naïve you are.'

Kostya stretched – his arms rapidly sprouting a covering of short fur, his skin turning dark and coarse.

'You deal with the staff,' he said in a shrill, piercing voice. 'If you get wind of anything, call me.'

He turned to me, his face distorted by the transformation, and smiled again:

'You know, Anton, a naïve Light One like you is the only kind a Dark One could ever really be friends with.'

He jumped down, flapping his leathery wings ponderously. The huge bat flew off into the night, a little awkwardly, but quickly enough.

There was a small rectangle of cardboard lying on the outside sill – a business card. I picked it up and read it:

'Konstantin. Research assistant, the Scientific Research Institute for Haemotological Problems.'

And then the phone numbers – work, home, mobile. I actually remembered the home number – Kostya was still living with his parents. Most vampires tend to have pretty strong family ties.

What had he been trying to tell me?

Why all the panic?

I switched on the light, lay down on the mattress and looked at the pale grey rectangles of the windows.

'If he becomes a genuine Other . . .'

How did Others appear in the world? No one knew. 'A random mutation', Las had called it – a perfectly adequate term. You were born a human being, you lived an ordinary life . . . until one of the Others sensed your ability to enter the Twilight and pump power out of it. After that you were 'guided'. Lovingly, carefully coaxed into the required spiritual condition, so that in a moment of powerful emotional agitation you would look at your shadow, and see it in a different way. See it lying there like a black rag, like a curtain you could pull up over yourself and then draw aside to enter another world.

The world of the Others.

The Twilight.

And the state you were in when you first found yourself in the Twilight – joyful and benign or miserable and angry – determined who you would be. What kind of power you would go on to draw from the Twilight . . . the Twilight that drinks power from ordinary people.

'If he becomes a genuine Other . . .'

There was always the possibility of coercive initiation. But only through the loss of true life and transformation into a walking corpse. A human being could become a vampire or a werewolf, and he would be forced to maintain his existence by taking the lives of human beings. So there was a route for the Dark Ones . . . but one that even they weren't particularly fond of.

Only what if it really was possible to become a magician?

What if there was a way for any human being to be transformed into an Other? To acquire long – very long – life and exceptional abilities. There was no doubt many people would want to do it.

And we wouldn't be against it either. There were so many fine people living in the world who were worthy of being Light Others.

Only the Dark Ones would start building up their ranks too . . .

Suddenly it struck me. It was no disaster that someone had revealed our secrets to a human being. It was no disaster that information could leak out. It was no disaster that the traitor knew the address of the Inquisition.

But this was a new twist in the spiral of endless war.

For centuries the Light Ones and Dark Ones had been shackled by the Treaty. We had the right to search for Others among human beings, even the right to nudge them in the right direction. But we were obliged to sift through tons of sand in our search for grains of gold. The balance was maintained.

Then suddenly here was a chance to transform thousands, millions of people into Others!

A football team wins the Cup Final – and a wave of magic surges across tens of thousands of exultant people, transforming them into Light Others.

And at the same moment the Day Watch issues a command to the fans of the team that has lost – and they're transformed into Dark Others.

That was what Kostya had had in mind. The immense temptation to shift the balance of power in your own favour at a single stroke. Of course, the consequences would be clear, both to the Dark Ones and us Light Ones. Of course, the two sides would adopt new amendments to the Treaty and restrict the initiation of human beings within acceptable limits. After all, the USA and the USSR had managed to keep their nuclear arms race within bounds . . .

I closed my eyes and shook my head. Semyon had once told me that the arms race was halted by the creation of the ultimate weapon. Two thermonuclear devices – that was all that was required – each of which could trigger a self-sustaining reaction of nuclear fusion. The American one was installed somewhere in Texas, the Russian one in Siberia. It was enough to explode either one of them – and the entire planet would be transformed into a ball of flame.

Only, of course, that state of affairs didn't suit us, so the weapon that was never meant to be used could never be activated. But the presidents didn't need to know that, they were only human beings . . .

Maybe the leaders of the Watches had 'magical bombs' like that?

And that was why the Inquisition, which was in on the secret, policed the observation of the Treaty so fervently?

Maybe.

But even so it would be better if it was impossible to initiate ordinary people . . .

Even in my drowsy state I winced at the implications. What did this mean, that I'd begun to think like a fully fledged Other? There are Others, and there are human beings – and they're second class. They can never enter the Twilight, they're not going to live more than a hundred years. And there's nothing you can do about it . . .

Yes, that was exactly the way I'd started to think. Finding a good human being with the natural aptitudes of an Other and bringing him or her over to your side – that was a joy. But turning *everyone* into Others was puerile nonsense, a dangerous and irresponsible delusion.

Now I had something to feel proud about. It had taken me less than ten years to finally stop being human.

My morning began in contemplation of the mysteries of the shower cubicle. Reason finally conquered soulless metal and I got a shower – with music playing, no less – and then concocted a breakfast out of crispbreads, salami and yoghurt. Feeling cheered by the sunshine, I settled down on the windowsill and ate with a view of the Moscow river. For some reason I recalled Kostya admitting that vampires can't look at the sun. Sunlight doesn't actually burn them, it just gives them an unpleasant sensation.

But I had no time for melancholy reflection on old acquaintances. I had to search for . . . for whom? The renegade Other? I was hardly in the best position to do that. His human client? A long, dreary business.

All right, I decided. Let's proceed according to the strict laws of the classic detective novel. What do we have? A clue. The letter sent from Assol. What does it give us? It doesn't give us anything. Unless perhaps someone saw the letter being posted three days ago. There's not much chance that they'd remember, of course . . .

What a fool I was! I even slapped myself on the forehead. Sure, it's no disgrace for an Other to forget about modern technology, Others aren't very fond of complicated technical gizmos. But I was a computer hardware specialist.

All the grounds of Assol were monitored by video cameras.

I put my suit on, knotted my tie and splashed on the eau de cologne that Ignat had chosen for me the day before. Dropped my phone into my inside pocket . . . 'Only dumb kids and sales assistants carry their mobiles on their belts' – that was one of Gesar's helpful little comments.

The phone was new and still unfamiliar. It had some games in it, a built-in disc player, a dictaphone and all sorts of other unnecessary nonsense.

I rode down to the lobby in the cool silence of the lift. And immediately caught sight of my new acquaintance from the night before – only this time he was looking really odd . . .

Las, wearing brand new blue overalls with Assol written on the back, was explaining something to a confused elderly man dressed the same way.

'This isn't a broom you've got here, okay! There's a computer in it, it tells you how dirty the tarmac is and the pressure of the cleaning solution . . . Come on, I'll show you . . .'

My feet automatically carried me after them.

Out in the yard, in front of the entrance to the lobby, there were two bright orange road-sweeping machines, with a tank of water, round brushes and a little glass cabin for the driver. There was something toy-like about the small vehicles, as if they'd come straight from Sunshine Town, where the happy baby girls and boys cheerfully clean their own miniature avenues.

Las clambered nimbly into one of the machines and the elderly man thrust himself halfway in after him. He listened to something Las said, nodded and set off towards the second cleaning unit.

'And if you're lazy, you'll spend the rest of your life as a junior yard-keeper!' I heard Las say. His machine set off, twirling its brushes merrily, turning circles on the tarmac surface. Before my eyes a yard that was already clean acquired an entirely sterile appearance.

Well, would you believe it!

So Las worked as a yard-keeper in the Assol complex, did he?

I tried to withdraw unobtrusively, so as not to embarrass him. But he had already spotted me, and he drove closer, waving his hand gleefully. The brushes started turning less vigorously.

'So you work here then?' I asked. I suddenly started having the most fantastic ideas – Las didn't live in Assol at all, he'd simply moved into an empty apartment for a while. There was no way anyone with a huge residence like that would go cleaning the yard!

'I earn a bit on the side,' Las explained calmly. 'It's good fun, I'm telling you! Ride round the yard for an hour in the morning, instead of your morning exercises, and they pay you wages for it. And not bad wages either.'

I didn't say anything.

'Do you like going on the rides in the park?' Las asked me. 'All those buggies, where you have to pay ten dollars for three minutes? Well, here they pay *you* the money. To enjoy yourself. Or take those computer games . . . sitting there, twitching that joystick about . . .'

'It all depends on whether they make you paint the fence . . .' I muttered.

'That's right,' Las agreed happily. 'But they don't make me do that. I get the same sort of buzz cleaning up the yard as Leo Tolstoy did from scything hay. Only no one has to wash it all again after me – unlike the count, whose peasants used to finish the job for him . . . I'm in their good books here, I get a regular bonus. So, do you fancy riding around too? I could get you a job, if you like. The professional yard-keepers just can't get the hang of this technical equipment.'

'I'll think about it,' I said, examining the briskly spinning brushes, the water spurting out of the nickel-plated nozzles, the gleaming cabin. Back when we were kids, which of us didn't want to drive a street-washing truck? Now, of course, after early childhood kids start dreaming about working as a banker or a hit man . . .

'Okay, think it over, but I've got work to do,' Las said amiably. And the machine set off round the yard, sweeping, washing and sucking up dirt. I heard singing from the cabin:

> The generation of yard-keepers and watchmen
> Have lost each other in the vast expanse of winter . . .
> They've all gone back home now.
> In our time, when every third man is a hero,
> They don't write articles,
> They don't send telegrams . . .

Dumbfounded, I went back to the lobby. I found out from the security guard where Assol's own post office was located and set off. The post office was open: there were three young female employees sitting behind the counter in the cosy little shop, and the postbox where the letter had been sent was standing right there.

The glass eyes of video cameras glittered just below the ceiling.

We could certainly use some professional investigators. They would have come up with this idea straight away.

I bought a postcard of a young chick jumping up and down in the tray of an incubator with the printed message 'I miss my family!' Not very amusing, but in any case I couldn't remember the mailing address of the village where my family was on holiday, so, with a mischievous smile, I sent the postcard to Gesar at home – I did know his address.

I chatted to the girls for a while – working in such an elite residential complex, they had to be polite, but on top of that they were bored – then left the post office and went to the security department on the first floor.

If I'd been able to use my abilities as an Other, I would have simply implanted in the security guards' minds the idea that they liked me – then I'd have been given access to all the video recordings. But I couldn't reveal who I was. And so I decided to employ the most universal motive for liking anyone – money.

Out of the money I'd been given I put together a hundred dollars in roubles – well, no one could expect more than that, could they? I entered the duty office, and there was a young guy in a formal suit, looking bored.

'Good day!' I greeted him, smiling radiantly.

The security man's expression indicated complete solidarity with my opinion concerning the quality of the day. I cast a quick sideways glance at the monitors in front of him – they showed images from at least ten television cameras. And he had to be able to call up a repeat run of any particular moment. If the images were saved to a hard disk (where else could they be saved?), then a recording from three days earlier might not have been transferred to the archive yet.

'I have a problem,' I said. 'Yesterday I received a rather amusing letter . . .' – I winked at him – 'from some girl. She lives here too, as far as I can tell.'

'A threatening letter?' the security man asked, pricking up his ears.

'No, no!' I protested. 'On the contrary . . . But my mysterious stranger is trying to remain incognito. Could I take a look to see who posted letters at the post office three days ago?'

The security man started thinking about it.

And then I spoiled everything. I put the money on the desk and said with a smile:

'I'd be very grateful to you . . .'

The young guy instantly turned to stone. I think he pressed something with his foot.

And ten seconds later two of his colleagues appeared, both extremely polite – which looked pretty funny, given their impressive dimensions – and insistently invited me to come in and see their boss.

There is after all a difference, and a serious one, between dealing with state officials and a private security firm.

It would have been interesting to see if they would have taken me to their boss by force. After all, they weren't the militia. But I thought it best not to aggravate the situation any further and did as my suited escorts asked.

The head of security looked at me reproachfully. He was already advanced in years and had clearly come from the agencies of state security.

'What were you thinking of, Mr Gorodetsky,' he said, holding up my pass to the Assol grounds, 'behaving as if you were in a state institution – if you'll pardon the expression?'

I got the impression that what he really wanted to do was snap my pass in two, call the guards and order them to throw me out of the elite complex.

I felt like saying I was sorry and I wouldn't do it again. Especially since I really was feeling ashamed.

Only that was the desire of the Light Magician Anton Gorodetsky, not of Mr A. Gorodetsky, the owner of a small firm trading in milk products.

'What exactly is the problem?' I asked. 'If it's not possible to do as I requested, they should have said so.'

'And what was the money for?' the head of security queried.

'What money?' I asked in surprise. 'Ah . . . your colleague thought I was offering him money?'

The head of security smiled.

'Absolutely not!' I said firmly. 'I wanted to get my handkerchief out of my pocket. My hay fever's really killing me today. And there was a load of small change in there, so I put it on the desk . . . but I didn't even get time to blow my nose.'

I think I overdid it a bit.

The stony-faced boss held out my pass and said very politely:

'The incident is closed. I'm sure you understand, Mr Gorodetsky, that private individuals are not permitted to view our security recordings.'

I sensed that what had stung the boss most was the phrase about 'small change'. Of course, he wasn't exactly poor, working in a place like that. But he wasn't so flush that he could call a hundred dollars small change.

I sighed and lowered my head.

'Forgive me for being so stupid. I really did try to offer some . . . remuneration. I've been running from one bureaucrat to another all this week, registering the firm . . . it was an automatic reflex.'

The security boss gave me a searching look. He seemed to have softened just a bit.

'It's my fault,' I admitted. 'I was just overwhelmed by curiosity. Would you believe I couldn't sleep half the night, I kept trying to guess . . .'

'I can see you didn't sleep,' the boss said, looking at me. And he couldn't resist asking – after all, human curiosity is ubiquitous, 'What is it you're so interested in?'

'My wife and daughter are at the dacha right now,' I said. 'I'm knocking myself out, trying to get the work on the apartment finished . . . and suddenly I get this letter. Anonymous. In a woman's handwriting. And the letter . . . well, how can I put it . . . it's a kilo of flirting and half a kilo of promises. A beautiful stranger is dreaming of getting to know you, it says, but she doesn't dare take the first step. If I'm observant enough to realise who the letter's from – then all I have to do is approach her . . .'

A glint of amusement appeared in his eyes.

'And your wife's at the dacha?' he asked.

'Yes, she is,' I said with a nod. 'Don't get the wrong idea . . . I've no ambitious plans. I'd just like to find out who this stranger is.'

'Do you have the letter with you?' the boss asked.

'I threw it away immediately,' I said. 'If my wife ever set eyes on it, I'd never be able to prove that nothing happened . . .'

'When was it sent?'

'Three days ago. From our post office.'

The boss thought for a moment.

'The letters there are collected once a day, in the evening,' I said. 'I don't think too many people go in there . . . only about five or six a day. If I could just have a look . . .'

The boss shook his head and smiled.

'Yes, I understand in principle it's not allowed . . .' I said sadly. 'Can't you at least take a look, eh? Maybe there wasn't a single woman there that day, and it's my neighbour's idea of a joke. He's like that . . . the jolly type.'

'From the tenth floor, you mean?' the boss asked, frowning.

I nodded:

'You take a look . . . just tell me if there was a woman there or not.'

'This letter is compromising for you, isn't it?' the boss said.

'To some extent,' I admitted. 'As far as my wife is concerned.'

'Well, then you have grounds for viewing the recording,' the boss decided.

'Thank you very much!' I exclaimed. 'Really, thank you!'

'You see how simple everything is?' said the boss, slowly pressing a key on his computer keyboard. 'And you go getting the money out . . . what Soviet sort of way is that to behave? Just a moment . . .'

I couldn't restrain myself, I got up and stood behind his shoulder. The boss didn't object. He was pretty excited – evidently there wasn't much work for him to do in the grounds of Assol.

The image of the post office appeared on the screen, first from one corner – an excellent view of what the counter girls were doing. Then from another corner – a view of the entrance and the postbox.

'Monday. Eight in the morning,' the boss said triumphantly. 'And now what? Are we going to sit and watch the screen for twelve hours?'

'Oh, of course,' I said, pretending to be disappointed. 'I never thought of that.'

'We press a key . . . no, this one here . . . And now what do we have?'

The image started flickering rapidly.

'What?' I asked, as if I'd never designed the same kind of system for our office.

'Movement search,' the boss declared.

We had our first taker at nine-thirty in the morning. Some oriental-looking worker came into the post office and posted a whole bundle of letters.

'Not your female stranger?' the boss quipped sarcastically. And then he explained. 'That's one of the men building the second block. They're always sending letters to Tashkent . . .'

I nodded.

The second visitor came in at quarter past one; I didn't know him. A very respectable-looking gent, with a bodyguard walking behind him.

The gentleman didn't post any letters. I didn't understand why he went in at all – maybe he was eyeing up the girls, or studying the layout at Assol.

And the third one was . . . Las!

'Oh!' the boss exclaimed. 'Now that's your neighbour, the jester, isn't it? The one who sings songs at night.'

I was obviously a very poor detective . . .

'That's him . . .' I whispered. 'But would he really . . .'

'Okay, let's watch a bit more,' the security boss said, taking pity on me.

Later on, after a two-hour break, people came piling in.

Another three residents sent off envelopes of some kind. All men, all very serious-looking.

And one woman. About seventy years old. Just before closing time. Plump, wearing a sumptuous dress and huge beads in bad taste. Her sparse grey hair was set in curls.

'Surely it couldn't be her?' the boss said, delighted. He got up and slapped me on the shoulder. 'Well, is there any point in looking for your mysterious flirt?'

'It's clear enough,' I said. 'It's a wind-up.'

'Never mind, it's nothing more than a harmless joke,' the security boss consoled me. 'And a request from me to you for the future . . . don't ever make such ambiguous gestures. Never take money out, if you don't intend to pay someone.'

I hung my head.

'We're the ones who corrupt people,' the boss said bitterly. 'Do you understand? We do it ourselves. Offer someone money once, twice . . . and the third time he asks you for it. And we complain – what is all this, and where did it come from? But you're a good man, I can see the light in you.'

I gaped at the boss in amazement.

'Yes, you are a good man,' said the boss. 'I trust my instinct. I saw all sorts in twenty years in the criminal investigation department. Don't do that again, all right? Don't sow evil in the world.'

It was a long time since I'd felt so ashamed.

A Light Magician being taught not to do evil!

'I'll try,' I said, looking the boss in the eye guiltily. 'Thanks very much for your help.'

He didn't answer. His eyes had turned glassy, as vacant as a little baby's. His mouth had opened slightly. His fingers had turned white, clenched tightly around the armrests of his chair.

The freeze. A fairly simple spell, very widely used.

There was someone standing by the window behind me. I couldn't see them, but I could sense them with my back . . .

I jerked to one side as quickly as I could. But I still felt the icy breath of the power aimed at me. No, it wasn't the freeze. But it was something similar, something out of the vampire's arsenal of tricks.

The power skidded across me and sank into the unfortunate security boss. The cover Gesar had put in place not only disguised me, it protected me too.

My shoulder smashed against the wall and I threw my hands out in front of me, but at the last second I pulled back and didn't strike. I blinked and raised the shadow of my eyelids up over my eyes.

Standing by the windows, grim-faced from effort, was a vampire. Tall, with the face of a well-bred European. A Higher Vampire, without the slightest doubt. And not as immature as Kostya. He was at least three hundred years old. And his power undoubtedly exceeded mine.

But not Gesar's! The vampire had not seen that I was really an Other. And now all those suppressed non-life instincts that Higher

Vampires can keep under control came bursting out. I don't know who he took me for. Maybe some special human being with reactions that could rival a vampire's, or a mythical half-blood – the child of a human woman and a male vampire – or for a rather less mythical warlock, a hunter of lower Others. But the vampire was clearly on the point of cutting loose and smashing everything around him. His features began melting like soft putty, changing into a bestial face with a heavy forehead, fangs sliding out of his upper jaw and razor-sharp claws springing from his fingers.

A crazed vampire is a terrible thing.

The only thing worse is a vampire poised and in control.

My reflexes saved me from a duel with a dubious outcome. I held back and didn't strike, and shouted out the traditional formula of arrest:

'Night Watch! Leave the Twilight!'

And immediately I heard a voice from the doorway.

'Stop, he's one of us!'

I was amazed how quickly the vampire normalised. The claws and the fangs were withdrawn, the face quivered, like jellied meat, assuming that reserved, noble expression of a prosperous European. And I remembered this European very well – from the glorious city of Prague, where they brew the best beer in the world and still have the finest Gothic architecture.

'Witiezslav?' I exclaimed. 'What do you think you're doing?'

And, of course, the person standing at the door was Edgar. The Dark Magician who had worked for a short while in the Moscow Day Watch before leaving to join the Inquisition.

'Anton, I beg your pardon!' The imperturbable Estonian was really embarrassed. 'A slight error. In pursuit of our common goal . . .'

Witiezslav was politeness itself.

'Our apologies, watchman. We did not recognise you.'

His gaze slid over me tenaciously and a note of admiration appeared in his voice.

'What a disguise . . . Congratulations, watchman. If that is your work, I bow to you.'

I didn't explain who had constructed my defences. It's not often that a Light Magician (or a Dark Magician, for that matter) gets a chance to give Inquisitors a good bawling-out.

'What have you done to this man?' I barked. 'He is under my protection!'

'It was necessary for our work, as my colleague has already said,' Witiezslav replied with a shrug. 'We're interested in the information from the video cameras.'

Edgar casually moved aside the chair with the frozen security boss in it and came closer. He smiled:

'Gorodetsky, everything's all right. We're all doing the same job, aren't we?'

'Do you have permission for . . . using methods like this?' I asked.

'We have permission for very many things,' Witiezslav replied frostily. 'You have no idea how many.'

That was it, he'd recovered his equilibrium. And he was set on confrontation. But of course – he'd very nearly given way to his instincts, lost his self-control, and for a Higher Vampire that's an unpardonable disgrace. A note of genuine, cold fury appeared in Witiezslav's voice:

'Would you like to test that, watchman?'

Of course, an Inquisitor can't allow anyone to yell at him. Only now there was no way I could back down either.

Edgar saved the situation. He raised his hands and exclaimed in emotional tones.

'It's my fault! I ought to have recognised Mr Gorodetsky. Witiezslav, it's all the result of my poor work. I'm sorry.'

I held out my hand to the vampire first.

'Fair enough, we are all doing the same job. I hadn't expected to see you here.'

I'd hit the bull's eye there. Witiezslav looked away for a moment. And he smiled very amiably as he shook my hand. The vampire's palm was warm . . . and I realised what that meant.

'Our colleague Witiezslav has come straight from the plane,' said Edgar.

'And he hasn't gone through temporary registration yet?' I asked.

No matter how powerful Witiezslav might be, no matter what position he might hold in the Inquisition, he was still a vampire. And he was obliged to go through the humiliating procedure of registration.

I didn't press the point too hard. Just tried to be helpful.

'We can complete all the formalities here,' I suggested. 'I have the right to do that.'

'Thank you,' the vampire said with a nod. 'But I'll call into your office. Proper procedure above all things.'

A shaky truce had been patched together.

'I've already looked through the recordings,' I said. 'Letters were posted three days ago by four men and one woman. And some construction worker posted a whole pile of letters. There are builders from Uzbekistan working here.'

'A good sign for your country,' Witiezslav said very politely. 'When the citizens of neighbouring states are used as manpower, it's an indication of economic growth.'

I could have explained to him what I thought about that. But I didn't.

'Would you like to see the recording?' I asked.

'Yes, I think so,' the vampire said.

Edgar stood aside.

I brought up the image of the post office on the monitor, then switched on 'movement search', and we watched all the local lovers of the epistolary genre once again.

'I know this one,' I said, pointing at Las. 'I'll find out today what it was he posted.'

'Do you suspect him?' asked Witiezslav.

'No,' I said and shook my head.

The vampire ran the tape through again. But this time the unfortunate security boss was set in front of the monitor, still under the spell.

'Who's this?' Witiezslav asked him.

'A resident,' he replied indifferently. 'Block one, sixteenth floor.'

He had a good memory. He named all the suspects, except the building worker with the pile of letters. As well as Las, the resident from the sixteenth floor and the old woman from the eleventh, letters had been posted by two of Assol's managers.

'We'll deal with the men,' Witiezslav decided. 'For a start. You check the old woman, Gorodetsky. All right?'

I shrugged. Collaboration was all very well, but I wasn't going to let anyone order me about.

Especially not a Dark One. And a vampire.

'It's easier for you,' Witiezslav explained. 'It's . . . hard for me to approach old people.'

The admission was frank and unexpected. I mumbled something in reply and didn't press him for any further explanation.

'I sense in them something that I don't have,' he went on to explain anyway. 'Mortality.'

'You envy them that?' I couldn't resist asking.

'It frightens me.' Witiezslav leaned down over the security chief and said: 'We're going to go now. You will sleep for five minutes and have beautiful dreams. When you wake up, you will forget our visit. You will only remember Anton . . . you will feel very friendly towards him. If Anton needs anything, you will give him any help you can.'

'There's no need . . .' I protested weakly.

'We are all working for the same cause,' the vampire reminded me. 'I know how hard it is to work undercover. Goodbye.'

And instantly he disappeared. Edgar gave a guilty smile and walked out of the door.

I left the office too, without waiting for the head of security to wake up.

CHAPTER 4

FATE, WHICH OUR magicians claim does not exist, was kind to me.

In Assol's vestibule (well, you really couldn't call that spacious hall a lobby,) I saw the old woman that the vampire had been afraid to approach. She was standing by the lift, gazing pensively at the buttons.

I glanced at the old woman through the Twilight, and realised that she was totally confused, almost in a panic. The well-trained security guards were no help here. On the outside the old woman seemed entirely calm and collected: I realised she was definitely a lady – not an ordinary old Russian woman at all. I set off decisively towards her.

'Excuse me, can I be of any help?' I asked.

She cast me a sideways glance. Not a glance of senile suspicion, more of embarrassment.

'I've forgotten where I live,' she confessed. 'Do you happen to know?'

'The eleventh floor,' I said. 'Allow me to show you the way.'

The grey curls with delicate pink skin showing through them swayed ever so slightly.

'Eighty years old,' said the old woman. 'I remember that . . . it's painful to remember it. But I do.'

I took the lady by the arm and led her towards the lift. One of the security men started walking towards us, but my aged companion shook her head:

'The gentleman's showing me the way . . .'

The gentleman did show her the way. The elderly lady recognised her own door and even quickened her step in delight. The apartment was not locked, it had been magnificently refurbished and furnished, and there was a lively girl about twenty years old striding to and fro in the hallway and complaining into a phone:

'Yes, I've looked downstairs! She slipped out again . . .'

The girl was delighted when we showed up. Only I'm afraid the sweet smile and the touching concern were mostly meant for me.

Good-looking young women don't take servants' jobs in homes like that because the money's good.

'Mashenka, bring us some tea,' said the old woman, interrupting the girl's prattling. She probably had no illusions either. 'In the large room.'

The girl went dashing obediently to the kitchen, but not before she had smiled once more and deliberately brushed her pert breasts against me as she said in my ear:

'She's got really bad . . . My name's Tamara.'

Somehow I didn't feel like introducing myself. I followed the old woman through into the 'large room'. Well, it was huge. With furniture from Stalin's time and clear traces of the work of an expensive designer. The walls were covered with black-and-white photographs – at first I even took them for elements of the design. But then I realised that the blindingly beautiful young woman with white teeth, wearing a flying helmet, was my elderly lady.

'I bombed the Fritzes,' the lady said modestly as she sat down at a round table covered with a maroon velvet tablecloth with tassels. 'Look, Kalinin himself presented me with that medal . . .'

Dumbfounded, I took a seat facing the former pilot.

Even in the best of cases people like that live out their final days in old state dachas or in monolithic, dilapidated Stalinist buildings. But not in an elite residential complex. She had dropped bombs on the fascists, not ferried the Reichstag's gold reserves back home to Russia.

'My grandson bought the apartment for me,' the old woman said, as if she had read my thoughts. 'A big apartment. I don't remember anything here . . . it all seems familiar, like it's mine, but I don't remember . . .'

I nodded. She had a good grandson, what could I say? Of course, transferring an expensive apartment to your war-heroine grandmother's name and then inheriting it later was a very clever way to do things. But in any case it was a good deed. Only the servant should have been chosen with more care. Not a twenty-year-old girl obsessed with the profitable capital investment of her pretty young face and good figure, but an older, reliable nurse . . .

The old woman looked pensively out of the window. She said:

'I'd be better off in those houses, the little ones . . . I'm more used to that . . .'

But I wasn't listening any more. I was looking at the table, heaped high with letters bearing the eye-catching stamp 'No longer at this address'. It was hardly surprising. The addressees included such figures as the old Soviet Union figurehead Kalinin, Generalissimus Joseph Stalin, Comrade Khrushchev and 'Dear Leonid Ilich Brezhnev'.

Our more recent national leaders had clearly not been retained in the old woman's memory.

I didn't need any Other abilities to guess what kind of letter the old woman had posted three days earlier.

'I can't bear having nothing to do,' she complained, catching my glance. 'I keep asking to be assigned to the schools, the flying colleges . . . so I can tell the young people what our life was like . . .'

I took a look at her through the Twilight anyway. And I almost exclaimed out loud.

The old pilot was a potential Other – maybe not a very powerful one, but it was crystal clear.

Only, to initiate her at that age . . . I couldn't imagine it. At sixty, at seventy . . . but at eighty?

The stress of it would kill her. She'd just fade away into the Twilight, an insane, insubstantial shadow.

You can't check everyone. Not even in Moscow, where there are so many watchmen.

And sometimes we recognise our brothers and sisters too late.

Tamara appeared carrying a tray set with dishes of biscuits and sweets, a teapot and beautiful old cups. She set the dishes down on the table without making a sound.

But the old woman was already dozing, still perched on her chair as firm and upright as ever.

I got up carefully and nodded to Tamara:

'I'll be going. You should keep a closer watch on her, you know she forgets where she lives.'

'But I never take my eyes off her,' Tamara replied, fluttering her eyelids. 'I'd never . . .'

I checked her too. No Other abilities at all.

An ordinary young woman. Even quite kind in her own way.

'Does she often write letters?' I asked with the faintest of smiles.

Taking the smile as sign of absolution, Tamara began smiling too:

'All the time! To Stalin, and Brezhnev . . . Isn't that hilarious?'

I didn't argue with her.

* * *

Of all the cafés and restaurants that Assol was crammed with, the only one open was the café in the supermarket. A very nice café, on the second-floor balcony above the checkouts. With an excellent view of the entire supermarket hall. It had to be a good place to drink a cup of coffee, mapping out your route for a pleasant stroll as you bought the groceries – doing your 'shopping': that terrible word, that monstrous Anglicism that has eaten its way into the Russian language, like a tick boring into its helpless prey.

That was where I had my lunch, trying not to feel horrified by the prices. Then I bought a double espresso, and a packet of cigarettes – which I smoke only very rarely – and tried to imagine that I was a detective.

Who had sent the letter?

The renegade Other or the Other's human client?

It didn't look like there was any advantage in it for either of them. And the scenario with another individual attempting to forestall the initiation was just too melodramatic.

Think, head, think! You've come across more confused situations than this before. We have a renegade Other. We have his client. The letter was sent to the Watches and to the Inquisition. So the letter was most likely sent by an Other. A powerful, intelligent, well-informed Other.

Then the question was: What for?

And I already had the answer: In order not to go through with this initiation. In order to deliver the client into our hands and not go through with his promise.

That meant it wasn't a matter of money. In some incomprehensible fashion the unknown client had acquired a hold over the Other. A hold so terrible and absolute that he could demand anything he wanted. An Other could never admit that a human being held that kind of power over him. So he was making a cunning knight's move . . .

Yes, yes, yes!

I lit a cigarette, took a sip of coffee, and slumped back grandly in the soft chair like I belonged there.

It was beginning to come together. How could an Other end up in bondage to a human being? An ordinary human being, even if he was rich, influential, intelligent . . .

There was only one possibility, and I didn't like it one little bit. Our mysterious renegade Other could have found himself in the position of the golden fish in the fairy tale. He could have given a human being his word of honour to grant him or her any wish at all. After all, the fish in the story hadn't expected the crazy old woman . . . that reminded me: I had to inform Gesar that I had discovered a potential Other . . . that the crazy old woman would want to become the Empress of the Sea.

And that brought me to the really upsetting part.

A vampire, or a werewolf, or a Dark Magician wouldn't give a damn about any promise.

They would give their word and then take it back again. And they'd tear the human's throat out if he tried to stand up for his rights.

So it was a Light Magician who had made the rash promise!

Could that really happen?

It could.

Easily. We were all a bit naïve, Kostya had been right about that. Our human weaknesses made us vulnerable – we could be trapped by our sense of guilt, all sorts of romantic notions . . .

And so the traitor was in our ranks. He had given his word – I wouldn't try to figure out why just yet. He was caught in a trap. If a Light Magician refused to carry out his promise, he would dematerialise . . .

Stop! There was another curious point here. I could promise a human being to do 'anything he wanted'. But if I was asked to do the impossible . . . well, I didn't know what exactly, not something that was difficult, or repugnant, or forbidden – but actually impossible . . . extinguish the sun, for instance, or turn a human being into an Other . . . What answer would I give? That it was impossible. No way. And I'd be right, and there wouldn't be any reason for me to dematerialise. And my human master would have to accept that. Ask for something else . . . Money, health, incredible sex appeal, good luck playing the stock market and a keen nose for danger. In general, the usual human pleasures that a powerful Other can provide.

But the renegade Other had panicked. He'd panicked badly enough to set both Watches and the Inquisition on his 'master' at the same time. He was backed into a corner, he was afraid of disappearing into the Twilight forever.

That meant that he really could turn a human being into an Other!

That meant the impossible was possible. The means existed. Not known to many, but they did exist . . .

I suddenly felt uneasy.

The traitor was one of our oldest and most knowledgeable magicians. Not necessarily a magician beyond classification, not necessarily someone who held a really important position. But an old hand with access to the greatest secrets . . .

For some reason I immediately thought of Semyon.

Semyon, the Light Magician who sometimes knew things that required the seal of the Avenging Fire to be applied to his body, to prevent him talking about them.

'I'm well into my second century . . .'

Maybe.

He knew a lot of things.

Who else did?

There was a whole bunch of old, experienced magicians who

didn't work in the Watch. Just got on with living in Moscow, watched TV, drank beer, went to football matches.

I didn't know them, that was the problem. Those wise old birds who had quit working didn't want to get involved in the endless war between the Watches.

And who could I turn to for Advice? Who could I expound my terrifying conjectures to? Gesar? Olga? Potentially they were on the suspect list themselves.

No, I didn't believe they could have blundered. After the rough deal she'd had from life, Olga – not to mention the arch-cunning Gesar – would never make a gaffe like that, they wouldn't make impossible promises to a human being. And Semyon couldn't do it either. Semyon was wise, in the primordial, folk meaning of the word. I couldn't believe he would slip up like this . . .

That meant it was another of our senior colleagues who had blundered.

And anyway, how would I look putting forward an accusation like that? 'I think the guilty party is one of us. A Light One. Most likely Semyon. Or Olga. Or even you, Gesar . . .'

How could I carry on going to work after that? How would I be able to look my colleagues in the face?

No, I couldn't come out with suspicions like that. I had to know for sure.

Somehow it felt awkward to call the waitress over. I walked to the counter and asked her to make me a fresh cup of coffee. Then I leaned against the railings and looked down.

Below me I spotted my acquaintance from the night before. The guitarist, collector of amusing T-shirts and happy owner of a large English toilet, was standing beside a small open pool full of live lobsters. Las's face reflected the intense workings of his thought. Finally he laughed and pushed his trolley towards the checkout.

I pricked up my ears.

Las unhurriedly set out his modest purchases on the moving belt, with a bottle of Czech absinthe towering over everything else. As he was paying, he said:

'You know, that pool of lobsters you have over there . . .'

The girl at the checkout smiled, every element of her posture confirming that there was a pool and there were live lobsters paddling in it, and a couple of arthropods would go remarkably well with absinthe, kefir and frozen pelmeni.

'Well,' Las continued imperturbably, 'I just saw one lobster climb on another's back, crawl out onto the edge and hide under those fridges over there.'

The girl started blinking rapidly. A minute later two security men and a sturdy female cleaner appeared at the checkout. After listening to the terrible tale of the escape, they rushed over to the fridges.

Las finished paying, glancing back into the hall every now and then.

The pursuit of the non-existent lobster was in full swing. The cleaner was poking her mop under the fridges, with the security men bustling around her. I heard one of them say:

'Drive it this way, towards me! I can almost see it already!'

Las moved towards the exit with a quiet smile on his face.

'Go easy with that poking. You'll dent its shell – it'll be damaged goods,' one of the security men warned.

Trying to wipe a smile unworthy of a Light Magician off my face, I took my coffee from the waitress. No, that guy wouldn't have cut letters out of newspapers with nail scissors. That would have been far too tedious.

My phone rang.

'Hi, Sveta,' I said.

'How are things going, Anton?'

Her voice sounded a bit less alarmed this time.

'I'm having a coffee. I've had a chat with my colleagues. From the competing firms.'

'Aha,' said Svetlana. 'Well done. Anton, do you need my help at all?'

'But you . . . you're not on the staff,' I said, perplexed.

'I don't give a damn!' Svetlana replied, flaring up instantly. 'It's you I'm concerned about, not the Watch!'

'No need yet,' I replied. 'How's Nadiushka?'

'She's helping me make borscht,' Svetlana said with a laugh. 'So dinner will be a bit late today. Shall I call her?'

'Uhuh,' I said, relaxing, and took a seat by the window.

But Nadya didn't take the phone, and she didn't want to talk to her daddy.

They can be stubborn like that at the age of two.

I talked to Svetlana a little bit longer. I felt like asking if her bad premonitions had disappeared, but I didn't. It was clear enough from her voice that they had.

I wound up the conversation, but I didn't put my phone away. There was no point in calling the office. But what if I had a word with someone in a private capacity?

Well, I had to go into town, meet people, keep the wheels of my business turning, sign new contracts, didn't I?

I dialled Semyon's number.

It was time to stop playing the sleuth. Light Ones don't lie to each other.

For meetings that are not entirely business, but not exactly personal either, the best places are small pubs, with five or six tables at most. There was a time when Moscow didn't have any places like that. Public catering always meant premises large enough for a full-scale bash.

But we have them now.

This particular entirely unremarkable pub-café was right in the very centre, on Solyanka Street. A door in the wall leading straight in from the street, five tables, a little bar – back at the Assol complex even the bars in the apartments were more impressive.

And there was nothing special about the clientele. It wasn't one of those special-interest clubs that Gesar loved to collect – scuba-divers get together here, and recidivist cat-burglars there . . .

And the cuisine had no pretensions of any kind. Two types of draught beer, other alcoholic drinks, sausages out of a microwave and French fries. Booze and junk.

Maybe that was why Semyon had suggested meeting in this café? He fitted right in. And I didn't exactly stand out from the crowd either . . .

Noisily blowing the froth off his Klin Gold beer – I'd only ever seen that done in old movies – Semyon took a mouthful and looked at me amiably:

'Let's hear it.'

'You know about the crisis?' I asked, taking the bull by the horns straight away.

'Which crisis is that?' Semyon asked.

'The one with the anonymous letters.'

Semyon nodded. He even added something:

'I've just completed the temporary registration of our visitor from Prague.'

'This is what I think,' I said, twirling my beer mug round on the clean tablecloth. 'They were sent by an Other.'

'Sure they were!' said Semyon. 'You drink your beer. If you want, I'll sober you up afterwards.'

'You can't, I'm shielded.'

Semyon screwed his eyes up and looked at me. And he agreed that yes, I was shielded and it was beyond his powers to break through a magic-proof shell installed by none other than Gesar himself.

'Well then,' I went on, 'if they were sent by an Other, what is he trying to achieve?'

'The isolation or elimination of his human client,' Semyon said calmly. 'Evidently he must have rashly promised to make him an Other. So now he can't back out of it.'

All my heroic intellectual efforts had been pointless. Without even working on the case, Semyon had figured it all out in his own head.

'It's a Light Other,' I said.

'Why?' asked Semyon, surprised.

'A Dark Other has plenty of other ways to go back on a promise.'

Semyon thought for a while, chewed on a potato straw and said yes, it looked that way. But he wouldn't entirely rule out any involvement by Dark Ones. Because even Dark Ones could swear a rash oath that there was no way to get round. For instance, swear on the Dark, call the primordial power to bear witness. After that, they couldn't wriggle out of it.

'Agreed,' I said. 'But even so, the chances are greater that one of us has slipped up.'

Semyon nodded and declared:

'Not me.'

I looked away.

'Don't you get upset,' Semyon said in a melancholy voice. 'You've got the right idea and you're doing the right thing. We could have slipped up. Even I could have blundered. Thanks for asking me to talk, and not just running to the boss . . . I give you my word, Light Magician Anton Gorodetsky, that I did not send these letters and I do not know who sent them.'

'You know, I'm really glad about that,' I said honestly.

'Not nearly as glad as I am,' Semyon laughed. 'I'll tell you something, the Other who did this has got some nerve. He hasn't just got the Watches involved in this mess, he's dragged the Inquisition into it as well. To do that, you either have to be way out of control, or calculate every last little detail. If it's the first, he's done for, but if it's the second, he'll squirm his way out of it. I'd lay two to one he'll squirm his way out.'

'Semyon, is it true that an ordinary human being can be turned into an Other after all?' I asked. Honesty is the best policy.

'I don't know,' Semyon replied and shook his head. 'I used to believe it was impossible. But if recent events are anything to go by, there's some kind of loophole. Very narrow, pretty nasty, but still a loophole.'

'Why nasty?' I asked, seizing on his words.

'Because otherwise we would have made use of it. What a coup, for instance, to make the President one of your own! And not just the President, but everyone who has any kind of influence. There'd be an amendment to the Treaty, determining the procedure for initiation, and there'd be the same stand-off, only at a new level.'

'But I thought it had been absolutely forbidden,' I admitted. 'The Higher Others got together and agreed not to disrupt the balance . . . threatened each other with the ultimate weapon . . .'

'With what?' Semyon asked, astonished.

'You know, the ultimate weapon. Remember, you told me about the incredibly powerful thermonuclear bombs? We have one, the Americans have one . . . There must be something of the sort in magic too . . .'

Semyon started laughing:

'What nonsense, Anton! There aren't any bombs like that, it's all fantasy, fairy tales! Learn some physics! There isn't enough heavy water in the oceans for a self-sustaining thermonuclear reaction.'

'Then why did you tell me that?'

'We were spinning all sorts of yarns at the time. I never thought you'd believe it . . .'

'Ah, dammit,' I muttered and took a mouthful of beer. 'And you know, after that I couldn't sleep at night . . .'

'There is no ultimate weapon, you can sleep easy,' Semyon laughed. 'No real one and no magical one. And if we accept that it is possible to initiate ordinary people after all, then the procedure is extremely difficult and disgusting, with unpleasant side effects. In general, no one wants to get their hands dirty. Neither us nor the Dark Ones.'

'And you don't know about any such procedure?' I asked, just to make sure.

'I don't.' Semyon thought for a moment. 'No, I definitely don't. Reveal myself to people, give them orders or, say, recruit them as volunteers – I've done it all. But as for turning someone into an Other when you want to, I've never heard of that.'

Another dead end.

I nodded, gazing gloomily into my beer mug.

'No need to knock yourself out,' Semyon advised me. 'There are only two possibilities. This Other is either a fool or he's very cunning. In the first case the Dark Ones or the Inquisitors will find him. In the second case they won't, but they will find the human being and teach him not to wish for such strange things. Similar cases have been known.'

'What am I going to do?' I asked. 'I must admit the Assol complex is interesting, it's fun to live there. Especially on expenses.'

'Then enjoy it,' Semyon said calmly. 'Or is your pride offended? Do you want to out-gallop everyone else and find the traitor first?'

'I don't like leaving things half-done,' I admitted.

Semyon laughed:

'All I've been doing for the last hundred years is leaving things half-done . . . There was the little business of the hoodoo laid on the rich peasant Besputnov's cattle, in the Kostroma province. What a case that was, Anton! A mystery. A tight web of intrigue. It was magical all right, but it was all done so cunningly . . . the hoodoo was applied via a field of hemp.'

'Do cattle actually eat hemp?' I asked, intrigued despite myself.

'Ah, who'd let them? The peasant Besputnov used to make rope out of that hemp. And he used the rope to lead his cows around. And the hex went through it that way. A cunning hoodoo, slow and thorough. And not a single registered Other for a hundred miles around. I moved into the little village and started searching for the evildoer . . .'

'Did they really work that thoroughly back then?' I asked, amazed. 'Sending in a watchman for the sake of some peasant and his cattle?'

Semyon smiled:

'I did all sorts of work back then. This peasant's son was an Other, and he asked us to step in to help his father, who was so depressed he almost made himself a noose out of that rope . . . So I moved in, all on my ownsome, got myself some property, even started cosying up to a certain little widow lady. But at the same time I was searching. And I realised I was on the trail of an ancient witch, very well disguised, not a member of any Watches and not registered anywhere. It was really fascinating. Just imagine: a witch who was two or three hundred years old! She had accumulated as much power as a first-grade magician! And there I was playing at Nat Pinkerton . . . detecting . . . I felt ashamed somehow to call in the Higher Magicians to help. And gradually, bit by bit, I turned up clues, and put together a list of suspects. One of them was actually the attractive young widow . . .'

'Well?' I asked, entranced. Semyon certainly liked to stretch the truth a bit, but this story seemed like the real thing.

'That's all there is,' Semyon sighed. 'There was a rebellion in Petrograd. Then the revolution. So you can imagine, there were more important things to deal with than cunning witches. Human blood was flowing in rivers. I was recalled. I wanted to go back and find the old hag, but I never had the time. And then they flooded the entire village and everybody was resettled. Maybe that witch is dead by now.'

'Frustrating,' I said.

Semyon nodded:

'And I've got an entire wagonload of stories like that. So there's no need for you to go sweating your guts out on this one.'

'If you were a Dark One,' I admitted, 'I'd definitely think you were trying to divert suspicion from yourself.'

Semyon just smiled.

'I'm not a Dark One, Anton. As you know perfectly well.'

'And you don't know anything about the initiation of human beings,' I sighed. 'I was really hoping . . .'

Semyon turned serious.

'Anton, let me tell you something. The girl I loved more than anything in the whole world died in 1921. She died of old age.'

I looked at him, but didn't dare risk a smile. Semyon wasn't joking.

'If I'd known how to make her an Other . . .' Semyon whispered, gazing off into the distance. 'If I'd only known . . . I revealed myself to her as an Other. I did everything for her. She was never ill. At the age of seventy, she looked thirty at the most. Even in hungry Petrograd she never wanted for anything . . . the permits she had used to strike Red Army men dumb . . . I had her credentials signed by Lenin himself. But I couldn't give her my length of life. That's not in our power.' He looked into my eyes sombrely. 'If I'd known how to initiate Lubov Petrovna, I wouldn't have asked anybody's permission. I'd have gone through anything. I'd have dematerialised myself – but I'd have made her into an Other . . .'

Semyon stood up and sighed:

'But now, to be quite honest, it doesn't matter to me. Whether people can be transformed into Others or not simply doesn't concern me. And it shouldn't concern you either. Your wife's an Other. Your daughter's an Other. All that happiness for one person? Gesar himself can't even dream of anything like it.'

He walked out, but I sat at the table for a while longer, finishing my beer. The owner of the café – who was also the waiter, the chef and the barman – never even looked in my direction. When Semyon came in, he had hung a magical screen round the table.

What had I been thinking of, really?

There were two Inquisitors beavering away. The talented vampire Kostya was circling the Assol complex in the form of a bat. They'd figure it out, they were bound to discover who had wanted to become an Other. And they'd either find the individual who had sent the letters, or they wouldn't.

What difference did that make to me?

The woman I loved was an Other. And more than that, she had voluntarily abandoned her work in the Watch, a brilliant career as a Great Enchantress. All for an idiot like me. So that I wouldn't get hung up about being stuck for ever at my basic second grade of power.

And Nadiushka was an Other too. I'd never have to go through the horror suffered by an Other whose child grows up, grows old and dies. Sooner or later we would reveal Nadienka's true nature to her. She would want to be a Great One, no doubt about it. And she would be the very Greatest. Maybe she would even do something to make this imperfect world better.

But here I was playing at spies, like a little child. Worrying myself sick about succeeding in my mission, instead of dropping in on my friendly neighbour in the evening or relaxing – strictly for purposes of camouflage – in the casino.

I got up, put the money on the table and walked out. In an hour or two the screen would disperse, the owner of the café would see the money and the empty glasses and remember a couple of ordinary-looking guys drinking beer there.

CHAPTER 5

I SPENT HALF a day doing things that were strictly off limits and no use to anyone. Kostya would probably have pulled a wry face and informed me what he thought of my naïvity.

First I went back to Assol to change into jeans and a simple shirt, and then I set off in the direction of the nearest normal courtyard – towards the dreary, nine-storey prefabricated buildings. There, to my delight, I discovered a football pitch, with senior-school-age loafers kicking a ball around on it. There were a few young men there as well, in fact. Even though the recently concluded World Cup had been, to put it mildly, an inglorious one for our team, it had still had a positive effect. In the few courtyards that still survived, the spirit that had seemed lost was reviving.

I was put on a team. The side that had only one adult – with an impressive paunch, but extremely agile and frisky. I'm not a very good player, but these guys weren't World Cup material either.

For about an hour I ran around on the dusty, trampled earth, yelling and shooting at the goal made out of rusty wire mesh, even scoring a few times. Once a huge senior-school hulk deftly dumped me on the ground and gave me an amiable smile.

But I didn't take offence or get upset.

When the game tailed off – of its own accord, somehow – I went into the nearest shop, bought some mineral water and beer and – for the very youngest footballers – Baikal fizzy drink. Of course, they would have preferred Coca-Cola, but it's time we stopped drinking that foreign poison

The only thing bothering me was the realisation that excessive generosity would arouse all kinds of suspicions. So I had to be moderate in my good deeds.

After saying goodbye to the players, I walked as far as the river beach and enjoyed a swim in the water that was dirty, but cool. The pompous palace spires of the Assol complex towered up into the sky on one side.

Well, let them . . . I didn't care.

The funniest thing of all, I realised, was that in my place any Dark Magician could have done exactly the same thing. Maybe not one of the really young ones still into pleasures previously out of reach, like fresh oysters and expensive prostitutes. But a Dark One who had already lived a bit and come to understand that everything in the world was nothing but vanity, the vanity of vanities, in fact.

And he would have scampered round that pitch, yelling and kicking the ball, and hissing at the teenagers' clumsy attempts to swear: 'Hey, watch your lip, kid!' And afterwards he would have gone to the beach, and splashed about in the muddy water, and laid on the grass, looking up at the sky . . .

Where was it, that dividing line? Okay, with the lower Dark Ones, everything was clear. They were non-life. They had to kill in order to survive. And there was nothing any verbal gymnastics could do about that. They were Evil.

But where was the real boundary?

And why did it sometimes seem on the part of dissolving? Like now, at a time when the only problem was one single human being who wanted to become an Other? Just one, that was all! But just look at the resources that had been thrown into the search. Dark Ones, Light Ones, the Inquisition . . . And I wasn't the only one working on this business, I was just a pawn who had been advanced, carrying out local reconnaissance work. Gesar was wrinkling his brow, Zabulon knitting his eyebrows, Witiezslav scowling and baring those teeth. A human wanted to become an Other – hunt him down, get him!

But who wouldn't want it?

Not the eternal hunger of the vampires, not the insane fits of the werewolves, but the full, complete life of a magician. With everything that ordinary people had.

Only better.

You're not afraid anyone will steal the expensive stereo from your car when you leave it unwatched.

You don't get sick with flu, and if you come down with some vile incurable disease, the Dark Sorcerers or the Light Healers are at your service.

You don't wonder how you're going to survive until pay day.

You don't feel afraid of dark streets at night or drunken bums.

You're not even afraid of the militia.

You're certain your child will get home safely from school and not run into some crazy maniac in the front hallway . . .

Yes, of course, that was where the real problem lay. Your nearest and dearest were safe, they were even excluded from the vampire lottery. Only you couldn't save them from old age and death.

But after all, that was still a long way off. Somewhere in the future, far ahead.

On the whole it was far better to be an Other.

What's more, you wouldn't gain anything if you refused initiation, even your human relatives would be right to call you a fool. After all, if you became an Other, you'd be able to help them out. Like that story of Semyon's . . . someone put a hex on a peasant's cows, and his Other son had an investigator sent in to help him. Blood is thicker than water, after all, your own flesh and blood is dearest. Nothing to be done about that . . .

I jerked upright as if I'd been electrocuted. I jumped to my feet and stared up at the buildings of the Assol complex.

What reason could a Light Magician have for making a rash promise to do absolutely anything?

There was only one reason.

That was it, the lead.

'Have you come up with something, Anton?' a voice asked behind my back.

I turned round and looked into the black lenses of Kostya's glasses. He was wearing just bathing trunks – appropriate attire for the beach – and a child's white panama hat perched on the back of his head like a skullcap (no doubt he'd taken it away from some toddler without any qualms of conscience) as well as the dark glasses.

'Finding the sun hot?' I asked spitefully.

'It's oppressive. Hanging up there in the sky like a flat-iron . . . Why, aren't you feeling hot?'

'Sure,' I admitted. 'But it's a different kind of heat.'

'Can we manage without the sarcasm?' Kostya asked. He sat down on the sand and fastidiously tossed aside a cigarette butt from near his feet. 'I only go swimming at night now. But this time I came . . . to have a word with you.'

I felt ashamed. The person sitting in front of me was a moody young man, it made no difference that he was undead. And I still remembered the gloomy teenager hovering uncertainly at the door of my apartment. 'You shouldn't invite me in, I'm a vampire, I could come in the night and bite you . . .'

And that boy had held out for a pretty long time. He'd drunk pig's blood and donors' blood. He'd dreamed of becoming alive again. 'Like Pinocchio' – he must have read Collodi or seen the movie *AI*, but anyway he'd found the right comparison.

If only Gesar hadn't detailed me to hunt vampires . . .

No, that was nonsense. Nature would have taken its course. And Kostya would have been given his licence.

And in any case I had no right to scoff at him. I had one huge advantage – I was alive.

I could approach old people without feeling ashamed. Yes, without any shame, because Witiezslav hadn't been honest with me. It wasn't fear or revulsion that had made him avoid the old woman.

It was shame.

'Sorry, Kostya,' I said and lay down on the sand beside him. 'Let's talk.'

'It seems to me that the permanent residents at Assol have nothing to do with it,' Kostya began gloomily. 'The client is only there occasionally.'

'We'll have to check them all,' I said faking a sigh.

'That's only the start. We have to find the traitor.'

'We are looking.'

'I can see the way you're looking . . . Realised that he's one of yours, have you?'

'How do you make that out?' I protested indignantly. 'Some Dark One could quite easily have blundered . . .'

We discussed the situation for a while. We seemed to have reached the same conclusions simultaneously.

Only now I was just half a step ahead. And I had no intention of helping Kostya out.

'The letter was posted with the heap of letters that builder brought to the post office,' said Kostya, not suspecting how cunning I was being. 'Nothing could be easier. All those *Gastarbeiters* live in an old school, they use it as a hostel. They put all their letters on the attendant's table on the ground floor. In the morning someone goes to the post office and posts them. It would be no problem for an Other to get into the hostel and divert the attention of the attendant . . . or simply wait for him to go to the toilet. Then drop the letter into the general pile. And there you go! No leads.'

'Simple and effective,' I agreed.

'In the Light Ones' style,' Kostya said with a frown. 'Get someone else to do the dirty work for you.'

For some reason I didn't take offence. I just smiled mockingly and turned over on to my back, looking up at the sky and the glorious yellow sun.

'Okay, we do the same . . .' Kostya muttered.

I didn't say anything.

'Come on, tell me, haven't you ever used people for your operations?' Kostya asked crossly.

'Sometimes. Used them, but never put them in danger.'

'And in this case the Other has done exactly the same,' Kostya said, forgetting his comment about the 'dirty work'.

'What I'm wondering is . . . does it make any sense to follow this trail any further? So far the traitor has covered all his tracks thoroughly. We'll end up chasing a phantom . . .'

'They say a couple of days ago two security guards at Assol thought they saw something ghastly in the bushes,' I said. 'They even opened fire.'

Kostya's eyes blazed.

'Have you already checked it out?'

'No,' I said. 'I'm shielded, undercover, there's no way I can.'

'Is it okay if I check it out?' Kostya asked eagerly. 'Listen, I'll mention that it was you . . .'

'Go ahead,' I said magnanimously.

'Thanks, Anton,' said Kostya, breaking into a broad smile and giving me a hefty punch on the shoulder. 'You're a decent guy after all. Thanks.'

'Do a good job,' I couldn't resist saying, 'and maybe you'll jump the queue to get another licence.'

Kostya fell silent and his face turned sour. He stared hard at the river.

'How many people did you kill to become a Higher Vampire?' I asked.

'What's that to you?'

'I'm just . . . curious.'

'Check out your archives some time and take a look,' Kostya said with a crooked smile. 'Is it really that hard?'

Of course, it wasn't that hard. But I'd never looked at Kostya's file. I didn't really want to know . . .

'Uncle Kostya, give me my hat!' a squeaky voice demanded nearby.

I glanced sideways at the little girl, about four years old, who had come running up to Kostya. So he really had been teasing a child, and he'd stolen her hat . . .

Kostya obediently removed the panama from his head and gave it to her.

'Will you come again tonight?' the girl asked, glancing at me and pouting. 'Will you tell me a story?'

'Uhuh,' Kostya said with a nod.

The girl beamed and ran off to a young woman who was collecting her things together a little distance away. The sand kicked up from under her heels.

'You've lost your mind!' I roared, sitting up. 'I'll reduce you to dust right here!'

My expression must have been pretty terrifying. Kostya was quick to answer:

'What is it? What's wrong with you, Anton? She's my niece! Her mother's my cousin! They live in Strogino, and I'm staying with them for the time being, so I don't have to drag myself all the way across town.'

That brought me up short.

'What, did you think I was sucking her blood?' Kostya asked, still looking at me warily. 'Go and check. There aren't any bites. She's my niece, understand? For her sake I'd take out anyone myself!'

'Pah!' I said and spat. 'What else could I think? "Will you come again tonight?", "Will you tell me a story?" . . .'

'A typical Light One,' Kostya said more calmly. 'Since I'm a vampire I must be a bastard, right?'

Our fragile truce wasn't exactly over, but it had reverted to the normal state of cold war. Kostya sat there fuming, and I sat there cursing myself for jumping to conclusions. They didn't issue licences for children under the age of twelve, and Kostya wasn't such a fool as to hunt without a licence.

But it had just slipped out . . .

'You've got a little daughter,' Kostya said, suddenly catching on. 'The same age, right?'

'Younger,' I replied. 'And prettier.'

'Obviously, your own are always prettier,' Kostya laughed. 'All right, Gorodetsky. I understand. Let's forget it. And thanks for the lead.'

'That's okay,' I said. 'Maybe those security men didn't see anything after all. They'd been drinking vodka or smoking dope . . .'

'We'll check it out,' Kostya said cheerfully. 'We'll check everything out.'

He rubbed the back of his head with his open hand and stood up.

'Time to go?' I asked.

'It's getting to me,' Kostya answered, squinting upwards. 'I'm disappearing.'

And he did just that, disappeared, after first averting the eyes of everyone there. There was just a dim shadow left hanging in the air for a second.

'Show-off,' I said and turned back over on to my stomach.

To be honest, I was feeling hot too. But I decided on principle not to leave with a Dark One.

I still had a few things to think through before I went to the Assol security office.

Witiezslav had done a really good job. When I turned up the head of security broke into a broad, friendly smile.

'Oh, look who's come to see us!' he declared, shoving some papers off to one side. 'Tea, coffee?'

'Coffee,' I decided.

'Andrei, bring us some coffee,' the boss commanded. 'And a lemon.'

And he reached into the safe and produced a bottle of good Georgian cognac.

The security man who had shown me into the boss's office was a little disconcerted, but he didn't argue.

'Any questions?' the boss asked as he deftly sliced the lemon. 'Will you have some cognac, Anton? It's good, I promise!'

And I didn't even know what his name was . . . I liked the former boss of security better. The way he'd treated me had been sincere.

But the former security boss would never have given me the information I was counting on getting now.

'I need to take a look at the personal files of all the residents,' I said. And I added with a smile: 'In a building like this you must keep a check on everyone, right?'

'Of course,' the boss agreed readily. 'Money's all very fine, but there are some serious people intending to live here, and we don't want any thugs or bandits . . . You want all the personal files?'

'The lot,' I said. 'For everyone who's bought an apartment here, regardless of whether they've moved in yet or not.'

'The files on the real owners or the people the apartments are registered to?' he asked politely.

'The real owners.'

The boss nodded and reached into the safe again.

Ten minutes later I was sitting at his desk and leafing through the files – all very neat and not too thick. Out of natural curiosity I started with myself.

'Do you need me here any more?' the security boss asked.

'No, thanks.' I eyed the number of files. 'I'll need about an hour.'

The boss went out, closing the door quietly behind him.

And I got stuck into my reading.

Anton Gordoetsky, it emerged, was married to Svetlana Gorodetskaya and had a two-year-old daughter, Nadezhda Gorodetskaya. Anton Gorodetsky had a small business – a firm trading in dairy products. Milk, kefir, cottage cheese and yoghurts . . .

I knew the firm. A standard Night Watch subsidiary that earned money for us. There were about twenty of them around Moscow, and their employees were perfectly ordinary human beings who never suspected where the profits really went.

It was all pretty modest and simple, cute. Like the old promo jingle for milk – 'On the meadow, on the meadow, who is grazing on the meadow?' That's right, Others. Well, I couldn't really deal in vodka, could I?

I put my file to one side and started on the other residents.

Naturally not all the information about the people was there, it couldn't have been. After all, no private security service, even in the most luxurious residential complex, is any match for the KGB.

But I didn't need much. Basic information about their relatives. In the first instance, their parents.

First I set aside those whose parents were alive and well and put the files on people whose parents were dead in a different pile.

I was particularly interested in anyone who had been raised in a children's home – there were two of those – and anyone with a stroke through the columns headed 'Father' or 'Mother'.

There were eight of those.

I laid these files out in front of me and started studying them closely.

Immediately I weeded out one ex-orphanage boy who, to judge from his file, had criminal connections. He had been out of the country for the last year and, despite appeals from law enforcement agencies, had no intention of coming back.

Then I sifted out two from incomplete families.

One of them turned out to be a weak Dark Magician known to me from a trivial old case. The Dark Ones were bound to be giving him the third degree already. If they hadn't come up with anything, the guy was in the clear.

The other was a rather well-known variety artiste who, I knew – again quite by chance – had been touring for the last three months in the USA, Germany and Israel. Probably earning money for the finishing work on his apartment.

That left seven. A good number. For the time being I could focus on them.

I opened the files and began reading them closely. Two women, five men . . . Which of them might be worth considering?

'Roman Lvovich Khlopov, forty-two, businessman . . .' The face didn't arouse any associations. Maybe he was the one? Maybe . . .

'Andrei Ivanovich Komarenko, thirty-one, businessman . . .' Oh, what a strong-willed face! And still fairly young . . . Was it him? Possibly . . . No, impossible! I set the businessman Komarenko's file aside. A man in his early thirties who donated serious money like that to building churches and was distinguished by 'intense religious feeling' wouldn't want to be transformed into an Other.

'Timur Borisovich Ravenbakh, sixty-one, businessman . . .' Rather young-looking for his age. And if he met Timur Borisovich, even the strong-willed youngster Andrei Ivanovich Komarenko would have lowered his eyes. The face was familiar, either from TV, or somewhere else . . .

I set the file aside. Then my hands started to sweat. A cold tremor ran down my back.

No, it wasn't from TV, or rather, not only from TV, that I remembered that face . . .

It couldn't be!

'It can't be!' I said, repeating my thought out loud. I poured myself some cognac and tossed it down. I looked at Timur Borisovich's face – a calm, intelligent, slightly eastern face.

It couldn't be.

I opened the file and started reading. Born in Tashkent. Father . . . unknown. Mother . . . died at the very end of the war, when little Timur was not even five. Raised in a children's home. Graduated from a junior technical college and then a construction institute. Made his career through Komsomol connections. Somehow managed to avoid joining the Party. Founded one of the first construction co-operatives in the USSR, which actually did far more business trading in imported paving stones and plumbing fixtures than constructing buildings. Moved to Moscow . . . founded a firm . . . engaged in politics . . . was never . . . never a member of . . . was never employed as . . . a wife, a divorce, a second wife . . .

I'd found the human client.

And the most terrible thing about it was that I'd found the renegade Other at the same time.

The discovery was so unexpected, it felt as if the universe had collapsed around me.

'How could you!' I said reproachfully. 'How could you . . . boss . . .'

Because if you made Timur Borisovich ten or fifteen years younger, he would have been a dead ringer for Gesar, or Boris Ignatievich as he was known to the world, who sixty years ago had lived in that region . . . Tashkent, Samarkand and other parts of Central Asia . . .

What astonished me most of all was not my boss's transgression. Gesar a criminal? The idea was so incredible, it didn't even provoke any response.

I was shaken by how easily the boss had been caught out.

So sixty-one years earlier a child had been born to Gesar in distant Uzbekistan. Then Gesar had been offered a job in Moscow. But the child's mother, an ordinary human being, had died in the turmoil of war. And the little human being, whose father was a Great Magician, had ended up in a children's home . . .

All sorts of things happen. Gesar might not even have known that Timur existed. Or he could have known, but for some reason or other not have played any part in his life. But then the old man had felt a tug at his heartstrings, and he'd met with his son, who was already old, and he'd made a rash promise . . .

And that was certainly amazing!

Gesar had been intriguing for hundreds, thousands of years. Every single word he spoke was carefully weighed. And then he pulled a stunt like this?

Incredible.

But a fact.

You didn't have to be an expert in physiognomy to recognise Timur Borisovich and Boris Ignatievich as close relatives. Even if I kept quiet, the Dark Ones would make the same discovery. Or the Inquisition would. They'd put the screws on the elderly businessman . . . But why bother with the screws? We weren't vicious racketeers. We were Others. Witiezslav would look into his eyes, or Zabulon would click his fingers, and Timur Borisovich would spill the whole story as if he were at confession.

And what would happen to Gesar?

I thought about it. Well, if he admitted that he did send the letter . . . then there hadn't been any evil intent on his part . . . and in general he had the right to reveal himself to a human being.

I spent a little while running through the points of the Treaty in my mind, the amendments and refinements, the precedents and exceptions, the references and footnotes . . .

The result was pretty amusing.

Gesar would be punished, but not very severely. The maximum penalty would be an official rebuke from the European Office of the Night Watch. And something menacing, but almost meaningless, from the Inquisition. Gesar wouldn't even lose his job.

Only . . .

I imagined what merriment there would be in the Day Watch. How Zabulon would smile. How sincerely Dark Ones would start to enquire after Gesar's family affairs and send greetings to his little human son.

Of course, after living the number of years that Gesar had, anyone would grow a thick skin, and learn how to shrug off ridicule.

But I wouldn't have liked to be in his place right then.

And our guys wouldn't go easy on the irony either. No, no one would actually reproach Gesar for committing a blunder. Or badmouth him behind his back.

But there would be smirks. And bemused head-shaking. And

whispers – 'the Great One's getting old after all, getting old . . .'

I didn't have any puppyish adoration or wide-eyed admiration left for Gesar. Our views differed on so many things. And there were some things I still couldn't forgive him for . . .

But to pull a stupid stunt like this!

'What on earth were you thinking of, Great One?' I said. I put all the files back in the open safe and poured myself another glass of cognac.

Could I help Gesar?

How?

Get to Timur Borisovich first?

And then what? Cast a spell of silence on him? They'd remove it, someone would be found who could.

What if I forced the businessman to leave Russia? To go on the run, as if all the city's criminal groups and law enforcement agencies were after him?

It would serve him right. Let him spend the rest of his life hunting seals or knocking coconuts off palm trees! So he wanted to be the Emperor of the Sea . . .

I picked up the phone and entered the number of our office's exchange, dialled the additional digits, and was put straight through to the IT lab.

'Yes?' it was Tolik's voice.

'Tolik, run a check on someone for me. Quick.'

'Tell me the name and I'll run it,' Tolik answered, unsurprised at my request.

I listed everything I'd found out about Timur Borisovich.

'Ha! So what else do you need apart from that?' Tolya asked. 'Which side he sleeps on, or the last time he visited the dentist?'

'Where he is right now,' I said dourly.

Tolik laughed, but I heard the brisk rattle of a keyboard at the other end of the line.

'He has a mobile phone,' I said just in case.

'Don't teach your grandmother . . . He has two mobiles . . . And they're both . . . they're . . . Right, just a moment, I'll superimpose the map . . .'

I waited.

'At the Assol residential complex. And not even the CIA could tell you more precisely than that, the positioning isn't accurate enough.'

'I owe you a bottle,' I said, and hung up. Jumped to my feet. But then . . . what was the rush? I was sitting in front of the observation services monitor, wasn't I?

I didn't have to search for long.

Timur Borisovich was just getting into the lift, followed by a couple of men with stony faces. Two bodyguards. Or a bodyguard and a driver who doubled up as a second bodyguard.

I switched off the monitor and dashed out into the corridor just in time to bump into the head of security.

'Got what you wanted?' he asked, beaming.

'Uhuh,' I said, nodding on the run.

'Need any help?' he shouted after me eagerly.

I just shook my head.

CHAPTER 6

THE LIFT SEEMED to take an unbearably long time creeping up to the twentieth floor. I managed to think up and reject several plans on the way. It was the bodyguards who complicated the whole business.

I'd have to improvise. And if necessary, breach my disguise a little.

I rang the doorbell for ages, peering into the electronic eye of the 'spy-hole'. Eventually something clicked and a voice from the concealed intercom said:

'Yes?'

'You're flooding me out!' I blurted, trying to sound as agitated as possible. 'The frescoes on my ceiling have run! The water's swilling about in the grand pianos!'

Where the hell did I get those frescoes and pianos?

'What grand pianos?' the voice asked suspiciously.

How was I supposed to know what kinds of grand pianos there are? Black and expensive. Or white and even more expensive . . .

'Viennese pianos! With curvy legs!' I blurted out.

'Not the ones in the bushes then?' the voice asked me with blunt irony.

I looked down at my feet. That damned multiple point lighting . . . there weren't even any proper shadows!

I reached my hand out towards the door and just caught a faint glimpse of a shadow on the pinkish wood bound with armour-plate steel.

And I pulled the shadow towards me.

My hand plunged into the Twilight, and I followed.

The world was transformed, becoming colourless and grey. A dense silence descended, only disturbed by the buzzing of the electronic innards of the 'spy-hole' and the intercom.

I was in the Twilight, that strange world to which only the Others know the way. The world from which our Power is drawn.

I could see the pale shadows of the wary bodyguards through the door, their auras flickering an alarmed crimson colour above their heads. And now I could have reached out with my thoughts, given the order – and they would have opened the door for me.

But I preferred to walk straight through the door.

The security guards were genuinely alarmed – one of them had a pistol in his hand, the other was reaching incredibly slowly for his holster.

I touched the security guards, running my thumb across their solid foreheads. Sleep, sleep, sleep . . . You are very tired. You have to lie down and sleep right now. Sleep for at least an hour. Sleep very soundly. And have pleasant dreams.

One guard went limp immediately, the other resisted for a fraction of a second. I'd have to check him later to see if he was an Other, you could never tell . . .

Then I emerged from the Twilight. The world acquired colour and sped up. I heard music coming from somewhere.

The two guards were slumping like stuffed sacks onto the expensive Persian rug spread out just inside the door.

I managed to catch both of them at once and lay them down fairly gently.

And then I set off towards the sound of a violin playing in a minor key.

Now this apartment had been done up in real style. Everything gleamed and shone, everything had been carefully considered so that it harmonised with the whole. It must have taken a top designer to do all this. The owner hadn't hammered a single nail into any of these walls. He'd probably never even expressed any desire to do so . . . just muttered in approval or dissatisfaction as he looked through the colour sketches, and jabbed his finger at a few of the pictures – then forgotten about the apartment for six months.

It turned out that Timur Borisovich had come to the Assol building to relax for a while in the jacuzzi. And a genuine Jacuzzi at that, not a hydro-massage bath from some other less famous firm. Only his face, so painfully reminiscent of Gesar's, protruded above the frothing surface of the water. An expensive suit was carelessly thrown across the back of a chair – the bathroom was big enough for chairs, a coffee table, a spacious sauna and this jacuzzi, which was like a small swimming pool.

No doubt about it, genes are a remarkable thing. Gesar's son couldn't become an Other, but in his human life he enjoyed every possible boon.

I walked in, got my bearings in those wide, open spaces and approached the bath. Timur Borisovich looked at me and frowned. But he didn't make any sudden movements.

'Your bodyguards are sleeping,' I said. 'I assume you have an alarm button or a pistol somewhere within easy reach. Don't try to use it, it won't help.'

'There's no alarm button here,' Timur Borisovich growled, and his voice sounded like Gesar's. 'I'm not paranoid . . . So you must be an Other?'

Right. Apparently it was full and frank confession time.

I laughed.

'Yes, I am. I'm glad no long explanations will be required.'

Timur Borisovich snorted. He asked:

'Do I have to get out? Or can we talk like this?'

'This is fine,' I said generously. 'Do you mind?'

The Great Magician's offspring nodded, and I pulled up a chair and sat down, heartlessly creasing his expensive suit.

'Do you understand why I'm here?'

'You don't look anything like a vampire,' said Timur Borisovich. 'Probably a magician? A Light Magician?'

I nodded.

'You've come to initiate me,' Timur Borisovich decided. 'Was it too much trouble to phone first?'

Oh, calamity . . . He didn't understand a thing after all.

'Who promised you would be initiated?' I asked sharply.

Timur Borisovich frowned. He muttered:

'I see . . . here we go again. What did you come here for?'

'I'm investigating the unsanctioned dissemination of secret information,' I said.

'But you're an Other? Not from state security?' Timur Borisovich asked anxiously.

'Unfortunately for you, I'm not from state security. Tell me absolutely honestly who promised you would be initiated, and when.'

'You'll sense it if I lie,' Timur Borisovich said simply.

'Of course.'

'Oh Lord, all I wanted was just to spend a couple of hours in peace!' Timur Borisovich exclaimed in a pained voice. 'Problems here, conflicts there . . . and when I climb into the bath, in comes a serious young man looking for answers!'

I waited. I didn't bother to point out that I wasn't simply a man.

'A week ago, I had a meeting with . . .' Timur Borisovich hesitated, '. . . a meeting, in rather strange circumstances . . . with a certain gentleman . . .'

'What did he look like?' I asked. 'No need to describe him, just picture him to yourself.'

A gleam of curiosity appeared in Timur Borisovich's eyes. He looked at me hard.

'What?' I exclaimed, bewildered.

I had good reason to be . . .

If I could trust the mental image that had appeared in the businessman's mind (and why not?), then the person who had come to talk to him was the now little known but once famous movie actor Oleg Strizhenov.

'Oleg Strizhenov.' Timur Borisovich snorted. 'Still young and handsome. I thought there was something badly wrong with my head. But he said it was just a disguise . . .'

So that was it. Gesar had had enough wits to disguise himself. Well then . . . that improved our chances.

Feeling a bit more cheerful, I said;

'Go on. Then what happened?'

'That were-creature,' said Timur Borisovich, inadvertently confusing our terminology, 'gave me a lot of help with a certain matter. I'd got involved in a bad business . . . entirely by chance. If I hadn't been told a few things, I wouldn't be lying here now.'

'So you were helped.'

'Helped big time,' Timur Borisovich said with a nod. 'So naturally I got curious. Another time we had a real heart-to-heart. Remembered old Tashkent and talked about the old films . . . And then this phoney Strizhenov told me about the Others, and said he was a relative of mine. So he'd be happy to do anything at all for me. Free and for gratis, no return favours required.'

'So?' I asked, urging him on.

'Well, I'm not an idiot,' Timur Borisovich said with a shrug. 'You don't ask golden fishes for three wishes, you ask for unlimited power. Or at the very least for a pool full of golden fishes. I asked him to make me an Other, like him. Then this "Strizhenov" started getting edgy and hopping about like he was on a red-hot skillet. Said it couldn't be done. But I could tell he was lying. It can be done! So I asked him to make a real effort to turn me into an Other . . .'

He was telling the truth. Every single word. But he wasn't quite telling me the whole story.

'It *is* impossible to make you into an Other,' I explained. 'You're an ordinary human being. I'm sorry, but there's no way you'll ever be an Other.'

Timur Borisovich snorted again.

'It's . . . well, if you like, it's in the genes,' I explained. 'Timur Borisovich, did you realise that your contact was caught in a trap? That he had formulated his proposal wrongly, and as a result he was obliged to do something for you that's impossible?'

The self-confident businessman had nothing to say to that.

'You did,' I said. 'I can see that you did. And you still went on demanding?'

'I told you – it can be done!' said Timur Borisovich, raising his voice. 'I can feel it! I can tell when someone's lying just as well as you can! And I didn't make any threats, I only asked!'

'It was probably your father who came to see you,' I said. 'Do you realise that?'

Timur Borisovich froze in his seething jacuzzi.

'He wanted to help you all right,' I said. 'But he can't do this. And your demand is literally killing him. Do you understand that?'

Timur Borisovich shook his head.

'The promise he gave was too vague,' I said. 'You took him at his word, and if he fails to carry out his promise, then he'll die. Do you understand?'

'Is that one of your rules?'

'It's a corollary of power,' I said curtly. 'For the Light Ones.'

'Where was he all that time, my dad?' Timur Borisovich asked with genuine sorrow in his voice. 'I suppose he must still be young? Why did he come to me when my grandchildren are already married?'

'Believe me, he couldn't have come sooner,' I replied. 'Most likely he didn't even know about you. It just happened that way. But now you're killing him. Your own father.'

Timur Borisovich was silent.

But I was exultant. This businessman lounging in his jacuzzi wasn't a hardened scoundrel. He'd grown up in the East, and the word 'father' meant a lot to him.

No matter what.

'Tell him that I withdraw my . . . request,' Timur Borisovich muttered. 'If he doesn't want to . . . then to hell with him . . . He could simply have come and told me everything honestly. He didn't need to send his staff.'

'Are you sure I'm one of his staff?'

'Yes. I don't know who my dad is. But he's some big wheel in those Watches of yours.'

I'd done it! I'd removed the sword of Damocles that had been hanging over Gesar's head!

Maybe that was why he'd sent me to Assol? Because he knew I could do it.

'Timur Borisovich, one more request,' I went on, striking while the iron was hot. 'You have to disappear for a while, get out of town. Certain facts have become known . . . there are Others on your trail, apart from me. Including Dark Ones. They'll make trouble for you, and . . . for your father.'

Timur Borisovich jerked himself upright in his bath.

'What else are you going to order me to do?'

'I could order you,' I explained, 'just as easily as your bodyguards. And you'd go dashing to the airport without your trousers. But I'm asking you, Timur Borisovich. You've already done one good thing by agreeing to withdraw your demand. Take the next step. Please.'

'Do you realise what kind of ideas people get about businessmen who take off without warning to God knows where?'

'I can imagine.'

Timur Borisovich grunted and suddenly looked older somehow. I felt ashamed. But I carried on waiting.

'I'd like to talk . . . to him.'

'I think that'll be okay,' I agreed. 'But first you have to disappear.'

'Turn around,' Timur Borisovich muttered.

I turned around obediently. Because I believed I wouldn't get a heavy nickel-plated soap-dish across the back of my head.

And that entirely groundless trust saved me.

Because I glanced at the wall through the Twilight – to make sure the bodyguards were still sleeping peacefully by the door. And I saw a fleeting shadow, moving far too quickly for a human being.

And what's more, the shadow was moving through the wall. Not walking normally, like a magician, but gliding like a vampire.

By the time Kostya was in the bathroom, I'd already set my face into the calm, mocking expression appropriate for a Light watchman who's got the better of a Dark One.

'You!' said Kostya. In the Twilight his body gave off a light vapour. Vampires generally look different in the Twilight world, but Kostya still looked a lot like a human being. Amazing for a Higher Vampire.

'Of course,' I said. My words seemed to sink into wet cotton wool. 'What are you doing here?'

Kostya hesitated, but he answered honestly:

'I sensed you using power. So I knew you must have found something . . . Someone.'

He turned his gaze on Timur Borisovich and asked:

'Is this the blackmailer?'

There was no point in lying now. Or in trying to hide the businessman either.

'Yes,' I said. 'I've got him to withdraw his demands.'

'How?'

'I lied, told him it was his own father who promised to turn him into an Other. And now his father's in serious trouble . . . He felt ashamed and withdrew his demands.'

Kostya frowned.

'I'm planning to send him as far as possible out of harm's way,' I lied, inspired. 'He can settle down somewhere in the Dominican Republic.'

'That's only half of the investigation,' Kostya said sullenly. 'I think you Light Ones are protecting one of your own.'

'We are, or I am?'

'You are, Anton. Finding the human being isn't the most important thing. We need the one who spoke out of turn. The one who promised to initiate him.'

'But he doesn't know anything!' I protested. 'I checked his memory, there's nothing there. The traitor came to him disguised as a movie actor from the last century. And he didn't leave any clues.'

'We'll see about that,' Kostya decided. 'Let him get his trousers on, and I'll take him in.'

How about that for cheek!

'I found him, and he's going with me!' I barked.

'And I think you were going to cover up the clues,' Kostya said with quiet menace.

Behind our backs the old man was slowly towelling himself off, without even the slightest idea of the conversation we were having in the Twilight. And we glared at each other, neither of us willing to back off.

'He's going with me,' I repeated.

'Fight you for him?' Kostya asked, almost cheerfully.

In a single gliding movement he was there beside me. He glanced into my eyes, and in the Twilight his eyes glittered with red fire.

He really wanted this fight.

He'd been wanting it for years. To finally convince himself that truth was on the side of the Higher Vampire Konstantin, and not the naïve youth Kostya, who had dreamed of freeing himself from the curse and becoming human again . . .

'I'll annihilate you,' I whispered.

Kostya just laughed:

'Shall we find out?'

I looked down at my feet. The shadow was barely visible, but I raised it – and slipped down into the next level of the Twilight. Where the walls of the building were mere hints in the mist and space was filled with a low, disconcerting drone.

But I only held the advantage for a brief moment.

Kostya appeared at the second level immediately after me. And now he had changed a great deal – his face looked like a skull with the skin stretched tight over it, his eyes were sunken and his ears long and pointed.

'I've really learned a lot,' Kostya whispered. 'Well then, who's the suspect going with?'

And then another voice spoke:

'I have a proposal that will suit everyone.'

Witiezslav materialised in the grey mist. His body was also distorted, and it was steaming, like a lump of dry ice in the sun.

I shuddered – the Prague vampire had emerged from the third level of the Twilight, from depths that were beyond my reach. Just how powerful was he?

Edgar appeared after Witiezslav. The journey to the third level had been a serious effort for the magician – he was staggering and breathing heavily.

'He's going with us,' Witiezslav continued. 'We are not inclined to suspect Anton Gorodetsky of any criminal intent. But we take note of the Day Watch's suspicions. The investigation is transferred to the Inquisition.'

Kostya didn't reply.

I didn't say anything either. Apart from the fact that Witiezslav was well within his rights, there was no way I could oppose him.

'Shall we go back, gentlemen?' Witiezslav proposed. 'It's a little bleak down here.'

And a second later we were back standing in the spacious bathroom, where Timur Borisovich was hopping from one foot to the other as he tried to get into his underpants.

Witiezslav gave him time to pull up his underwear. It was only when the businessman heard something and turned round, then saw our little group and shouted out in surprise that Witiezslav cast a cold glance at him.

Timur Borisovich went limp. Edgar leapt to his side and lowered the limp body into a chair.

'You say he doesn't know who the traitor is,' Witiezslav said, surveying the businessman curiously. 'What a remarkably familiar face . . . It suggests certain rather interesting conjectures to me.'

I said nothing.

'You can be proud of yourself, Anton,' Witiezslav went on. 'What you said made perfect sense. I believe this man's father really does serve in a Watch. The Night Watch.'

Kostya laughed. Of course, he didn't much like Witezslav's

decision. Kostya would have preferred to deliver Gesar's offspring to the Day Watch. But the way things were suited him pretty well too.

'Could the all-knowing Gesar really have committed such a blunder?' he asked in delight. 'How interesting . . .'

Witiezslav looked at him, and Kostya stopped short.

'Anyone can blunder,' Witiezslav said in a quiet voice. 'Even a magician beyond classification. But . . .'

He fixed his gaze on me:

'Can you ask Gesar to come here?'

I shrugged. It was a stupid question, of course I could. And so could Witiezslav.

'I don't like what's going on here,' Witezslav said in that same quiet voice. 'I don't like it at all. Someone here is bluffing far too brazenly.'

He ran his piercing, inhuman glance over all of us. Something had put him on his guard, but exactly what was it?

'I'll contact my chief,' Kostya said in a tone that brooked no denial.

Witiezslav didn't object. He was looking at Timur Borisovich and frowning.

I took out my phone and dialled Gesar's number.

'Someone's trying to make fools of us all,' said Witiezslav, his fury starting to break through. 'And that someone . . .'

'Tell him to get dressed,' I said as I listened to the beeping of the phone. 'Or do we have to humiliate an old man and take him in his underpants?'

Witiezslav didn't move a muscle, but Timur Borisovich stood up and started getting dressed, as if he were sleepwalking.

Edgar sidled up to me and asked sympathetically:

'Isn't he answering? In his place I'd . . .'

'It will be a long time before anyone offers you a place like that,' Witiezslav commented. 'If you can't see how we've been set up . . .'

If the look on Edgar's face was anything to go by, he couldn't see a thing. And neither could I, or Kostya, who had rolled his eyes back and up and was whispering something silently.

'Yes, Anton . . .' Gesar said when he answered. 'Anything interesting?'

'I've found the man who was promised he could be turned into an Other,' I said, forcing out the words with difficulty.

Total silence fell in the bathroom. Everyone seemed to be straining to hear the faint sound from my phone.

'Excellent!' Gesar exclaimed. 'Well done! Now get in touch with the investigators from the Day Watch and the Inquisition straight away. Let them join in. That Czech vampire, Witiezslav, is around there somewhere. The old guy's on the ball, even if he doesn't have any sense of humour . . . but that's a misfortune suffered by all vampires.'

Witiezslav turned towards me. His face had turned to stone and his eyes were blazing. He'd heard everything.

And I would have bet a crate of Czech beer to a bottle of triple cologne that Gesar knew perfectly well that Witiezslav was standing there beside me.

'Witiezslav is already here,' I said. 'And so is Edgar and . . . the investigator from the Dark Ones.'

'Great!' Gesar was delighted. 'Ask our visitor from Prague to put up a portal for me . . . if he can manage that, of course. I'll drop over to see you.'

I put the phone away and looked at Witiezslav. To be honest, I felt Gesar had overdone it a bit.

But how could I know how things stood between the old Light Magician and the vampire Inquisitor? And what scores they had to settle with each other?

'You heard him,' I said evasively.

'Tell me again,' Witiezslav replied curtly.

'The head of the Night Watch of Moscow, the Most Lucent Magician Gesar, requests you to put up a portal for him. If that is within your power, of course.'

Witiezslav simply glanced to one side and a narrow, bright doorway appeared in the air above the bubbling jacuzzi. Anyone stepping out through that strange door was bound to end up in the water.

'No problem,' Witiezslav said coolly. 'Edgar . . .'

The former Dark Magician looked devotedly into his eyes.

'The file on this man . . .' Witiezslav nodded towards Timur Borisovich, who was lazily knotting his necktie. 'It's probably downstairs, in the security office.'

Edgar disappeared. To save time, he went to get the file through the Twilight.

And a moment later Gesar appeared in the bathroom.

Only he didn't appear through the portal, but beside it, stepping down neatly onto the marble floor.

'I'm really getting old,' he sighed. 'I missed the door . . .'

He looked at Witiezslav and broke into a broad smile.

'Well, just look who's here! Why didn't you drop in to see me?'

'I've been busy,' Witiezslav answered curtly. 'I think we need to resolve a few matters that have come up, as quickly as possible . . .'

'You've been spending too much time in the office,' Gesar sighed. 'You've become a total bureaucrat . . . Well, what do we have here?'

'There he is,' I put in.

Gesar gave me a smile of approval and looked at Timur Borisovich.

There was a sudden hush. Kostya had gone quiet after finishing his silent conversation with Zabulon, who was in no hurry to put in an appearance. Witiezslav had turned to stone. I was trying not even to breathe.

'That's curious,' said Gesar. He went over to Timur Borisovich, who was staring blankly straight ahead, and touched his arm. He heaved a sigh: 'Ai-ai-ai . . .'

'Do you know this man, Most Lucent Gesar?' Witiezslav asked.

Gesar turned towards us with an expression of profound sadness, and asked bitterly:

'Tell me, have you completely lost your grip? This is my own flesh and blood, Witiezslav! This is my son!'

'Really?' Witiezslav asked ironically.

Gesar took no more notice of him. He put his arms round the old man, who from the human point of view could have been his father. He stroked his cheeks affectionately and whispered:

'Where have you been all these years, my little one . . . and we end up meeting like this . . . They told me you'd died . . . they said it was diphtheria . . .'

'My heartfelt congratulations, Gesar,' said Witiezslav. 'But I should like to receive an explanation.'

Edgar reappeared in the bathroom. Perspiring, clutching a folder in his hands.

Still hugging his old son, Gesar replied:

'It's a simple story. Before the war I worked all over Uzbekistan. Samarkand, Bukhara, Tashkent . . . I was married. Then I was recalled to Moscow. I knew I'd had a son, but I never saw him. There was no time for that . . . there was a war on. Then the boy's mother died. And I lost track of him.'

'Not even *you* were able to find him?' Witiezslav asked suspiciously.

'Not even me. According to the documents, he had died. Of diphtheria . . .'

'This is like a Mexican soap opera,' Edgar protested. 'Most Lucent Gesar, do you claim never to have met this man?'

'Never,' Gesar said sadly.

'You have never spoken to him, never, in contravention of all the rules, offered to help him become an Other?' Edgar persisted.

Gesar looked at the magician ironically.

'Esteemed Inqusitor, if anyone knows, you should, that a human being cannot become an Other.'

'Answer the question!' said Edgar, half-asking, half-ordering.

'I have never seen him, never spoken to him and never made any promises to him. I did not send the letters to the Watches and the Inquisition. I did not ask anyone to meet with him or send those letters. The Light bears witness to my words!' Gesar rapped out. He flung out his hand – and for an instant a petal of white fire blossomed on it. 'Are you casting doubt on what I say? Claiming that I am the traitor?'

Gesar had grown taller, as if some spring had straightened out inside him. You could have hammered nails into that look in his eyes.

'Are you accusing me?' Gesar continued, raising his voice. 'You, Edgar? Or you, Witiezslav?'

Kostya was too slow to back away and he was caught in that withering glance:

'Or you, vampire-boy?'

Even I felt like hiding. But deep in my heart I was laughing. Gesar had put one over on everyone. I didn't know how he'd managed it, but he had.

'We would not dare even to surmise such a thing, Most Lucent Gesar,' said Witiezslav, the first to bow his head. 'Edgar, your questions were phrased impolitely.'

'I apologise,' Edgar said, hanging his head. 'Forgive me, Most Lucent Gesar. I am profoundly sorry.'

Kostya was gazing around in panic. Was he waiting for Zabulon? No, that wasn't likely. On the contrary, he was hoping the Dark One's chief wouldn't turn up for his share of the taunts.

And Zabulon wouldn't turn up, I realised that. A European vampire who, for all his great power and centuries-old wisdom, had lost his touch for intrigue, might fall into a trap. But Zabulon had realised straight away that Gesar wouldn't leave himself open so stupidly.

'You have attacked my son,' Gesar said sadly. 'Who cast the spell of paralysis on him? You, Konstantin?'

'No!' Kostya exclaimed, panic-stricken.

'I did,' Witiezslav said dourly. 'Shall I remove it?'

'Remove it?' Gesar barked. 'You have used magic on my boy! Can you imagine what a shock that is, at his age? Eh? And who will he become now, after the initiation? A Dark One?'

My eyes almost popped out of my head. Kostya gave a faint squeal. Edgar clamped his jaws shut.

We must all have looked at Timur Borisovich through the Twilight at exactly the same moment.

The aura of a potential Other was quite unmistakable.

Timur Borisovich had no need to expose himself to the fangs of a vampire or a werewolf. He could become a perfectly respectable magician. Fourth- or fifth-grade.

Unfortunately, most likely a Dark Magician . . . But . . .

'And now what am I to do?' Gesar continued. 'You have attacked my little child, frightened him, crushed his will . . .

The superannuated 'little child' was scrabbling feebly at his necktie, still trying to tie the Windsor knot as neatly as possible.

'Is he going to become a Dark One now?' Gesar asked indignantly. 'Well? This was all planned, was it? Gesar's son a Dark Magician?'

'I'm sure he would have become a Dark One in any case . . .' said Witiezslav. 'With his way of life . . .'

'You have subdued his will, urged him towards the Dark, and now you make claims like that?' Gesar said in a menacing whisper. 'Does the Inquisition believe it has the right to violate the Treaty? Or is this a strictly personal attack? Haven't you got over Karslbad yet? We can continue this conversation, Witiezslav. This may not be Krasnaya Kupal'nya, but we still have plenty of space for a duel.'

Witiezslav wavered for a second, trying to withstand Gesar's stare.

Then he gave in:

'My apologies, Gesar. I had no idea that this man was a potential Other. Everything indicated quite the opposite . . . those letters . . .'

'And what now?' Gesar snapped.

'The Inquisition acknowledges its . . . its haste . . .' Witiezslav said. 'The Moscow Night Watch is entitled to take this . . . this man under its tutelage.'

'To carry out his remoralisation?' Gesar asked. 'To initiate him after he has turned to the Light?'

'Yes,' Witiezslav said in a whisper.

'Well then, let us consider this dispute settled,' Gesar said with a smile, slapping Witiezslav on the shoulder. 'Don't be upset. We all make mistakes sometimes. The important thing is to put them right, isn't it?'

My, that old European bloodsucker certainly had iron self-control.

'That's right, Gesar,' he said sadly.

'By the way, have you caught the renegade Other?' Gesar asked.

Witiezslav shook his head.

'What's in my little boy's memory?' Gesar wondered aloud. He looked at Timur Borisovich, already standing there fully dressed. 'Ai-ai-ai . . . Oleg Strizhenov. A 1960s movie star. What an audacious disguise!'

'So it would seem the traitor is fond of old Russian movies?' asked Witiezslav.

'Indeed. Personally I would have preferred Innokenty Smoktunovsky,' Gesar replied. 'Or Oleg Dal. Witiezslav, this case is a dead-end. The traitor hasn't left any leads.'

'And you can't even imagine who he is?' Witiezslav asked.

'I can imagine,' Gesar said with a nod. 'There are thousands of Others in Moscow. Any one of them could have assumed someone else's appearance. Does the Inquisition wish to check the memory of all the Others in the city?'

Witiezslav frowned.

'No, it can't be done,' Gesar agreed. 'I can't even vouch for my own colleagues, and the Others who don't serve in the Watches will refuse point blank.'

'We'll set an ambush,' Edgar declared. 'And if the traitor shows up again . . .'

'He won't show up,' Witiezslav said wearily. 'He has no need to now.'

Gesar smiled, looking at the gloomy vampire. Then the smile disappeared from his face.

'Now will you please leave my son's apartment? I'll be expecting you in my office to sign the report. At seven o'clock this evening.'

Witiezslav nodded and disappeared, only to reappear a moment later, looking slightly confused.

'On foot, on foot,' Gesar said. 'I've shielded off the Twilight here. Just to be on the safe side.'

I trudged off after the Inquisitors and Kostya – boy, was he happy to be out of there and on his way!

'Anton,' Gesar called after me. 'Thank you. You did a good job. Call in to see me this evening.'

I didn't answer. We walked past the bodyguards, still dead to the world, and I attentively scanned the aura of the one I'd thought seemed doubtful.

No, not an Other after all. A human being.

I'd be doubly careful about that from now on.

Witiezslav said nothing, engrossed in thought, leaving Kostya and Edgar to fiddle with the locks. Then he cast a sideways glance in my direction and asked:

'Will you offer us a cup of coffee, watchman?'

I nodded. Why not?

We'd worked together on the same job. And we'd all been duped together, no matter what token compliments Gesar might have paid me.

CHAPTER 7

WE MADE A curious group – a young vampire from the Day Watch, two Inquisitors and a Light Magician.

All standing together in a big, empty apartment waiting for the water in the microwave to boil so we could make instant coffee. I'd even allowed Kostya to come in, and now he was sitting on the inside of the windowsill.

Witiezslav was the only one who just couldn't sit still.

'I'm not used to Russia any more,' he said, striding up and down in front of the window. 'I've lost the feel of the place. The country's unrecognisable.'

'Yes, the country's changing. New houses being built, new roads . . .' I exclaimed enthusiastically.

'Spare me your irony, watchman,' Witiezslav interrupted. 'That's not what I'm talking about. For seventy years the Others in your country had the strongest discipline of all. Even the Watches remained within the bounds of propriety.'

'And now it's like everything's gone crazy?' I asked shrewdly.

Witiezslav didn't answer that.

I felt ashamed. No matter what he was like, this Prague vampire from the Inquisition, today he had been thoroughly hoodwinked and bamboozled. It was the first time I'd seen the Inquisition humiliated. Even Gesar . . . well, he wasn't exactly afraid of it, but he acknowledged it as an insuperable force.

Then suddenly he had outwitted it. And with elegant ease.

Had something changed in the world? Had the Inquisition become a third side . . . just one more side in the game? Dark Ones, Light Ones and the Inquisition?

Or Dark Ones, Light Ones and the Twilight?

The water in the glass teapot began to seethe and bubble. I poured the boiling water into the cups standing along the windowsill. Set out the coffee, sugar and a carton of milk.

'Gorodetsky, do you realise that today the Treaty was violated?' Witiezslav asked suddenly.

I shrugged.

'You don't have to answer,' Witiezslav said. 'I already know you've understood the whole thing. An individual from the Moscow Night Watch provoked the Inquisition into acting injudiciously, after which he was granted the right to recruit a certain individual to the side of the Light. I don't think he will be of any great help to the Night Watch.'

I didn't think so either. Timur Borisovich wouldn't bother to learn how to use the Twilight Power. He'd have long life, the ability to do little magic tricks, to see his business partners' secret thoughts, to dodge bullets . . . That would be enough for him. Okay, you had to assume his firm would transfer large sums into the Night Watch account on a regular basis. And the businessman would become a better person, he would do some kind of charity work . . . pay for the upkeep of a polar bear in the zoo and ten orphans in a children's home.

But even so, it wasn't worth a quarrel with the Inquisition.

'Ignominious,' Witiezslav said bitterly. 'The abuse of an official position for personal ends.'

I couldn't help snorting.

'What's so funny?' Witiezslav asked guardedly.

'I think Gesar was right. You really have been shuffling papers around for too long.'

'So you think there's nothing wrong with all this?' Witiezslav asked. 'There's no call for outrage?'

'A man – okay, so he's not the best man in the world – will become a Light One,' I said. 'Now he will never do evil to anyone. On the contrary. So why should I be indignant?'

'Leave it, Witiezslav,' Edgar said quietly. 'Gorodetsky doesn't understand a thing. He's too young.'

Witiezslav nodded and took a sip of coffee. He said gloomily:

'I thought you were different from the rest of this Light fraternity. That it was the substance you cared about, not the form.'

That really wound me up.

'Yes, the substance is important to me, Witiezslav. And the substance here is that you're a vampire! And you, Edgar, are a Dark Magician! I don't know where you see a violation of the Treaty, but I'm sure there wouldn't have been any charges brought against Zabulon!'

'Light Magician . . .' Witiezslav hissed. 'Adept of the Light . . . All we do is maintain the balance, is that clear? And even Zabulon would have ended up facing a tribunal if he'd pulled a stunt like this.'

But there was no stopping me now.

'Zabulon has done lots of things. He tried to kill my wife. He tried to kill me. He's constantly urging people towards the Dark. You say one of our side acted dishonestly in outwitting the cheat? Well, maybe it was dishonest, but it was right. You're always so outraged when you get your own counterfeit coin back . . . well, that's easily fixed. Start playing fair for a change.'

'Your fairness and ours are two different things,' Edgar put in. 'Witiezslav, let's go.'

The vampire nodded and put down his unfinished cup of coffee.

'Thank you for the coffee, Light One. I return to you the invitation to enter.'

And the two Inquisitors walked out, leaving just Kostya, sitting silently on the windowsill and finishing his coffee.

'Moralists!' I said angrily. 'Or do you think they're right too?'

Kostya smiled:

'No, of course not. They got what they deserve. It's high time the Inquisition was taken down a peg or two . . . I'm just sorry it was Gesar who did it, and not Zabulon.'

'Gesar didn't do anything,' I said stubbornly. 'He swore, didn't you hear him?'

Kostya shrugged:

'I've no idea how he set everything up. But it was his plot. Zabulon was right to wait it out. He's a cunning old fox, all right . . . You know what surprises me?'

'What?' I asked cautiously. Somehow I didn't find Kostya's support very inspiring.

'What difference is there at all between us? We intrigue to drag the little people we want over to our side. And you do exactly the same. Gesar wanted to make his son a Light One – and he did it. Good for him! I've got no complaints.'

Kostya was smiling.

'Who do you think was right in the Second World War?' I asked.

'What are you getting at?' Kostya was tense now, naturally expecting a trick.

'Just answer the question.'

'Our side was right,' Kostya said patriotically. 'And, by the way, some vampires and werewolves fought in the war. Two of them were even awarded the order of Hero of the Soviet Union.'

'And just why was our side right? Stalin would have been happy enough to swallow up the whole of Europe. We bombed cities full of civilians, and pillaged museums, and shot deserters . . .'

'Because it was our side! That's why it was right!'

'Well then, now it's *our* side that's right. And our side is the Light Ones.'

'You mean, that's the way you see it,' Kostya objected. 'And you refuse to consider any other point of view?'

I nodded.

'Ha . . .' Kostya said contemptuously. 'Come up with at least one logical argument.'

'We don't drink blood,' I said.

Kostya put his cup down and stood up.

'Thank you for the hospitality. I return to you the invitation to enter.'

And I was left alone – in a big, empty apartment, with just the dirty cups, the open microwave and the water cooling in the glass teapot . . .

Why had I heated it in the microwave? A single pass with my hands and the water would have boiled right there in the cups.

I took my mobile phone out and dialled Svetlana's number. There was no answer. She must have gone for a walk with Nadiushka and left her phone in her room again.

Deep down I wasn't feeling nearly as sure of myself as I'd tried to make out.

In what way were we really better after all? Intriguing, fighting, deceiving? I needed the answer, I needed to hear it again. And not from that smart-alec Gesar, with his way of weaving words into fancy lace patterns. And not from myself either – I didn't trust myself any more. I needed the answer from someone I did trust.

But I also needed to understand how Gesar had tricked the Inquisition.

Because if he had sworn on the Light, and lied . . .

Then what was I fighting for?

'Oh, to hell with the . . .' I began and stopped short. Don't curse – they taught us that in the first few days after initiation. And I'd almost let rip.

Let the whole business be. Just let it be.

And at that moment someone rang the doorbell – as if they'd guessed this was a bad time for me to be left alone.

'Yes!' I shouted across the room, remembering that I hadn't locked the door.

It opened a bit and my neighbour Las stuck his head in. He glanced around and asked:

'Okay to come in? I'm not interrupting anything?'

'No, that's fine, come in.'

Las walked into the room and took a look around.

'Nah, it's not so bad in here . . . only you need to get a toilet installed . . . All right if I grab a quick shower? Now or this evening . . . I really enjoyed it.'

I stuck my hand in my pocket and felt for my bunch of keys. Imagined the keys swelling and splitting . . .

I tossed Las the new set.

'Here, catch!'

'What are these for?' Las asked, inspecting the keys.

'I have to go away. Use the place in the meantime.'

'Oh no, the first decent guy to move in . . .' Las replied, disappointed. 'What a shame! Are you leaving soon?'

'Straight away,' I said. I'd suddenly realised how much I wanted to see Sveta and Nadya. 'Maybe I'll be back.'

'And maybe not?'

I nodded.

'What a shame!' Las repeated, moving closer. 'I saw your mini-disc player somewhere around the place . . . here.'

I took the disc he was holding out to me.

'*Combat Implants*,' Las explained. 'My album. Only don't play it when there are women or children present.'

'I won't.' I twirled the disc in my hands. 'Thanks.'

'Have you got problems or something?' Las asked. 'Sorry if I'm sticking my nose in, but you're looking pretty low.'

'No, it's nothing,' I said, shaking myself. 'I'm just missing my daughter. I'll be off in a minute . . . she's with my wife at the dacha, and I've got all this work to do here . . .'

'A sacred duty,' Las said approvingly. 'A child must not be left without attention. At least if her mother's with her, that's the most important thing.'

I looked at Las.

'The mother's most important for a child,' Las said, with the air of a Vysotsky, Piaget or some other doyen of child psychology. 'It's biologically determined. What we males mostly do is take care of the female. And the female takes care of the child.'

I was let into Timur Borisovich's apartment without any arguments. The bodyguards looked perfectly all right and probably didn't have the slightest idea about recent events.

Gesar and his new-found son were drinking tea in the study. The study was large – I'd even be tempted to call it huge – with a massive desk and heaps of all sorts of amusing trinkets on the shelves of the antique cabinets. It was amazing how similar their tastes were. Timur Borisovich's study was just like his father's office.

'Come in, young man,' Timur Borisovich said, and smiled at me. 'You see, everything's been worked out.'

He cast a quick glance at Gesar and added:

'He's still young, hot-headed . . .'

'That's for sure,' Gesar said with a nod. 'What's happened, Anton?'

'I need to have a word,' I said. 'In private.'

Gesar sighed and looked at his son, who stood up:

'I'll go and see my blockheads. No point in them just sitting on their backsides here. I'll find them something to do.'

Timur Borisovich went out, and I was left alone with Gesar.

'Well, what's happened, Gorodetsky?' he asked wearily.

'Can we speak freely?'

'Yes.'

'You didn't want to see your son become a Dark Magician, did you?' I asked.

'Would you like to see your Nadiushka as a Dark Enchantress?' said Gesar, answering a question with a question.

'But Timur was certain to become a Dark One,' I went on. 'You needed to be granted the right to his remoralisation. And for that the Dark Ones or, even better, the Inquisition had to panic and apply unreasonable force to your son.'

'And that's what happened,' said Gesar. 'All right, Gorodetsky, are you trying to accuse me of anything?'

'No, I'm trying to understand.'

'You saw me swear on the Light. I hadn't met Timur before. I didn't promise him anything, I didn't send the letters. And I didn't engage anyone to do these things.'

No, Gesar wasn't making excuses. And he wasn't trying to pull the wool over my eyes. It was as if he was setting out the terms of a problem – waiting with relish to see what answer his pupil would give.

'Witiezslav only needed to ask one more question,' he said. 'But apparently that question was too human for him . . .'

Gesar blinked rapidly.

'The mother,' I said.

'Witiezslav killed his own mother,' Gesar explained. 'Not with deliberate intent. He was a young vampire and he couldn't control himself. But . . . ever since then he has tried not even to say that word.'

'Who is Timur's mother?'

'There ought to be a name in the file.'

'There could be any name at all in the file. It says that Timur's mother disappeared at the end of the war . . . but I know a female Other who spent the time since then trapped in the body of a bird. As far as people knew, she had died.'

Gesar was silent.

'Could you really not find him any sooner?'

'We were sure that Timka had died,' Gesar said quietly. 'Olga was the one who didn't want to accept it. And when she was rehabilitated, she went on looking . . .'

'She found her son. And made him a rash promise,' I concluded.

'It's permissible for women to give way to their feelings,' Gesar said dryly. 'Even the wisest of women. And men exist to protect their woman and their child. To organise everything on a serious, rational basis.'

I nodded.

'Do you blame me?' Gesar asked curiously 'Anton?'

'Who am I to blame you?' I asked. 'I have a daughter who's a Light Other. And I wouldn't want to let the Dark have her.'

'Thank you, Anton.' Gesar nodded and relaxed visibly. 'I'm glad you understand that.'

'I just wonder how far you would have gone for your son and Olga,' I said. 'You know Svetlana had a premonition? Some kind of danger for me.'

Gesar shrugged.

'Premonitions are pretty unreliable.'

'What if I'd decided to tell the Inquisition the truth?' I went on. 'Decided to leave the Watch and join the Inquisition . . . What then?'

'You didn't leave,' Gesar said. 'Despite all Witiezslav's hints. What else, Anton? I can tell you've got another question you want to ask.'

'How did your son turn out to be an Other?' I asked. 'It's a lottery. It's rare for a family of Others to have a child who's an Other.'

'Anton, either go to Witiezslav and present him with your conclusions,' Gesar said in a low voice, 'or get out and go to Svetlana, as you were planning to do. Spare me this interrogation.'

'Aren't you afraid the Inquisition will think it all through and figure out what happened?' I carried on.

'No, I'm not. In three hours Witiezslav will sign a document closing the investigation. They won't open the case again. They're already up to their ears in shit.'

'Good luck with remoralising Timur,' I said.

And I headed for the door.

'You still have another week's leave. Spend some time with your family,' Gesar called after me.

At first I was going to reply proudly that I didn't need any handouts.

But I stopped myself in time.

What the heck!

'Two weeks,' I said. 'At this stage I've got at least a month of compensatory leave coming.'

Gesar didn't say a word.

EPILOGUE

I DECIDED TO return the BMW after I got back from leave. After all . . .

The road surface was brand new – the highway here used to be all potholes, with a few connecting stretches of good road; now it was stretches of good road, only occasionally interrupted by potholes – so the car coasted comfortably at high speed.

It's good to be an Other.

I knew I wouldn't get caught in traffic. I knew a dump-truck with a drunk driver wouldn't suddenly swerve in front of me. If I ran out of petrol, I could pour water into the tank and turn it into fuel.

Who wouldn't want a life like that for his own child?

What right did I have to blame Gesar and Olga for anything?

The stereo in the car was brand-new, with a minidisc slot. At first I was going to stick *Combat Implants* into it, then I decided I was in the mood for something more lyrical.

I put on The White Guard.

> I don't know what you have decided.
> I don't know how things are there with you,

An angel has sewed the sky shut with thread,
Dark blue and light blue . . .
I don't remember the taste of loss,
I have no strength to resist evil,
Every time I walk out the door,
I walk towards your warmth . . .

My mobile phone rang. And the intelligent stereo immediately turned down its own volume.

'Sveta?' I asked.

'You're hard to reach, Anton.'

Svetlana's voice was calm. That meant everything was all right. And that was the most important thing.

'I couldn't get through to you either,' I admitted.

'Must be fluctuations in the ether,' Svetlana laughed. 'What happened half an hour ago?'

'Nothing special. I had a talk with Gesar.'

'Is everything okay?'

'Yes.'

'I had a premonition. That you were walking close to the edge.'

I nodded, watching the road. I have a clever wife, Gesar. Her premonitions are reliable.

'And everything's all right now?' I asked, just to make sure.

'Now everything's all right.'

'Sveta . . .' I asked, holding the wheel with one hand. 'What should you do when you're not sure if you've done the right thing? If you're tormented over whether you're right or not.'

'Join the Dark Ones,' Svetlana replied without any hesitation. 'They're never tormented.'

'And that's the whole answer?'

'It's the only answer there is. And all the difference there is between Light Ones and Dark Ones. You can call it conscience, you can call it a moral sense. It comes down to the same thing.'

'I have this feeling,' I complained, 'as if the time of order is coming to an end. Do you understand? And I don't know what's coming next. Not a dark time, not a light time . . . not even the time of the Inquisitors . . .'

'It's nobody's time, Anton,' said Svetlana. 'That's all it is, nobody's time. You're right, something's coming. Something's going to happen in the world. But not right this minute.'

'Talk to me, Sveta,' I asked her. 'I've still got half an hour to drive. Talk to me for that half-hour, okay?'

'I haven't got much money left on my mobile,' Svetlana answered doubtfully.

'I can call you back,' I suggested. 'I'm on an assignment, I've got a company mobile. Gesar can pay the bill.'

'And won't your conscience torment you?' she laughed.

'I gave it a good drilling today.'

'All right, don't call back, I'll put a spell on my mobile,' said Svetlana. Maybe she was joking, maybe she was serious. I can't always tell.

'Then talk to me,' I said. 'Tell me what's going to happen when I get there. What Nadiushka's going to say. What you're going to say. What your mother's going to say. What's going to happen to us.'

'Everything's going to be fine,' said Svetlana. 'I'll be happy, and so will Nadya. And my mother will be happy . . .'

I drove the car, contravening the strict rules of the state highway patrol by pressing the mobile phone to my ear with one hand. Trucks came hurtling towards me and past me on the other side of the road.

I listened to what Svetlana was saying.

And from the speakers the quiet female voice carried on singing:

When you come back, everything will be different,
How shall we recognise each other . . .
When you come back,
But I am not your wife or even your friend.
When you come back to me,
Who loved you so madly in the past,
When you come back,
You will see the lots were cast long ago, and not by us . . .

Story Two

NOBODY'S SPACE

PROLOGUE

HOLIDAYS IN THE countryside near Moscow have always been the prerogative of the rich or the poor. It's only the middle classes that prefer Turkish hotels on inclusive tariffs offering 'as much as you can drink', a torrid Spanish siesta or the neat and tidy coast of Croatia. The middle classes don't like to take their holidays in Central Russia.

But then, the middle classes in Russia aren't very big.

In any case, the profession of biology teacher, even in a prestigious Moscow grammar school, has nothing whatever to do with the middle classes. And if the teacher is female, if her swine of a husband left her three years ago for another woman, who has no intention of encroaching on the mother's right to bring up her two children, then Turkish hotels are no more than an idle fantasy.

It was a good thing the children had not yet reached the terrible teenage years and were still genuinely delighted by the old dacha, the little stream and the forest that started just beyond the fence.

What was not so good was the way the elder child, a daughter, took her senior status so seriously. At the age of ten you can be pretty good at keeping an eye on your little five-year-old brother splashing about in the stream, but there's no way you ought to go wandering deep into the forest with him, relying on the knowledge you've gleaned from a school textbook on nature studies.

As yet, however, ten-year-old Ksyusha had no idea that they were lost. She walked blithely on along the forest path that she could barely even make out, holding her brother tightly by the hand as she told him a story:

'And then they hammered more pine stakes through him. They hammered one stake into his forehead, and another into his stomach! But he got up out of his coffin and said: 'You can't kill me anyway! I've been dead for ages already! My name is . . .'

Her brother started whingeing quietly.

'Okay, okay, I was joking,' Ksyusha said more seriously. 'He fell down and died. They buried him and went off to celebrate.'

'I'm f-f-frightened,' Romka confessed. He wasn't stammering because he was afraid, though – he always stammered. 'Don't t-tell me any m-m-more, all right?'

'All right,' said Ksyusha, looking round. She could still see the path behind them, but ahead it was completely lost under fallen pine needles and rotting leaves. The forest had suddenly become gloomy and menacing. Nothing at all like it was near the village where their mother had rented their summer dacha – an old house that no one lived in any more. They'd better turn back, before it was too late. As a caring older sister, Ksyusha realised that.

'Let's go home, or mum will tell us off.'

'A doggy,' her brother said suddenly. 'Look, a doggy!'

Ksyusha turned round.

There really was a dog standing behind her. A large, grey dog with big teeth. Looking at her with its mouth open, just as if it was smiling.

'I want a doggy like that,' Romka said without stumbling over the words at all, and looked at his sister proudly.

Ksyusha was a city girl and she'd only ever seen wolves in

pictures. And in the zoo as well, only those were an exotic species from somewhere in Asia . . .

But now she felt suddenly afraid.

'Let's go, let's go,' she said quietly, tightening her grip on Romka's hand. 'It's someone else's doggy, you can't play with it.'

Something in her voice must have frightened her brother, frightened him so badly that instead of complaining, he clutched his sister's hand even tighter and followed her without a murmur.

The grey creature stood still for a moment, and then set off after the children at a slow, deliberate walk.

'It's f-following us,' said Romka, looking back. 'Ksyusha, is it a w-wolf?'

'It's a doggy,' said Ksyusha. 'Only don't run, okay? Dogs bite people who run!'

The animal made a coughing sound, as if it was laughing.

'Run!' shouted Ksyusha, and they set off at random, forcing their way through the forest, through the prickly bushes that grasped at them, past an incredibly big anthill as tall as a grown-up, past a row of moss-covered tree-stumps where someone had once cut down ten trees and dragged them away.

The creature kept disappearing and appearing again. Behind them, on the right, on the left. And every now and then it made a noise like a cough . . . or a laugh.

'It's laughing!' Romka shouted through his tears.

It disappeared. Ksyusha stopped beside an immense pine tree, clutching Romka tight against her. Her little brother had given up on sissy stuff like that a long time ago, but this time he didn't struggle, just pressed his back against his sister, put his hands over his eyes in fear and repeated quietly over and over again:

'I'm n-not afraid, I'm n-not afraid. There's no one there.'

'There's no one there,' Ksyusha confirmed. 'And you stop that whining! The wol . . . the doggy had puppies here. She was just driving us away from her puppies. All right? We're going home now.'

'Let's go!' Romka agreed and took his hands away from his eyes. 'Oh, the puppies!'

His fear disappeared instantly the moment he saw the cubs coming out of the bushes. There were three of them – grey with big foreheads and soft eyes.

'P-puppies!' Romka exclaimed in delight.

Ksyusha jerked to one side in panic. The pine she was standing against wouldn't let her go – her calico dress was stuck to the resin on its bark. Ksyusha tugged harder and the cloth tore with a crack and came unstuck.

Then she saw the wolf standing behind her, smiling.

'We have to climb up the tree . . .' Ksyusha whispered.

The wolf laughed.

'Does she want us to play with the puppies?' Romka asked hopefully.

The wolf shook its head. As if it was answering: 'No, no. I want the puppies to play with you . . .'

And then Ksyusha started shouting – so loudly and piercingly that even the wolf took a step backwards and wrinkled up its muzzle.

'Go away, go away!' Ksyusha shouted, forgetting that she was already a big, brave girl.

'Don't shout like that,' she heard a voice say behind her. 'You'll wake up the entire forest . . .'

The children turned round with renewed hope. Standing beside the cubs was a woman – beautiful, with black hair, barefoot and wearing a long linen dress.

The wolf growled menacingly.

'Don't be silly,' said the woman. She leaned down and picked up one of the cubs – it dangled limply in her hands, as if it had fallen asleep. The other two froze on the spot. 'Now who do we have here?'

Paying no more attention to the children, the wolf moved sullenly towards the woman, who started chanting:

> Dense wolf's thickets dark with fear,
> There's no way you can hide in here . . .

The wolf stopped.

> The truth and lie I both can see,
> Now, who do you look like to me?

. . . the woman concluded, looking at the wolf.

It bared its teeth.

'Ai-ai-ai . . .' said the woman. 'Now what are we going to do?'

'Go . . . a . . . way,' the wolf barked. 'Go . . . a . . . way . . . witch.'

The woman dropped the cub on the soft moss. As if they had suddenly woken from a trance, the cubs dashed across to the wolf in panic and jostled under its belly.

> Three blades of grass, a birch-bark strip,
> And one wolfberry from a branch,
> A drop of blood, of tears a drip,
> And skin of goat, of hair a lock:
> I have mixed them in my crock,
> Brewed my potion in advance . . .

The wolf began backing away, with the cubs following.

> You have no strength, you have no chance,
> My spell will pierce you like a lance

. . . the woman declared triumphantly.

Then four grey bolts of lightning – one large and three small – seemed to flash from the clearing into the bushes. Tufts of grey fur and shreds of skin were left swirling in the air. And there was a sudden sharp smell, as if a whole pack of dogs was standing there, drying off after the rain.

'Aunty, are y-you a w-witch?' Romka asked in a hushed voice.

The woman laughed. She walked up to them and took them by the hand.

'Come along.'

The hut wasn't standing on chicken legs, like the one in the fairy tale, and Romka was disappointed. It was a perfectly ordinary log house with small windows and a tiny porch.

'Have you got a b-bathhouse here?' Romka asked, looking around.

'Why do you want a bathhouse?' the woman replied. 'Do you want to get washed?'

'F-first of all you have to heat up the b-bathhouse really hot, then f-feed us, before you can eat us,' Romka said seriously.

Ksyusha tugged on his hand. But the woman didn't take offence – she laughed.

'I think you're confusing me with Baba-Yaga, aren't you? Do you mind if I don't heat up the bathhouse? I haven't got one anyway. And I'm not going to eat you.'

'No, I don't mind,' Romka said, relieved.

The inside of the house didn't look like a place any self-respecting Baba-Yaga could live either. There was a clock with dangling weights ticking on the whitewashed wall, a beautiful chandelier with velvet tassels, and a small Philips television standing on a shaky dresser. There was a Russian stove too, but it was heaped up with all sorts of clutter, and it was obvious that it was a very long time since any bold young heroes or little children had been roasted in it. The only thing with a serious and forbidding look to it was a large bookcase full of old books. Ksyusha went over and looked at the spines of the books. Her mother had always told her that the first thing a cultured person should do in someone else's house was to look at her host's books, and then at everything else.

But the books were worn and she could hardly make out the titles, and she didn't understand even the ones she could read, although they were all in Russian. Her mother had books like that too: 'Helminthology', 'Ethnogenesis' . . . Ksyusha sighed and walked away from the bookcase.

Romka was already sitting at the table and the witch was pouring hot water from a white electric kettle into his cup.

'Would you like a cup of tea?' she asked in a kind voice. 'It's good, made from forest herbs . . .'

'It is g-good,' Romka confirmed, although he was more concerned with dipping hard little bread rings into honey than drinking his tea. 'S-sit down, Ksyusha.'

Ksyusha sat down and accepted a cup politely.

The tea really was good. The witch drank some herself, smiling and looking at the children.

'Are we going to turn into little goats when we've drunk our tea?' Romka suddenly asked.

'Why?' the witch asked in surprise.

'Because you'll put a spell on us,' he explained. 'You'll turn us into little goats and eat us up.'

Clearly he did not completely trust their mysterious rescuer yet.

'Now, why would I want to turn you into smelly little goats and then eat you?' the witch asked indignantly. 'If I wanted to eat you, I'd eat you as you are, without turning you into anything else.'

Romka pouted sulkily, and Ksyusha hissed:

'Drink your tea and be quiet! Some wizard or other . . .'

They didn't turn into goats, the tea tasted good, and the bread rings and honey tasted even better. The witch asked Ksyusha all about how she was doing in school. She agreed that fourth grade was absolutely terrible, not like third grade at all. She scolded Romka for slurping his tea. She asked Ksyusha how long her brother had had a stammer. And then she told them she wasn't a witch at all. She was a botanist, and collected all sorts of rare herbs in the forest. And, of course, she knew which herbs the wolves were afraid of.

'But why did the wolf talk?' Romka asked doubtfully.

'It didn't talk at all,' the botanist-witch retorted. 'It barked, and you thought it was talking. Isn't that right?'

Ksyusha thought about it and decided that was the way it had really been.

'I'll show you to the edge of the forest,' said the woman. 'You can see the village from there. And don't come into the forest any more, or the wolves will eat you!'

Romka thought for a moment and then offered to help her gather herbs. Only she would have to give him a special herb to keep the wolves away, so they wouldn't eat him. And one to keep bears away, just in case. And she could give him one to keep lions away too, because the forest here was just like in Africa.

'No herbs for you!' the woman said strictly. 'They're very rare herbs, in the Red Book of threatened species. You can't just go pulling them up.'

'I know about the Red Book,' Romka said, delighted. 'Tell me more, please.'

The woman looked at the clock and shook her head. Well-mannered Ksyusha immediately said it was time to go.

The woman gave each of the children a piece of honeycomb

to take with them and showed them to the edge of the forest – it turned out to be very close.

'And don't you set foot in the forest again!' the woman repeated sternly. 'If I'm not there, the wolf will eat you.'

As they headed down the hill towards the village, the children looked back several times.

At first the woman was standing there, watching them walk away. But then she disappeared.

'She is a witch really, isn't she, Ksyusha?' Romka asked.

'She's a botanist!' Ksyusha said, taking the woman's side. Then she exclaimed in surprise: 'You're not stammering any more!'

'I am stam-stam-stammering!' said Romka, playing the fool. 'I didn't really need to stammer before, I was just joking.'

CHAPTER 1

WHERE DO WE get the idea that milk straight from the cow tastes good?

It must be something we learn in junior school. Some memorable phrase from the textbook *Our Native Tongue*, about how wonderful milk tastes, straight from the cow. And the naïve city kids believe it.

In fact, milk straight from the cow tastes rather peculiar. But after it's been left to stand in the cellar for a day and cooled off – now that's a different matter. Even those poor souls who lack the necessary digestive enzymes drink it. And there are plenty of them, by the way: as far as mother nature's concerned, adults have no business drinking milk, it's children who need it . . .

But people usually don't pay much attention to nature's opinion.

And Others pay even less.

I reached for the jug and poured myself another glass. Cold, with a smooth layer of cream . . . why does boiling make the cream – the best part of milk – so smooth? I took a big gulp. No more, I had to leave some for Sveta and Nadiushka. The whole village – it was quite big, with fifty houses – had just one cow. It was a good thing there was at least one . . . and I had a strong suspicion that the humble Raika had Svetlana to thank for her magnificent yields. Her owner, Granny Sasha, already an old woman at forty, also owned the pig Borka, the goat Mishka and a gaggle of miscellaneous, nameless poultry, but she had no real reason to feel proud. Svetlana just wanted her daughter to drink genuine milk. That was why the cow was never ill. Granny Sasha could have fed her sawdust and it wouldn't have changed a thing.

But genuine milk really is good. Never mind the characters in the ads – they can arrive in a village with their cartons of milk and that jolly gleam in their eyes and say 'The real thing!' as often as they like. They're paid money to do that. And it makes things easier for the peasants, who stopped keeping any kind of livestock themselves long ago. They can just carry on slagging off the 'democrats' and the 'city folk' and not worry about raising cows any more.

I put down my empty glass and sprawled back in a hammock hanging between two trees. The locals must have thought I was a real bourgeois. Arriving in a fancy car, bringing my wife lots of strange foreign groceries, spending the whole day lounging in a hammock with a book . . . In a place where everybody generally spent the whole day roaming about, searching for a drop of something to fix their hangovers . . .

'Hello, Anton Sergeevich,' someone said over the top of the fence – it was Kolya, a local drunk. He might as well have been reading my thoughts – and how had he remembered my name?

'How was the drive?'

'Hello, Kolya,' I greeted him in lordly fashion, not making the slightest attempt to get up out of the hammock. He wouldn't appreciate it in any case. That wasn't what he'd come for. 'It was fine, thanks.'

'Need any help with anything, around the house and garden?' Kolya asked vaguely. 'I thought, you know, I'd just come and ask . . .'

I closed my eyes – the sun, already sinking towards the horizon, glowed blood-red through my eyelids.

There was nothing I could do. Not the slightest thing. A sixth- or seventh-degree intervention would have been enough to free the poor devil Kolya from his hankering for alcohol, cure his cirrhosis and inspire him with a desire to work, instead of drinking vodka and thrashing his wife.

What if I had defied all the stipulations of the Treaty and made that intervention in secret? A brief gesture of the hand . . . And then what? There wasn't any work in the village. And nobody in the city wanted Kolya, a former collective farm mechanic. Kolya didn't have any money to start his own business. He couldn't even buy a piglet.

So he'd slope off again to look for moonshine, getting by on money from odd jobs, and working off his anger on his wife, who drank as much as he did and was just as weary of everything. It wasn't the man I needed to heal, it was the entire planet.

Or at least this particular sixth part of the planet. The part with the proud name of Russia.

'Anton Sergeevich, I'm desperate . . .' Kolya said pathetically.

Who needs a cured alcoholic in a dying village where the collective farm has fallen apart and the only private farmer was burned out three times before he took the hint?

'Kolya,' I said, 'didn't you have some kind of special trade in the army? A tank driver?'

Did we have any paid professional soldiers at all? It would be better if he went to the Caucasus, rather than just dropping dead in a year's time from all that cheap moonshine . . .

'I wasn't in the army,' Kolya said in a miserable voice. 'They wouldn't take me. They were short of mechanics here back then, they kept giving me deferrals, and then I got too old . . . Anton Sergeevich, if you want somebody's face smashed in, I can still do that all right! Don't you worry! I'll tear them to pieces!'

'Kolya,' I asked him, 'would you take a look at my car's engine? I thought it was knocking a bit yesterday.'

'Sure, I'll take a look,' said Kolya, brightening up. 'You know, I . . .'

'Take the keys.' I tossed him the bunch. 'And I owe you a bottle.'

Kolya broke into a happy smile:

'Would you like me to wash it too? It must have cost a lot . . . and these roads of ours . . .'

'Thanks,' I said. 'I'd be very grateful.'

'Only I don't want any vodka,' Kolya suddenly said, and I started in surprise. What was this, had the world gone mad? 'It's got no taste to it . . . now a little bottle of homebrew . . .'

'Done,' I said. Delighted, Kolya opened the gate and set off towards the small barn in which I'd parked the car the evening before.

And then Svetlana came out of the house – I didn't see her, but I sensed her. That meant Nadiushka had settled down and was enjoying a sweet after-lunch nap. Sveta came over, stood at the head of the hammock and paused for a moment, then she put her cool hand on my forehead and asked:

'Bored?'

'Uhuh,' I mumbled. 'Sveta, there's nothing I can do. Not a single thing. How can you stand it here?'

'I've been coming to this village since I was a child,' Svetlana said. 'I remember Uncle Kolya when he was still all right. Young and happy. He used to give me rides on his tractor when I was still a little snot-nose. He was sober. He used to sing songs. Can you imagine that?'

'Were things better before?' I asked

'People drank less,' Svetlana replied laconically. 'Anton, why didn't you remoralise him? You were going to – I felt a tremor run through the Twilight. There aren't any Watch members here . . . except you.'

'Give a dog a bone and how long does it last?' I answered churlishly. 'I'm sorry . . . Uncle Kolya's not where we need to start.'

'No, he's not,' Svetlana agreed. 'But then any intervention in the activities of the authorities is prohibited by the Treaty. "Humans deal with their own affairs, Others deal with theirs . . .".'

I didn't say anything. Yes, it was prohibited. Because it was the simplest and surest way of directing the mass of humanity towards Good or Evil. Which was a violation of the equilibrium. There had been kings and presidents in history who were Others. And it had always ended in appalling wars . . .

'You'll just be miserable here, Anton . . .' said Svetlana. 'Let's go back to town.'

'But Nadiushka loves it here,' I objected. 'And you wanted to stay here another week, didn't you?'

'But you're fretting . . . Why don't you go on your own? You'll feel happier in town.'

'Anybody would think you wanted to get rid of me,' I growled. 'That you had a lover here.'

Svetlana snorted.

'Can you suggest a single candidate?'

'No,' I said, after a moment's reflection. 'Except maybe one of the holidaymakers . . .'

'This is a kingdom of women,' Svetlana retorted. 'They're either single mothers, or they're here to give the children some fresh air and exercise while their husbands are slaving away. That reminds me, Anton. There was one strange thing that happened here . . .'

'Yes?' I asked, intrigued. If Svetlana called something 'strange' . . .

'You remember Anna Viktorovna called to see me yesterday?'

'The teacher?' I laughed. Anna Viktorovna was such a typical schoolmistress, she should have been in the old Soviet film *The Muddle*. 'I thought she came over to see your mother.'

'Both of us. She has two kids – a little boy, Romka, he's five, and Ksyusha, who's ten.'

'Good,' I said, giving Anna Viktorovna my seal of approval.

'Don't try to be funny. Two days ago the children got lost in the forest.'

My drowsiness suddenly evaporated and I sat up in the hammock, grasping a tree with one hand. I looked at Svetlana:

'Why didn't you tell me straight away? The Treaty's all very well, but . . .'

'Don't worry, they got lost, but then they turned up again. They came home on their own in the evening.'

'Well, that's strange,' I couldn't resist saying. 'Children who stayed in the forest for an extra couple of hours! Don't tell me – they actually like wild strawberries?'

'When their mother started giving them what for, they told her they got lost,' Svetlana went on, ignoring me. 'And they met a wolf. The wolf drove them through the forest – and straight to some wolf cubs . . .'

'I see . . .' I murmured. I felt a vague flutter of alarm in my chest.

'Anyway, the children were in a real panic. But then a woman appeared and recited some lines of verse to the wolf, and it ran away. The woman took them to her house, gave them some tea and showed them to the edge of the forest. She said she was a botanist and she knew special herbs that wolves are afraid of . . .'

'Childish fantasies,' I snapped. 'Are the kids all right?'

'Absolutely.'

'And there I was, expecting foul play,' I said, and lay back down. 'Did you check them for magic?'

'They're completely clean,' said Svetlana. 'Not the slightest trace.'

'Fantasies. Maybe they did get a fright from someone . . . perhaps even a wolf. And some woman did lead them out of the forest. The kids were lucky, but take a belt to them . . .'

'The young one, Romka, used to stammer. Quite badly. Now he speaks without the slightest problem. He rattles on, recites poetry . . .'

I thought for a moment. Then I asked:

'Can stammering be cured? By suggestion, you know, hypnosis? . . . Or some other way?'

'There is no cure for it. Like the common cold. And any doctor who promises to stop you stammering with hypnosis is a quack. Of course, if it was some kind of reactive neurosis, then . . .'

'Spare me the terminology,' I asked here. 'So there is no cure. What about folk medicine?'

'Nothing, except maybe some wild Others . . . Can you cure stammering?'

'Even bedwetting,' I muttered. 'And incontinence. But Sveta, you didn't sense any magic, did you?'

'But the stammer's gone.'

'That can only mean one thing,' I said reluctantly. I sighed and got up out of the hammock. 'Sveta, this is not good. A witch. With power even greater than yours. And you're first-grade!'

Svetlana nodded. I didn't often mention the fact that her power exceeded my own. It was the main thing that came between us . . . that could really come between us some day.

And in any case, Svetlana had deliberately withdrawn from the Night Watch. Otherwise, she would already have been an enchantress beyond classification.

'But nothing happened to the children,' I went on. 'No odious wizard pawed the little girl, no evil witch made soup out of the little boy . . . No, if this is a witch, why such kindness?'

'Witches don't have any compulsion to indulge in cannibalism or sexual aggression,' Svetlana said pompously, as if she was giving a lecture. 'All their actions are determined by plain egotism. If a witch was *really* hungry, she might eat a human being. For the simple reason that she doesn't think of herself as human. But otherwise, why not help the children? It didn't cost her anything. She led them out of the forest and cured the little boy's stammer as well. After all, she probably has children of her own. You'd feed a homeless puppy, wouldn't you?'

'I don't like it,' I confessed. 'A witch as powerful as that? They don't often reach first-grade, do they?'

'Very rarely.' Svetlana gave me a quizzical look. 'Anton, do you have a clear idea of the difference between a witch and an enchantress?'

'I've worked with them,' I said curtly. 'I know.'

But Svetlana wasn't satisfied with that.

'An enchantress works with the Twilight directly and draws power from it. A witch uses accessories, material objects charged with a greater or lesser degree of Power. All the magical artefacts that exist in the world were created by witches or warlocks – you could call them their artificial limbs. Artefacts can be things or elements of the body that are dead – hair, long fingernails . . . That's why a witch is harmless if you undress her and shave off all her hair, but you have to gag an enchantress and tie her hands.'

'For sure nobody's ever going to gag you,' I laughed. 'Sveta, why are you lecturing me like this? I'm no Great Magician, but I know the elementary facts, I don't need reminding.'

'I'm sorry, I didn't mean to upset you,' Svetlana apologised quickly.

I looked at her and saw the pain in her eyes.

What a brute I was! How long could I go on taking out my insecurities on the woman I loved? I was worse than any Dark One . . .

'Sveta, forgive me . . .' I whispered and touched her hand. 'Forgive a stupid fool.'

'I'm no better myself,' Svetlana admitted. 'Really, why am I lecturing you on the basics? You deal with witches every day in the Watch . . .'

Peace had been restored, and I was quick to reply:

'With ones as powerful as this? Come on, in the whole of Moscow there's only one first-grade witch, and she retired ages ago . . . What are we going to do, Sveta?'

'There is no actual reason to interfere,' she replied thoughtfully. 'The children are all right, the boy's even better off than he was before. But there are still two questions that need to be answered. First, where did the strange wolf that drove the children towards the cubs come from?'

'That's if it *was* a wolf,' I remarked.

'If it was,' Svetlana agreed. 'But the children's story hangs together well . . . The second question is whether the witch is registered in this locality or not, and what her record is like . . .'

'We'll soon find out,' I said, taking out my mobile phone.

Five minutes later I had the answer. There was nothing in the Night Watch records about any witches in the area.

Ten minutes later I walked out of the garden, armed with instructions and advice from my wife – in her capacity as a potential Great Enchantress. On my way past the barn, I glanced in through the open doors – Kolya was hovering over the open bonnet of the car, and there were some parts lying on a newspaper spread out on the ground. Holy Moses . . . all I'd done was mention a knocking sound in the engine!

And Uncle Kolya was singing, crooning quietly to himself:

> We're not stokers and not carpenters either,
> But we're not bitter, we have no regrets!

Those were clearly the only lines he could remember. He kept repeating them as he rummaged around enthusiastically in the engine:

> We're not stokers and not carpenters either,
> But we're not bitter, we have no regrets!

When he spotted me, he called out happily:

'This is going to cost you more than half a litre, Antosha! Those Japs have completely lost it, the things they've done to the diesel engine, I can hardly bear to look!'

'They're not Japanese, they're Germans,' I corrected him.

'Germans?' Kolya said. 'Ah, right, it's a BMW, and I've only fixed Subarus before . . . I was wondering why everything was done different . . . Never mind, I'll put it right! Only my head's humming, the son of a bitch . . .'

'Look in on Sveta, she'll pour you a drop,' I said, accepting the inevitable.

'No.' Kolya shook his head. 'Not while I'm working, no way . . . Our first farm chairman taught me that – while you're messing with the metal, not a single drop! You go, go on. I've got enough here to keep me busy till evening.'

Mentally bidding farewell to the car, I walked out into the dusty, hot street.

Little Romka was absolutely delighted at my visit. I walked in just as Anna Viktorovna was about to suffer ignominious defeat in the battle of the afternoon nap. Romka, a skinny, suntanned little kid, was bouncing up and down on the springy bed and yelling ecstatically:

'I don't want to sleep by the wall! My knees get all bent!'

'What am I supposed to do with him?' asked Anna Viktorovna, glad to see me. 'Hello, Anton. Tell me, does your Nadienka behave like this?'

'No,' I lied.

Romka stopped jumping up and down and pricked up his ears.

'Why don't you take him and keep him?' Anna Viktorovna suggested craftily. 'What do I want with a silly dunce like him? You seem like a strict man, you'll teach him how to behave. He can look after Nadienka, wash her nappies, wash the floors for you, put the rubbish out . . .'

As she said all this Anna Viktorovna kept winking at me emphatically, as if I really might take her suggestion seriously and carry off little Romka as an underage slave.

'I'll think about it,' I said, to support her educational efforts. 'If he just won't do anything he's told, we'll take him for re-education. We've had worse cases, and they turned out as meek as lambs!'

'No, you won't take me!' Romka said boldly, but he stopped bouncing, sat down on the bed and pulled the blanket up over his legs. 'What would he want with a silly dunce like me?'

'Then I'll put you in a boarding school,' Anna Viktorovna threatened.

'Only heartless people put children in boarding schools,' said Romka, clearly repeating a phrase he'd heard somewhere. 'But you're not heartless.'

'What am I supposed to do with him?' Anna Viktorovna repeated rhetorically. 'Can I offer you some cold kvass?'

'Me too, me too!' Romka squealed, but a stern glance from his mother shut him up.

'Thank you,' I said with a nod. 'Actually it was this silly dunce that I came to see you about . . .'

'What has he been up to?' asked Anna Viktorovna, taking a businesslike approach.

'It's just that Sveta told me about their adventures . . . about the wolf. I'm a hunter, and the thing is . . .'

A minute later I was sitting at the table with a glass of cold kvass, the centre of attention.

'Yes, I know what they say, but I'm a teacher,' Anna Viktorovna was saying. 'They say wolves help clean up the forest . . . only that's not true, of course, a wolf doesn't just kill sick animals, it kills any animals it can get . . . But it's still a living creature. A wolf's not to blame for being a wolf. But here – right next to the village! Chasing children! It drove them towards the cubs, do you realise what that means?'

I nodded.

'It was teaching the cubs to hunt.' Anna Viktorovna's eyes lit up, either with fear or that mother's fury that sends wolves and bears running for the bushes. 'What was it – a man-eater?'

'It couldn't have been,' I said. 'There haven't been any cases of wolves attacking people round here. There haven't even been any reports of wolves living in these parts for a long time . . . most likely it was a feral dog. But I want to check.'

'Yes, check,' Anna Viktorovna said firmly. 'And if . . . even if it's a dog. If the children didn't imagine the whole thing . . .'

I nodded again.

'Shoot it,' Anna Viktorovna requested. Then she added in a whisper: 'I can't sleep at night . . . for imagining . . . what could have happened.'

'It was a doggy!' Romka piped up from the bed.

'Hush!' Anna Viktorovna shouted at him. 'All right then, come here. Tell the nice man what happened.'

Romka didn't need to be asked twice. He got down off the bed, came over to us, clambered up onto my knees with a very serious air and looked into my eyes searchingly.

I ruffled up his coarse, sun-bleached hair.

'So this is what happened . . .' Romka began contentedly.

Anna Viktorovna looked at him in a very sad sort of way. I

could understand her. It was these little children's father that I couldn't understand. All sorts of things can happen. So they were separated. But how could anyone just cancel his children out of his life and be happy just to pay maintenance?

'We walked and walked, you know, we were out for a walk,' Romka told us with agonising slowness. 'And after we walked for a while we reached the forest. And then Ksyusha started telling me scary stories . . .'

I listened to his story very carefully. Well, the 'scary stories' might be one more reason to believe the whole business was imagined. But the child was speaking perfectly clearly, except for repeating a few words, which was usual for a child his age; there was nothing to find fault with.

Just to be on the safe side, I scanned the boy's aura. A little human being. A good little human being, and I wanted to believe he would grow up into a good adult. Not the slightest sign of any Other potential. And no traces of magical influence.

But then, if Svetlana hadn't spotted anything, what could I expect, with my second-grade abilities?

'And then the wolf laughed out loud!' Romka exclaimed, throwing his hands up in the air in glee.

'Weren't you frightened?' I asked.

To my surprise, Romka thought about that for a long time. Then he said:

'Yes, I was. I'm small, and the wolf was big. And I didn't have a stick. And then I stopped being afraid.'

'So you're not afraid of the wolf now?' I asked. After an adventure like that, any normal child would have developed a stammer, but Romka had lost his.

'Not a bit,' said the boy. 'Oh, now you've put me off. What part did I get to?'

'The part where the wolf laughed,' I said with a smile.

'Just exactly like a man,' said Romka.

So that was it. It was a long time since I'd had any dealings with werewolves. Especially werewolves as brazen as this . . . hunting children, only a hundred kilometres from Moscow. Had they been counting on the fact that there was no Night Watch in the village? Even then, the district office checked every missing person case. They had a very skilful, specialised magician for that. From the normal human viewpoint what he did was pure charlatanism – he looked at photographs, and then either put them aside or phoned the operations office and said in an embarrassed voice: 'I think I've got something here . . . I'm not quite sure what . . .'

And then we would swing into action, drive out to the country, find the signs . . . and the signs would be terrible, but we're used to that. Then the werewolves would probably resist arrest, and someone – it could easily be me – would wave his hand. And a jangling grey haze would go creeping through the Twilight . . .

We rarely took their kind alive. But this time I really wanted to.

'And what I think as well,' Romka said thoughtfully, 'is that the wolf said something. I think so, I think so . . . Only he didn't talk, I know wolves don't talk, do they? But I dream that he did talk.'

'And what did he say?' I asked cautiously.

'Go a-way, witch!' Romka said, trying in vain to imitate a hoarse bass voice.

Right. Now I could issue the warrant for a search. Or at least request help from Moscow.

It was a werewolf, no doubt about it. But fortunately for the children, there was a witch there too.

A powerful witch.

Very powerful.

She hadn't just driven away the werewolf – she'd tidied up the children's memories without leaving any trace. Only she hadn't gone in deep. She hadn't expected there would be a vigilant watchman in the village. The boy didn't remember anything when he was awake, but in his dream – there it was. 'Go away, witch!'

How very interesting!

'Thank you, Romka.' I held out my hand to him. 'I'll go to the forest and take a look.'

'But aren't you afraid? Have you got a gun?' he asked eagerly.

'Yes.'

'Show it to me!'

'It's at home,' Anna Viktorovna said strictly. 'And guns aren't toys for children!'

Romka sighed and asked plaintively:

'Only don't shoot the cubs, all right? Better bring me one and I'll train it as a dog! Or two, one for me, one for Ksyusha!'

'Roman!' Anna Viktorovna snapped in a voice of iron.

I found Ksyusha at the pond, as her mother said I would. A covey of girls was sunbathing beside a pack of boys, and the gibes were flying in both directions. The boy sunbathers were old enough not to pull the girls' plaits any more, but they still didn't understand what girls were any good for.

When I arrived everyone stopped talking and stared at me warily. I hadn't put in an appearance at the village before.

'Ksyusha?' I asked the little girl I thought I'd seen in the street with Romka.

The serious girl in a dark blue swimsuit looked at me, nodded and said politely:

'Hi . . . hello.'

'Hello. I'm Anton, Svetlana Nazarova's husband. Do you know her?' I asked.

'What's your daughter's name?' Ksyusha asked suspiciously.

'Nadya.'

'Yes, I know,' she said with a nod, getting up off the sand. 'You want to talk about the wolves, right?'

I smiled.

'That's right.'

She glanced at the boys. The boys, not the girls.

'Uhuh, that's Nadya's dad,' said a freckle-faced kid who was obviously from the village. 'My dad's fixing your car right now.'

He looked round proudly at his friends.

'We can talk here,' I said to reassure the children. It was terrible, of course, to see normal kids living in normal families being so cautious.

But it was better that they were.

'We went for a walk in the forest,' Ksyusha began, standing to attention in front of me. I thought for a moment and sat down on the sand – then the girl sat down too. Anna Viktorovna certainly knew how to bring up her children. 'It was my fault we got lost . . .'

One of the village kids giggled. But quietly. After the business with the wolves Ksyusha was probably the most popular girl with the boys in first class.

In principle she didn't tell me anything new. And there were no traces of magic on her either. Only the mention of a bookcase 'with old books' made me prick up my ears.

'Do you remember any of the book titles?' I asked.

Ksyusha shook her head.

'Try to remember,' I asked her. I looked down at my feet, at my long, irregular shadow.

The shadow rose up obediently to meet me.

And the cool, grey Twilight accepted me.

It's always a pleasure to look at children from the Twilight.

Even the most intimidated and unhappy of them still have auras without any of the malice and bitterness that adults are shrouded in.

I apologised mentally to the kids – after all, they hadn't asked me to do what I was going to do. And I ran the lightest possible, imperceptible touch across them. Just to remove the slight traces of Evil that had already stuck to them.

And then I stroked Ksyusha's hair and whispered:

'Remember, little girl . . .'

I wouldn't be able to remove the block put in place by the witch, if she was more powerful than me, or at least equal in power. But fortunately for me, the witch had been very gentle with their minds.

I emerged from the Twilight and the air hit me like a blast from a stove. The summer had really turned out hot.

'I remember!' Ksyusha said triumphantly. 'One book was called *Aliada Ansata*.'

I frowned.

That book wasn't a herbarium . . . or at least it wasn't an ordinary witch's herbarium, it was particularly heinous. It even had a few vile uses for dandelions.

'And *Kassagar Garsarra*,' Ksyusha continued.

Some of the children giggled. But uncertainly.

'How was it written?' I asked. 'In Latin letters? You know, like English?'

'No, in Russian,' she replied. 'In really funny, old letters.'

I'd never heard of a Russian translation of that manuscript, which was extremely rare even among the Dark Ones. It couldn't be printed, the magic of the spells wouldn't be preserved. It could only be copied out by hand. And only in blood. Not the blood of a virgin or a young innocent, those were erroneous beliefs introduced later, and modern copies like that were no use at all. The *Kassagar Garsarra* was still believed to exist only in Arabic, Spanish, Latin and Old German. A magician who rewrote the book had to use his own blood – a separate jab for every spell. And it was a thick book . . .

And Power was lost with the blood.

It was enough to make me feel proud of Russian witches for producing even one fanatic like that.

'Is that all?' I asked

'*Fuaran*.'

'There's no such book, it's an invention . . .' I replied automatically: 'What did you say? *Fuaran*?'

'Yes, *Fuaran*,' Ksyusha repeated.

There wasn't really anything too horrible in that book. But in all the textbooks it was mentioned as an imaginary invention. According to legend, it contained instructions on how to turn a human child into a witch or a warlock. Detailed instructions that supposedly worked.

But that was impossible!

Wasn't it, Gesar?

'Wonderful books,' I said.

'They're books on botany, are they?' Ksyusha asked.

'Yes,' I confirmed. 'Like catalogues, kind of. *Aliada Ansata* tells you where to look for various kinds of herbs . . . and so on. Well, thank you, Ksyusha.'

There were interesting things going on around here! Right here, just outside Moscow, a powerful witch sitting in the dark depths of the forest . . . though hardly – it was only a small stretch of forest . . . with a library of extremely rare books on Dark magic. And sometimes she saved children from dim-witted werewolves, for which I was very grateful. But books like that were supposed to be registered on a special list – kept by both Watches and the Inquisition. Because the Power that stood behind them was immense, and dangerous.

'I owe you a chocolate bar,' I told the girl. 'You told me your story really well.'

Ksyusha didn't make any fuss, she just said 'thank you'. Then she seemed to lose all interest in the conversation.

Since the little girl was older, the witch had obviously brain-washed her more thoroughly. Only she'd forgotten about the books the witch had seen.

And that made me feel a bit less worried.

CHAPTER 2

GESAR LISTENED TO me carefully. He asked questions to clarify a few things and then said nothing, just sighed and groaned. I lounged in the hammock with the phone in my hands, telling him all the details . . . the only thing I didn't tell him was that the witch had the book *Fuaran*.

'Good work, Anton,' Gesar told me eventually. 'Well done. I see you remain vigilant.'

'What shall I do?' I asked.

'The witch must be found,' he said. 'She hasn't done any harm, but she has to be registered. You know, just . . . usual procedure.'

'And the werewolves?' I asked.

'Most likely a group from Moscow,' Gesar commented dryly. 'I'll order a check on all werewolves with three or more werewolf children.'

'There were only three cubs,' I reminded him.

'The werewolf might only have taken the older ones hunting,' Gesar explained. 'They usually have large families . . . Are there any suspicious holidaymakers in the village? An adult with three or more children?'

'No,' I replied regretfully. 'Sveta and I thought of that straight away . . . Anna Viktorovna is the only one who came with two, and all the rest either have no children or just one. The birth rate's critically low in Russia . . .'

'I am aware of the demographic situation, thank you,' Gesar interrupted sardonically. 'What about the locals?'

'There are some large families, but Svetlana knows all the local people well. Nothing suspicious, just ordinary types.'

'So they're outsiders,' Gesar concluded. 'As I understand it, no one has disappeared from the village. Are there any holiday hotels or rest homes nearby?'

'Yes,' I confirmed. 'On the far side of the river, about five kilometres away, there's a Young Pioneers' camp, or whatever it is they call them now . . . I've already checked, everything's in order, the children are all in place. And they wouldn't let them come across the river, it's a military-style camp, very strict. Lights out, reveille, five minutes to dress. Don't worry about that.'

Gesar grunted in dissatisfaction and asked me:

'Do you need any help, Anton?'

I thought about it. It was the most important question that I hadn't been able to answer so far.

'I don't know. It looks as though the witch is more powerful than me. But I'm not going there to kill her . . . and she must sense that.'

Somewhere in Moscow, Gesar pondered something. Then he declared:

'Have Svetlana check the probability lines. If the danger to you is only slight, then try yourself. If it's more than ten or twelve per cent . . . then . . .' He hesitated for a moment, then finished briskly. 'Ilya and Semyon will come. Or Danila and Farid. Three of you will be able to manage.'

I smiled. You're thinking about something else, Gesar. About something completely different. You're hoping that if anything goes wrong, Svetlana will back me up. And then maybe come back to the Night Watch . . .

'And then, you've got Svetlana,' Gesar concluded. 'You understand the whole business. So get on with it and report back as necessary.'

'Yes sir, *mon générale*,' I rapped.

'In terms of military rank, lieutenant-colonel, my title would be at least generalissimus. Now get on with the job,' Gesar retorted.

I put my phone away and took a minute to classify grades of Power in terms of military ranks. Seventh grade – private . . . sixth – sergeant . . . fifth – lieutenant . . . fourth – captain . . . third – major . . . second – lieutenant-colonel . . . first – colonel.

That was right – if you didn't introduce unnecessary differentiations or divide ranks into junior and senior, then I would be a lieutenant-colonel – and a general would be an ordinary magician beyond classification.

But Gesar was no ordinary magician.

The gate slammed shut and Ludmila Ivanovna came into the garden. My mother-in-law. With Nadiushka skeetering restlessly around her. The moment my daughter was in the garden, she came dashing across to the hammock.

She wasn't initiated, but she could sense her parents. And there were plenty of things she could do that any ordinary two-year-olds couldn't. She wasn't afraid of any animals, and they loved her. Dogs and cats simply fawned on her . . .

And mosquitoes didn't bite her.

'Daddy,' Nadya said, scrambling up on top of me. 'We went for a walk.'

'Hello, Ludmila Ivanovna,' I said to my mother-in-law. Just to be on the safe side. We'd already exchanged greetings that morning.

'Taking a rest?' my mother-in-law asked dubiously.

We got along fine, really. Not like in the old jokes about mothers-in-law. But somehow I had the feeling that she always suspected me of something. Of being an Other, maybe . . . if there was any way she could know about the Others.

'Just a quick one,' I said cheerfully. 'Did you go far, Nadya?'

'Yes, very far.'

'Are you tired?'

'Yes,' Nadya said. 'But Grandma's more tired than me!'

Ludmila Ivanovna stood there for a second, apparently wondering whether a blockhead like me could be trusted with his own daughter. She decided to risk it, and went into the house.

'Where are you going?' Nadiushka asked, clutching my hand tightly.

'Did I say I was going anywhere?' I asked in surprise.

'No, you didn't say . . .' she admitted and ruffled her hair with her hand. 'But you are going?'

'Yes, I am,' I confessed.

That's the way things are, if a child is a potential Other so powerful that she has the ability to foresee the future from birth. A year earlier Nadya had started crying a week before she actually started teething.

'La-la-la . . .' Nadya sang, looking at the fence. 'But the fence needs painting!'

'Did Grandma say that?' I asked.

'Yes. If we had a real man, he'd paint the fence,' Nadiushka repeated laboriously. 'But we haven't got a real man, so Grandma's going to have to paint it.'

I sighed.

Oh these terrible dacha fanatics! When people got old, why did they always develop a passion for gardening, scrabbling in the earth? Were they trying to get used to it?

'Grandma's joking,' I said, and thumped my chest. 'We do have a real man here, and he'll paint the fence! If necessary, he'll paint all the fences in the village!'

'A real man,' Nadya repeated, laughing.

I buried my face in her fine hair and blew. Nadiushka started giggling and kicking out at the same time. I winked at Svetlana as she came out of the house, and lowered my daughter to the ground.

'Run to Mummy.'

'No, better go to Grandma,' said Svetlana, sweeping Nadya up in her arms. 'For a drink of milk.'

'I don't want milk!'

'You have to,' Svetlana retorted.

And Nadiushka didn't argue any more, she set off meekly to the kitchen. Even ordinary human mothers and children have a strange, unspoken understanding with each other. So what could you expect from our family? Nadya could sense perfectly well when she could play up, and when it wasn't even worth trying.

'What did Gesar say?' Svetlana asked, sitting down beside me. The hammock started to sway.

'He gave me a choice. I can look for the witch on my own, or I can call in assistance. Will you help me decide?'

'Look at the future for you?' Svetlana asked.

'Yes.'

Svetlana closed her eyes and lay back in the hammock. I pulled up her legs and put them across my knees. From the outside it looked perfectly idyllic. An attractive woman lying in a hammock, resting. Her husband sitting beside her, playfully stroking her thigh.

I can look into the future too, but not nearly as well as Svetlana. It's not my speciality, so would have taken me a lot longer to do. And my forecast would have been unreliable.

Svetlana opened her eyes and looked at me.

'Well?' I asked impatiently.

'Don't stop, keep stroking,' she said with a smile. 'You're in the clear. I don't see any danger at all.'

'The witch is evidently weary of her evildoing,' I laughed. 'All right, then. I'll issue her a verbal warning for not being registered.'

'It's her library that bothers me,' Svetlana confessed. 'Why would she hide away in the back of beyond, with books like that?'

'Maybe she just doesn't like the city?' I suggested. 'She needs the forest, fresh air . . .'

'Then why just outside Moscow? She should go away to Siberia, where the environment's less polluted and the rarest herbs grow. Or to the Far East.'

'She's local,' I laughed. 'Patriotic about her own little homeland.'

'Something's not right,' Svetlana said peevishly. 'I still can't get over that business with Gesar . . . and then suddenly this witch!'

'What's so strange about the Gesar business?' I asked with a shrug. 'He wanted to make his son into a Light One. I for one don't blame him. Imagine how guilty he must feel. He thought the child had died . . .'

Svetlana smiled ironically:

'At this moment Nadiushka's sitting on a stool, dangling her legs and saying she wants the skin taken off her milk.'

'So . . . ?' I asked, puzzled.

'I can sense where she is and what's happening to her,' Svetlana explained. 'Because she's my daughter. And I'm not as powerful as Gesar or Olga . . .'

'They thought the boy had died . . .' I muttered.

'That could never happen,' Svetlana said firmly. 'Gesar's not a block of stone, he's got feelings. He would have sensed that the boy was alive. Olga certainly would have. He's her flesh and blood . . . she couldn't have believed that her child had died. And if they knew he was alive, the rest was straightforward enough. Gesar has the power, and he had it fifty years ago, to turn the entire country upside down in order to find his son.'

'You mean they deliberately didn't look for him?' I asked, but Svetlana didn't answer. 'Or . . .'

'Or,' Svetlana agreed, 'the boy really was an ordinary human being. In that case everything fits. They could have believed he was dead and found him entirely by chance.'

'The *Fuaran*,' I said. 'Maybe this witch is somehow connected with what happened at the Assol complex?'

Svetlana shrugged and sighed:

'Anton, I want desperately to go into the forest with you, find this kind botanist lady and subject her to intensive interrogation.'

'But you're not going to,' I said.

'No, I'm not. I swore I wouldn't get involved in Night Watch operations.'

I understood everything. I shared the resentment Svetlana felt towards Gesar. And in any case I preferred not to take Svetlana with me . . . it wasn't her job, to go traipsing through the forest looking for witches.

But how much simpler and easier it would have been to work together.

I sighed and stood up.

'Right then, I won't put it off any longer. The heat's eased off, so it's time I took a stroll in the forest.'

'It's almost evening,' Svetlana remarked.

'I won't be far away. The children said the hut was really near.'

Svetlana nodded.

'All right. Just wait a minute and I'll make you some sandwiches. And fill a flask with compote.'

While I was waiting, I took a cautious peep into the barn. And I almost flipped. Not only had Kolya taken half the diesel engine apart and laid the pieces out on the floor, he now had another local drunk, Andryukha or Seryoga, rummaging away beside him. They were so absorbed in their confrontation with German technology that the 'little bottle' soft-hearted Svetlana had brought for them was still standing there unopened. Kolya was crooning an old folk ditty to himself:

My very best friend and I
Worked on a diesel engine . . .

I tiptoed away from the shed.

To hell with the car anyway . . .

Svetlana kitted me out as if I wasn't just going for a walk along the edge of the forest, but was about to be parachuted into the middle of the Siberian taiga.

Sandwiches in a plastic bag, a flask of compote, a sturdy penknife, matches, a box of salt, two apples and a torch.

And she'd also checked that my mobile phone was charged. Bearing in mind the forest's minuscule dimensions, that wasn't a bad idea. In an emergency I could always climb a tree – then the signal would be bound to reach the network.

It was my idea to take the minidisc player. And as I strolled towards the forest, I listened to The Hibernation of the Beasts:

The medieval city sleeps, the worn-out granite trembles,
The night maintains its silence out of fear of death.

The medieval city sleeps, the dull and washed-out colours
Speak to you like some distant echo – but don't trust it.
In libraries books sleep, storehouses are bloated with barrels,
And geniuses lose their minds on the night watch,
And darkness averages, levels everything: bridges, canals and houses,
Capitols and prisons, all in a single pattern . . .

I wasn't really expecting to find the witch that evening. I ought to have gone in the morning, and with a team. But I really wanted to locate the suspect myself!

And to take a look at that book, the *Fuaran*.

I stood at the edge of the forest for a while, looking at the world through the Twilight. Nothing out of the ordinary. Not the slightest trace of magic. Except that in the distance, above our house, there was a bright white glow. A first-grade enchantress can be seen from a long way off . . .

Okay, let's go in deeper.

I raised my shadow from the ground and stepped into the Twilight.

The forest was transformed into an eddying haze, a phantom. Only the very largest of the trees were represented in the Twilight world.

Now, where had the kids come out of the forest?

I found their tracks fairly quickly. A couple of days later and the faint footprints would have faded away, but they were still visible. Children leave clear tracks, they have a lot of power in them. Only pregnant women leave tracks that are clearer.

There were no tracks from the 'female botanist'. They could have faded already. But it was more likely that this witch had long been in the habit of not leaving any tracks.

Yet she hadn't erased the children's tracks. Why not? An oversight? That traditional Russian sloppiness? Or was it deliberate?

Well, I wasn't going to guess.

I recorded the children's footprints in my memory and left the Twilight. I couldn't see the tracks any more, but I could sense which way they were leading. Now I was ready to set off.

First I disguised myself thoroughly. Of course, the disguise was no match for the shell that Gesar had encased me in, but a magician less powerful than me would take me for a human being. Maybe we were overestimating the witch's abilities?

I spent the first half-hour vigilantly surveying the area, inspecting every suspicious bush through the Twilight, sometimes pronouncing simple search spells. In general working by the book, a disciplined Other conducting a search.

Then I got bored of that. I was in a forest – only a small one, and maybe not one that was in great shape, but it was at least unspoiled by tourists. Maybe the forest was unspoiled because it was only fifty square kilometres. There were all kinds of small forest wildlife here, like squirrels, hares and foxes. There weren't any wolves at all, of course – real ones, that is, rather than werewolves. Fine – we could get along without wolves. There was plenty of free food around – I stopped by some wild raspberry bushes and spent ten minutes picking the slightly withered, sweet berries. Then I came across an entire colony of white cep mushrooms. More than a colony – it was a genuine mushroom megalopolis. Huge white mushrooms, not worm-eaten, no rubbishy little ones or different kinds. I'd had no idea there was treasure like that to be found only a couple of kilometres from the village.

I hesitated. If I picked all those mushrooms, I could take them home and dump them on the table, to my mother-in-law's amazement and Svetlana's delight. How Nadya would squeal in ecstasy and boast to the neighbours' kids about her clever dad!

Then I thought that I couldn't sneak a haul like that back to the house without being seen, which would mean the whole village would go dashing off, hunting for mushrooms. Including the local drunks, who would be happy to sell them on the side of the main road and buy vodka with the earnings. And the grannies, who mostly supported themselves by gathering wild food. And all the local kids.

But somewhere in this forest there were werewolves on the prowl . . .

'They'll never believe me,' I said miserably, looking at the mushroom patch.

I felt a craving for fried white mushrooms. I swallowed hard and carried on following the track.

And five minutes later I came out at a small log-built house.

Everything was just as the children had described it. A little house, tiny windows, no fence, no outbuildings, no vegetable patches. Nobody ever builds houses like that in the forest. Even the dingiest little watchman's hut has to have a lean-to shed for firewood.

'Hey, anybody home?' I shouted. 'Hello?'

Nobody answered.

'Little hut, little hut,' I muttered, citing the fairy tale. 'Turn your back to the forest and your front to me . . .'

The hut as it was stayed. But then, it was already facing me anyway. I suddenly felt very foolish.

It was time to stop playing stupid games. I'd go in and wait for the mistress of the house, if she wasn't home . . .

I walked up to the door and touched the rusty iron handle – and at that very moment, as if someone had been waiting for that touch, the door opened.

'Good day,' said a woman about thirty years old.

A very beautiful woman . . .

Somehow, from what Romka and Ksyusha had told me, I'd expected her to be older. They hadn't really said anything about her appearance, and I'd pictured some average image of 'just a woman'. That was stupid of me . . . of course, for children as young as them, 'beautiful' meant 'wearing a bright-coloured dress'. In another year or two, Ksyusha would probably have said with delight and admiration in her voice: 'The lady was so beautiful!' and compared her with the latest teenage girl's idol.

But she was wearing a check shirt, the kind that men and women can wear.

Tall – but not so tall as to make a man of average height feel insecure. Slim – but not at all skinny. Legs so long and straight I felt like shouting: 'Why the hell did you put jeans on, you fool, get into a miniskirt!' Breasts – well, no doubt some men prefer to see two huge silicone melons, and some take delight in chests as flat as a boy's. But in this particular matter any normal man should go for the golden mean. Hands . . . well, I don't know exactly how hands can be erotic. But hers certainly were. Somehow they made you think that just one touch from those slender fingers and . . .

With a figure like that, a beautiful face is an optional extra. But she was lovely. Hair as black as pitch, large eyes that smiled and enticed. All her features were regular, with just some tiny deviation from perfection that was invisible to the eye, but nonetheless allowed you to see her as a living woman and not a work of art.

'Er . . . h-hello,' I whispered.

What was wrong with me? Anyone would think I'd been raised on an uninhabited island and never seen a woman before.

She beamed at me.

'You're Romka's dad, are you?'

'What?' I asked, confused.

The woman was slightly embarrassed.

'I'm sorry. The other day a little boy got lost in the forest, I showed him the way back to the village. He stammered too . . . a little bit. So I thought . . .'

'I don't usually stammer,' I mumbled. 'I'm usually always spouting all sorts of nonsense. But I wasn't expecting to meet such a beautiful woman in the forest, and I just choked up.'

The 'beautiful woman' laughed:

'Oh, and are those words nonsense too? Or the truth?'

'The truth,' I confessed.

'Won't you come in?' She stepped back into the house. 'And thank you very much. Round here compliments are hard to come by . . .'

'Well, you won't meet people here very often,' I observed, walking into the house and looking around.

Not a trace of magic. A rather strange interior for a house in a forest, but then you come across all sorts of things. True, there was a bookcase with old volumes in it . . . But there were no indications that my hostess was an Other.

'There are two villages near here,' the woman explained. 'The one I took the children back to and another, a bit larger. I go there to buy groceries, the shop's always open. But it's still not a good place for compliments.'

She smiled again.

'My name's Arina. Not Irina – Arina.'

'Anton,' I replied. And then I showed off my schoolboy literary erudition. 'Arina, like Pushkin's nanny?'

'Precisely, I was named after her,' the woman said, still smiling. 'My father was Alexander Sergeevich, like Pushkin, and naturally my mother was crazy about the poet. You could say she was a fanatic. So that's where I got my name . . .'

'But why not Anna, after Anna Kern? Or Natalya, after Natalya Goncharova?'

Arina shook her head.

'Oh, that wouldn't do . . . My mother believed all those women played a disastrous role in Pushkin's life. Yes, they served as a source of inspiration, but he suffered greatly as a man . . . But the nanny . . . she made no claims on her Sasha, she loved him devotedly.'

'Are you a literary specialist?' I asked, putting out a feeler.

'What would a literary specialist be doing here?' Arina laughed. 'Have a seat, I'll make some tea, it's really good, with herbs. Everyone's gone crazy just recently about maté and rooibosch and those other foreign teas. But we Russians don't need all those exotic brews. We have enough herbs of our own. Or just ordinary black tea – we're not Chinese, why should we drink green water? Or forest herbs. Here, try this . . .'

'You're a botanist,' I said dejectedly.

'Correct!' Arina laughed. 'Are you sure you're not Romka's dad?'

'No, I'm . . .' I hesitated for a moment, and then said the most convenient thing that came to mind, 'I'm a friend of his mother's. Thank you very much for saving the children.'

'Oh, sure, I really saved them!' Arina said and smiled again. She was standing with her back to me, sprinkling dry herbs into a teapot – a pinch of one, a tiny bit of another, a spoonful of a third . . . my gaze automatically came to rest on the section of those worn jeans that outlined her firm backside. And somehow it was immediately clear that it was taut, without any sign of that favourite city lady's ailment, cellulite. 'Ksyusha's a bright girl, they'd have found their own way out.'

'What about the wolves?' I asked.

'What wolves, Anton?' Arina looked at me in amazement. 'I explained that to them – it was a stray dog. Where would wolves come from in a small forest like this?'

'A stray dog with puppies is dangerous too,' I observed.

'Well, maybe you're right.' Arina sighed. 'But even so, I don't think it would have attacked the children; an animal has to go completely mad to do something like that. People are far more dangerous than animals.'

I couldn't argue with that.

'Don't you find it boring out here in the wilderness?' I asked, changing the subject.

'I'm not stuck here all the time,' Arina laughed. 'I come for the summer, I'm writing a dissertation: "The ethnogenesis of certain species of crucifers in the central region of Russia".'

'For a doctorate?' I asked, feeling rather envious. I was still disappointed that I'd never finished writing mine, because I'd become an Other, and all those scholarly games had suddenly seemed boring. They were boring – but even so I felt sad.

'Post-doctoral,' Arina replied with understandable pride. 'I'm thinking of presenting it this winter.'

'Is that your research library you have with you?' I asked, nodding at the bookshelf.

'Yes,' said Arina, nodding in reply. 'It was a stupid thing to do, of course, to drag all the books here. But I got a lift from . . . a friend. In a jeep. So I took the opportunity and brought along my whole library.'

I tried to imagine whether a jeep could get through this forest. It looked as though there was a fairly wide track starting just at the back of the house . . . maybe it could get through . . .

I went over to the bookcase and inspected the books closely.

It really was a rich library for a botanical scholar. There were some old volumes from the early part of the last century, with forewords singing the praises of the Party, and Comrade Stalin in particular. And some even older ones, pre-revolutionary. And lots of simple well-thumbed volumes published twenty or thirty years earlier.

'A lot of them are just lumber,' Arina said without turning round. 'The only place for them is in some bibliophile's collection. But somehow I can't bring myself to sell them.'

I nodded gloomily, glancing at the bookcase through the Twilight. Nothing suspicious. No magic. Old books on botany.

Or an illusion created so artfully that I couldn't see through it.

'Sit down, the tea's ready,' said Arina.

I sat down on a squeaky Viennese chair, picked up my cup of tea and sniffed at it.

The smell was glorious. It smelt like ordinary good-quality tea, with a bit of citrus, and a bit of mint. But I would have bet my life that the brew didn't contain any tea leaves, or citron, or plain ordinary mint.

'Well,' Arina said with a smile. 'Why don't you try it?'

She sat down facing me and leaned forward slightly. My gaze involuntarily slipped down to the open collar revealing her suntanned cleavage. I wondered if 'the friend with a jeep' was her lover? Or simply a colleague, another botanist? Oh sure! A botanist with a jeep . . .

What was wrong with me?

'It's hot,' I said, holding the cup in my hands. 'I'll let it cool off a bit.'

Arina nodded.

'It's handy to have an electric kettle,' I added. 'It boils quickly. But where do you get your power from? I didn't notice any wires round the house.'

Arina flinched.

'An underground cable?' she suggested plaintively.

'Oh no,' I said, holding the cup at a distance and carefully pouring the brew onto the floor. 'That answer won't do. Think again.'

Arina tossed her head in annoyance:

'What a disaster! And over such a little thing . . .'

'It's always the little things that give you away,' I said sympathetically. I stood up. 'Night Watch of the City of Moscow, Anton Gorodetsky. I demand that you immediately remove the illusion!'

Arina didn't answer.

'Your refusal to co-operate will be interpreted as a violation of the Treaty,' I reminded her.

Arina blinked. And disappeared.

So that was the way it was going to be . . .

I raised my shadow with a glance, reached towards it, and the cool Twilight embraced me.

The little house hadn't changed at all.

Except that Arina wasn't there.

I concentrated hard. It was too dim and grey to find my shadow. But I finally managed to find it and stepped down to the second level of the Twilight.

The grey mist thickened and the air was filled with a heady, distant drone. A cold shudder ran across my skin. This time the little house had changed – and radically. It had turned into an old peasant hut; the walls were bare logs, overgrown with moss. Instead of glass, there were sheets of semi-transparent mica in the windows. The furniture was cruder and older, the Viennese chair I was sitting in had become a sawn-off log. Only the distinguished scholarly bookcase hadn't changed. However, the books in it were rapidly changing their appearance, the false letters were dropping to the floor, the leatherette spines were changing to real leather . . .

I still couldn't see Arina. There was only a vague, dim silhouette hovering somewhere close to the bookcase, a fleeting, transparent shadow . . . the witch had retreated to the third level of the Twilight.

In theory I could go there too.

Only in practice, I'd never tried. For a second-grade magician, that meant straining his powers to the absolute extreme.

Right now I was too angry with the cunning witch to care. She had tried to enchant me, to put a love spell on me . . . the old hag!

I stood by the darkened window, catching the faint droplets of light that penetrated to the second level of the Twilight. And I found, or at least I thought I found, the faintest of shadows on the floor . . .

The hardest thing was spotting it. When I did, the shadow behaved as I wanted, swirling up towards me and opening the way through.

I stepped down to the third level of the Twilight.

Into a strange sort of house, woven together out of the branches and thick trunks of trees.

There were no more books, and no furniture. Just a nest of branches.

And Arina, standing there facing me.

How old she was!

She wasn't hunched and crooked, like Baba-Yaga in the fairy tale. She was still tall and upright. But her skin was wrinkled like the bark of a tree and her eyes had sunk deep into her head. The only garment she was wearing was a dirty, shapeless sackcloth smock, and her shrivelled breasts dangled like empty pouches behind its deep neckline. She was bald, with just a single tress of hair jutting out from the crown of her head like a Red Indian forelock.

'Night Watch!' I repeated, the words emerging slowly and reluctantly from my mouth. 'Leave the Twilight! This is your final warning!'

What could I have done, considering that she could dive to the third level of the Twilight so easily? I don't know. Maybe nothing . . .

She didn't offer any more resistance, but took a step forward – and disappeared.

It cost me a significant effort to move back up to the second level. It was usually easier to leave the Twilight, but the third level had drawn Power out of me as if I was some ignorant novice.

Arina was waiting for me on the second level. She had already assumed her former appearance. She nodded, and moved on – to the normal, calm and cosy human world . . .

I had to try twice, streaming with cold sweat, before managing to raise my shadow.

CHAPTER 3

ARINA WAS SITTING on a chair, with her hands resting modestly on her knees. She wasn't smiling any more, and in general she was as meek as a lamb.

'Can we manage without any more hocus-pocus from now on?' I asked as I emerged into the real world. My back was wet and my legs were trembling slightly.

'Can I stay in this form, watchman?' Arina asked in a low voice.

'What for?' I replied, unable to resist taking petty revenge. 'I've already seen the real you.'

'Who's to say what's real in this world?' Arina said pensively. 'It all depends on your point of view . . . Regard my request as simple female caprice, Light One.'

'And the attempt to enchant me – was that caprice too?'

Arina shot a bright, defiant glance at me and said:

'Yes. I realise that my Twilight appearance . . . but here and now, this is what I am! And I have all the human feelings. Including the desire to please.'

'All right, stay like that,' I growled. 'I can't say I'm exactly dreaming of a repeat performance . . . Remove the illusion from the magical objects.'

'As you wish, Light One.' Arina ran her hand over her hair, adjusting the style.

And the little house changed just a bit.

Now instead of the teapot, there was a small birch-wood tub standing on the table, with steam still rising from it. The TV was still there, but the wire no longer ran to an illusory power socket; instead it was stuck into a large brownish tomato.

'Clever,' I remarked, nodding at the TV. 'How often do you have to change the vegetables?'

'Tomatoes – every day,' the witch said with a shrug. 'A head of cabbage works for two or three days.'

I'd never seen such an ingenious way of producing electricity before. Sure, it's possible in theory, but in practice . . .

But I was more interested in the books in the bookcase. I walked over and took out the first small volume that came to hand, a slim one in a paper cover.

Hawthorn and Its Practical Use in Everyday Witchcraft.

The book had been printed on something like a rotary printer. Published the previous year. It gave the print run – two hundred copies. It even had an ISBN. But the publishing house was unfamiliar, TP Ltd.

'A genuine botanical text . . . Do you people really print your own books?' I asked admiringly.

'Sometimes,' the witch said modestly. 'You can't copy everything out by hand.'

'Copying by hand isn't the worst of it,' I remarked. 'Sometimes things are written in blood . . .'

I took *Kassagar Garsarra* down from the shelf.

'In my own blood, mind,' Arina said laconically. 'No abominations.'

'This book itself is an abomination,' I remarked. 'Well well . . . "Setting people against each other without excessive effort" . . .'

'Why are you trying to incriminate me?' Arina asked, irritated now. 'Those are all academic editions. Antiques. I haven't stirred up trouble for anybody.'

'Really?' I said, leafing through the book. '"Soothing kidney ailments, driving out dropsy . . ." Okay, we'll let you have that.'

'You wouldn't accuse someone who was reading De Sade of planning torture, would you?' Arina snapped. 'That's our history. All sorts of different spells. Not divided into destructive and positive ones.'

I cleared my throat. Basically she was right. The fact that there were all sorts of different magical recipes collected together in the book didn't constitute a crime in itself. There were things like . . . 'How to relieve the pain of a woman in childbirth without harming the child'. But then right beside that was 'Killing the foetus without harming the woman' and 'Killing the foetus together with the woman'.

Everything the way it always was with the Dark Ones.

Despite these foul recipes and the attempt to enchant me, there was something I liked about Arina. In the first place, there was the way she'd dealt with the children. There was no doubt that a smart old witch could easily have found some monstrous use for them. And then . . . there was something melancholy and lonely about her – despite all her power, despite her valuable library and attractive human form.

'What have I done wrong?' Arina asked peevishly. 'Come on, don't string it out, sorcerer!'

'Are you registered?' I asked.

'Why, am I a vampire or a werewolf?' Arina asked in reply. 'Now he wants to put a seal on me . . . the very idea . . .'

'No one's talking about a seal,' I reassured her. 'It's just that all magicians of the first-grade and higher are obliged to inform the district centre of their place of residence. So that their movements will not be interpreted as hostile actions . . .'

'I'm not an enchantress, I'm a witch!'

'Magicians, enchantresses and Others of equivalent power . . .' I recited wearily. 'You are on the territory of the Moscow Watch. You were obliged to inform us.'

'There was never any of that before,' the witch muttered. 'The foremost sorcerers told each other about themselves, the vampires and werewolves were registered . . . and everybody left us alone.'

That sounded strange.

'When was "before"?' I asked.

'In '31,' the witch said reluctantly.

'You've been living here since 1931?' I said, unable to believe my ears. 'Arina . . .'

'I've been living here for two years. Before that . . .' She frowned. 'It doesn't matter where I was before that. I didn't hear about the new laws.'

Maybe she was actually telling the truth. It sometimes happens like that with old Others, especially those who don't work in the Watches. They hide themselves away somewhere in the back of beyond, way out in the taiga or the forest, and sit there for decades at a time, until the boredom just gets too much.

'And two years ago you decided to move here?' I asked, trying to get things straight.

'Yes. What would an old fool like me want with the city?' Arina laughed. 'I just sit here and watch TV, read books. Catching up on what I've missed. I found an old friend of mine who sends me books from Moscow.'

'Well, all right,' I said. 'Then it's just the normal procedure. Have you got a sheet of paper?'

'Yes.'

'Write a statement. Your name, where you're from, year of birth, year of initiation, if you've ever served in a Watch, what grade of Power you possess.'

Arina obediently found a piece of paper and a pencil. I frowned, but I didn't offer her my ball-point pen. She could write it with a goose quill if she wanted.

'When was the last time you registered or made your location known to the official agencies of the Watches? Where have you been since then?'

'I won't write it,' said Arina, putting her pencil down. 'All this new-fangled paper-scribbling . . . Whose business is it where I've been warming my old bones?'

'Arina, stop talking like an old peasant woman,' I told her. 'You were speaking perfectly normally before.'

'I was in disguise,' Arina declared without batting an eyelid. 'Oh, very well. But you have to drop that bureaucratic tone too.'

She rapidly covered the entire sheet with close, neat handwriting. Then handed it to me.

She wasn't as old as I'd been expecting. Less than two hundred years. Her mother had been a peasant, her father was unknown, none of her relatives were Others. She had been initiated as a girl of eleven by a Dark Magician or, as Arina stubbornly referred to him, a sorcerer. Someone not local, German in origin. At the same time he had deflowered and abused her, which for some reason she found necessary to write down, adding 'the lascivious wretch'. So that was it. This 'German' had taken her as his servant and student – in every respect. Evidently he hadn't been too bright or too gentle – by the age of thirteen the girl had acquired enough power to vanquish her mentor in a fair duel and dematerialise him. And he had been a fourth-grade magician, by the way. After that she had come under the surveillance of the Watches of that time. But she had no other criminal acts in her record – if her statement was to be believed, that is. She didn't like cities, she had lived in villages and made her living by using petty witchcraft.

After the revolution several attempts had been made to 'dekulakise her' as part of the communists war against rich peasants . . . the peasants had realised she was a witch and decided to set the Soviet Secret Police onto her. Mausers and magic, would you believe it! Magic had won out, but things couldn't go on like that forever. In 1931 Arina had . . .

I looked up at the witch and asked:

'Seriously?'

'I went into hibernation,' Arina said calmly. 'I realised the red plague was going to last a long time. I could have chosen to sleep for six, eighteen or sixty years. We witches always have to take a lot of conditions into account. Six years or eighteen was too short for the communists. I went to sleep for sixty years.'

She hesitated, and then confessed:

'It was here that I slept. I protected my hut as securely as I could, so that no human being or Other could come close.'

Now I understood. Those were bad times. Others were killed almost as often as ordinary people. It wasn't too hard to go missing.

'You didn't tell anyone you were sleeping here?' I asked. 'None of your friends . . .'

Arina laughed:

'If I'd told anyone, you wouldn't be here talking to me, Light One.'

'Why?'

She nodded towards the bookcase:

'That's my entire fortune. And it's a substantial one. A great temptation.'

I folded the statement and put it in my pocket. Then I said:

'It is. But there's still one rare book I didn't spot.'

'Which one?' the witch asked in surprise.

'*Fuaran*.'

Arina snorted.

'Such a big boy, and you believe in fairy stories . . . There is no such book.'

'Aha. And the little girl made up that title all on her own.'

'I didn't clear her memory,' Arina sighed. 'Tell me, after that what's the point in doing good deeds?'

'Where's the book?' I asked sharply.

'Third shelf down, fourth volume from the left,' Arina said irritably. 'Did you leave your eyes at home?'

I walked across to the bookcase

Fuaran!

Written in big gold letters on black leather.

I took the book out and looked triumphantly at the witch.

Arina was smiling.

I looked at the title on the front cover – *Fuaran: fantasy or fact?* The word 'Fuaran' was in large print, the others were smaller.

I looked at the spine.

Now I saw it. The smaller letters had faded and crumbled away.

'A rare book,' Arina admitted. 'Thirteen copies were printed in St Petersburg in 1913, at the printing works of His Imperial Highness. Printed properly, at night when the moon was full. I don't know how many of them have survived.'

Could a frightened little girl have seen only the single word printed in big letters?

Of course she could!

'What's going to happen to me now?' Arina asked woefully. 'What rights do I have?'

I sighed, sat down at the table and turned the pages of the 'fake Fuaran'. It was an interesting book, no doubt about it.

'Nothing's going to happen to you,' I told her. 'You helped the children. The Night Watch is grateful to you for that.'

'Why do people wrong for no reason?' the witch muttered. 'You're only harming yourself . . .'

'In view of that fact, and also the special circumstances of your life . . .' I searched my memory, trying to recall the paragraphs, footnotes and comments. 'In view of all of this, you will not suffer any punishment. There's just one question . . . what is your grade of Power?'

'I wrote the answer "I don't know",' Arina answered calmly. 'How can you measure that?'

'At least approximately?'

'When I went to sleep, I was on the first rank,' the witch admitted with a certain pride. 'But now I've probably moved beyond all the ranks.'

That had to be right. That was why I hadn't been able to penetrate her illusion.

'Do you intend to work in the Day Watch?'

'What can they show me that I haven't seen before?' Arina asked indignantly. 'Especially as Zabulon's worked his way up to the top. Hasn't he?'

'Yes,' I confirmed. 'Why does that surprise you? Surely you don't think he isn't powerful enough?'

'He was never short of Power,' Arina said, frowning. 'It's just that he abandons his own people far too easily. His girlfriends . . . he never lived with any of them for more than ten years, something always happened . . . and the stupid young fools still kept leaping into his bed anyway. And he really hates Ukrainians and Lithuanians. When there's dirty work to be done, he calls in a brigade from Ukraine, and gets them to do it for him. If someone has to take a risk, then a Lithuanian will be at the top of the list. I thought he wouldn't last in the job with habits like that.' Arina suddenly laughed. 'Obviously he's become an expert at avoiding trouble. Good for him!'

'Yes, good for him,' I said sourly. 'If you're not going to work in the Day Watch structures, and you continue to live as an ordinary civilian, you are granted the right to perform certain magical actions . . . for personal purposes. Each year – twelve seventh-degree interventions, six sixth-degree interventions, three fifth-degree interventions and one fourth-degree intervention. Every two years – one third-degree intervention. Every four years – one second-degree intervention.'

I stopped.

Arina enquired:

'And first-degree interventions?'

'The maximum grade of power permitted to Others not in service with the Watches is limited to their previous grade,' I commented spitefully. 'If you undergo an examination and are registered as a witch beyond classification, then once every sixteen years you will be granted the right to use first-degree magic. By arrangement with the Watches and the Inquisition, naturally. First-degree magic is a very serious business.'

The witch smirked. It was a strange kind of smirk, just like an old woman's, and it looked unpleasant on that beautiful young face.

'I'll get by without the first-degree one way or another. If I understand correctly, the limitations only apply to magic directed against people?'

'Against people and Others,' I confirmed. 'You can do whatever you like with yourself and inanimate objects.'

'Well, thanks for that, at least,' Arina said. 'You know, I'm sorry I tried to enchant you, Light One. You don't seem too bad. Almost like us.'

That dubious compliment made me cringe.

'One more question,' I said. 'Who were those werewolves?'

Arina paused. Then she asked:

'Why, has the law been changed?'

'What law?' I asked, trying to play the fool.

'The old law. A Dark One is not obliged to inform on a Dark One. Or a Light One on a Light One . . .'

'There is such a law,' I admitted.

'Well then, you catch the werewolves yourself. They may be bloodthirsty fools, but I won't give them away.'

She said it with firm confidence. I had nothing to pressure her with – she hadn't assisted the werewolves, quite the reverse.

'As for the magical acts directed against me . . .' I thought for a moment. 'Never mind, I forgive you for that.'

'Just like that?' the witch asked, surprised.

'Just like that. I'm pleased I was able to resist them.'

The witch snorted:

'You think you resisted them, all on your own? . . . Your wife's an enchantress, I'm not blind. She put a spell on you so that no woman could seduce you.'

'That's a lie,' I replied calmly.

'Yes, it is,' the witch admitted. 'Well done. Enchantment's got nothing to do with it, it's just that you love her. Well, my best wishes to your wife and daughter. If you happen to meet Zabulon, tell him he always was an ass and still is.'

'With pleasure,' I promised. Well, good for the old witch! She wasn't afraid to badmouth Zabulon. 'And what shall I tell Gesar?'

'I'm not sending him any greetings,' Arina said contemptuously. 'What business could a village idiot like me have with great Tibetan magicians?'

I stood there, looking at this strange woman – so beautiful in her human form, so repulsive in her true shape. A witch, a mighty witch. But I couldn't say she was spiteful or malicious – she was a jumble of just about everything.

'Don't you get miserable here on your own, Grandma?' I asked.

'Are you trying to insult me?'

'Not in the least. I have learned a few things, after all.'

Arina nodded, but didn't answer.

'You didn't want to seduce me at all, and you don't have any physical desires left,' I went on. 'It's not the same for witches as for enchantresses. You're an old woman and you feel like an old woman, you couldn't give a damn about men. But then, you could carry on as an old woman for another thousand years. So you were only trying to seduce me for sport.'

In the blink of an eye Arina was transformed, changed into a neat, clean old woman with ruddy cheeks and a slight stoop, bright, lively eyes, a mouth with only a few teeth missing and tidily arranged grey hair. She asked:

'Is that better?'

'Yes, I suppose so,' I said, feeling slightly disappointed. After all, her previous form had been very attractive.

'I used to be like this . . . a hundred years ago,' said the witch. 'And I was the way you first saw me . . . once. I was so lovely at sixteen. Ah, Light One, what a happy, beautiful girl I used to be! Even if I was a witch . . . Do you know how and why we age?'

'I heard something about it once,' I admitted.

'It's the price for moving up in rank.' Once again she used the old-fashioned word that had been displaced in recent years by the term 'grade'. 'A witch can stay young in body. Only then you'll be stuck on third rank for ever. We're more closely linked with nature, and nature doesn't like falsehood. Do you understand?'

'I understand,' I said

Arina nodded:

'Well then, Light One . . . be glad that your wife's an enchantress. You've dealt fairly with me, I won't deny that. Would a present be all right?'

'No,' I said and shook my head. 'I'm on duty. And a present from a witch . . .'

'I understand. I don't want to give *you* a present. It's for your wife.'

That set me back. Arina hobbled spryly across to a trunk bound with strips of iron, standing where there had been an ordinary chest of drawers before, opened the lid and put her hands inside. A moment later she came back to me, holding a small ivory comb.

'Take it, watchman. With no spite or dark intent, not for sorrow or for care. Make me a shadow if I lie, may I be scattered in the air.'

'What is it?' I asked.

'A wonder.' Arina furrowed her brow. 'What do they call them nowadays . . . an artefact!'

'But what's it for?'

'Don't you have enough power to see?' Arina asked slyly. 'Your wife will understand. And what do you want explanations for, Light One? I'll just lie, and you'll believe me. You're not as powerful as I am, you know that.'

I bit my tongue and said nothing. After all . . . I'd insulted her a few times. And now I'd been given the answer I deserved.

'Take it, don't be afraid,' Arina repeated. 'Baba-Yaga might be wicked, but she helps fine young heroes.'

What was my problem, really?

'It would be better if you handed over the werewolves,' I said, taking the comb. 'I accept your present only as an intermediary, and this gift does not impose any obligations on anyone.'

'A cunning young fellow,' Arina chuckled. 'But as for the wolves . . . I'm sorry. You understand, I know you do. I won't give them away. By the way, you can take the book. Borrow it, to check. You have that right, don't you?'

It was only then I realised I was still holding *Fuaran: fantasy or fact?* in my left hand.

'For expert examination, temporarily, within the terms of my rights as a watchman,' I said glumly.

The old harridan could lead me by the nose. If she hadn't wanted me to, I wouldn't have noticed the book I'd accidentally stolen until I got home. She would have had a perfect right to complain to the Watches about the theft of a valuable 'wonder'.

When I left the house, I saw the night was already pitch-black. And I had at least two or three hours of staggering through the forest ahead of me.

But the moment I stepped down from the porch, a ghostly blue light appeared in the air ahead of me. I sighed and looked back at the little house, with electric light glowing brightly in its windows. Arina hadn't come out to show me the way – but the blue light danced invitingly in the air.

I followed it.

Five minutes later I heard the lazy yapping of dogs.

And just ten minutes after that, I reached the outskirts of the village.

The most annoying thing about it all was that not once in all that time did I sense the slightest trace of magic.

CHAPTER 4

THE CAR IN the barn had been returned to its former appearance. But I didn't dare get into the driving seat to check how the diesel engine had survived its long ordeal at the hands of the farm mechanics. I walked quietly through into the house and listened – my mother-in-law was already asleep in her room, but there was the faint glow of a night light in ours.

I opened the door and went in.

'Did everything go all right?' Svetlana asked. The way she asked, it was hardly even a question. She could sense everything perfectly well without words.

'Pretty much,' I said and nodded. I looked at Nadiushka's little bed – our daughter was fast asleep. 'I didn't find the werewolves. But I had a talk with the witch.'

'Tell me about it,' said Svetlana. She was sitting on the bed in her nightdress, with a thick book lying beside her – *The Moomintrolls*. Either she'd been reading to Nadya, who would listen to anything as she was falling asleep, even a list of building materials, as long as it was read by her mother. Or she'd decided to relax in bed herself with a good book.

I took my shoes off, got undressed and lay down beside her. And started telling her everything.

Svetlana frowned a few times. And smiled a few times. But when I repeated the witch's words about my wife putting a spell on me, she was genuinely upset.

'I never did!' she exclaimed in a trembling voice. 'Ask Gesar . . . He can see all my spells . . . I never even thought about doing anything of the sort!'

'I know,' I reassured her. 'The witch admitted it was a lie.'

'Actually . . . I did think about it,' Svetlana said suddenly, with a laugh. 'You can't help thinking things . . . but it was just a silly idea, nothing serious. When Olga and I were talking about men, a long time ago . . .'

'Do you miss the Watch?' I couldn't help asking.

'Yes,' Svetlana admitted. 'But let's not talk about that . . . Well done, Anton! You got to the third level of the Twilight?'

I nodded.

'First-grade power . . .' Svetlana said uncertainly.

'No, I know my limits,' I objected. 'Second. Honest second grade. That's my ceiling. Let's not talk about that either, okay?'

'All right, let's talk about the witch,' Svetlana said with a smile. 'So she went into hibernation? I've heard of that, but it's still very rare. You could write an article about it.'

'Who for? A newspaper? *Arguments and Facts*? A witch has been discovered who slept for sixty years in the forest outside Moscow?'

'For the Night Watch information bulletin,' Svetlana suggested. 'Anyway, we really ought to put out our own newspaper. It would have to be a different text for normal people . . . anything you like. Something narrowly specialised. *The Russian Aquarium Herald*, say. How to breed cyclids and set up an aquarium with flowing water in your apartment.'

'How do you know about things like that?' I asked in amazement, and then stopped short. I remembered that her first husband, whom I'd never even seen, was a big fan of aquariums.

'I just happened to remember,' Svetlana said, frowning. 'But any Other, even a pretty feeble one, has to be able to see the real text.'

'I've already thought of the first headline,' I said.

We both smiled.

'Show me that "artefact",' Svetlana said.

I reached across to my clothes and took out the comb, wrapped in a handkerchief.

'I can't see any magic in it,' I admitted.

Svetlana held the comb in her hands for a while.

'Well?' I asked. 'What should we do? Throw it over one shoulder, then wait for a forest to spring up?'

'You're not supposed to see anything,' said Svetlana, smiling. 'And it's not a matter of power, the witch was just making fun of you. Maybe even Gesar wouldn't see anything . . . it's not for men.'

She raised the comb to her hair and began combing it smoothly and gently. She said casually:

'Just imagine . . . it's summer, hot, you're tired, you didn't sleep last night, you've been working all day . . . But you've just had a swim in cool water, someone's given you a massage, you've had a good meal and a glass of fine wine. And now you're feeling much better . . .'

'It improves the mood?' I guessed. 'Counters fatigue?'

'Exclusively for women,' Svetlana replied. 'It's old, at least three hundred years old. It must have been a present from some powerful magician to a woman he loved. Perhaps even a human woman . . .'

She looked at me and her eyes were glowing. She said in a soft voice:

'And it's supposed to make a woman attractive. Irresistible. Alluring. Does it work?'

I looked at her for a second – then glanced at the night light and put it out.

Svetlana herself erected the magic canopy that deadens all sound.

I woke up early in the morning, before five. But to my amazement, I felt perfectly fresh – just like some woman who owns a magic comb and has combed her hair to her heart's content. I was in the mood for great deeds. And a good solid breakfast.

I didn't wake anyone, just rummaged about in the kitchen, broke a couple of pieces off a long loaf of bread and found a small plastic bag of sliced salami. I filled a large mug with home-made kvass and took everything outside.

It was light already, but the village was quiet and still. There was no one hurrying to the morning milking – the cowsheds had stood empty for five years already. No one was hurrying anywhere at all . . .

I sighed and sat down on the grass under the apple tree that had stopped bearing fruit a very, very long time ago. I ate the huge sandwich and drank the kvass. And to complete my comfort, I got the book *Fuaran* from the room – by magic, through the window. I was hoping my mother-in-law was asleep and wouldn't notice the levitating volume.

As I ate my second sandwich, I became increasingly engrossed in reading.

It was truly fascinating!

At the time the book was written, they didn't have any of those clever little words like 'genes' and 'mutations' and other bits of biological wisdom that we try to use nowadays to explain the nature of Others. So the team of witches who worked on the book – there were five of them, but only their first names were given – had used terms like 'affinity for sorcery' and 'change of nature'. One of the authors listed was Arina, something the witch had modestly failed to mention the day before.

First of all the learned witches discussed at length the very nature of the Others. Their conclusion was that the 'affinity for sorcery' existed inside every human. The level of this 'affinity' was different for everyone. As a reference point one could take the natural degree of magic dispersed throughout the world. If a person's 'affinity' was higher than the average global level, then he or she would be a perfectly ordinary human being. He or she wouldn't be able to enter the Twilight, and would only occasionally feel anything strange, as a result of fluctuations in the natural level of magic. But if a person's 'affinity' was *less intense* than that of the surrounding world, he or she would be able to make use of the Twilight.

It all sounded pretty strange. I'd always thought of Others as individuals with strongly developed magical abilities. But the point of view expressed here was the exact opposite of that.

In fact, the following amusing comparison was used as an example: say the temperature throughout the entire world is thirty-six point five degrees. Then most people with a body temperature higher than that will radiate heat outwards and 'warm up nature'. But the small number of people who have a body temperature lower than thirty-six point five will start absorbing heat. And since they receive a constant influx of power, they will be able to make use of it, while people with far warmer temperatures carry on aimlessly 'heating nature'.

An interesting theory. I'd read several other attempts to explain how we came to be different from ordinary people. But I'd never come across one like this. There was something almost offensive about it.

But what difference did it make? The result was still the same. There were people, and there were Others . . .

I carried on reading.

The second chapter was devoted to the differences between 'magicians and enchantresses' and 'witches and wizards'. Back then, apparently, they didn't use the term 'wizard' for Dark Magicians, but only for 'witches of the male sex' – Others who habitually make use of artefacts. It was an interesting article, and I got the feeling it had been written by Arina herself. Essentially it all came down to the fact that there was no real difference. An enchantress operated directly with the Twilight, pumping power out of it to perform certain magical actions. A witch first created certain 'charms' that accumulated Twilight power and were capable of working independently for a long time. Enchantresses and magicians had the advantage of not needing any contrivances – no staffs or rings, books or amulets. Witches and wizards had the advantage that, once they had created a successful artefact, they could use it to accumulate immense reserves of power, which it would be very difficult to draw out of the Twilight instantaneously. The conclusion was obvious, and Arina expressed it in so many words: a rational magician would never despise artefacts, and an intelligent wizard would try to learn to work with the Twilight directly. In the author's opinion, 'in a hundred years' time we shall see that even the greatest and most arrogant magicians will not disdain the use of amulets, and even the most orthodox of witches will not regard it as detrimental to enter the Twilight'.

Well, that prediction had come true to the very letter. Most of the Night Watch staff were magicians. But we made regular use of artefacts . . .

I went into the kitchen, made myself another couple of sandwiches and poured myself some kvass. I looked at the clock – six in the morning. Dogs had begun barking somewhere, but the village still hadn't woken up.

The third chapter dealt with the numerous attempts made by Others to turn a human being into an Other (as a rule, Others had been motivated by love or greed) and attempts by human beings who had learned the truth in one way or another to become Others.

There was a detailed analysis of the story of Gilles de Retz, Joan of Arc's sword-bearer. Joan was a very weak Dark Other, 'a witch of the seventh rank', which, by the way, did not prevent her from performing deeds that were, for the most part, noble. Joan's death was described in very vague terms, there was even a hint that she might have averted the inquisitors' eyes and escaped from her pyre. I decided that was pretty doubtful: Joan had violated the Treaty by using her magic to interfere in human affairs, so our Inquisition would have been keeping an eye on her execution too. There was no way you could avert their eyes . . . But the story of that poor devil Gilles de Retz was described in much greater detail. Either out of love or sheer scatterbrain foolishness, Joan told him all about the nature of the Others. And the young knight, so famous for his noble courage and chivalry, totally lost it. He decided that magical Power could be taken from ordinary people – young, healthy people. All you had to do was torture them, become a cannibal and appeal to the Dark powers for help . . . In effect, the man decided to become a Dark Other. And he tortured several hundred women and children to death, for which (as well as the offence of not paying his taxes), he was eventually burned at the stake too.

It was clear from the text that even the witches didn't approve of that kind of behaviour. There were scathing attacks on the blabbermouth Joan and unflattering epithets applied to her crazy sword-bearer. The conclusion was presented in dry, academic terms – there was no way to use the 'affinity for sorcery' possessed by ordinary people to transform anyone into an Other. After all, an Other was distinguished, not by an elevated level of this 'affinity' that the bloodthirsty Gilles de Retz, in his foolishnness, had tried to increase, but by a lower level. And so all of his murderous experiments had only made him more and more human . . .

It sounded rather convincing. I scratched the back of my head. So . . . it turned out that I was far less gifted for magic than the hopeless alcoholic Kolya? And only thanks to that lack of ability was I able to make use of the Twilight? Well, try to figure that out.

And Svetlana, it turned out, had an even lower level of 'affinity'?

And theoretically Nadiushka had no gift for magic at all? And that was why the power simply flooded into her the way it did – here, take it and use it?

Oh, those witches, they were really smart!

The next chapter discussed whether it was possible to raise the level of Power in nature, so that a larger number of people would become Others. The conclusion was disappointing – it wasn't possible. After all, Power was not only used by Others, who in principle could refrain from magical actions temporarily. Power was also gleefully consumed by blue moss, the only plant known to live at the first level of the Twilight. If there was more Power, the twilight moss would grow more abundantly . . . And there might be other consumers of Power at the deeper levels of the Twilight . . . So the level of Power was a constant – I laughed out loud at finding that word in the archaic book.

All this was followed by the actual story of the book *Fuaran*. The title was derived from the name of an ancient eastern witch who wanted desperately to turn her daughter into an Other. The witch experimented for a long time – first she went down the same path as Gilles de Retz, then she realised her mistake and began trying to increase the level of Power in nature. In fact, she followed every false trail, and eventually realised that she needed to 'reduce her daughter's affinity for sorcery'. According to the rumours, her attempts to do this were recorded in *Fuaran*. The situation was complicated by the fact that in those times the nature of the 'affinity' was unknown – but then it wasn't known at the time this book was written either, and the situation still hadn't changed today. Nonetheless, through a process of trial and error, the witch succeeded in turning her daughter into an Other!

Unfortunately for the witch, a great discovery like that attracted the interest of every single Other. Back then there was no Treaty, no Watches and no Inquisition, and so everyone who heard rumours of the miracle made a dash to get their hands on the formula. For a while Fuaran and her daughter managed to beat off the attacks – apparently the already mighty witch had not only turned her daughter into a powerful Other, but also increased her own grade of power. The aggrieved Others banded together into an army of magicians, with no division between Dark Ones and Light Ones, struck all together and wiped out the family of witches in a terrible battle. In her final hour Fuaran fought desperately for her life – she even transformed her human servants into Others . . . but although they acquired power, they were too disoriented and unskilled. One of the servants turned out to be cleverer than the others, and didn't hang around, but just grabbed the book and ran. By the time the victorious magicians realised that the witch's 'laboratory notes' had disappeared (essentially that was all *Fuaran* was, lab notes), the fugitive's tracks were already cold. The fruitless search for the book went on for a long time. Occasionally someone would claim that he had met the runaway servant, who had become a rather powerful Other, and that they had seen the book and looked through it. Counterfeit books also appeared, some of them produced by crazy followers of the witch, some by Other swindlers. All the cases were thoroughly analysed and documented in the book.

The final chapter contained a discussion of the theme 'What did Fuaran invent?' The authors had no doubt that she really had succeeded, but they believed the book had been lost forever. The reluctant conclusion was that her discovery was so fortuitous and original that its essential nature was impossible to guess.

But what surprised me most of all was the brief résumé – if the book *Fuaran* still existed, it was the duty of every Other to destroy it immediately, 'for reasons clear to everyone, despite the substantial temptation and motives of personal gain . . .'

Oh, those Dark Ones! How they clung to their great power!

I closed the book and started walking round the yard. I looked into the barn again, and decided once more not to risk turning on the car's engine.

Fuaran and her book had existed. The witches had been certain of that. I had to allow for the possibility of a hoax, but in my heart I didn't really believe it.

So the theoretical possibility of transforming a human being into an Other did exist!

That made sense of what had happened at Assol. Gesar and Olga's son had been a human being – as Others' children usually were. That was why the Great Ones hadn't been able to find him. But when they had found him, they'd turned him into an Other, then set up the whole show . . . they hadn't even been afraid to deceive the Inquisition.

I lay down in the hammock and took out my minidisc player. Pressed the random selection switch and closed my eyes. I felt like switching off completely, filling my ears with something meaningless . . .

But I was unlucky. I got Picnic.

Oh no, this makes me want to laugh,
There is no window here, the door's corroded;
The Grand Inquisitor himself
Has come to torture me.
The Inquisitor squats down,

Picks up an instrument:
'Tell me everything you know,
And you'll feel better soon'.
I'm sure he wants to open me up
Like a simple suitcase, he knows one thing:
Even the very emptiest of the emptiest
Has a false bottom, a false bottom.

I don't enjoy coincidences like that. Even the most ordinary people can influence reality, they're just not capable of directing their power. Everybody's familiar with the feeling – when buses turn up just as you need them; when the songs playing on the radio link to your thoughts; when you get phone calls from people you were just thinking about . . . There is a very simple way of checking if you're getting close to the abilities of an Other. If for several days in a row when you happen to glance at the clock you see the figures 11.11, 22.22 or 00.00, it means your connection with the Twilight is becoming more intense. On days like that you shouldn't ignore your premonitions and intuitions.

But that's just small-scale human stuff. In Others the connection is just as unconscious as in people, but it's far more pronounced. I really didn't like the fact that the song about the Grand Inquisitor had turned up at precisely that moment . . .

If I had had more strength
I would have told him: 'Dear fellow,
I do not know who I am, where I am,
What forces rule this world;
And the labyrinths of long streets
Have snared my wandering feet . . .'
The Inquisitor does not trust me,
He gives the screw a turn

I'm sure he wants to open me up
Like a simple suitcase, he knows one thing:
Even the very emptiest of the emptiest
Has a false bottom, a false bottom.

Aha. And I would have liked to know what forces rule this world too . . .

Someone patted me gently on the shoulder.

'I'm not asleep, Sveta,' I said. And opened my eyes.

The Inquisitor Edgar shook his head, smiling reticently. I read his lips:

'Sorry, Anton, but I'm not Sveta.'

Despite the heat, Edgar was wearing a suit, a tie and polished shoes without a single speck of dust on them. And in these city clothes he still didn't look ridiculous. That's Baltic blood for you.

'What the hell!' I barked, tumbling out of the hammock. 'Edgar?'

Edgar waited patiently. I pulled out my earphones, caught my breath and declared:

'I'm on holiday. According to the rules, harassing an employee of the Night Watch while he is off duty . . .'

'Anton, I just dropped in to see you,' he replied. 'You don't mind, do you?'

I didn't dislike Edgar. He'd never be a Light One, but his move to the Inquisition inspired respect. If Edgar wanted to have a word with me, I'd be happy to meet him any time.

But not at the dacha where Sveta and Nadiushka were on holiday.

'Yes, I mind,' I said sternly. 'If you don't have an official warrant, get off my land!'

I pointed with an impossibly absurd gesture to the crooked picket fence. My land . . . what a grand-sounding phrase.

Edgar sighed. And slowly reached for something in his inside pocket.

I knew what it was. But it was too late to start back-pedalling now.

The warrant from the Moscow Office of the Inquisition said that 'for purposes of an official investigation we hereby command the employee of the Moscow Night Watch, Anton Gorodetsky, Light Magician of the second rank, to afford every possible assistance to Edgar, Inquisitor of the second rank'. It was the first time I'd ever seen an actual warrant from the Inquisition, and so a few petty details stuck in my mind: the Inquisitors continued to define power in the old-style 'ranks', they weren't ashamed to use a phrase like 'hereby command', and they called each other only by their first names even in official documents.

And then I noticed the most important part, at the bottom. The seal of the Night Watch and a flourish in Gesar's handwriting: 'I have been informed and consent'.

How about that!

'What if I refuse?' I asked. 'I don't much like being 'hereby commanded'.

Edgar frowned and peered at the document. He said:

'Our secretary's just turned three hundred. Don't take offence, Anton. It's nothing but archaic terminology. Like "rank".'

'And is doing without surnames another part of old tradition?' I asked. 'I'm just curious.'

Edgar glanced at the piece of paper, perplexed. He frowned again. Then he said irritably, beginning to draw out his vowels in the Baltic style:

'Why-y that old hag . . . She forgot my surname and she was too proud to ask.'

'Then I have good grounds for throwing this warrant on the compost heap.' I looked round the plot of land for a compost heap, but didn't find one. 'Or down the toilet. The instruction doesn't have your surname on it, so it has no force, right?'

Edgar didn't answer.

'And what's in store for me if I refuse to co-operate?' I asked.

'Nothing too serious,' Edgar said glumly. 'Even if I bring a new warrant. A complaint to your immediate superior, punishment at his discretion . . .'

'So your intimidating document comes down to a request for help?'

'Yes,' said Edgar and nodded.

I was relishing the situation. The terrible Inquisition that green novices used for frightening each other with, had turned out to be a toothless old crone!

'What's happened?' I asked. 'I'm on holiday, do you realise that? With my wife and daughter. And my mother-in-law too. I'm not working.'

'That didn't stop you going to see Arina,' said Edgar, without batting an eyelid.

It served me right. Never, ever, let your guard down.

'That relates to my direct professional responsibilities,' I retorted. 'Protecting people and monitoring the activities of Dark Ones. Always and everywhere. By the way, how do you know about Arina?'

Now it was Edgar's turn to smile and take his time.

'Gesar informed us,' he said eventually. 'You called him yesterday and reported in, didn't you? Since this is an unusual situation, Gesar felt it was his duty to warn the Inquisition. As a token of our unfailing friendly relations.'

I didn't understand a thing.

Was the witch somehow mixed up in that business with Gesar's son?

'I have to call him,' I said, walking demonstratively towards the house. Edgar remained standing docilely beside the hammock. He even peered briefly at a plastic chair, but decided it wasn't clean enough.

I waited with the mobile phone pressed against my ear.

'Yes, what is it, Anton?'

'Edgar's come to see me . . .'

'Yes, yes, yes,' Gesar said absent-mindedly. 'Yesterday, after your report, I decided I ought to inform the Inquisition about the witch. If you feel like it, help him out. If you don't, just send him you know where. His warrant is drawn up incorrectly, did you notice?'

'Yes, I did,' I said, glancing sideways in Edgar's direction. 'Boss, what about those werewolves?'

'We're checking,' Gesar replied after a brief hesitation. 'A dead end so far.'

'And something else, about that witch . . .' I glanced down at the 'book about the book'. 'I requisitioned a rather amusing book from her . . . *Fuaran: fantasy or fact?*.'

'Yes, yes, I've read it,' Gesar said amiably. 'Now if you'd found the genuine *Fuaran*, then you'd really deserve a medal. Is that all, Anton?'

'Yes,' I said. Gesar hung up.

Edgar was waiting patiently.

I walked up to him, paused theatrically for a moment and asked:

'What is the purpose of your investigation? And what do you want from me?'

'You are going to co-operate, Anton?' Edgar exclaimed, genuinely delighted. 'My investigation concerns the witch Arina, whom you discovered. I need you to show me how to get to her.'

'What business does the Inquisition have with that old bag of bones?' I enquired. 'I don't see the slightest indication of any crime here. Not even from the Night Watch's point of view.'

Edgar hesitated. He wanted to lie – and at the same time, he realised that I would sense it if he did. Our powers were more or less equal, and even his Inquisitor's gimmicks wouldn't necessarily work.

'We have some old leads on the witch,' the Dark Magician

admitted. 'On file from back in the 1930s. The Inquisition has a number of questions for her.'

I nodded. I'd been bothered from the start by her story about being persecuted by the malicious NKVD. All sorts of things happened back then, the peasants could have kicked up a racket to attempt to try to get even with a witch. But they could only have tried. A trick like that might work with a lower-grade Other. But not with a witch of such great power . . .

'Okay, we'll go to see her,' I agreed. 'Would you like some breakfast, Edgar?'

'I wouldn't say no,' the Dark Magician replied frankly. 'Er . . . Will your wife object?'

'Let's ask her,' I said.

It was an interesting breakfast. The Inquisitor felt out of place and tried awkwardly to crack jokes, at the same time as paying compliments to Svetlana and Ludmila Ivanovna, talking baby-talk to Nadiushka and praising the simple omelette.

Clever little Nadiushka took a close look at 'Uncle Edgar', shook her head and said:

'You're different.'

After that she never left her mother's side.

Svetlana found Edgar's visit amusing. She asked him innocent questions, recalled the story of the Mirror* and in general behaved as if she was entertaining a colleague from work and a good comrade.

But Ludmila Ivanovna was delighted with Edgar. She liked the way he dressed and spoke. The way he held his fork in his left hand and his knife in his right made her ecstatic. Anyone would have thought the rest of us were eating with our hands. And the fact that Edgar firmly refused 'a little glass for the appetite'

* See *The Day Watch*, Story One

provoked a reproachful glance in my direction, as if I was in the habit of gulping down a couple of glasses of vodka every morning.

And so Edgar and I set out feeling well fed, but slightly irritated. I was irritated by my mother-in-law's fawning raptures, and he seemed to be irritated by her attention.

'Can you tell me what the charges against the witch are?' I asked as we approached the edge of the forest.

'Well, after all, I suppose we did drink to *Brüderschaft* back in Prague that time,' Edgar reminded me. 'Why don't we address each other less formally? Or is my new job . . .'

'It's no worse than your job in the Day Watch,' I laughed. 'Okay, at ease.'

Edgar was satisfied with that and didn't drag things out any longer.

'Arina is a powerful and respected witch . . . within their narrow circles. You know how it is, Anton, every group has its own hierarchy. Gesar can mock Witiezslav as much as he likes, but as far as vampires are concerned, he's the most powerful there is. Arina occupies a similar sort of position among the witches. An extremely high one.'

I nodded. My new acquaintance was clearly no simple witch.

'The Day Watch asked her to work for them more than once,' Edgar continued. 'Just as insistently as your side fought for Svetlana . . . please don't take offence, Anton.'

I wasn't offended in the slightest . . .

'The witch refused point-blank. Okay, that's her right. Especially as she did collaborate on a temporary basis in certain situations. But early last century, shortly after the socialist revolution, an unpleasant event took place . . .'

He paused. As we entered the forest, I set off with rather ostentatious confidence, and Edgar followed. Looking absurd in his city suit, the Dark Magician clambered fearlessly through the bushes and the gullies. He didn't even loosen his tie . . .

'At the time the Watches were fighting for the right to conduct a social experiment,' Edgar told me. 'Communism, as you know, was invented by the Light Ones . . .'

'And subverted by the Dark Ones,' I couldn't resist adding.

'Oh, come on, Anton,' Edgar said resentfully. 'We didn't subvert anything. People chose for themselves what kind of society to build. Anyway, Arina was asked to collaborate. She agreed to carry out . . . a certain mission. The interests of the Dark Ones and the Light Ones were involved, as well as the witch's. Both sides were in agreement over the . . . mission. They were both counting on winning out in the end. The Inquisition was keeping an eye on things, but there was no reason to intervene. It was all happening with the agreement of both Watches.'

This was interesting. What kind of mission could it have been, if it was approved equally by Dark Ones and Light Ones?

'Arina carried out her mission brilliantly,' Edgar continued. 'She was even awarded special privileges from the Watches. If I'm not mistaken, the Light Ones granted her the right to use second-degree magic.'

This was serious stuff. I nodded and took note of the information.

'But after a while the Inquisition began having doubts about the legality of Arina's actions,' Edgar said drily. 'The suspicion arose that in the course of her work she had fallen under the influence of one of the sides and acted in its interests.'

'And that side was?'

'The Light Ones,' Edgar said sombrely. 'A witch, helping the Light ones – incredible, isn't it? That's why it took so long for them to get round to suspecting her, but the circumstantial evidence of treachery was just too strong . . . The Inquisition summoned Arina . . . for an interview. And then she just disappeared. The search for her went on for some time, but in those days – you know the way things were . . .'

'What was it she did?' I asked, not really expecting an answer.

Edgar sighed and replied:

'Intervened in the minds of human beings . . . Total remoralisation.'

I gulped. What interest could Dark Ones have in that?

'Surprised?' Edgar growled. 'Do you have a clear idea of what remoralisation actually is?'

'I've carried one out. On myself.'

Edgar gaped at me, dumbstruck, for a few seconds and then nodded:

'Ah . . . yes, of course. Then you won't need much explanation. Remoralisation is a relative process, not an absolute one. Whatever you might say, there is no absolute standard of morality in the world. So remoralisation makes a person act absolutely ethically, but only within the limits of his own basic morality. To put it crudely, a cannibal in the jungle who doesn't think eating his enemy is a crime will calmly continue with his dinner. But he won't do anything that his morality forbids.'

'I'm aware of that,' I said.

'Well then, this remoralisation wasn't entirely relative. The communist ideology was implanted in people's minds . . . you've probably heard about many of them, but the names aren't important for purposes of the case.'

'The moral code of the builder of communism,' I said with a wry laugh.

'That hadn't been invented yet,' Edgar replied very seriously. 'But let's say something very similar. These people started to behave entirely in accordance with the idealised model of communist ethics.'

'I can understand the interest of the Night Watch in all this,' I said. 'The principles of communism are certainly attractive . . . But where did the Dark Ones' interest lie?'

'The Dark Ones wished to demonstrate that imposing a non-viable system of ethics would not produce anything good. That the victims of the experiment would either go insane, or be killed, or start acting contrary to their remoralisation.'

I nodded. What an experiment! Never mind those Nazi medics who mutilated people's bodies. It was souls that had gone under the knife here . . .

'Are you outraged by the Light Ones' behaviour?' Edgar asked suggestively.

'No.' I shook my head. 'I'm sure they didn't mean to harm anyone. They hoped the experiment would lead to the building of a new, happy society.'

'Were you ever a member of the Communist Party?' Edgar asked with a grin.

'I was only a Young Pioneer. Look, I get the idea of the experiment. But why did they bring in a witch to do it?'

'In this case it was far more efficient to use witchcraft than magic,' Edgar explained. 'The experiment was aimed at thousands of people of every possible age and social group. Can you imagine the forces that magicians would have needed to assemble? A witch was able to do it all by using potions.'

'Did she put them in the water supply, or what?'

'In bread. They got her a job in a bread-making plant,' Edgar laughed. 'She actually proposed a new, more efficient way of baking bread – with the addition of various herbs. And she even won a special bonus for it.'

'I see. And what was Arina's interest in all this?'

Edgar snorted. He jumped nimbly over a fallen tree and looked into my eyes.

'Do you have to ask, Anton? Who wouldn't like to fool about with magic as powerful as that? And she even had permission from the Watches and the Inquisition!'

'I suppose so . . .' I muttered. 'So, there was an experiment . . . And the result?'

'As should have been expected,' Edgar said, his eyes glinting with irony. 'Some of them went insane, took to drink or killed themselves. Some were repressed – for over-zealous devotion to their ideals. And some found ways to get round the remoralisation.'

'The Dark Ones were proved right?' I asked, so stunned that I stopped dead in my tracks. 'But even so the Inquisition considers that the witch corrupted the spell, acting on instructions from the Light Ones?'

Edgar nodded.

'That's raving lunacy,' I said, walking on. 'Utter nonsense! The Dark Ones effectively proved their point. And you say the Light Ones were to blame!'

'Not all the Light Ones,' Edgar replied imperturbably. 'One particular individual . . . maybe a small group. Why they did it, I don't know. But the Inquisition is dissatisfied. The objectivity of the experiment was compromised, the balance of power was undermined, some kind of long-term, obscure intrigue was launched . . .'

'Aha,' I said with a nod. 'If there's intriguing involved, let's put it all down to Gesar.'

'I didn't mention any names,' Edgar said quickly. 'I don't know any. And allow me to remind you that at that time the highly respected Gesar was working in Central Asia, so it would be absurd to charge him with anything . . .'

He sighed – perhaps remembering recent events at the Assol complex?

'But you want to find out the truth?' I asked.

'Absolutely!' Edgar said. 'Thousands of people were forcibly turned to the Light – that is a crime against the Day Watch. All those people came to harm – that is a crime against the Night

Watch. The social experiment authorised by the Inquisition was disrupted – that is a crime . . .'

'I get the idea,' I interrupted. 'I must say, I find this story extremely unsavoury.'

'You'll help me to uncover the truth?' Edgar asked. And he smiled.

'Yes,' I said, with no hesitation. 'It's a crime.'

We shook hands.

'Do we have to tramp much further?' the Inquisitor asked.

I looked round and was glad to recognise the familiar features of the clearing where I'd seen that amazing bed of mushrooms the day before.

Today, however, there wasn't a single mushroom left.

'We're almost there,' I reassured the Dark Magician. 'Let's just hope the lady of the house is at home . . .'

CHAPTER 5

ARINA WAS BREWING a potion – just as any self-respecting witch should – in her little house in the forest. Standing by the stove with the oven-fork in her hands, holding a cast-iron pot that was giving off clouds of greenish fumes. And muttering:

> Spindle tree, white furze – a pinch,
> Rocky cliff sand – quite a sprinkling
> Heather branch and skeleton of finch
> Pustule squeezings – just an inkling.

Edgar and I went in and stood by the door, but the witch didn't seem to notice us. She carried on standing with her back to us, shaking the pot and chanting:

> More white furze and spindle tree,
> Three tail feathers from an eagle . . .

Edgar cleared his throat and continued:

Kneecaps of a bumble bee,
And the collar off my beagle?

Arina started violently and exclaimed:

'Oh, good heavens above!'

It sounded perfectly natural . . . but somehow I knew for sure that the witch had been expecting us.

'Hello, Arina,' Edgar said without expression. 'Inquisition. Please stop working your spells.'

Arina deftly thrust the pot into the stove and only then turned round. This time she looked about forty – a sturdy, full-fleshed, beautiful countrywoman. And very annoyed. She put her hands on her hips and exclaimed peevishly:

'And hello to you, Mr Inquisitor! Why are you interfering with the spell? Am I supposed to catch the finches and pluck the eagle's feathers all over again?'

'Your ditties are no more than a way of remembering the amounts of the various ingredients and the right sequence of actions,' Edgar replied, unmoved. 'You'd already finished brewing the light footfall potion, my words could not possibly have interfered with it. Sit down, Arina. Why not take the weight off your feet?'

'How's that supposed to improve things?' Arina replied sullenly and walked across to the table. She sat down and wiped her hands on her apron with its pattern of daisies and cornflowers. Then she glanced sideways at me.

'Good morning, Arina,' I said. 'Edgar asked me to act as his guide. You don't mind, do you?'

'If I did mind, you'd have ended up in the swamp!' Arina answered in a slightly offended tone. 'Well, I'm listening, Mr Inquisitor Edgar. What business is it that brings you here?'

Edgar sat down facing Arina. He reached under the flap of his jacket and pulled out a leather folder. How had he managed to fit that under there?

'You were sent a summons, Arina,' the Inquisitor said in a soft voice. 'Did you receive it?'

The witch started thinking. Edgar opened his folder and showed her a narrow strip of yellow paper.

'1931!' the witch gasped. 'Oh, all those years ago . . . No, I never received it. I've already explained to the gentleman from the Night Watch that I went to sleep. The Secret Police were trying to frame me . . .'

'The Secret Police are not exactly the most terrible thing in the life of an Other,' said Edgar. 'Very far from it, in fact . . . So, you received the summons . . .'

'I didn't receive it,' Arina said quickly.

'You didn't receive it,' Edgar corrected himself. 'Well, let's accept that. The messenger never came back . . . I suppose anything could have happened to a civilian employee in the bleak Moscow forests.'

Arina said nothing.

I stood by the door, watching. I was curious. An Inquisitor's job is like any watchman's but there was something special about this situation. A Dark Magician interrogating a Dark Witch. And one who was far more powerful than him, a fact that Edgar couldn't fail to appreciate.

But he had the Inquisition standing behind him. And when you're faced with that, you can't count on any help from your 'own' Watch.

'Let us consider that you have now received the summons,' Edgar went on. 'I have been instructed to conduct a preliminary interview with you before any final decisions are taken . . . so . . .'

He took out another piece of paper, glanced at it and asked:

'In the month of March, 1931, were you working at the First Moscow Bread Combine?'

'I was,' Arina said, and nodded.

'For what purpose?'

Arina looked at me.

'He has been informed,' said Edgar. 'Answer the question.'

'I was approached by the leaders of the Night Watch and the Day Watch of Moscow,' Arina said with a sigh. 'The Others wished to know how people would behave if they tried to live in strict conformity with communist ideals. Since both Watches wanted the same thing, and the Inquisition supported their request, I agreed. I never have liked cities, they're always . . .'

'Please stick to the point,' Edgar told her.

'I carried out the task,' Arina said, finishing her story in a rush. 'I brewed the potion, and it was added to the fine white bread for two weeks. That's all! I was thanked by the two Watches, I left my job at the factory and went home. And then the Secret Police started going absolutely . . .'

'You can write about your difficult relations with the organs of state security in your memoirs!' Edgar suddenly barked. 'What interests me is why you altered the formula.'

Arina slowly got to her feet. Her eyes glittered with fury and her voice thundered as loud as if she were King Kong's mate:

'Remember, this, young man! Arina has never made any mistakes in her spells! Never!'

Edgar remained unimpressed.

'I didn't say you made a mistake. You deliberately altered the formula. And as a result . . .' He paused dramatically.

'What, as a result?' Arina asked, outraged. 'They checked the potion when it was ready. The effect was exactly what was required.'

'As a result, the potion took effect immediately,' said Edgar. 'The Night Watch has never been a collection of fools and idealists. The

Light Ones realised that all ten thousand experimental subjects would be doomed if they made an instant switch to communist morality. The potion was supposed to take effect gradually, so that the remoralisation would peak at full power ten years later, in the spring of 1941.'

'That's right,' Arina said soberly. 'And that's the way it was made.'

'The potion had an almost instantaneous effect,' said Edgar. 'We couldn't work out what was happening at first, but after a year the number of experimental subjects had been reduced by half. Less than a hundred of them survived until 1941 – the ones who managed to overcome the remoralisation . . . to demonstrate moral flexibility.'

'Oh, what a terrible thing,' Arina exclaimed, throwing her hands up in the air. 'How awful . . . I feel so sorry for those poor people . . .' She sat down. Then looked across at me and asked: 'Well, Light One, do you think I was working for the Dark Ones too?'

If she was lying, it was very convincing. I shrugged.

'Everything was done correctly,' Arina said, remaining stubborn. 'The basic ingredients were mixed into the flour . . . do you know how difficult it was in those years to carry out any subversive activity? The retardant in the potion was plain sugar . . .' Suddenly she flung her hands up and stared at Edgar triumphantly. 'That's what went wrong! Those were hungry years, the workers at the combine stole the sugar . . . That's why it worked too fast . . .'

'An interesting theory,' said Edgar, shuffling his papers.

'I'm not to blame for any of this,' Arina declared firmly. 'The plan for the operation was agreed. If the wise men of the Watches failed to think of a simple thing like that, then whose fault is it?'

'That would be all very well,' said Edgar, lifting up another sheet of paper. 'Except that you conducted the first experiment on the workers at the bakery. Here's your report, recognise it? After that, they couldn't have stolen the sugar. So there's only one explanation – you deliberately sabotaged the operation.'

'Why don't we consider some other explanations?' Arina asked plaintively. 'For instance . . .'

'For instance – your friend Louisa's report,' Edgar suggested. 'About how, during the operation, she happened by chance to see you in the company of an unidentified Light Magician near the stand at the race track. About how you argued and haggled, until eventually the Light One handed you some kind of package, and you nodded and shook hands. Louisa even heard the words: 'I'll do it, and in less than a year . . .' Let me remind you that for the duration of the experiment you were forbidden to have any contact with Others. Weren't you?'

'Yes,' said Arina, bowing her head. 'Is Lushka still alive?'

'Unfortunately not,' said Edgar. 'But her testimony was recorded and witnessed.'

'A pity . . .' Arina murmured. She didn't say why it was a pity exactly. But it wasn't too hard to guess that Louisa was fortunate not to be around any longer.

'Can you explain which Light One you met with, what you promised to do and what you received from him?'

Arina raised her head and smiled bitterly at me. She said:

'What a muddle . . . I'm always getting in a muddle . . . over little things. Like that kettle . . .'

'Arina, I am obliged to deliver you for further questioning,' said Edgar. 'In the name of the Inquisition . . .'

'Try it, second-ranker,' Arina said derisively.

And she disappeared.

'She's withdrawn into the Twilight!' I shouted, tearing myself away from the wall and looking round for my shadow. But Edgar delayed for a second, making sure that the witch hadn't averted our eyes.

We appeared at the first level almost simultaneously. I was a little wary of looking at Edgar – what would the Twilight world transform him into?

It wasn't too bad, he'd hardly changed at all. His hair had just thinned out a bit.

'Deeper!' I waved my hand insistently. Edgar moved his head, raised his open hand to his face – and his palm seemed to suck all of him in.

Impressive. Inquisitors' gimmicks.

At the second level, where the house turned into a log hut, we stopped and looked at each other. Of course, Arina wasn't there.

'She's gone down to the third level . . .' Edgar whispered. His hair had now completely disappeared and his skull had stretched out, like a duck's egg. Even so, he still looked almost human.

'Can you do it?' I asked.

'I managed it once,' Edgar answered honestly. Our breath turned to steam. It didn't feel all that cold yet, but there was an insidious chill in the air . . .

'And I managed it once,' I admitted.

We hesitated, like overconfident swimmers who have suddenly realised that the river in front of them is too turbulent and too cold. And neither of us dared take the first step.

'Anton, will you help?' Edgar asked eventually.

I nodded. Why else had I come dashing into the Twilight?

'Let's go,' said the Inquisitor, gazing down intently at his feet.

A few moments later we stepped into the third level – a place where only first-grade magicians were supposed to go.

The witch wasn't there.

'Well, that's inventive,' Edgar whispered. The house of branches really was impressive. 'Anton, she built this herself . . . she can stay down here for a long time.'

Slowly – the space around us resisted sudden movements – I walked over to the wall, parted the branches and looked out.

It was nothing like the human world.

There were glittering clouds drifting across the sky – like steel filings suspended in glycerine. Instead of the sun there was a broad cloud of crimson flame way up high – the only spot of colour in the hazy grey gloom. On all sides, as far as the horizon, there were low, contorted trees, the same ones the witch had used to build her house. But then, were they really trees? There were no leaves, just a fantastic tangle of branches . . .

'Anton, she's gone deeper. She's beyond classification,' Edgar said behind me. I turned and looked at the magician. Dark-grey skin, a bald, elongated skull, sunken eyes . . . But still human eyes. 'How do I look?' Edgar asked and bared his teeth in a smile. I wished he hadn't – his teeth were sharp cones, like a shark's.

'Not great,' I admitted. 'I suppose I don't look any better?'

'It's only an appearance,' Edgar replied casually. 'Are you holding up okay?'

I was. My second immersion in the lower depths of the Twilight was going more smoothly.

'We have to go to the fourth level,' said Edgar. His eyes were human, but with a fanatical gleam.

'Are you beyond classification then?' I asked him. 'Edgar, it's hard for me even to go back!'

'We can combine our powers, watchman!'

'How?' I was perplexed. Both the Dark Ones and the Light Ones have the concept of a 'Circle of Power'. But it's a dangerous thing, and it requires at least three or four Others . . . and anyway, how could we combine Light Power and Dark Power?

'That's my problem!' said Edgar, and began shaking his head about. 'Anton, she'll get away! She'll get away on the fourth level! Trust me!'

'A Dark One?'

'An Inquisitor,' the magician barked. 'I'm an Inquisitor, do you understand? Anton, trust me, I ord . . .' Edgar stopped short and then continued in a different tone: 'I'm asking you, please!'

I don't know what made me do it. The excitement of the hunt? The desire to catch a witch who had destroyed thousands of people's lives? The way the Inquisitor asked?

Or maybe a simple desire to see the fourth level? The most mysterious depths of the Twilight, which even Gesar visited only rarely, and where Svetlana had never been?

'What do I do?' I asked.

Edgar's face lit up. He reached out his hand – the fingers ended in blunt, hooked claws – and said:

'In the name of the Treaty, by the equilibrium that I maintain, I summon the Light and the Dark . . . and request power . . . in the name of the Dark!'

He gazed insistently at me and I also held out my hand, and said:

'In the name of the Light . . .'

In part this was like the swearing of an oath between a Dark One and a Light One. But only in part. No petal of flame sprang up in my hand, no patch of darkness appeared on Edgar's open palm. It all happened on the outside – the grey, blurred world around us suddenly acquired clarity. No colours appeared, we were still in the Twilight. But there were shadows. It was like a TV screen with the colour turned right down, when you suddenly turn up the brightness and contrast.

'Our right has been acknowledged . . .' Edgar whispered, gazing around. His face looked genuinely happy. 'Our right has been acknowledged, Anton!'

'And what if it hadn't been?' I asked cautiously.

'All sorts of things could have happened . . . But our right has been acknowledged, hasn't it? Let's go!'

In the new 'high-contrast' Twilight it was much easier to move around. I raised my shadow as easily as in the ordinary world.

And found myself where only magicians beyond classification have any right to go.

The trees – if they really were trees – had disappeared. All around us the world was as level and flat as the old medieval pancake Earth, supported on the backs of three whales. Featureless terrain, an endless plain of sand . . . I bent down and ran a handful of the sand through my fingers. It was grey, as everything in the Twilight was supposed to be. But there were embryonic colours discernible in its greyness – smoky mother-of-pearl, coloured sparks, golden grains . . .

'She's got away,' Edgar said right in my ear. He stretched out an arm that had become surprisingly long and slim.

I looked in that direction and saw a grey silhouette way off in the distance, dashing away at great speed. I could only see the witch because the plain was so flat, and she was moving in immense leaps, soaring into the air and flying over the ground ten metres at a time, throwing her arms out and moving her legs in a strange way, like a happy child skipping across a meadow in spring.

'She must have drunk her own potion,' I guessed. I couldn't think of any other way she could have leapt like that.

'Yes. She knew what she was doing when she brewed it,' said Edgar. He swung his arm and flung something after Arina.

A string of balls of flame went hurtling after the witch. A group fireball, a standard battle spell for the Watches But this was some special Inquisitors' version.

A few charges burst before they reached the witch. One accelerated sharply and reached her, touched her back and exploded, shrouding the witch in fire. But the flames immediately went out and, without even turning round, she tossed something behind her, and a pool of liquid that glimmered like mercury spread out at that spot. As they flew over the pool, the remaining charges lost speed and height, plunged into the liquid and disappeared.

'Witches' tricks,' Edgar said in disgust. 'Anton!'

'Eh? What?' I asked, with my eyes still fixed on Arina as she disappeared into the distance.

'Time for us to be going. The power was only granted in order to catch the witch, and the hunt's over. We'll never catch up with her.'

I looked upwards. The crimson cloud that had shone at the previous level of the Twilight was gone. The entire sky glowed an even pinkish-white colour.

How strange. Colours appeared again here . . .

'Edgar, are there any more levels?' I asked.

'There always are.' Edgar was clearly starting to feel worried. 'Come on, Anton! Come on, or we'll get stuck here.'

He was right, the world around us was already losing contrast, wreathing itself in grey vapour. But the colours were still there – the mother-of-pearl sand and the pinkish sky . . .

Already feeling the cold prickling of the Twilight on my skin, I followed Edgar up to the third level. As if it had been waiting for that moment, the world finally lost all its colour and became grey space, filled with a cold, roaring wind. Holding each other's hands – not in order to exchange power, which is almost impossible, but in order to stay on our feet – we made several attempts to return to the second level. The 'trees' on all sides were breaking with a barely audible cracking sound, and the witch's bivouac tumbled onto its side as we kept searching and searching for our shadows. I don't even remember the moment when the Twilight parted in front of me and allowed me back through into the second level. It seemed almost normal, not frightening at all . . .

We sat there on the clean-scraped wooden floor, breathing heavily. We were in an equally bad way, the Dark Inquisitor and the Light Watchman.

'Here.' Edgar put his hand awkwardly into his pocket and brought out a block of Guardsman chocolate. 'Eat that.'

'What about you?' I asked, tearing off the wrapper.

'I've got more.' Edgar rummaged in his pockets for a long time and finally found another pack of chocolate – Inspiration this time. He started unwrapping the fingers of chocolate one at a time.

We ate greedily. The Twilight draws the strength out of you – and it's not just a matter of magical power, it even affects something as basic as your blood sugar level. That's about all we've managed to discover about the Twilight, using the methods of modern science. Everything else is still as much of a mystery as ever.

'Edgar, how many levels are there to the Twilight?'

He finished chewing another piece of chocolate and answered:

'I know of five. This is the first time I've been on the fourth.'

'And what's down there, on the fifth level?'

'All I know is that it exists, watchman. No more than that. I didn't even know anything about the fourth level, until now.'

'Colours came back there,' I said. 'It's . . . completely different. Isn't it?'

'Uhuh,' Edgar mumbled. 'Different. That's not for us to worry about, Anton. It's beyond our powers. You should be proud you've been down to the fourth, not all first-grade magicians have gone that deep.'

'But you can?'

'If needs be, in the line of duty,' Edgar admitted. 'After all, it's not necessarily the most powerful who join the Inquisition. And we have to be able to stand up to a crazy magician beyond classification, right?'

'If Gesar or Zabulon ever go crazy, we won't be able to stand up to them,' I said. 'We couldn't even manage the witch.'

Edgar thought for a moment and agreed that the Moscow

Office of the Inquisition wasn't really up to dealing with Gesar and Zabulon. But only if they happened to violate the Treaty simultaneously. Otherwise Gesar would be glad to help neutralise Zabulon, and Zabulon would be glad to help neutralise Gesar. That was the way the Inquisition worked.

'Now what do we do about the witch?' I asked.

'Look for her,' Edgar said briskly. 'I've already been in touch with my people, they'll cordon off the district. Can I count on your continued assistance?'

I thought for a moment.

'No, Edgar. Arina's a Dark One. Obviously she did do something terrible . . . seventy-odd years ago. But if she was exploited by Light Ones . . .'

'So you're going to carry on sticking to your own side,' Edgar said in disgust. 'Anton, do you really not understand? There is no Light or Dark in a pure sense. Your two watches are just like the Democrats and Republicans in America. They quarrel, they argue, but in the evening they hold cocktail parties together.'

'It's not evening yet.'

'It's always evening,' Edgar replied bleakly. 'Believe me, I was a law-abiding Dark One. Until I was driven into . . . until I left the Watch to join the Inquisition. And you know what I think now?'

'Tell me.'

'Power of night and power of day – same old nonsense anyway. I don't see any difference between Zabulon and Gesar any more. But I like you . . . as a human being. If you joined the Inquisition, I'd be glad to work with you.'

I laughed:

'Trying to recruit me?'

'Yes, any watchman has the right to join the Inquisition. No one has the right to hold you back. They don't even have a right to try to change your mind.'

'Thanks, but I don't need to have my mind changed. I'm not planning to join the Inquisition.'

Edgar groaned as he got up off the floor. He dusted down his suit, although there wasn't a single speck of dust, or a crease, anywhere on it.

'That suit of yours is enchanted,' I said.

'I just know how to wear it. And it's good material.' Edgar went over to the bookcase, took out a book and leafed through it. Then another, and another . . . He said enviously: 'What a library! Narrowly specialised, but even so . . .'

'I thought *Fuaran* was here too,' I admitted.

Edgar just laughed.

'What are we going to do about the hut?' I asked.

'There, see – you're still thinking like my ally,' Edgar promptly remarked. 'I'll put spells of protection and watchfulness on it, what else? The experts will be here in two or three hours. They'll give everything a thorough going-over. Shall we go?'

'Don't you feel like rummaging around a bit yourself?' I asked.

Edgar looked around carefully and said he didn't. That the little house could be hiding lots of nasty surprises left by the cunning witch. And that digging through the belongings of a witch beyond classification was a job that could be dangerous for your health . . . better leave it to those who had it in their job description.

I waited while Edgar put up several spells of watchfulness round the hut – he didn't need any help. And we set off for the village.

The way back took a lot longer, as if some elusive magic that had helped us find our way to the witch's house had disappeared. Edgar was far more garrulous now – maybe my help had inclined him to talk more freely?

He told me about his training, how he had been taught to use Light power as well as Dark. And about the other Inquisition trainees – they had included two Ukrainian Light Enchantresses, a Hungarian werewolf, a Dutch magician and many different sorts of Others. He said the rumours about the Inquisition's special vaults overflowing with magical artefacts were greatly exaggerated: there were plenty of artefacts, but most of them had lost their magical power long ago and were no good for anything any more. And he told me about the parties the trainees had organised in their free time . . .

It was all very entertaining, but I knew perfectly well where Edgar was headed. So I started recalling the years of my own training with elaborate enthusiasm, bringing up various amusing incidents from the history of the Night Watch, including Semyon's historical tall tales . . .

Edgar sighed and I went quiet. In any case, we'd already reached the edge of the forest. Edgar stopped.

'I'll wait for my colleagues,' he said. 'They should be here any minute now. Even Witiezslav postponed his departure and promised to call over.'

I wasn't in any great hurry to invite the Inquisitor back – especially not along with a Higher Vampire. I nodded, but couldn't help asking:

'How do you think everything's going to turn out?'

'I raised the alarm in time, so the witch can't leave this district,' Edgar said guardedly. 'The trackers move in now, we'll check everything and arrest Arina. Put her on trial. If you're needed, you'll be called as a witness.'

I didn't completely share Edgar's optimism, but I nodded. He should know better than me what the Inquisition was capable of.

'And the werewolves?'

'That's the Night Watch's prerogative, right?' Edgar said, answering a question with a question. 'If we come across them, we'll let you know, but we won't make a special point of chasing them through the forest. What makes you think they're still here anyway? Typical city types, out in the countryside for a spot of hunting. You should keep a closer eye on your clients, Anton.'

'Somehow I have the feeling they're still here,' I muttered. I really did think so, although I couldn't explain why I was so sure. There was no trace of them in the village . . . and werewolves rarely spend more than twenty-four hours in their wolves' bodies.

'Check the nearby villages,' Edgar advised me. 'At least the one the witch used to go to for her groceries. But really it's a waste of time. After an unsuccessful hunt they just tuck their tails between their legs and go into hiding. I know their type.'

I nodded – it was good advice, even though it was pretty basic. I should have gone round the outlying areas straight away, rather than trying to catch the toothless old witch. Some detective I was – I'd got too interested in that book *Fuaran*. What I should do was pay more attention to the routine, boring work. Preventive measures were best, as they used to proclaim so correctly in Soviet times.

'Good luck, Edgar,' I said.

'And good luck to you, Anton.' Edgar thought for a moment and added: 'It's a strange situation that's come up – both Watches are mixed up in this business with the witch. You pretty much represent the interests of the Night Watch. I think that Zabulon will send someone too . . . before the situation is resolved.'

I sighed. Things were going from bad to worse.

'I think I can guess who he'll send,' I said. 'Zabulon enjoys causing me petty aggravation.'

'You ought to be glad he hasn't set his mind to serious aggravation,' Edgar said dourly. 'But you'll have to put up with the petty stuff. Nobody has the power to change another person's nature; your friend is a Dark One and he'll die a Dark One.'

'Kostya's already dead. And he's not a person, he's a vampire.'

'What's the difference?' Edgar asked gloomily. He stuck his hands into the pockets of those expensive trousers that he wore so well and hunched his shoulders as he watched the red sun sinking behind the horizon. 'It's all the same in this world, watchman . . .'

Serving in the Inquisition definitely had a strange effect on Others. It made them take a nihilistic view of life. And spout meaningless phrases.

'Good luck,' I repeated and set off down the hill. Edgar lay down on the grass, mercilessly creasing his suit, and gazed up at the sky.

CHAPTER 6

HALFWAY BACK TO the house I met Ksyusha and Romka, striding briskly along the dusty street, holding hands. I waved to them and Ksyusha immediately shouted out:

'Your Nadiushka's gone for a walk to the river with her granny!'

I laughed. Ludmila Ivanovna didn't very often hear herself called 'granny' – and like any other fifty-year-old Moscow woman, she hated the very sound of it.

'Well, I hope they enjoy it,' I said.

'Have you found the wolves yet?' Romka shouted.

'No, your wolves have run away,' I answered.

Maybe, for strictly psychotherapeutic purposes, I ought to have said that I'd caught the wolves and handed them over to the zoo? But then, the little boy didn't seem to be suffering from any lingering fears after his encounter with the werewolves. Arina had done a good job there.

Greeting the small number of villagers I met along the way, I walked to our house. Svetlana had occupied my hammock – with a bottle of beer and the book *Fuaran: fact or fiction* open at the final pages.

'Interesting?' I asked.

'Uhuh,' Svetlana said with a nod. She was drinking the beer rustic fashion, straight from the bottle. 'It's more fun that Tove Jansson's *Moominpappa at Sea*. Now I understand why they didn't print all the stories about the Moomintrolls before. The last ones aren't for children at all. Tove Jansson was obviously suffering from depression when she wrote them.'

'An author has the right to get depressed too,' I said.

'Not if she writes children's books, she doesn't!' Svetlana exclaimed sternly. 'Children's books should be heart-warming. Otherwise it's just like a tractor driver ploughing a field crookedly and then saying: "Ah, I was feeling depressed, it was more interesting to drive round in circles". Or a doctor who prescribes a patient a combined laxative and sleeping draft and then ex-plains: "I'm feeling a bit low, I thought it would cheer me up a bit".'

She reached out to the table and put down the fake *Fuaran*.

'You're very strict, Mother,' I said with a shake of my head.

'That's why I'm strict – because I'm a mother,' Svetlana replied in the same tone. 'I was only joking. The books are still wonderful anyway. Only the last ones are very sad.'

'Nadiushka and your mother have gone for a walk to the river,' I said.

'Did you see them?'

'No Ksyusha said: "Your Nadia and her granny have gone for a walk . . .".'

Svetlana tittered. But then she pulled a frightened face.

'Don't tell my mother that! She'll be upset.'

'Do you think I'm tired of living?'

'Why don't you tell me how your hike went?'

'The witch got away,' I said. 'We chased her down to the fourth level of the Twilight, but she still got away.'

'The fourth?' Svetlana's eyes flashed. 'Are you serious?'

I sat down beside her – the hammock swayed indignantly and

the trees creaked, but they held. I gave her a short account of our adventures.

'And I've never been to the fourth level . . .' Svetlana said thoughtfully. 'How interesting . . . The colours come back?'

'I even thought there were some smells.'

Svetlana nodded absent-mindedly:

'Yes, I've heard rumours about that . . . Very interesting.'

I kept quiet for a few seconds. And then I said:

'Svetlana, you ought to go back to the Watch.'

She didn't object as usual. She didn't say anything at all. Encouraged, I went on:

'You can't live at half-power. Sooner or later you . . .'

'Let's not talk about it, Anton. I don't want to be a Great Enchantress,' Svetlana explained with a wry grin. 'A little bit of domestic magic, that's all I need.'

The gate slammed shut – Ludmila Ivanovna had come back. I glanced quickly at her and was about to look away – then I stared at her, puzzled.

My mother-in-law was glowing. Anybody might have thought that she'd just put some uppity salesgirl in a shop firmly in her place, found a hundred roubles in the street and shaken hands with her beloved TV host Leonid Yakubovich.

She was even walking differently – with light steps, her shoulders held straight and her chin held high. She was smiling blissfully and singing in a soft voice:

> We were born to make a fairy tale come true . . .

I shook my head hard to clear it. My mother-in-law smiled sweetly at us, waved her hand and in two strides she was past us and heading for the house.

'Mum!' Svetlana shouted to her, jumping up. 'Mum!'

My mother-in-law stopped and looked at her – with that same blissful smile.

'Are you feeling all right, Mum?' Svetlana asked.

'Wonderful!' Ludmila Ivanovna replied affectionately.

'Mum, where's Nadiushka?' Svetlana asked, raising her voice slightly.

'She's gone for a walk with a friend,' she answered, unmoved.

I shuddered. Svetlana exclaimed:

'What do you mean? It's evening already . . . children can't go walking on their own . . . with what friend?'

'With a friend of mine,' my mother-in-law explained, still smiling. 'Don't worry. You don't think I'm so stupid as to let our little girl go off on her own, do you?'

'What friend of yours?' Svetlana screamed. 'Mum! What's wrong with you? Who's Nadia with?'

The smile on my mother-in-law's face began slowly dissolving, giving way to an uncertain expression.

'With that . . . that . . .' She frowned. 'With Arina. My friend . . . Arina . . . my friend?'

I was too slow to catch exactly what Svetlana did – I just felt a chill tremor run over my skin as the Twilight was parted. Svetlana leaned towards her mother, who froze with her mouth open, swallowing air in small gulps.

Reading people's thoughts is pretty difficult, it's much easier to make them speak. But we can take an instant snapshot of thought information from close relatives in exactly the same way as we do between ourselves for the sake of speed.

But then, I didn't need the information anyway.

I understood everything already.

And I didn't even feel afraid – just empty. As if the entire world had frozen over and stopped dead.

'Go to bed!' Svetlana shouted at her mother. Ludmila Ivanovna turned and walked towards the house like a zombie.

Svetlana looked at me. Her expression was very calm, which made it hard for me to pull myself together. After all, a man feels a lot stronger when his woman is frightened.

'Arina just came up and blew on her. Took Nadienka by the hand and went off into the forest,' Svetlana blurted out. 'And my mother's been walking around for the past hour, the stupid fool!'

That was when I realised Svetlana was on the verge of hysterics.

I managed to pull myself together.

'What could she do against the witch?' I grabbed Svetlana by the shoulders and shook her. 'Your mother's only a human being!'

Tears welled up briefly in Svetlana's eyes and then immediately disappeared. Suddenly she gently pushed me away and said:

'Stand back, Anton, or you'll get caught . . . you can hardly stay on your feet as it is . . .'

I didn't try to argue. After my adventures with Edgar I wasn't going to be any help. There was hardly any power left in me, I had nothing left to share with Svetlana.

I stepped back and put my arms round the trunk of the stunted apple tree that had given up fruiting years ago. I closed my eyes.

The world around me shuddered.

And I felt the Twilight shift and stir.

Svetlana didn't gather power from people around her, as I would have done. She had enough of her own – obstinately neglected, unused . . . and constantly accumulating. They say that after giving birth female Others experience a colossal influx of power, but I hadn't noticed any changes in Svetlana at the time. It had all seemed to vanish; it was being hidden, saved up – as it turned out – for a rainy day.

The world was losing its colours. I realised I was falling into the Twilight, the first level: the intensity of the magic was so great that nothing even slightly magical could remain in human reality. The book *Fuaran: fact or fiction* fell through the rough board table and hit the ground with a thump. Three houses away clumps of blue moss, the emotional parasite that lives in the Twilight, flared up on the roof and were instantly consumed by flames.

Svetlana was enveloped in a white glow. She was moving her hands quickly, as if she were knitting with invisible yarn. A moment later, the yarn became visible, as threads as fine as gossamer streamed away from her hands and spread out, driven by a non-existent wind. A storm began raging around her, and then subsided as the thousands of glittering threads flew off into the distance in all directions.

'What?' I shouted. 'Sveta!'

I knew the spell she had just used. I could even have cast a 'snowy web' myself – maybe not so efficiently or rapidly, but still . . .

Svetlana didn't answer. She raised her hands to the sky, as if she was praying. But we don't believe in any gods, or in God. We are our own gods and our own demons.

A rainbow sphere, like an oversize soap bubble, parted from Svetlana's hands and drifted majestically up into the sky. The bubble expanded, rotating slowly on its axis. A dark red spot on the translucent rainbow film reminded me of Jupiter. When the red spot rotated to face me, I felt a cold, searing touch, like a breath of icy wind.

Svetlana had created the 'eye of the magician'. First grade again . . . but to create it immediately after the 'snowy web'!

The third spell followed with no perceptible pause, and I realised Svetlana had been holding it in readiness for a long time, for occasions precisely like this. She released a flock of ghostly matt-white birds from her hands. You could have called them doves, except that their beaks were too large and sharp, too rapacious.

I didn't know this spell at all.

Svetlana lowered her hands. And the Twilight settled back down. It came creeping back to us, touching our skin with its cautious, predatory chill.

I emerged into the ordinary world.

Followed by Svetlana.

Here nothing had changed. The open cover of the book lying on the ground hadn't even slammed shut yet.

But all the dogs in the village were yapping, howling and barking.

'Sveta, what?' I asked, dashing towards her.

She turned to me, and her eyes were clouded. Her invisible magical envoys were still dispersing. And then, as they dematerialised tens and hundreds of kilometres away from us, they sent back their final reports.

I knew what they said.

'Nothing . . .' Svetlana whispered. 'Nothing anywhere. No Nadiushka . . . no witch . . .'

Her eyes came back to life. That meant the magical cobweb had decayed, the white birds had fallen to earth and dissolved, the rainbow sphere had burst in the sky.

'Nothing anywhere,' Svetlana repeated. 'Anton . . . We need to calm down.'

'She couldn't have gone far,' I said. 'And she hasn't done anything bad to Nadya, believe me!'

'A hostage?' Svetlana asked. I read hope in her face.

'The Inquisition have the district sealed off. They have their own methods, even Arina won't get past the cordons.'

'Yes . . .' Svetlana whispered. 'I see.'

'To get away, she needs outside help,' I said, unsure whether I was trying to convince Sveta or myself. 'She's not going to get it voluntarily. So she's decided to blackmail us.'

'Will we be able to satisfy her demands?' Svetlana, taking the bull by the horns straight away, without bothering to ask if we would want to satisfy them . . . What else could we do? We'd do anything . . . if we could.

'We have to wait for the demands.'

Svetlana nodded.

'Yes . . . wait. But what for, exactly? A call?'

Immediately she flung her hand up and looked at the window of the bedroom.

An instant later the comb that Arina had given her broke the glass as it came flying through the window. Svetlana caught it in her hand as if it was some insect. She looked at the comb for several seconds, then grimaced and ran it through her hair.

I heard a low, good-humoured laugh. And somewhere inside my head Arina's voice said:

'Hello there, sweetheart. So we meet at last. Did my present come in handy?'

'Remember, you old wretch . . .' Svetlana began, holding the comb out in front of her.

'I know, I know, my darling. I know everything, and I shan't forget. If I harm a single little hair on Nadienka's head, you'll follow me to the ends of the earth, drag me back up from the fifth level of the Twilight, tear me asunder, chop me into little pieces and feed me to the pigs. I know everything you want to say. And I believe you'd do it too.'

Arina's voice was serious. She wasn't mocking us, but explaining perfectly calmly what she wanted us to do. And Svetlana waited silently keeping the comb in her hand. When the witch had finished, she said:

'All right. Then let's not waste any time. I want to speak to Nadiushka.'

'Nadienka, say hello to Mummy,' Arina said.

We heard a perfectly cheerful voice say:

'Hello!'

'Nadiushka, is everything all right?' Svetlana asked cautiously.

'Uhuh . . .' Nadya replied.

Then Arina immediately started speaking again:

'Enchantress, I won't do your daughter any harm, just as long as you don't do anything stupid. I don't want much from you – lead me out of the encirclement and you'll get your daughter back.'

'Arina,' I said, taking Svetlana by the hand, 'the district is cordoned off by the Inquisition. Do you understand that?'

'I wouldn't have asked for help otherwise,' Arina replied coolly. 'Think, sorcerer! There's a weak board in every fence and a tear in every net. Lead me through, and I'll return your daughter.'

'And what if I can't?'

'Then it's all the same to me,' Arina said succinctly. 'I'll try to fight my way out. And I'm sorry, but I'll have to kill your little girl.'

'What for?' I asked in a very calm voice. 'What good will that do you?'

'What good?' Arina asked in astonishment. 'If I manage to break out, next time everyone will know that I'm not joking. And then again . . . I know someone who likes to have others do his dirty work for him. He'll pay me well for the death of your little girl.'

'We'll try,' said Svetlana, squeezing my hand tightly. 'Do you hear me, witch? Don't touch the child, we'll save you!'

'We're agreed then,' said Arina, sounding almost happy. 'So think how I can get past the cordons. You have three hours. If you think of something sooner, enchantress, then pick up the comb and comb your hair again.'

'Only don't touch Nadiushka!' Svetlana shouted in a trembling voice.

Immediately she made a swift pass with her left hand.

The comb was instantly covered in a crust of ice. Svetlana dropped it on the table and muttered:

'The disgusting creature . . . Anton?'

We looked at each other for a second, as if we were tossing the initiative backwards and forwards, like a ball.

I spoke first:

'Sveta, this is really risky. She can't handle us both in open combat. So she leaves herself exposed if she gives Nadya back.'

'We'll find her a corridor . . . a way out . . .' my wife whispered. 'She can get beyond the cordons and leave Nadienka there. I'll find her straight away. She can even go to another town and leave her there. I'll open a portal . . . I know how. I can do that! I'd be there in a minute!'

'That's right,' I said with a nod. 'In a minute. And then what? The witch won't have time to go far. As soon as Nadya's with us, you'll want to find Arina and dematerialise her.'

Svetlana nodded:

'Blow her to pieces, not dematerialise her . . . The smart thing for the witch to do would be to use our help, but kill Nadya anyway. Anton, what should we do? Summon Gesar?'

'What if she senses it?' I asked.

'Can't we phone him?' Sveta suggested.

I thought about it and agreed. After all, Arina had fallen well behind the times. Would she even guess that we could contact Gesar by non-magical means, using a mobile phone?

Svetlana's phone was still in the house. She dragged it out like the comb, with another casual pass of her hand, then looked at me again. I nodded.

It was time to ask for help. Time to demand help. The full might of the Moscow Night Watch. In the final analysis, Gesar had plans of his own for Nadya that we knew nothing about . . .

'Wait!' a voice called to us from the gate. We swung round, probably throwing our hands up too hastily into a combat pose. For us this was no longer the ordinary, human world. We were living in the world of the Others, where the power of your spells and the speed of your reactions decide everything.

But we didn't have to fight.

There was a young man standing at the gate, with three children behind him – two boys and a girl. They were all dressed in greyish-green, semi-military clothes that looked like the uniform of a routed army. The man was about twenty-five, the children about ten. He couldn't have been their father, or even their brother – their faces were too dissimilar.

They had only one thing in common – their dark auras. Wild and shaggy, totally out of keeping with their likeable faces and short, neat hairstyles.

'I see our werewolves have come calling,' I muttered.

The man inclined his head briefly to confirm that I was right.

What a fool I was!

I'd been looking for an adult with three children, but I hadn't bothered to check the Young Pioneer camp.

'Come to give yourselves up?' Svetlana asked frostily. 'You've chosen a bad time.'

No matter how weak they were as Others, they must have felt the recent vortex of power – and the incredible might radiating from Svetlana, which left no chance for werewolves, vampires or any other lower Dark Ones. Sveta could have buried them up to their necks in the ground with a single wave of her hand.

'Wait!' the man said quickly. 'Listen to what we have to say! My name's Igor. I'm . . . I'm a registered Dark Other, sixth grade.'

'What town?' Svetlana asked curtly.

'Sergiev Posad.'

'And the children?' she asked, continuing her interrogation.

'Petya's from Zvenigorod, Anton's from Moscow, Galya's from Kolomna . . .'

'Are they registered?' Svetlana asked. She clearly wanted to hear the answer 'No', and that would have sealed Igor's fate.

The boys pulled up their shirts without speaking. The girl hesitated for a moment, but then unfastened her top button.

They all had seals.

'That won't do you much good,' Svetlana muttered. 'Go into the shed and wait for the field operatives. You can explain to a tribunal why you took the cubs hunting humans.'

But Igor shook his head again, with an expression of genuine concern – and not for himself, which was surprising.

'Wait! Please! This is important! You have a daughter, don't you? A little Other girl, a Light One, two or three years old?'

'We saw where they took her,' the boy with my name said in a quiet voice.

I moved Sveta aside and stepped forward. I asked:

'What do you want?'

We already knew what the werewolves wanted. And the werewolves knew that we understood. The sad thing about it was they could tell we'd be willing to deal.

But there are always little details worth talking through.

'A charge of minor negligence,' Igor said quickly. 'While we were out walking we inadvertently allowed ourselves to be seen by human children and frightened them.'

'You were hunting, you beast!' Svetlana burst out. 'You and the cubs were hunting human children!'

'No!' said Igor, shaking his head. 'The kids got a bit frolicsome and decided to play a game with the human children. I arrived on the scene and pulled them away. It was my fault, I wasn't watching them closely enough.'

His calculations were precisely right. I couldn't have ignored what had happened, even if I wanted to. The facts were already out. It was just a matter of how to classify the incident. Attempted murder almost certainly meant dematerialisation for Igor and intensive supervision for the cubs. Minor negligence meant no more than a report, a fine and 'special supervision' of his subsequent behaviour.

'All right,' I said hastily, so that Svetlana couldn't get in before me. 'If you help us, you can have your "minor negligence".'

I wanted to be responsible for saying it.

Igor relaxed. He'd probably been expecting the deal to take longer.

'Galya, tell them,' he ordered. He explained: 'She saw it . . . Galya's a fidget, she just can't sit still . . .'

Svetlana walked over to the girl. And I gestured for Igor to move aside. He tensed up again, but followed me meekly.

'A few questions,' I explained. 'And I advise you to answer honestly.'

Igor nodded.

'How were you granted the right to initiate three children who weren't yours?' I asked, swallowing the words 'you bastard' that were begging to be added.

'They were all incurably ill,' Igor answered. 'I was studying in medical college, on practical training in a children's cancer ward . . . all three of them were dying from leukaemia. There was a doctor there who was an Other. A Light One. He suggested it to me . . . I bite all three of them and turn them into werewolves, and they recover. And by way of return he receives the right to heal a few other children.'

I said nothing. I remembered the incident from about a year earlier. An utterly outrageous case of open collusion between a Dark One and a Light One, which both Watches had preferred to hush up. The Light One had saved about twenty children, making the most of such a rare opportunity to heal. The Dark Ones had received three werewolves. A small exchange. Everyone was happy, including the children and their parents. A few additional amendments to the Treaty had been adopted to avoid similar cases in the future. Everyone had preferred to forget the precedent as quickly as possible.

'Do you blame me?' Igor asked.

'It's not for me to blame you,' I whispered. 'All right. Whatever your motives might have been . . . never mind that. The second question. Why did you take them out hunting? Don't lie this time, don't lie! You were hunting! You were planning to violate the Treaty!'

'I got carried away,' Igor answered calmly. 'What point is there in lying? I took the cubs out for a walk, and deliberately chose the most remote area. Then suddenly there were those little children . . . Alive. They smelled good. One thing led to another. As for the cubs . . . they only caught their first rabbit this year, got their first taste of blood.'

And then he smiled – a guilty, embarrassed, even sincere smile. He explained:

'Your mind works quite differently in an animal body. Next time I'll be more careful.'

'All right,' I said.

What else could I say? Nadiushka's life was hanging by a thread. Even if he was lying, I wasn't going to start prying.

'Anton!' Svetlana called to me. 'Catch!'

I looked at her – and the images came crowding into my mind.

. . . A beautiful woman in a long, old woman's dress with a bright-coloured Pavlovsk shawl . . .

. . . Walking beside her, a little girl . . . falling behind . . . the woman picks her up in her arms . . .

. . . Along the riverbank . . .

. . . Grass . . . tall grass . . . why is it so tall – above my head . . .

. . . I jump over a stream – with all four paws, put my nose to the ground, pick up the trail with my animal instincts . . .

. . . A stunted patch of trees, merging into a hummocky field . . . trenches, ditches . . .

. . . A smell . . . what a strange smell this land gives off . . . it's thrilling . . . and it makes me want to squeeze my tail between my legs . . .

. . . The woman with the little girl in her arms goes down into a deep trench . . .

. . . Back . . . back . . . it's the same witch, the same one, that's her scent . . .

'What is it?' Svetlana asked. 'If it's not far away, why didn't I find them?'

'A battlefield,' I whispered, shaking the images of what the little wolf-girl had seen out of my head. 'The front line ran just past here, Sveta. The earth there is soaked in blood. You have to look for something specific to find anything at all. It's like trying to probe the Kremlin with magic.'

Igor came up, cleared his throat politely and asked:

'Is everything all right then? Maybe we could wait for the investigators at the camp? We don't really need to rush things, our session there ends in a week, and I can report to the Night Watch to explain everything . . .'

I was thinking. Trying to correlate what I'd seen with the map of the area that I'd summoned up in my memory. Twenty kilometres . . . the witch hadn't simply walked there with Nadiushka. She'd shortened the journey – witches can do that. We wouldn't catch her in a car, mine wasn't a jeep, after all, and there wasn't a single Niva or UAZ four-wheel drive in the whole village. What you really needed for those roads was a tractor . . .

But I could enter the Twilight.

Or even better, make myself faster.

'Sveta,' I said and looked in her eyes. 'You've got to stay here.'

'What?'

'The witch is no fool. She won't give us three hours to think. She'll get in touch sooner than that. With you – she's not expecting anything remarkable from me. You stay here, and when the witch contacts you, talk to her. Tell her I've gone to prepare the corridor through the encirclement . . . Lie, tell her anything. Then I'll summon you and distract her.'

'You won't manage it,' said Svetlana. 'Anton, you're not strong enough to withstand her. And I don't know how quickly I'll be able to open a portal. I'm not even sure I'll be able to. I've never tried, only read about it. Anton!'

'I won't be alone,' I replied. 'Right, Igor?'

He turned pale and started shaking his head.

'Hey, watchman . . . That's not what we agreed!'

'We agreed that you would help,' I reminded him. 'We didn't define what counts as help. Well?'

Igor cast a sideways glance at his young wards. He frowned and said:

'You're a real swine, watchman . . . It's easier for me to fight a magician than a witch. All her magic comes from the earth. It cuts straight to the quick . . .'

'Never mind, we'll be together,' I said. 'The five of us.'

The cubs – I forced myself to think about them only as cubs – glanced at each other. Galya jabbed Petya in the side with her fist and whispered something.

'What do you need them for?' Igor asked, raising his voice. 'Watchman! They're only children!'

'Werewolf cubs,' I corrected him, 'who almost ate human children. Do you want to atone for your guilt? Get off with a caution? Then stop yapping!'

'Uncle Igor, we're not afraid,' Petya said unexpectedly.

The young Anton backed him up.

'We'll go with you!'

They looked at me calmly, without resentment. Clearly they hadn't expected anything else.

'They can't do anything more . . .' said Igor. 'Watchman . . .'

'That's okay. If they distract the witch, that will be a help. Now transform!'

Svetlana turned away. But she didn't say anything.

The werewolves began getting undressed silently. The little girl was the only one who looked around shyly and went behind a currant bush, the others weren't embarrassed.

Out of the corner of my eye I saw a village woman walking along the road, carrying a bucket filled with potatoes. She'd probably dug them up out of the collective farm field. When she saw what was happening inside the fence, she stopped, but I couldn't give a damn about her right then. I wasn't in great shape as it was, I had no power to waste on chance witnesses. I needed to learn to run. To run fast, so that I could keep up with the wolves.

'Let me help,' said Svetlana. She moved her open hand through the air, and I felt a pleasant ache fill my body and strength start flooding into my legs. I instantly felt hot, as if I'd stepped into an overheated sauna. 'Pace' is a simple spell, but it has to be used with great caution. Catch the cardiac muscle as well as the legs, and you'll give yourself a heart attack.

Beside me Igor began groaning and arched over with his hands and feet on the ground and his spine reaching towards the sky, as if it had snapped in half. So that was where all the old folktales about having to jump over a rotten tree stump came from . . . His skin turned dark, broke out in a bright red rash, then sprouted clumps of damp, rapidly growing fur.

'Quickly!' I shouted. The air coming out of my mouth was hot and damp, I could see my breath steaming, as if there was a frost. It was unbearably difficult to stand still – my body craved movement.

It was good to see that the werewolves felt the same.

The large wolf grinned. For some reason his teeth were the last thing to change. The human teeth in a wolf's mouth looked comical, and at the same time horrific. I suddenly had the strange thought that werewolves had to manage without fillings and crowns.

But then, I realised, their bodies are a lot stronger than human ones. Werewolves don't suffer from tooth decay.

'Let's-s-s go . . .' the wolf barked with a lisp. 'It's hot.'

The cubs ran up to the wolf, yelping – they were wet too, as if they'd been sweating. One of them still had human eyes, but I couldn't tell if it was one of the boys or the girl.

'Let's run!' I said.

And I tore off, without looking back at Svetlana, without thinking about whether anyone would see us or not. I could sort that out later. Or Svetlana would erase our tracks.

But the streets were empty, even the woman with the bucket had gone. Maybe Svetlana had driven everybody back home? It would be good if she had. It's a strange sight – a man running faster than nature allows, and four wolves running along with him.

My legs seemed to carry me on of their own accord. The ten-league boots in children's fairy tales and Baron Münchhausen's fleet-footed friend – these are the reflections in human myth of this little piece of magic. Only the fairy tales don't tell you how much the pounding of the road against your feet hurts . . .

After about a minute we turned towards the river and it was easier running over soft earth. I stayed beside the wolf, like some considerate storybook Prince Ivan who didn't want to exhaust his grey friend. The cubs fell behind – it was harder for them. Werewolves are very strong, but their speed doesn't come from magic.

'What ideas . . . have you . . . come up with?' the wolf barked. 'What are . . . you going . . . to do?'

If only I knew the answer to that.

A battle between Others is the manipulation of the Power dissolved in the Twilight. I was a second-grade magician – which is pretty high. Arina was way beyond all frameworks of classification. But Arina was a witch, and that was an advantage and a disadvantage at the same time. She couldn't have taken all her charms and talismans and amulets with her . . . only a few little things. But on the other hand, she could draw power directly from nature. In the city, her powers decreased, but here they increased. For really serious magic she needed to use some particular amulet, and that took time . . . but the charge of accumulated power in an amulet could be monstrously strong.

I couldn't tell. There were too many variables. I wouldn't even have tried to predict the outcome of a fight between Arina and Gesar. The Great Magician would probably win, but it wouldn't be easy.

And what could I use against the witch?

Speed?

She'd withdraw into the Twilight, where she felt a lot more confident. And with every successive level, I'd get slower and slower.

Surprise?

To some degree. After all, I was hoping Arina wasn't expecting me.

Simple brute force? Smash her over the head with a rock?

To do that, I had to get close to her.

Everything suggested that I had to sneak up on her and get as close as possible. And the moment the witch was distracted, attack. With a crude, primitive punch.

'Listen!' I shouted to the wolf. 'When we get close, I'll withdraw into the Twilight. I'll go on ahead and creep up on the witch. You advance in the open. When she starts talking to you and gets distracted, I'll attack. Help me then.'

'All r-r-right,' the wolf growled, saying nothing about what he really thought of the plan.

CHAPTER 7

WAS THIS SPOT still marked on maps of the Second World War? Maybe it was a battlefield well known to historians and celebrated in all the books, a place where two armies had once clashed in a bloody, murderous conflict – and the juggernaut of the blitzkrieg had shuddered to a halt and been rolled back?

Or maybe it was one of our obscure, unknown fields of shame, where the crack German units had trampled into the mud the untrained and poorly armed volunteers thrown in against them? A place only remembered in the archives of the Ministry of Defence?

I didn't know my history very well, but it was probably the latter. This place was too deserted, too bleak and dead. An abandoned patch of dirt that not even the collective farms had coveted.

In our country we don't like to erect monuments on battlefields where we were defeated.

Maybe that's because our victories weren't all that slick either?

I stood on the bank of the narrow river and looked at the area of dead ground. It wasn't all that big: a strip of land between the forest and the river, about a kilometre wide and ten kilometres long. Not so very many people had been killed here. More likely hundreds than thousands.

But then, how could you really say that wasn't many?

The field was utterly deserted. I couldn't see anybody with my normal vision, and a glance through the Twilight hadn't revealed anything either.

Then I picked up my shadow – the sun was setting behind me – and entered the Twilight.

At the first level the ground was overgrown with blue moss, but not too thickly. The usual scraggy clumps, clutching greedily at faint echoes of human emotion.

There was one thing that put me on my guard. The moss seemed to run in rings round one particular spot. I knew that it could move, creeping along slowly but stubbornly towards its food.

And in this place there was only one possible reason for it to form into circles.

I set off through the thick grey haze. The human world was visible through it all around me, like a faded, poorly exposed black-and-white photograph. It was cold and cheerless – I was losing energy with every second I spent here. But there was a positive side to that. Not even Arina could stay in the Twilight constantly. She could glance into the first level from the ordinary world, but even that required Power.

And right now she was in no position to be reckless and wasteful with the Power she had stored up over the years.

At the first level the terrain is almost unchanged. Here too I had earth under my feet, ruts and humps. But I discovered something else. I could see, or rather, sense, the old weapons in the ground. Not every one, of course, only those that had actually killed. Half-decayed sub-machine guns, slightly better preserved rifles . . . There were more rifles.

About a hundred metres from Arina I hunkered down and started running in a squat. The spell Svetlana had put on me was still working, or I would soon have been out of breath. About fifty metres away I lay down and started to crawl. The ground was damp, and I was instantly coated with mud. At least I knew that when I left the Twilight the mud would simply drop off. The blue moss began stirring, uncertain what to do – move closer to me or crawl away from any possible danger. That was bad. Arina might realise what was agitating it.

And then, very close to me, only about five metres away, a head with long black hair began rising slowly from the densely overgrown ground. The trench was so narrow, it looked as if Arina was emerging straight from the earth.

I froze.

But Arina wasn't looking in my direction. Her body rose up very slowly until it was completely erect – she seemed to be sitting on the bottom of the old trench. Then she raised her hand theatrically to shade her eyes, as if she was saluting. I realised she was looking through the Twilight.

Fortunately not at me.

My press-ganged recruits were getting close.

How beautifully they ran! Even through the Twilight their movement looked fast, the only difference was that they hung in the air too long when they leapt. The wise old wolf was leading the way, with the cubs behind him.

A human being would have been frightened.

Arina laughed. She put her hands on her hips, for all the world like a young peasant woman from Ukraine watching her good-for-nothing husband approach with his drinking companions. She spoke, and low, rumbling sounds began drifting through the air. She was in no hurry to enter the Twilight.

I moved back into the human world.

'. . . stupid loudmouths!' I heard. 'Wasn't what you got last time enough for you?'

The wolves slowed to a walk and stopped about twenty metres away.

The leader stepped forward and barked:

'Witch! . . . Talk . . . We have to talk!'

'Talk away, grey wolf,' Arina said amiably.

Igor couldn't distract the witch for long, I knew that. Any moment now she would plunge into the Twilight and take a proper look around her.

But where was Nadiushka?

'Give us . . . the little girl . . .' the wolf half-shouted, half-howled. 'The Light One . . . is on the rampage . . . give us the girl . . . or it will . . . be worse for you . . .'

'Do you really think you can threaten me?' Arina asked in surprise. 'Have you completely lost your wits? Who would give a child to wolves? Leave while you still can!'

Strange, she seemed to be dragging things out.

'Is the child . . . alive?' the wolf asked in a slightly clearer voice.

'Nadenka, are you alive?' Arina asked, looking down towards the ground. She stooped, lifted my little girl out of the trench and set her on the surface.

I caught my breath. Nadenka didn't look frightened or tired at all. She seemed to be enjoying what was happening – a lot more than her walks with Grandma.

But she was close to the witch, too close.

'Wolfie!' said Nadya, looking at the werewolf. She reached her hand out to him and laughed happily.

The werewolf started wagging his tail.

It only lasted a few seconds, then Igor tensed up, his fur bristled, and once again we were watching a wild beast, not a tame dog. But even so, it had happened – a werewolf had fawned on a two-year-old girl, an uninitiated Other.

'Wolfie,' Arina agreed. 'Nadenka, look to see who else is here. Close your eyes and look. The way I taught you.'

Nadiushka cheerfully put her hands over her eyes. And began turning in my direction.

The witch was initiating her.

If Nadiushka really had learned to look through the Twilight . . .

My daughter turned towards me. She smiled.

'Daddy . . .'

I realised two things.

First, Arina knew perfectly well that I was nearby. The witch had been toying with me.

Second, Nadiushka wasn't looking through the Twilight. She had parted her fingers and looked through them.

I immediately withdrew into the Twilight. I was in such a nervous state that I plunged straight through to the second level – into that desolate cotton-wool silence and those pale-grey shadows.

Arina's aura was blazing orange and turquoise. Nadiushka's head was surrounded by a glowing, pure white halo – like a beacon beaming light into space: a potential Other. A Light One. With immense Power.

And the werewolves, who had started to run now, were bundles of red and crimson, fury and spite, hunger and fear . . .

'Svetlana!' I shouted into the grey space, into the soft silence. 'Come!'

I marked the spot for the portal simply – flinging pure Power into the Twilight, like stretching out a string of fire, a landing corridor. From me to Arina.

And at the same time I leapt up and started to run, so that Nadiushka wouldn't be between Arina and me, scattering from my fingers spells that I had learned a long time ago.

'Freeze' – a localised halt in time.

'Opium' – sleep.

'Triple blade' – the crudest and simplest of all the combat spells.

'Thanatos' – death.

I had no hope any of them would work. These things could only be effective when you were facing a very weak opponent. An Other with superior powers would parry the blows, whether he was in the Twilight or the human world.

All I wanted to do was distract the witch and slow her down. Overload her defences, which had to be based on amulets and talismans. All these fireworks were only calculated to identify a breach in those defences.

My 'freeze' seemed to disappear into nowhere.

The 'sleep' spell ricocheted off and shot up into the sky. I hoped there weren't any aeroplanes overhead.

The 'triple blade' struck home and the glittering blades sliced into the witch. But to her the triple blade was a mere scratch.

Things went worst of all with the summons to death. I had good reason to be fond of this piece of magic, so dangerously close to the spells of the Dark Ones. But even in the ordinary world, Arina still had time to hold out her hand. And the little bundle of grey mist that paralysed the will and stopped the heart landed obediently in her open palm.

Arina looked at me through the Twilight, smiling. Her hand was hovering over Nadiushka's head, and the grey bundle was slowly oozing between her fingers.

I leapt towards them – if I couldn't turn the blow aside, at least I could take it myself . . .

But Arina was already on the second level of the Twilight, moving fast. She looked blindingly beautiful. A movement of her fingers crumpled my spell, and she casually tossed it at the wolves.

'Don't be in such a hurry . . .' the witch chanted in a sing-song voice. In the silence of the second level her words were like thunder – and my legs betrayed me. I slumped to my knees just a step away from Arina and Nadiushka.

'Don't touch her!' I shouted.

'Didn't I ask you,' the witch said in a quiet voice, 'to help me get away? What's one old witch more or less to you?'

'I don't trust you!'

Arina nodded wearily:

'You're right not to trust me . . . And now what am I to do, sorcerer?'

Her hand slid across her skirt and tore a sprig of dried berries from her belt. She tossed them into the blazing white lights, black smoke billowed up and the marker for the portal disappeared.

Svetlana was too late.

'You leave me no choice, Light One,' Arina said with a grim expression. 'Do you understand? I'll have to kill you, and then your daughter's no use to me any more. What were you thinking of, with your second grade?'

At that instant a glittering white sword-blade struck Arina from behind, protruded for an instant from her chest, then drew back in obedience to some invisible hand.

'A-a-a-agh . . .' the witch groaned, slumping forward.

Then the grey gloom parted to let Svetlana through.

The witch seemed to have recovered from the blow already. She retreated, jigging backwards and keeping her eyes fixed on Svetlana. The slit that had been burned through her dress was smoking, but she wasn't bleeding. And the look on her face seemed more like admiration than hatred.

'My, my . . . Great One . . .' Arina cackled. 'Did I miscalculate then?'

Svetlana didn't answer. I could never have imagined such intense hatred in her face – any man would have died just looking into her eyes. She was clutching a white sword in her right hand, and the fingers of her left were working the air, as if she was assembling an invisible Rubik's cube.

The Twilight turned a little darker. A rainbow sphere sprang up around Nadiushka. Svetlana's next pass was for me – my body recovered the power of movement. I jumped up and started circling behind the witch. I was only a bit player in this war.

'Which level did you come from, you fidget?' the witch asked almost amiably. 'Could it really be the fourth? I was keeping an eye on the third . . .'

I sensed that the answer was incredibly important to her.

'From the fifth,' Svetlana replied.

'That's really bad . . .' the witch muttered. 'That's a mother's fury for you . . .' She squinted at me out of the corner of her eye, then fixed her gaze on Svetlana again. 'Don't you go gossiping about what you saw down there . . .'

'I don't need you to tell me,' Svetlana said.

The witch nodded and began working her hands very rapidly, tearing out her hair. I didn't know if Svetlana was expecting this, but I decided it would be a good idea to jump back. It was a good thing I did – a black blizzard sprang up and began swirling round the witch, as if every hair had been transformed into a slim, sharp blade of black steel. The witch began advancing on Svetlana, who tossed her white sword at her – the blades sliced it to pieces and extinguished it, but then a transparent shield appeared, floating in the air in front of Svetlana.

I thought it must be 'Luzhin's Shield'.

The blades shattered against it almost instantly, without a sound.

'Oh, Lord . . .' Arina wailed. It was strange, but I didn't have the slightest doubt that she was sincere. Yet at the same time she was playing to her audience.

In other words, to me.

'Surrender, you wretch!' said Svetlana. 'While I'll still let you, surrender!'

'But how about . . . how about this?' Arina declared. 'Eh?'

This time she didn't reach for her amulets. She just started crooning her clumsy doggerel:

> Dust to dust collect and bind,
> Arms and legs with power filling,
> Be my trusty servants willing.
> Or you'll be scattered to the wind.

I'd been expecting anything at all from Arina. Except this. Genuine necromancers are very rare, even among the Dark Ones.

The dead were slowly rising out of the earth.

The German soldiers of the Second World War were going back into battle.

Four skeletons dressed in tatters – all their flesh had disappeared long ago and there was earth packed between their bones – stood in a ring round Arina. Another came staggering blindly towards me, clumsily waving its fingerless hands – the bones had rotted clean away. The ludicrous zombie shed pieces of itself at every step. Three equally wretched monsters started towards Svetlana. One of them was even holding a black sub-machine gun that had lost its magazine.

'Think you can raise the Red Army?' Arina taunted Svetlana.

She shouldn't have done that – Svetlana froze as if she had turned to stone. Then she hissed through her teeth:

'My grandfather fought in the war. Was this supposed to frighten me?'

I didn't understand what she did next. I would have used the 'grey prayer', but she used something from the higher levels of magic beyond my reach. The zombies crumbled to dust.

Svetlana and Arina were left staring at each other in silence.

The joking was over.

The enchantress and the witch clashed in a straightforward duel of Power.

I took advantage of the brief pause to gather my own strength. If Svetlana faltered, then I would strike.

But it was Arina who faltered.

First of all, her dress was torn off. That might have had a demoralising effect – on a man.

Then the witch began ageing rapidly. Her luxuriant black hair shrank to a pitiful grey tuft. Her breasts drooped and stretched, her arms and legs withered. She was like a monster from a children's story.

And there were no special effects here.

'Your name!' Svetlana shouted.

Arina didn't hesitate for long.

Her toothless mouth quivered and she mumbled:

'Arina . . . I am in your power, sorceress . . .'

It was only then that Svetlana relaxed – and suddenly seemed to wilt. I walked round the subdued Arina and took hold of my wife's arm.

'It's all right . . . I'm okay,' Svetlana said with a smile. 'We did it.'

The old crone – it was impossible to think of her as Arina – gazed at us sadly.

'Will you allow her to assume her former shape?' I asked.

'Why, was she more attractive then?' said Svetlana, attempting to joke.

'She'll die of old age in a moment,' I said. 'She's over two hundred years old.'

'Let her croak . . .' Svetlana muttered. She glowered at Arina. 'Witch! I grant you the right to become younger!'

Arina's body rapidly straightened up and filled with life. The witch gulped at the air greedily. She looked at me:

'Thank you, sorcerer . . .'

'Let's get out of here,' Svetlana ordered. 'And no stupid tricks . . . I grant you only the right to leave the Twilight!'

Now all the witch's power that had not been stripped away with her clothes and amulets was completely under Svetlana's control. To coin a phrase, Svetlana had her finger on the trigger.

'Sorcerer . . .' said Arina, keeping her eyes fixed on me. 'First remove the shield from your daughter. There is a grenade with the pin drawn lying under her feet. It will explode at any moment.'

Svetlana cried out.

I dashed to the rainbow globe and struck it, breaking through the Sphere of Negation. Beneath it there were another two shields. I tore them away crudely, working with raw energy. From the second level of the Twilight I couldn't see anything.

I found my shadow and shot back up to the first level. Everything was clear there, not a trace of the blue moss – the raging battle had burned it away completely.

And almost immediately I saw the old 'pineapple' lying under Nadiushka's foot. Arina had left it there as she plunged into the Twilight. Her insurance policy . . .

The pin was pulled out. Somewhere inside the grenade the fuse was burning away agonisingly slowly, and in the human world three or four seconds had already elapsed . . .

The casualty range was two hundred metres.

If it exploded inside the shields, there would be nothing left of Nadiushka but a bloody pulp . . .

I picked up the grenade. It's very difficult to work with objects of the real world when you are in the Twilight. At least the grenade had a distinct Twilight double – the same ribs and ridges, smeared with mud and rust . . .

Should I throw it away?

No.

In the human world it wouldn't go far. And if I took it into the Twilight, it would explode instantly.

I couldn't think of anything better to do than slice the grenade in half, as if I was trying to stone an avocado. Then I sliced it again into several pieces, searching for the small, glowing string of the slow fuse among the metal and explosive. My phantom knife, a blade of pure Power, chopped through the grenade like a ripe tomato.

Finally I found it – a tiny little spark already creeping close to the detonator. I extinguished it with my fingers.

And then I tumbled out into the human world. Soaked in sweat, my legs trembling so badly that I was barely able to stand. I shook my hand – the burnt fingers were stinging.

'Just give a man a chance to tinker with anything mechanical,' Arina said scathingly when she appeared after me. I ought to have shut her inside the shield and let her be blown to pieces. Or I could have cast a frost on her and left her frozen solid until the next day . . .

'Daddy, teach me how to hide like that,' said Nadiushka, none the worse for her adventure. Then she spotted Arina and said indignantly: 'Aunty, don't be silly! You can't walk around with no clothes on!'

'How many times have I told you not to talk to grown-ups like that!' Svetlana exclaimed. Then she grabbed hold of Nadiushka's hands and started kissing her.

A scene from a madhouse . . .

If my mother-in-law had been there, she'd have had a few things to say . . .

I sat down on the edge of the trench, longing for a smoke. And I wanted a drink. And something to eat. And a sleep. But at the very least, a smoke.

'I won't do it again,' Nadya babbled 'Look, wolfie's poorly!'

It was only then that I remembered about the werewolves, and looked round.

The wolf was lying on the ground, his paws twitching feebly.

'I'm sorry, sorcerer,' said Arina. 'I threw your death spell at the wolf. There was no time to think.'

I looked at Svetlana. 'Thanatos' doesn't necessarily mean certain death. The spell can be removed.

'I'm drained . . .' Svetlana said in a low voice. 'I've no strength left.'

'I'll save the filthy creature if you like,' Arina suggested. 'It's not hard for me to do.'

We looked at each other.

'Why did you tell us about the grenade?' I asked.

'What good will it do me if she dies?' Arina replied indifferently.

'She'll be a Great Light One,' said Svetlana. 'The Greatest of all!'

'Well, let her.' Arina smiled. 'Maybe she'll remember her Aunty Arina, who told her about herbs and flowers . . . Don't worry. No one will ever make her into a Dark One. She's no simple child, the magic in her is too strong . . . What shall I do with the wolf?'

'Save him,' Svetlana said simply.

Arina nodded. Then suddenly she said to me:

'There's a bag over there in the trench . . . with cigarettes and food. I prepared this hideaway a long time ago.'

The witch worked on Igor for about ten minutes. First she drove away the growling cubs, who ran off to one side and tried to change back into children, and when they couldn't they lay down in the bushes. Then she started whispering something, all the while plucking first one plant, then another. She shouted at the cubs and they ran off and came back with twigs and roots in their teeth.

Svetlana and I looked at each other but said nothing. Everything was perfectly clear anyway. I finished my second cigarette, rolled a third between my hands to soften it and took a block of chocolate out of the black fabric bag. Apart from cigarettes, chocolate and a wad of sterling – what a prudent witch! – the bag was empty.

Somehow I'd been hoping to find the *Fuaran*.

'Witch!' Svetlana shouted when the werewolf got to his feet, still trembling. 'Come here!'

Arina came back to us, swinging her hips daintily and not even slightly embarrassed at being naked. The werewolf also lay down close to us. He was breathing heavily, and the cubs crowded round and started licking him. Svetlana winced at the sight, then turned to look at Arina.

'What are you accused of?'

'On the instructions of an unidentified Light One I modified the recipe for a potion and so ruined a joint experiment by the Inquisition, the Night Watch and the Day Watch.'

'Did you do it?'

'Yes,' Arina admitted blithely.

'What for?'

'Ever since the revolution I'd been dreaming of doing real damage to the reds.'

'Don't lie,' said Svetlana, frowning. 'You couldn't give a damn for the reds or the whites. Why did you take the risk?'

'What difference does that make, sorceress?' Arina sighed.

'A big one. In the first place, for you.'

The witch threw her head back and looked up at me, then at Svetlana. Her eyelids were trembling.

'Aunty Arina, are you feeling sad?' Nadiushka asked. Then she glanced sideways at her mother and put her hands over her own mouth.

'Yes,' the witch replied.

At that moment I really didn't want Arina to fall into the clutches of the Inquisition.

'The experiment was supported by all the Others,' Arina said. 'The Dark Ones believed that the appearance of thousands of convinced communists in the leadership of the country – the bread plant's output mostly went to the Kremlin and the People's Commissariats – wouldn't improve anything. On the contrary, it would provoke hostility towards the Soviets from the rest of the world. But the Light Ones believed that after a hard but victorious war against Germany – the likelihood of that was evident to the clairvoyants by then – the Soviet Union could become a genuinely attractive society. There was a secret report . . . essentially people would have built communism by 1980 . . .'

'And made maize the basic animal-feed crop,' Svetlana snorted.

'Don't talk drivel, sorceress,' the witch retorted calmly. 'I don't remember about any maize, but they were supposed to build a city on the moon in the 1970s. And fly to Mars, and something else. The whole of Europe would have been communist. And not under constraint either. By now here on earth we'd have had a huge Soviet Union, a huge United States . . . I think Britain, Canada and Australia were part of it . . . China was left on its own.'

'So the Light Ones miscalculated?' I asked.

'No.' Arina shook her head. 'They didn't miscalculate. Of course, the blood would have flowed in rivers. But what came at the end of it all wouldn't have been too bad. Far better than all the regimes we have now . . . The Light Ones overlooked something else. If things had gone that way, then round about now people would have learned that the Others existed.'

'I see,' said Svetlana. Nadiushka was squirming restlessly on her knees – bored of sitting, she wanted to go to the 'wolfie'.

'That's why the . . . unidentified Light One . . .' – Arina smiled – 'who had the wits to calculate the future more thoroughly than all the rest, came to me. We met a few times and discussed the situation. The problem was that the experiment had been planned not just by Higher Others, who could appreciate the danger of our being exposed, but also by a large number of first- and second-grade magicians . . . even some third- and fourth-grade ones. The project was extremely popular . . . in order to cancel it officially, full information would have had to be given to thousands of Others. There was no way that could be done.'

'I understand,' said Svetlana.

But I didn't understand a thing!

We conceal our existence from people because we're afraid. There are too few of us, and no magic is strong enough to guarantee our survival if a new campaign of 'witch hunts' begins. But in this wonderful, benign future that Arina said could already have happened would we really have been in any danger?

'That's why we decided to sabotage the experiment,' Arina continued. 'It increased the numbers killed in the Second World War, but reduced the numbers who died in the export of revolution to Europe and Northern Africa. It came out more or less even . . . of course, now life in Russia isn't as sweet and easy as it should have been. But who ever said that happiness is measured by a full stomach?'

'Oh sure!' I exclaimed, unable to restrain myself. 'Any teacher in a town on the Volga or miner in Ukraine will agree with you there.'

'Happiness should be sought in spiritual wealth!' Arina rebuked me. 'And not in baths filled with bubbles, or a heated privy. And at least people don't know about the Others!'

I held my tongue. The woman in front of us was not simply guilty – she ought to have been dragged to the tribunal on a rope and stoned along the way! A city on the moon? Okay, if we didn't have a city on the moon, we could do without it. But even our ordinary cities were barely alive, and the entire world was still wary of us . . .

'Poor thing,' said Svetlana. 'Did you suffer a lot?'

At first I thought she was mocking Arina.

The witch thought the same.

'Are you sympathising or scoffing?' she asked.

'Sympathising,' Svetlana answered.

'I don't feel sorry for the little people, don't get the wrong idea,' the witch hissed. 'But I do feel sorry for the country. It's my country, whatever it's like, all of it! But things turned out for the best. We'll carry on living, we won't die out. People will give birth to new people, they'll build cities and plough the fields.'

'It wasn't the secret police you were hiding from in your hibernation,' Svetlana said unexpectedly. 'And not even the Inquisition. You would have talked your way out of it somehow, I can sense it . . . You didn't want to see what was happening to Russia after your sabotage.'

Arina said nothing.

Svetlana looked at me and asked:

'What are we going to do now?'

'You decide,' I said, not really understanding the question.

'Where were you going to run to?' Svetlana asked.

'Siberia,' Arina replied calmly. 'That's the way things are done in Russia – they either exile you to Siberia, or you flee there yourself. I'll choose a nice clean little village and settle down somewhere just outside it. I'll earn my own living . . . find myself a man.' She ran one hand over her magnificent breasts with a smile. 'I'll wait for twenty years, see what happens. And at the same time I'll think about what to tell the Inquisition if they catch me.'

'You can't get past the cordons on your own,' Svetlana muttered. 'And I doubt if we can get you through.'

'I'll . . . hide her . . .' the werewolf coughed hoarsely. 'I . . . owe . . . her . . .'

Arina narrowed her eyes and asked:

'For what, for healing you?'

'No . . . not for that . . .' the werewolf replied vaguely. 'I'll lead you . . . through the forest . . . to the camp . . . hide you there . . . later you'll . . . get away.'

'Nobody's going to . . .' I began. But Svetlana gently put her hand against my lips, as if she was comforting Nadiushka.

'Anton, it's the best way. It's best if Arina gets away. After all, she didn't touch Nadienka, did she?'

I started shaking my head. This was rubbish, crazy nonsense! Had the witch somehow managed to take control of Svetlana's mind?

'It's the best way,' Svetlana insisted.

Then she turned to Arina:

'Witch, swear me an oath that you will never again take the life of a human or an Other!'

'I cannot swear such an oath,' said Arina, shaking her head.

'Swear me an oath that for the next hundred years you will not take the life of a human or an Other unless they threaten your own life . . . and you have no other means to defend yourself!' Svetlana concluded after a short pause.

'Now, that's a different matter,' Arina said and smiled. 'Now I can see that our Great One has matured a bit . . . It's not much fun spending a century without any teeth. But even so, I obey. May the Dark bear me witness!'

She raised her open hand, and a small patch of darkness appeared for a moment on her palm. All the werewolves, the adult and the cubs, began to howl.

'I return your Power to you,' Svetlana said before I could stop her.

And Arina disappeared.

I jumped to my feet and stood beside Svetlana. I still had a little Power left, enough to strike a couple of times, but what did the witch care about blows like that?

Suddenly Arina reappeared in front of us, smiling. She was already dressed, and I think she had even brushed her hair.

'I could still fix you without any killing!' she gloated. 'I could paralyse you or make you ugly.'

'You could,' Svetlana agreed. 'No doubt. Only what would be the point?'

For a brief moment Arina's eyes were filled with such intense melancholy that I felt my heart ache.

'There isn't any point, sorceress. Well then, goodbye. I don't remember kindnesses, but I'm not ashamed to say thank you . . . so thank you, Great One. It will be hard for you now.'

'I already know that,' Svetlana said quietly.

Arina's gaze came to rest on me and she smiled flirtatiously:

'And goodbye to you, sorcerer. Don't feel sorry for me, I don't like that. Ah . . . what a pity you love your wife . . .'

She knelt down and held her hand out to Nadiushka.

Svetlana didn't stop her.

'Goodbye, little girl,' the witch said merrily. 'I'm a wicked old aunty, but I wish you well. Whoever it was that sketched out your destiny was no fool . . . no fool at all . . . maybe you'll succeed where we failed? I have a little present for you . . .' She glanced at Svetlana.

Svetlana nodded.

Arina took hold of Nadiushka's finger. She muttered:

'Shall I wish you Power? You have plenty of Power already. They've given you everything . . . and plenty of everything . . .

But you like flowers, don't you? Then take this gift from me – how to use flowers and herbs. That will come in handy even for a Light Enchantress.'

'Goodbye, Aunty Arina,' Nadiushka said softly. 'Thank you.'

The witch looked at me again. I was dumbfounded, totally confused, I didn't understand a thing. Then she turned to the werewolves.

'Well then, lead on, grey wolf!' she exclaimed.

The wolf cubs went dashing after the witch and their mentor. One filthy little beast even stopped beside a bush, lifted his leg and sprayed it defiantly. Nadiushka giggled.

'Svetlana,' I whispered. 'They're getting away . . .'

'Let them go,' she replied. 'Let them.'

Then she turned towards me.

'What's happened?' I asked, looking into her eyes. 'What and when?'

'Let's go home,' said Svetlana. 'We . . . we need to have a talk, Anton. A serious talk.'

How I hate those words!

They never lead to anything good.

EPILOGUE

MY MOTHER-IN-LAW clucked and fussed over Nadiushka as she put her to bed.

'Ah, you little story-teller, what an imagination . . .'

'I did go for a walk with the aunty,' my daughter protested sleepily.

'You did, of course you did . . .' Ludmila Ivanovna agreed happily.

Svetlana winced. Sooner or later all Others are obliged to manipulate their relatives' memories.

And there's nothing pleasant about that.

Of course, we do have a choice. We could reveal the truth – or part of the truth – to our nearest and dearest.

But that doesn't lead to good results either.

'Good night, little daughter,' said Svetlana.

'Off you go, go on,' my mother-in-law sniffed. 'You've worn my little girl out, exhausted her, the poor sweetheart . . .'

We left the room and Svetlana closed the door firmly. It was quiet, the only sound was the pendulum clock creaking on the wall.

'All that namby-pamby talk,' I said. 'You can't treat a child like that . . .'

'A girl you can,' Svetlana said, dismissing my opinion. 'Especially if she's only two. Anton . . . let's go into the garden.'

'The garden, all right, the garden it is,' I agreed cheerfully. 'Let's go.'

We walked over to the hammock and sat down next to each other. I could feel Svetlana trying to pull away, hard as that is in a hammock.

'Start at the very beginning,' I advised her.

'At the beginning . . .' Svetlana sighed. 'At the beginning . . . that's not possible. Everything's too tangled.'

'Then explain why you let the witch go.'

'She knows too much, Anton. If there's a trial . . . if it all comes out . . .'

'But she's a criminal!'

'Arina didn't do anything bad to us,' Svetlana said quietly, as if she was trying to convince herself. 'I don't think she's bloodthirsty at all. Most witches are genuinely malevolent, but there are some like her . . .'

'I give up!' I said, raising my hands in the air. 'She kept the werewolves in line, and she didn't hurt Nadya. A genuine Arina Rodionovna, she really is. What about the disruption of the experiment?'

'She explained that.'

'What did she explain? That almost a hundred years of Russian history was flushed down the tubes? That instead of a normal society, a bureaucratic dictatorship was built . . . with all the consequences that flow from that?'

'You heard what she said – that would have meant people finding out about us!'

I gave a deep sigh and tried to gather my thoughts.

'Sveta . . . think about what you're saying. Five years ago you were a human being yourself! We are still human . . . only we're more advanced. Like a new twist in the spiral of evolution. If people had found out, it wouldn't have mattered.'

'We're not more advanced,' Svetlana said with a shake of her head. 'Anton, when you called me . . . I guessed that the witch would be watching the Twilight, so I jumped straight to the fifth level. Apart from Gesar and Olga, I don't think any of our Light Ones have ever been there. . .'

She stopped. I realised this was what Svetlana wanted to talk about. Something that was truly terrible.

'What's down there, Sveta?' I whispered.

'I was there for quite a while,' Svetlana went on. 'I discovered a few things. Just how doesn't matter right now.'

'And?'

'Everything it says in the witch's book is right, Anton. We're not genuine magicians. We don't have greater abilities than ordinary people. We're exactly like the blue moss at the first level of the Twilight. Remember that example from the book about body temperature and the temperature of the surroundings? All people have a magical temperature of thirty-six point six. Some who are very lucky, or unlucky, have a fever – their temperature is higher. And all that energy, all that power, warms the world. Our body temperature is below the norm. We absorb power that isn't ours and redistribute it. We're parasites. A weak Other like Egor has a temperature of thirty-four. Yours is, say, twenty. Mine is ten.'

I had my answer prepared. I'd already thought about this, just as soon as I'd finished reading the book.

'But so what, Sveta? What of it? People can't use their power. We can. So what's the point?'

'The point is that people will never come to terms with that. Even the best and the kindest always look enviously at those who have been given more. At the sportsmen, the handsome men and beautiful women, the geniuses and the ones with talent. But they can't complain about it . . . it's fate, chance. Imagine that you're an ordinary human being. Perfectly ordinary. Suddenly you discover that some people live for hundreds of years, can predict the future, heal diseases and put a hex on you. Quite seriously, all for real! And all at your expense! We're parasites, Anton. Exactly like the vampires. Exactly like the blue moss. If it gets out, and if they invent some new instrument that can distinguish Others from normal people, they'll start hunting us and exterminating us. And if we band together and create our own state, they'll drop atom bombs on us.'

'Divide and protect . . .' I whispered, citing the Night Watch's main mantra.

'That's right. Divide and protect, not people from Dark Ones, but people from Others in general.'

I laughed and looked up into the night sky, remembering myself when I was a little younger, walking along a dark street to a rendezvous with vampires. With a passionate heart, clean hands and a cool, empty head . . .

'We've talked so many times about what the difference is between us and the Dark Ones,' Svetlana said in a low voice. 'I've found one way of putting it. We're good shepherds. We watch over the flock. And I suppose that means a lot. Only we mustn't deceive ourselves or anyone else. There'll never be a time when all people become Others. We'll never reveal our kind to them. And we'll never allow people to build a more or less decent society. Capitalism, communism . . . that's not the point. The only world that will ever suit us is one in which people are preoccupied with the size of the trough and the quality of the hay. Because the moment they lift their heads out of the trough, and look round and see us, we'll be finished.'

I gazed into the sky and toyed with Svetlana's hand as it lay there on my knees. Just a hand, warm and limp . . . and only a short while ago it been raining down bolts of lightning on the witch who had sabotaged Russia . . .

The limp hand of a Great Enchantress, who had only half as much magic as me.

'And there's nothing to be done,' Svetlana whispered. 'The Watches won't let the ordinary people out of the cattle-shed. In the States there'll be huge feeding troughs that make you want to dive in over your head. Somewhere over in Uruguay, there'll be sparse grass on the mountain pastures, so people have no time to look up at the sky. The only thing we can do is choose the prettiest cattle-shed and paint it a nice bright colour.'

'What if you tell the Others all this?'

'It won't bother the Dark Ones at all. And the Light Ones will come to terms with it. I learned a truth I didn't want to know, Anton – and I've come to terms with it. Maybe I shouldn't have told you. But that would have been dishonest. As if you were part of the herd too.'

'Sveta . . .' I looked at the faint glow of the night light in the window. 'What's Nadiushka's magical temperature?'

She hesitated before she answered.

'Zero.'

'The Greatest of the Great . . .' I said.

'Absolutely no magic in her at all . . .' said Svetlana.

'So now what do we do?'

'Carry on living,' Svetlana said simply. 'I'm an Other . . . it's too late now to pretend to be innocent. I take Power from people or I draw it from the Twilight – either way, it's not my Power. But I'm not to blame for that.'

'Sveta, I'm going to Gesar. Right now. I'm leaving the Watch.'

'I know. Go.'

I got up and steadied the swaying hammock. It was dark, and I couldn't see Svetlana's face.

'Go, Anton,' she repeated. 'It's going to be hard for us to look into each other's eyes. We need time to get used to this.'

'What's down there, on the fifth level?' I asked.

'It's best if you don't know.'

'All right. I'll ask Gesar.'

'Let him tell you . . . if he wants to.'

I leaned down and touched her cheek – it was wet with tears.

'It's shameful . . .' she whispered. 'Shameful . . . to be a parasite.'

'Hang in there . . .'

'I am.'

When I went into the barn, I heard a door close – Svetlana had gone back into the house. Without bothering to switch on the light, I got into the car and pulled the door shut.

Right then, what had Uncle Kolya done with it? Should I start it or shouldn't I?

The car started first time and the engine began purring quietly. I switched on the dipped beams and drove out of the barn.

What about the rules of concealment?

To hell with them. Why should the shepherd hide from the flock?

I opened the gates with a brief wave of my hand, without getting out of the car. I drove out into the street and stepped on the accelerator. The village looked empty and lifeless. Someone had sprinkled sleeping pills in the sheep's feed.

The car tore out onto the country road. I switched to full beams and put my foot down. The wind rushed in through the open window.

I felt for the remote control on the steering wheel and switched on the minidisc player.

I entered this windy city without a cloak.
And it wound round my throat just like ivy.
The serpent's coils fettered my soul.
I see a black sun, beneath which I shall never shed a tear.
I am slipping out of character. I am insolent, unfair.
What can a rabbit hope for in a boa constrictor's throat?

> The serpent's coils only feel tight at first,
> I see a black sun, and dreams the same colour.
> I cannot tell sins from virtues, even to save my life.
> They're removing the witnesses, turning us to snakes.
> And I am willing to rot under any flag,
> Prepared to slither, zigzagging across the ground,
> And even sing of love, up to my throat in vomit,
> If that is what my Motherland requires.

A light appeared up ahead, somewhere near the slip road onto the motorway. I screwed up my eyes and looked through the Twilight. There was a temporary militia barrier across the road. And two men waiting beside it, with two Others.

Dark Others.

I smiled and slowed down.

> My brain is a beehive with ants instead of bees.
> The bullet's centre of gravity is displaced towards love.
> But the serpent's coils are armour plating.
> I see a black sun. A sun that hates me.
> I could have surrendered without a fight, caught in the devil's jaws.
> But I'll die on my feet – the coils will not let me fall.
> The serpent's coils – my brace and my shell.
> I see a black sun. And it hurts my eyes.

I stopped right in front of the barrier and waited for the motorway patrolman holding an automatic rifle to his chest. The Inquisition were never too choosy when it came to recruiting people for security cordons.

I handed the militiaman my licence and documents for the car, and turned the sound down.

I looked at the Others.

The first was an Inquisitor I didn't know, a lean, elderly Asiatic type. I'd have said he was at the second or third grade of Power, but with Inquisitors it's harder to tell.

The second was a Dark One I knew very well, from the Moscow Day Watch. The vampire Kostya.

'We're looking for a witch,' said the Inquisitor. The militiamen took no notice of the Others. The militiamen had been ordered not to see.

'Arina's not here,' I replied. 'Is Edgar in charge of the drag-net?'

The Inquisitor nodded.

'Ask him about me. Anton Gorodetsky, Night Watch.'

'I know him,' Kostya said casually, leaning down towards the Inquisitor. 'A law-abiding Light One . . .'

'Proceed,' said the patrolman, handing back my documents.

'You can drive on,' the Inquisitor said with a nod. 'There'll be more security posts down the road.'

I nodded and drove out onto the motorway.

Kostya stood there, watching me drive away.

I turned the sound up.

> I'm not for or against. I'm not good or evil.
> You've been damned lucky with me, my Motherland.
> Your serpent's coils are my home, my trap.
> I shall crawl under the sun.
> Under this cursed sun,
> From here to here, and then from here to here,
> From here to Judgement Day.

Story Three

NOBODY'S POWER

PROLOGUE

HE DIDN'T OFTEN dream.

And right now he wasn't even asleep. Even so, it was almost a dream, almost like one of those sweet visions in the instant before waking . . .

A light, pure vision, almost like a child's.

'Scavenging engines . . . key to start position . . .'

The silvery column of the rocket shrouded in light mist.

Flames dancing under the thruster nozzles.

Every Russian child dreams of being a cosmonaut – until he hears that question for the tenth time: 'What do you want to be, a cosmonaut?'

Some stop dreaming about outer space when they become Others.

The Twilight is more interesting than other planets. Their newly discovered Power has a stronger gravitational pull than the fame of a cosmonaut.

But now he was dreaming of a rocket – an absurd, old-fashioned rocket rising up into the sky.

The Earth floating beneath his feet – or is it above his head?

The thick quartz glass of the porthole.

Strange dreams for an Other, surely?

The Earth . . . a veil of clouds . . . the lights of the cities . . . people.

Millions of them. Billions.

And him – watching them from orbit.

An Other in space . . . what could be more ludicrous? Except maybe Other versus Alien. He had watched a science fiction film once, and suddenly found himself thinking that now was just the right moment for brave Ripley to slip into the Twilight – and then strike out and smash those unwieldy, helpless monsters.

The thought immediately made him laugh.

There weren't any Others up there.

But space *was* up there. Only he hadn't realised what it was for until now.

Now he understood.

He closed his eyes, dreaming about the small Earth rotating slowly under his feet.

Every child dreams of being a giant – until he starts to wonder what the point is.

Now he knew everything.

The parts of the jigsaw all fitted together.

His own destiny as an Other.

His crazy dream about space travel.

And the thick volume bound in human skin, its pages covered with neat cursive handwriting.

He picked up the book that was lying on the floorboards.

Opened it at the first page.

The letters had not faded. They were protected by a light but effective magic spell.

This language had not been heard on Earth for a long time. It would have reminded an Indologist of Sanskrit, but only a very few people would have known it was Paishachi.

But Others can read any dead language.

* * *

May the Elephant-Faced One preserve you, swaying his head first up, then down, like unto Shiva, swaying up and down on Mind! May Ganapati fill me with the sweet moisture of wisdom!

My name is Fuaran, I am a woman of the glorious city of Kanakapuri.

The Fulfiller of Desires, husband of Parvati, rewarded me generously in the days of my youth, granting me the ability to walk in the world of phantoms. While in our world a petal swirls in the air as it falls from a blossoming tree, in that world a whole day passes – such is its nature. And a great power lies concealed in that world.

He closed the *Fuaran*.

His heart was pounding.

A great power!

A power that had fallen from a witch's hands and disappeared almost two thousand years ago.

Owned by no one, concealed even from the Others.

Nobody's Power.

CHAPTER 1

I DROVE UP to the Night Watch building shortly after seven in the morning. The deadest time of all – the break between shifts. The field operatives who have been on night duty have handed in their reports and gone home and, following established Moscow tradition, the headquarters staff won't show up before nine.

They were changing shifts in the guard room too. The guards on their way out were signing some papers, those who had just arrived were studying the duty roster. I shook hands with all of them and walked through without any of the required checks. Strictly speaking, that was a breach of regulations . . . although this guard-post was primarily intended for checking ordinary people.

On the third floor the guards had already changed shifts. Garik was on duty and he made no exception for me, inspecting me through the Twilight and nodding for me to touch his amulet: an intricate image of a cockerel made out of gold wire. We called it 'Greetings to Dodon' after the king in Pushkin's fairy tale – in theory, if a Dark One touched the amulet, the cockerel would crow. Some wits claimed that if it sensed a Dark One, the cock would say in a human voice: 'How repulsive!'

Garik waited until he was done before giving me a friendly smile and shaking my hand.

'Is Gesar in his office?' I asked.

'Who knows where he is?' Garik replied.

He was right, that really was a stupid question. Higher Magicians move in mysterious ways.

'I thought you were supposed to be on leave . . .' Garik said. My strange question seemed to have put him on his guard.

'I got fed up relaxing. Like they say, Monday begins on Saturday . . .'

'And you look absolutely exhausted . . .' he went on, growing even more wary. 'Okay, come on . . . stroke the amulet again.'

I sent another greeting to Dodon, then stood still for a while as Garik checked my aura with another ingenious amulet made out of coloured glass.

'Sorry about that,' he said as he put the amulet away, adding in a slightly embarrassed voice: 'You're not yourself today.'

'I was on holiday in the country with Sveta, and a very old witch turned up,' I explained. 'And there was a pack of werewolves getting a bit out of hand. I had to go after the werewolves, and go after the witch . . .' I gestured despairingly. 'After a holiday like that I should be on sick leave.'

'So that's it,' said Garik, calming down. 'Put in an application, I think we still have some of our quota left for restoring powers.'

I shuddered and shook my head.

'No thanks. I'll manage on my own.'

After I said goodbye to Garik, I went up to the fourth floor. I stood outside Gesar's reception for a while, then knocked.

No one answered, and I went in.

The secretary wasn't at her desk, of course. The door into Gesar's office was firmly closed. But the little 'ready' light was blinking cheerfully on the coffee-maker, the computer was switched on and even the television was muttering away quietly on the news channel. The anchorman was reporting that another sandstorm had impeded the American forces in yet another peace-making mission, overturning several tanks and even bringing down two planes.

'And it beat up all the soldiers and took several of them prisoner too,' I couldn't resist adding.

What was this strange habit some Others had of watching TV? Either idiotic soap operas or the lies on the news. There was really only one word for it – 'people' . . .

Maybe the other word was 'cattle'?

But it isn't their fault. They are weak and divided. They are people, not cattle.

We are the cattle.

And people are the grass.

I stood there, leaning against the secretary's desk and looking out of the window at the clouds drifting over the city. Why was the sky so low in Moscow in summer? I'd never seen such low clouds anywhere else . . . except maybe for Moscow in winter . . .

'You can cut grass,' a voice said behind my back. 'Or you can tear it up by the roots. Which do you prefer?'

'Good morning, boss,' I said, turning round. 'I didn't think you were in.'

Gesar yawned. He was wearing slippers and a dressing-gown. I caught a glimpse of his pyjamas underneath it.

I would never have expected the Great Gesar to wear pyjamas covered with pictures of Disney cartoon characters. From Mickey Mouse and Donald Duck to Lilo and Stitch. How could a Great Magician, who had lived thousands of years and could read thoughts with such ease, wear pyjamas like that?

'I was sleeping,' Gesar said glumly. 'Sleeping peacefully. I went to bed at five.'

'Sorry, boss,' I said. Somehow, no other word but 'boss' came to mind. 'Was there a lot of work last night?'

'I was reading a book, an interesting one,' said Gesar, pressing switches on the coffee-maker. 'Black with sugar for me, milk and no sugar for you . . .'

'Something magical?' I enquired.

'No, dammit, Golovachev!' Gesar growled. 'When I retire I'm going to ask to be his co-author and write books! Take your coffee.'

I took the cup and followed Gesar into his office.

As usual, several new knick-knacks had appeared. In one cupboard there were lots of little figures of mice made of glass, tin and wood, ceramic goblets and steel knives. Propped up against the back wall of the cupboard was an old Civil Defense brochure with a photograph on its cover of a committee judging volunteers folding parachutes, and beside it there was a simple lithograph showing a green forest thicket.

For some reason – I couldn't understand exactly why – it all brought to mind the early years of school.

And hanging from the ceiling was a gold-coloured ice hockey helmet that looked exactly like a bald head. There were several darts stuck into it.

I glanced suspiciously at all these items, which might mean something very important, or absolutely nothing at all, and sat down in one of the visitors' chairs. I noticed a book with a bright cover lying in the wire-mesh wastepaper basket. Could Gesar really have been reading Golovachev? Taking a closer look I realised I was mistaken – the title of the book was *Masterpieces of World Science Fiction*.

'Drink your coffee, it cleans out the brain in the morning,' Gesar muttered in the same tone of annoyance. As he drank his own coffee, he slurped. I almost thought that if I gave him a saucer and some sugar lumps he'd start drinking it that way – straight from the saucer . . .

'I need answers to some questions, boss,' I said. 'A lot of questions.'

'You'll get them,' Gesar said with a nod.

'Others are much weaker magically than ordinary people.'

Gesar frowned.

'Nonsense. An oxymoron.'

'But isn't the magical Power of human beings . . .'

Gesar raised one finger and wagged it at me.

'Stop right there. Don't confuse potential energy and kinetic energy.'

Now it was my turn to keep quiet, while Gesar strode round the office with his coffee mug, pontificating in a leisurely fashion.

'First . . . Yes, all living things are capable of producing magical Power. All living things – not only human beings. Even animals, or grass. Is there any physical basis to this Power, can it be measured with a scientific instrument? I don't know. Possibly nobody ever will know. Second . . . No one can control their own Power. It dissipates into space and is absorbed by the Twilight, part is caught by the blue moss and part is intercepted by Others. Is that clear? There are two processes – the emission of your own Power and the absorption of Power that is not yours. The first process is involuntary and intensifies as you go deeper into the Twilight. The second is also, to a greater or lesser degree, typical of everybody – both human beings and Others. A sick child asks his mother: sit with me, rub my tummy! His mother strokes his tummy, and the pain goes away. The mother wants to help her child, and she is able to direct part of her Power to produce the desired effect. So-called psychics – human beings with truncated, castrated Other abilities – are not only able to influence people who are near and dear to them in a spontaneous outpouring of heightened emotion, but can heal other people or even put a curse on them. The Power that flows from them is more structured. No longer steam, but not yet ice – it's water. Third . . . We are Others. In us the balance of emission and absorption is displaced towards absorption.'

'What?' I exclaimed.

'Did you think it was all simple, like with vampires?' Gesar asked with an ironic smile. 'Do you think Others only take, without giving anything in exchange? No, we all give back the Power that we produce. But while an ordinary person's process of absorption and emission is in dynamic equilibrium, and the balance is occasionally disrupted as a result of emotional agitation, with us it's different. We are unbalanced from the very beginning. We absorb more from the surrounding world than we give back.'

'And we can juggle the remainder,' I said. 'Right?'

'We operate with the difference in potentials,' said Gesar, wagging his finger at me again. 'It doesn't matter what your "magical temperature" is – that was the term the witches used to use. You can actually generate a great deal of Power, and the rate at which it is emitted will increase in geometrical progression. There are Others like that . . . they give more back to the common pot than people do, but they also absorb very actively. They work on that difference in potentials.'

After a moment's pause, Gesar added a self-critical comment:

'But those are only rare cases, I admit. Far more often Others are less capable of producing magical Power than ordinary people, but equally or even more capable of absorbing it. We're not just crude vampires. We're donors too.'

'But why don't they teach us that?' I asked. 'Why?'

'Because in the most basic understanding of the process, we do, after all, consume Power that comes from someone else!' Gesar barked. 'Why did you come barging in here at such an early hour? To rant and rave and lecture me! How can this be true, that we simply consume the Power produced by people! And you have actually taken it directly, pumped it out, like a genuine vampire! When it was necessary, you didn't think twice. Off you went, in shining white armour, with sadness writ large on your noble visage! And behind you little children were crying!'*

He was right, of course. Partly.

But I had already worked in the Watch for long enough to know that a partial truth is also a lie.

'Teacher . . .' I said in a low voice, and Gesar started.

I had refused to be his pupil any more on that day when I gathered power from people.

'I'm listening, pupil,' he said, looking into my eyes.

'Surely it's not a question of how much Power we consume, but how much we give back,' I said. 'Teacher, isn't the goal of the Night Watch to divide and protect?'

Gesar nodded.

'To divide and protect until such time as people's morals improve and new Others will only turn to the Light?'

Gesar nodded again.

'And all people will become Others?'

'Rubbish.' Gesar shook his head. 'Whoever told you such nonsense? Can you find that phrase anywhere in even one of the Watches' documents? In the Great Treaty?'

I closed my eyes and looked at the words that sprang into view.

'We are Others . . .'

'No, it doesn't say that anywhere,' I admitted. 'But all our training, everything we do . . . it's all set up to create precisely that impression.'

'That impression is false.'

'Yes, but the self-deception is encouraged.'

* See *The Night Watch*, Story Three

Gesar heaved a deep sigh. He looked into my eyes. And said:

'Anton, everyone needs their life to have a meaning. A higher meaning. Both people and Others. Even if that meaning is false.'

'But it's a blind alley . . .' I whispered. 'Teacher, it's a blind alley. If we defeat the Dark Ones . . .'

'Then we'll defeat Evil. Egotism, selfishness, indifference.'

'But our own existence is egotism and selfishness too!'

'What do you suggest?' Gesar enquired politely.

I didn't answer.

'Do you have any objections to raise against the operational work of the Watches? Against monitoring the Dark Ones? Against helping people, and attempting to improve the social system?'

I suddenly realised how I could strike back.

'Teacher, what exactly did you give Arina in 1931? When you met her near the racetrack?'

'A piece of Chinese silk,' Gesar replied calmly. 'She's a woman, after all, she wanted beautiful clothes . . . and those were hard times. A friend of mine sent me the silk from Manchuria, and I couldn't really think what to do with it . . . Do you blame me?'

I nodded.

'Anton, I was opposed to wide-scale experimentation on human beings from the very beginning,' Gesar said, with obvious disgust. 'It was a foolish idea that had been kicking around since the nineteenth century. No wonder the Dark Ones agreed. It didn't bring any positive changes at all. Just more blood, war, famine, repression . . .'

He stopped speaking, jerked the drawer of his desk open with a crash and took out a cigar.

'But Russia would have been a prosperous country now . . .' I began.

'Bla-bla-bla . . .' Gesar shot back. 'Not Russia, the Eurasian Union. A prosperous social-democratic state. Vying with the Asian

Union, led by China, and the Conference of English-Speaking Countries, led by the United States. Five or six local nuclear conflicts every year . . . on the territory of Third World countries. A struggle for resources, an arms race far worse than what we have now . . .'

I was shattered and crushed. Totally blown away. But I still tried to object:

'Arina said something . . . about a city on the moon . . .'

'Yes, that's right,' Gesar said with a nod. 'There would have been cities on the moon. Around the nuclear missile bases. Do you read science fiction?'

I shrugged and cast a sideways glance at the book in the waste paper basket.

'What the American writers were writing about in the 1950s – that would all have happened,' Gesar explained. 'Yes, spaceships with nuclear drives . . . all military. You see, Anton, there were three ways that communism in Russia could have gone. The first led to a fine and wonderful society. But that's contrary to human nature. The second led to degeneration and self-destruction. That's what happened. The third way was a conversion to Scandinavian-type social-democracy, followed by the subjugation of most of Europe and North Africa. Alas, one of the consequences of following this path was the division of the world into three opposed blocks and – sooner or later – global war. But before that, people would have found out that the Others existed and wiped them out or brought them under control. I'm sorry, Anton, but I decided that was too high a price to pay for cities on the moon and a hundred different types of salami by 1980.'

'But now America . . .'

'You and your America,' Gesar said with a frown. 'Wait until 2006, and then we'll talk.'

I said nothing. I didn't even ask what it was Gesar had seen in the future, in 2006, which was already so near . . .

'I can appreciate your emotional torment,' said Gesar, reaching for his lighter. 'You won't think me too cynical if I light up now?'

'Have a glass of vodka, if you like, teacher,' I snarled back.

'I don't drink vodka in the morning,' Gesar started puffing to get his cigar lit. 'I understand your torment . . . your . . . doubts very well. I also do not regard the present situation as correct. But what's going to happen if we all fall into a melancholy depression and leave our jobs? I'll tell you what! The Dark Ones will be only too delighted to take on the role of shepherds of the human flock. They won't be embarrassed. They won't believe their luck . . . So make your mind up.'

'About what?'

'You came here intending to hand in your resignation,' Gesar replied, raising his voice. 'So make up your mind if you're staying in the Watch, or you think our goals aren't Light enough for you.'

'Where there's black, even grey looks white,' I replied.

Gesar snorted. He asked in a calmer voice:

'What's happening with Arina, did she get away?'

'Yes. She took Nadiushka hostage and demanded help from me and Svetlana.'

Not a single muscle even twitched in Gesar's face.

'The old hag has her principles, Anton. She can bluff with the best, but she would never harm a child. Trust me, I know her.'

'And what if her nerve cracked?' I asked, recalling the horrors I'd been through. 'She couldn't give a damn for the Watches, or the Inquisition. She's not even afraid of Zabulon.'

'Maybe not Zabulon . . .' Gesar laughed. 'I informed the Inquisition about Arina, but I contacted the witch as well. All official and above board, by the way. Everything's minuted. And she was warned about your family. Specially warned.'

This was unexpected.

I looked into Gesar's calm face and didn't know what to say.

'Arina and I have known and respected each other for a long time,' Gesar explained.

'How did you manage that?'

'What exactly?' Gesar asked in surprise. 'Mutual respect? Well, you see . . .'

'Every time I'm convinced that you're a villainous intriguer, you prove that I'm wrong within ten minutes. We're parasites on people? It turns out that it's all for their own good. The country's in ruins? Things could have been a lot worse. My daughter's in danger? She's in about as much danger as little Sasha Pushkin with his old nanny . . .'

Gesar's expression softened.

'Anton, a long, long time ago, I was a puny, snot-nosed kid.' He looked thoughtfully straight through me! 'Yes. Puny and snot-nosed. When I quarrelled with my mentors, whose names wouldn't mean anything to you, I was convinced that they were villainous intriguers too. But they always convinced me I was wrong. The centuries have gone by, and now I have my own pupils . . .'

He blew out a cloud of smoke and stopped speaking. What point was there in going on?

Centuries? Ha! Thousands of years – long enough to learn how to counter any outbursts from his subordinates. And do it so they would arrive fuming with indignation and leave filled with love and respect for their boss. Experience is a powerful thing. Far more powerful than magic.

'I'd really like to see you when you're not wearing any mask, boss,' I said.

Gesar smiled benignly.

'Tell me one thing at least, was your son an Other?' I asked. 'Or did you make him into one? I understand all that stuff about how the secret can't be revealed, it's better for everyone to think . . .'

Gesar's fist came crashing down onto the table. And he half-stood, leaning forward over his desk. 'How long are you going to go on harping on that subject?' he barked. 'Yes, Olga and I duped the Inquisition and won the right to remoralise Timur. He would have become a Dark One, and I couldn't allow that! Clear? Go and report me to the Inquisition if you like! But drop this ridiculous nonsense!'

For a brief moment I felt afraid. But Gesar started striding round his office again and gesticulating energetically, with his feet constantly coming out of his slippers.

'It's impossible to turn a human being into an Other. Impossible! There's no way. Would you like me to tell you the truth about your wife and daughter? Olga intervened in Svetlana's destiny. She used the second half of the Chalk of Destiny for her. But not even the Chalk of Destiny could have transformed your unborn daughter into an Other if she wasn't going to have been born an Other anyway. We only made her even more powerful, gave her absolute power.'

'I know,' I said with a nod.

'How?' Gesar asked, astonished.

'Arina gave me a hint.'

'She's a smart one,' Gesar said. He lowered his voice again. 'That's it! Now you know everything there is to know on the subject. A human being cannot become an Other. By employing the most powerful artefacts it is possible, in the early stages, or in advance, to make an Other more or less powerful, or incline him to the Light or the Dark . . . Within very narrow limits, Anton! If the boy Egor had not been neutral initially, we wouldn't have been able to erase his initiation to the Dark. If your daughter had not been meant to be born a Great Enchantress, we could never have made her into the Greatest of the Great. Before the vessel can be filled with Light or Dark, the vessel has to exist. It depends on us what will be poured into it, but we're not capable of creating the vessel itself. We can only work with the little things, the very tiniest things. And you think it's possible to turn a human being into an Other!'

'Boris Ignatievich,' I began, not knowing myself why I used his Russian name, 'forgive me if I'm talking nonsense. But I can't understand how you could have failed to find Timur earlier. He was your son and Olga's! Wouldn't you have been able to sense him? Even from a distance?'

At this point Gesar suddenly wilted. A strange expression, simultaneously guiltly and confused, appeared on his face.

'Anton, I may be an old plotter . . .' He paused. 'But do you really think I would allow my own son to grow up in a state orphanage, in poverty and suffering? Do you think I don't long for a little warmth and affection? To feel human? To play with my baby, to go to a football match with my little boy, to teach my teenager how to shave, to accept my young man into the Watch? Tell me one reason why I would have allowed my son to live and grow old so far away from me. Am I a bad father, a heartless old scoundrel? Maybe so. But then why did I decide to make him into an Other? Why would I want all that hassle?'

'But why didn't you find him sooner?' I exclaimed.

'Because when he was born he was a perfectly ordinary child. Not a trace of any Other potential.'

'It happens,' I said doubtfully.

Gesar nodded.

'You have doubts? Even I have doubts . . . I ought to have been able to sense even rudimentary traces of Power in Timur. But there weren't any . . .'

He spread his arms hopelessly. Then he sat down and muttered:

'So don't go attributing any imaginary miracles to me. I can't make Others out of ordinary people.' He paused, then suddenly added in a passionate voice: 'But you're right. I ought to have sensed him sooner. Okay, sometimes we only realise a stranger is an Other when he's already old. But my own son? The little boy I dandled in my arms, the boy I dreamed of seeing as an Other? I don't know. The initial signs must have been too weak . . . or else I must have gone crazy . . .'

'There is another possibility,' I said uncertainly.

Gesar looked at me suspiciously and shrugged.

'There's always more than one. What do you mean?'

'Someone knows how to transform ordinary people into Others. That someone found Timur and turned him into a potential Other. And then you sensed him . . .'

'Olga sensed him,' Gesar growled.

'All right, Olga sensed him. And you swung into action. You thought you were duping the Inquisition and the Dark Ones. But it was you being duped.'

Gesar snorted.

'Just try to accept, for one moment, that a human being can be turned into an Other!' I pleaded with him.

'But why was it done?' Gesar asked. 'I'm willing to believe the whole thing, but just explain why. To set Olga and me up for a fall? It doesn't look like it. Everything went without a hitch.'

'I don't know,' I admitted. As I stood up, I added vindictively: 'But if I were you I wouldn't let my guard down, boss. You're used to your own plots being the subtlest. But there's always more than one possibility.'

'Smart ass . . .' Gesar said, frowning. 'You get on back to Sveta . . . Hang on.'

He put his hand into the pocket of his dressing-gown and took out his mobile phone. It wasn't ringing, just vibrating nervously.

'Just a moment . . .' Gesar said, with a nod to me. And then he spoke into the phone, in a different voice: 'Yes!'

I tactfully moved away towards the cupboards and started studying the magical trinkets. Okay, so little models of monsters might serve to summon up the real thing. But what did he need a Tatar whip for? Something like Shahab's Lash?

'We'll be right there,' Gesar said curtly. His phone clicked shut. 'Anton!'

When I turned back to face Gesar, he was just finishing getting changed: as he ran his hands over his body, the dressing-gown and pyjamas changed their colour and texture and were transformed into a formal grey suit. With a final flourish of his hand, Gesar put a grey tie round his neck. Already tied in a neat Windsor knot. None of this was an illusion – Gesar really had created a suit out of his pyjamas.

'Anton, we have to take a little journey . . . to the wicked witch's house.'

'Have they caught her?' I asked, trying to make sense of my own feelings. I walked over to Gesar.

'No, worse than that. Yesterday evening while they were searching Arina's house they came across a secret hiding place.' Gesar waved his hand and a portal appeared, floating in the air. He added vaguely: 'There's already . . . quite a crowd there. Shall we go?'

'What's in the hiding place?' I exclaimed.

But Gesar was already pushing me into the glowing white oval.

'Brace yourself' were the final words of advice I heard from behind me.

The journey through a portal takes a certain amount of time – seconds, minutes, sometimes even hours. It's not the distance that matters, but the precision of focus. I didn't know who had put up the portal in Arina's house, and I didn't know how long I would be left hanging there in the milky-white void.

A secret hiding place in Arina's house. So what? All the Others created hiding places for magical objects in their apartments.

What could have startled Gesar like that? The boss had definitely seemed startled to me – his face had turned far too stony, too calm and composed.

I started imagining all sorts of horrors, like children's bodies in the basement. That would be a good reason for Gesar to panic, especially after being so certain that Arina would never touch Nadiushka.

No, that was impossible . . .

With that thought I tumbled out of the portal – straight into the middle of the small room in Arina's house.

It was really crowded in there.

'Move aside!' Kostya shouted and grabbed me by the arm. I barely had time to take a step before Gesar emerged from the portal.

'Greetings, Great One!' Zabulon said in a surprisingly polite voice, with no trace of his usual sarcasm.

I gazed around. Six Inquisitors I didn't know – wearing cloaks, with the hoods pulled forward over their faces, everything right and proper. Edgar, Zabulon and Kostya – nothing unexpected there. Svetlana! I looked at her fearfully, but she immediately shook her head reassuringly. That meant Nadya was okay.

'Who is conducting the investigation?' Gesar asked.

'A triumvirate,' Edgar replied briskly. 'Myself from the Inquisition, Zabulon from the Day Watch and . . .' He looked at Svetlana.

'I'll take it from here,' Gesar said with a nod. 'Thank you, Svetlana. I'm most grateful.'

I didn't need any explanations. Whatever had happened here, Svetlana had been the first Light One to appear – and she had begun to act on behalf of the Night Watch.

You could say she'd gone back to work.

'Shall I put you in the picture?' Edgar asked.

Gesar nodded.

'And Gorodetsky?' Edgar enquired.

'He's with me.'

'That's your right.' Edgar nodded to me. 'Well then, we have a quite exceptional occurrence here . . .'

Why was he telling us by speaking words?

I tried to ask Svetlana, reaching out to her with my mind . . .

And ran into a blank wall.

The Inquisition had blocked off the whole area. That was why they'd called Gesar on his mobile, and not contacted him telepathically. Whatever it was that had happened here, it had to be kept secret.

What Edgar said next confirmed what I was thinking.

'Since this event must be kept an absolute secret,' he said, 'I request everyone present to lower their defences and prepare to receive the seal of the Avenging Fire.'

I glanced sideways at Gesar – he was already unbuttoning his shirt. Zabulon, Svetlana, Kostya, even Edgar himself – they were all disrobing.

I pulled up my polo-neck sweater and resigned myself to what was to follow. The Avenging Fire . . .

'We here present swear never to divulge to anyone, at any time or in any place, what is revealed to us in the course of the investigation into this event!' said Edgar. 'I do so swear!'

'I do so swear!' Svetlana said and took hold of my hand.

'I do so swear,' I whispered.

'I do so swear . . . so swear . . . so swear . . .' said voices on every side.

'And if I should violate this oath of secrecy, may the hand of the Avenging Fire destroy me!' Edgar concluded.

There was a blindingly brilliant red flash from his fingers. A flaming imprint of his hand seemed to hover in the air, then it divided into twelve and the blazing palms started drifting towards us, very slowly. And that slow, deliberate movement was the most frightening thing of all.

The first one touched by the hand of the Avenging Fire was Edgar himself. The Inquisitor's face contorted, and several similar crimson handprints showed up for a moment on his skin.

Apparently it was painful . . .

Gesar and Zabulon bore the touch stoically and, unless my eyes deceived me, the numerous signs on their bodies were already woven into a dense pattern.

One of the Inquisitors squealed.

Apparently it was very painful . . .

The spell touched me, and I realised I had been wrong. It wasn't very painful. It was absolutely unbearable! It felt like I was being branded with a red-hot steel beam – and not just branded, but burned right through my body.

When the bloody mist cleared from in front of my eyes, I was surprised to see that I was still standing – unlike two of the Inquisitors.

'And they say giving birth is painful,' Svetlana said quietly as she buttoned up her blouse. 'Ha . . .'

'Allow me to remind you that if the seal is activated, it will be a lot more painful . . .' Edgar murmured. The Inquisitor had tears in his eyes. 'It's for the common good.'

'Cut the idle chatter!' Zabulon interrupted him. 'Since you're in charge now, try to behave appropriately.'

That was right, where was Witiezslav?

Had he flown back to Prague after all?

'Please follow me,' said Edgar. Still wincing, he walked towards the wall.

Hiding places can be set up in various ways. From the crudest

– the magical camouflage of a safe in a wall – up to a secure vault surrounded by powerful spells in the Twilight.

This hiding place was rather ingenious. For an instant, when Edgar walked into the wall, a narrow slit that looked too small for a man appeared in front of him. I immediately recalled this cunning and complicated method, a combination of magical illusion and the magic of displacement. Little sections of space – narrow strips along the wall – are gathered from within a contained space and magically combined into a single 'box-room'. It's a tricky business and rather dangerous, but Edgar walked into the secret space quite calmly.

'We won't all fit in,' Gesar muttered and squinted at the Inquisitors. 'You've already been in there, I believe? Wait here.'

Concerned that I might be stopped too, I stepped forward – and the wall obligingly parted in front of me. The defensive spells had already been broken.

The box-room turned out not to be so tiny after all. It even had a window, made in the same way – from strips 'cut' out of the other windows. The view through the window had a truly phantasmagorical appearance: a strip of forest, half a tree, a patch of sky, all jumbled up together in total disorder.

But there was something else in the box-room far more worthy of attention.

A good suit of close-textured grey cloth, a dandyish shirt – white silk with lace at the collar and the cuffs – an elegant tie in silver-grey with red flecks, and a pair of magnificent black leather shoes with white socks hanging out of them. All these things were lying on the floor in the middle of the box-room. I was sure that inside the suit there had to be silk underwear with hand-embroidered monograms.

But I didn't really feel any desire to root about amongst the clothes of Higher Vampire Witiezslav. The homogeneous grey dust that filled the suit and had spilled out around it was all that remained of the inspector from the European Office of the Inquisition.

Svetlana walked through into the box-room behind me, gasped and grabbed hold of my hand. Gesar groaned, Zabulon sighed – it even sounded sincere.

When Kostya came in last, he didn't make a sound. He just stood there as if in a trance, gazing at the pitiful remains of his fellow vampire.

'As you will, of course, understand,' Edgar began quietly, 'what has happened is appalling enough in itself. A Higher Vampire has been killed, quickly and with no signs of a struggle. I would assume that this is beyond even the powers of the respected Higher Magicians here present.'

'The Higher Magicians here present are not stupid enough to attack an agent of the Inquisition,' Gesar commented in a grave voice. 'However, if the Inquisition insists on verification . . .'

Edgar shook his head:

'No. I called you here precisely because I do not suspect you. I think it makes sense to ask your advice before I inform the European Office. After all, this is the territory of the Moscow Watches.'

Zabulon squatted down by the remains, scooped up a little of the dust in his hand, sniffed it and – I think – even touched his tongue to it. He stood up with a sigh and muttered:

'Witiezslav . . . I can't imagine who could have destroyed him. I would . . . I would have thought twice, no, three times, before engaging him in combat. And you, colleague?'

He looked at Gesar. Gesar took his time answering, surveying the dust with the enthusiasm of a young naturalist.

'Gesar?' Zabulon asked again.

'Yes, yes . . .' Gesar nodded. 'I could have done it. We actually had . . . certain disagreements. But to do it so swiftly . . . and so neatly . . .' Gesar shrugged and spread his hands. 'No, I couldn't have managed that. Alas. It even makes me feel rather envious.'

'The seal,' I reminded him cautiously. 'At temporary registration they apply a seal to vampires . . .'

Edgar looked at me as if I'd said something really stupid:

'But not to agents of the Inquisition.'

'And not to Higher Vampires!' Kostya added defiantly. 'The seal is only applied to petty riff-raff who can't control themselves, novice vampires and werewolves.'

'In fact, I've been meaning for a long time to raise the matter of removing these discriminatory restrictions,' Zabulon put in. 'The seal should not be applied to vampires and werewolves from the second grade upwards, or, better still, from the third . . .'

'Why don't we do away with mutual registration at the place of residence as well?' Gesar asked sarcastically.

'Stop arguing!' Edgar said with an unexpected note of authority in his voice. 'Gorodetsky's ignorance is no excuse for holding a debate! And apart from that, the termination of the vampire Witiezslav's existence is not the most terrible thing about all this.'

'What could be more terrible than an Other who kills Higher Others so effortlessly?' asked Zabulon.

'A book,' Edgar replied laconically. 'The *Fuaran*. The reason he was killed.'

CHAPTER 2

ZABULON GRINNED. HE clearly didn't believe a single word of what Edgar had just said.

Gesar seemed to be genuinely furious. It was hardly surprising. First I'd nettled him about the *Fuaran*, and now an Inquisitor was doing the same.

'My esteemed . . . European Inspector . . .' After a brief pause Gesar launched into a speech that was only moderately sarcastic. 'I am no less fascinated by mythology than you are. Among witches, stories about the *Fuaran* are very widespread, but we know perfectly well that they are no more than an attempt to add lustre to the reputation of their own . . . caste. There are exactly the same kind of folktales in the culture of werewolves, vampires and various kinds of Others who are fated to play a subordinate role in society. But we have a real problem here, and wandering off into the thickets of ancient superstition . . .'

Edgar interrupted him:

'I understand your point of view, Gesar. But the problem is that two hours ago Witiezslav called me on his mobile. While he was checking Arina's things, he stumbled across the secret room. Anyway . . . Witiezslav was very excited. He said the *Fuaran* was lying in the secret room, that it was genuine. I . . . must confess that I was sceptical. Witiezslav was an excitable character.'

Gesar shook his head doubtfully.

'I didn't come straight away,' Edgar went on. 'Especially since Witiezslav told me he was summoning Inquisition operatives from the security cordon.'

'Was he afraid of something?' Zabulon asked curtly.

'Witiezslav? I don't think so, not anything specific. It's standard procedure when an artefact of such great power is discovered. I completed my round of the security posts and was actually talking to Konstantin when our operatives reported that they had surrounded the house but could not sense Witiezslav's presence. I ordered them to enter – and they reported that there was no one inside. At that point I . . .' Edgar hesitated '. . . felt rather puzzled. Why would Witiezslav hide from his colleagues? I came as quickly as I could, with Kostya. It took us about forty minutes – we didn't want to go through the Twilight because we thought we might need all our Power when we got here – and our agents were unable to put up a reliable portal, there are too many magical artefacts here . . .'

'I see,' said Gesar. 'Go on.'

'There was a cordon round the house and two agents were on guard inside. We entered the secret room together and discovered Witiezslav's remains.'

'How long was Witiezslav left without protection?' Gesar asked, still sounding sceptical, but with a new note of interest in his voice.

'About an hour.'

'And for another forty minutes Inquisitors guarded his remains? There are six of them, third- and fourth-grade.' Gesar frowned. 'A powerful magician could have got through.'

'Unlikely,' said Edgar, shaking his head. 'Yes, they are third- and fourth-grade; Roman is the only one who's just about second-grade, but they're equipped with our guard amulets. Not even a Great One could have got through.'

'Then the killer must have been here before they arrived?'

'Most probably,' Edgar confirmed.

'A magician powerful enough to kill a Higher Vampire swiftly . . .' Gesar shook his head. 'I can only think of one candidate.'

'The witch,' Zabulon muttered. 'If she really did have the *Fuaran*, she might have come back for it.'

'First she abandoned it, and then came back?' Svetlana exclaimed. I realised she was trying to defend Arina. 'That's not logical!'

'Anton and I pursued her,' Edgar responded ingenuously. 'She fled in a panic. Clearly she didn't make a run for it immediately, as we assumed, but hid somewhere nearby. When Witiezslav found the book she sensed it and became frantic.'

Gesar gave Svetlana and me a dark look, but said nothing.

'Perhaps Witiezslav died without any help?' Svetlana persisted. 'He found the book, tried to work some spell in it . . . and was killed. There have been such cases.'

'Aha,' Zabulon said acidly, 'and in the meantime the book grew legs and ran away.'

'I wouldn't even exclude that possibility,' said Gesar, standing up for Svetlana. 'It could have sprouted legs, and it could have run away.'

Silence fell, and in the silence Zabulon's scoffing laugh sounded especially loud.

'Well, well! So we believe in the *Fuaran*?'

'I believe that someone killed a Higher Vampire with ease,' said Gesar. 'And that someone is not frightened of the Watches or the Inquisition. That very fact demands speedy and efficient investigation. Don't you agree, colleague?'

Zabulon nodded reluctantly.

'If we accept even for one moment that the *Fuaran* really was here . . .' Gesar shook his head. 'If all the rumours about this book are true . . .'

Zabulon nodded again.

Both Great Magicians froze, looking at each other. Either they were simply trying to stare each other down or, despite all the defences around them, they were managing somehow to conduct a magical conversation.

I walked over to the vampire's remains and squatted down.

A disagreeable sort. Disagreeable, even for a vampire.

But still one of us.

An Other.

Behind my back Edgar was burbling something about the need to bring in fresh reinforcements, and how catching Arina had now become a matter of vital importance. The witch was out of luck. An old violation of the Treaty, even on a grand scale, was one thing. Killing an Inquisitor was something else altogether.

All the facts stacked up against her. Who else was powerful enough to take out a Higher Vampire?

But somehow I didn't believe Arina was guilty . . .

For some reason, I didn't find Witiezslav's remains disgusting at all. Obviously there was nothing human left in him, not even a trace of bone. Grey dust, like damp cigarette ash, maintaining its form, but entirely homogeneous in structure. I touched something that looked a bit like a clenched fist, and was not at all surprised when the dust crumbled away, revealing a crumpled piece of paper.

'A note,' I said.

A deathly silence fell. Since there were no objections, I picked up the piece of paper, straightened it out and read it. And only then looked at the magicians.

They all looked so tense, it was as if they were expecting to hear me say: 'Witiezslav wrote down the name of his killer before he died . . . it was you!'

'Witiezslav didn't write this,' I said. 'It's Arina's writing, she wrote an explanatory note . . .'

'Read it out,' Edgar ordered.

'Dear Inquisitors,' I read in a loud voice. 'If you are reading this, it means that you are still pursuing issues from the past. I suggest a peaceful settlement. You get the book you have been looking for. I get a pardon.'

'So you were looking for it then?' Gesar asked in a very calm voice.

'The Inquisition tries to locate all artefacts,' Edgar replied calmly. 'Including those considered mythological.'

'Would she have got her pardon?' Svetlana asked unexpectedly.

Edgar looked at her in annoyance, but he answered:

'If the *Fuaran* had been lying here? It's not my decision to make, but the answer's probably yes. If it's the genuine *Fuaran*.'

'I'm inclined to think now that the book is the genuine article . . .' Gesar said in a quiet voice. 'Edgar, I'd like to consult with my colleagues.'

Edgar merely shrugged. The Inquisitor probably wasn't too keen on being left alone with Zabulon and Kostya, but his expression remained unchanged.

Svetlana and I followed Gesar.

The Inquisitors greeted us with suspicious glances, as if they thought we'd killed all the Dark Ones in the secret room. But it didn't bother Gesar.

'We're withdrawing for a conference,' he said casually, heading for the door. The Inquisitors glanced at each other, but they didn't argue – one of them just walked towards the secret room. But we were already out of the witch's house.

It seemed as if morning hadn't arrived yet, here in the dense heart of the forest. All around there was a mysterious semi-darkness, like the very first hour of dawn. I glanced up in surprise, and saw that the sky really was unnaturally grey: it was like looking through a pair of dark glasses. Apparently that was the manifestation in our world of the magical defences erected by the Inquisitors.

'Everything's falling apart . . .' Gesar muttered. 'Things are really bad . . .'

His gaze shifted rapidly from me to Svetlana and back. As if he couldn't decide which of us he needed.

'Was the *Fuaran* really there?' Svetlana asked.

'It seems so. Evidently the book exists.' Gesar pulled a wry face. 'This is bad, really bad . . .'

'We'll have to find the witch,' said Svetlana. 'If you want . . .'

Gesar shook his head. 'No, I don't want. Arina has to get away.'

'I understand,' I said, taking Svetlana by the hand. 'If they catch Arina, she might confess who that Light One was . . .'

'Arina doesn't know who that Light One was,' said Gesar, interrupting me. 'That Light One came to her in a mask. She can suspect and surmise, she might even be certain – but she doesn't have a single fact. It's something else that's worrying me . . .'

That was when I understood.

'The *Fuaran*?'

'Yes. That's why I ask you . . .'

Before he could finish, I hurriedly put in:

'We don't know where Arina is. Do we, Sveta?'

Svetlana frowned, but she shook her head in agreement.

'Thank you,' said Gesar. 'That's the first thing. Now for the second. We have to find the *Fuaran*. At any cost. They'll probably put a search party together. I want Anton to be our representative.'

'I'm more powerful,' Svetlana said quietly.

'That makes no difference at all.' Gesar shook his head. 'Not a scrap. I'll be needing you here, Svetlana.'

'What for?' she asked cautiously.

Gesar hesitated for a second. Then he said:

'To initiate Nadya if we should need to.'

'You're out of your mind,' Svetlana said in an icy voice. 'There's no way she can become an Other at her age and with her Power!'

'It might turn out that we have no other choice,' Gesar muttered. 'Svetlana, it's up to you. All I ask is that you stay with the child.'

'Don't worry about that,' Svetlana snapped. 'I won't take my eyes off her.'

'That's fine, then.' Gesar smiled and walked towards the door. 'Do come and join us, our Council at Fili is about to start.'

The moment the door closed behind him, Svetlana swung round to face me and demanded:

'Do you understand any of this?'

I nodded, and replied:

'Gesar was unable to find his own son. He really was just an ordinary human being. He only became an Other just recently.'

'Arina?'

'Looks like it. She emerged from hibernation and took a look around. Found out who was at the top . . .'

'And used the *Fuaran* to give Gesar a little secret present? She turned his son into an Other?' Svetlana shook her head. 'It makes no sense, why would she do that? They're not that close, surely?'

'But now Gesar will do everything possible to make sure they don't find Arina. She took out an insurance policy'

Svetlana screwed up her eyes and nodded.

'But listen, what about the Day Watch . . .'

'How do we know what she did for Zabulon?' I shrugged. 'Somehow I get the feeling the Day Watch won't go to any great lengths in looking for the witch either.'

'What a cunning old hag!' Svetlana said, without malice. 'I was wrong to think so little of witches. Did you understand that about Nadya?'

'No.'

What Gesar had said made simply no sense. Sometimes Other children were initiated at the age of five or six, but never any earlier than that. A child who has acquired the abilities of an Other but is unable to control them properly is a walking bomb. Especially an Other as powerful as Nadiushka. Even Gesar himself would be unable to stop our little girl if she got overexcited and started using her Power.

No, I had no idea what Gesar had meant.

'I'll pull his legs off and put them where his arms used to be,' Svetlana promised in a perfectly calm voice, 'if he even hints that we have to initiate Nadya. All right, shall we go?'

We linked arms – really wanting to feel close to each other at that moment – and went back into the house.

The Inquisitors whom chance had chosen to involve in the secret had been put back in the security cordon round the house, and the other six of us were sitting round the table.

Gesar was drinking tea that he'd made himself, by taking the witch's brew and adding herbs from her abundant reserves. I took a cup too. The tea smelled of mint and juniper, it was bitter and spicy, but bracing. No one else was tempted to drink it – Svetlana politely took a sip and put her cup down.

The note was lying on the table.

'Twenty-two or twenty-three hours ago,' said Zabulon, looking at the piece of paper. 'She wrote the note before your visit, Inquisitor.'

Edgar nodded and added reluctantly:

'Possibly . . . or just possibly, during our visit. It was hard for us, pursuing her in the depths of the Twilight – she would have had quite enough time to gather her wits and write a note.'

'Then we have no grounds for suspecting the witch,' Zabulon

muttered. 'She left the book in order to buy off her pursuers. She had no reason to come back for it and kill the Inquisitor.'

'Agreed,' Gesar said after a pause.

'A most astonishing unity of thought between Dark Ones and Light Ones,' said Edgar. 'You're frightening me, gentlemen.'

'This is no time for disagreements,' Zabulon replied. 'We have to find the killer and the book.'

They both definitely had their own reasons for protecting Arina.

'Good.' Edgar nodded. 'Let's go back to the beginning. Witiezslav calls me and tells me about the *Fuaran*. Nobody hears the conversation.'

'All mobile phone calls are monitored and recorded . . .' I put in.

'What are you suggesting, Anton?' Edgar looked at me ironically. 'That the human secret services are conducting a campaign against the Others? And when they heard about the book, they sent an agent here, and he killed a Higher Vampire?'

'Anton might not be that far off the mark,' Gesar said in my defence. 'You know, Edgar, every year we have to suppress human activity directed at exposing us. And you know about the special departments in the secret services . . .'

'We have people in them,' Edgar retorted. 'But even if we assume that they're searching for Others again, and that there's been a leak, Witiezslav's death is still a mystery. Not even James Bond could have crept up on him without being noticed.'

'Who's James Bond?' Zabulon enquired.

'That's another myth,' Gesar laughed. 'Contemporary mythology. Gentlemen, let us not waste time in idle discussion. The situation is perfectly clear. Witiezslav was killed by an Other. A powerful Other. And most likely someone he trusted.'

'He didn't trust anyone, not even me,' muttered Edgar. 'Suspicion is in a vampire's blood . . . pardon the pun.'

Nobody smiled. Kostya gave Edgar a moody glance, but said nothing.

'Are you suggesting we should check the memories of everyone here?' Gesar asked politely.

'Would you agree?' Edgar responded eagerly.

'No,' Gesar snapped. 'I appreciate the work done by the Inquisition, but there are limits.'

'Then we're stuck.' Edgar shrugged. 'Gentlemen, if you are not willing to co-operate . . .'

Svetlana cleared her throat delicately and asked:

'May I speak?'

'Yes, yes, of course.' Edgar nodded.

'I think we're on the wrong track,' said Svetlana. 'You have decided that we need to find the killer, and then we'll find the book. That's right, only we don't know who the killer is. Why don't we try to find the *Fuaran*? And then locate the killer through the book?'

'And how are you going to look for the book, Light One?' Zabulon asked ironically. 'Send for this James Bond?'

Svetlana reached out her hand and cautiously touched Arina's note.

'As I understand it, the witch put this note on the book. Perhaps even between its pages. The two things were in contact for some period of time, and the book is a very powerful magical object. If we summon up a simulacrum . . . the way that novice magicians are taught to do . . .'

She faltered under the gaze of the Higher Magicians and began to lose her thread. But both Zabulon and Gesar were looking at her encouragingly.

'Yes, there is magic like that,' Gesar murmured. 'Of course, I remember . . . they stole my horse once, and I was left with just the bridle . . .'

He stopped and shot a glance at Zabulon, then suggested in a friendly tone of voice:

'After you, Dark One. You create the simulacrum!'

'I'd prefer you to do it,' Zabulon replied with equal politeness. 'There'll be no unnecessary suspicion of deception.'

There was something wrong here. But what?

'Well then, as the old saying goes: 'First lash to the informer'!' Gesar responded cheerfully. Svetlana, your idea is accepted. Go ahead.'

Svetlana looked at Gesar in embarrassment:

'Boris Ignatievich . . . I'm sorry, these are such simple magical actions . . . It's such a long time since I performed them. Perhaps we ought to ask one of the junior magicians?'

So that was it . . . The Great Ones couldn't manage the basic elements of magic that were taught to beginners. They were confused and embarrassed – like academics who have been asked to multiply figures in a long column and write out letters in neat lines.

'Allow me,' I said. Without waiting for an answer, I reached out one hand towards the note. I half-closed my eyelids so that the shadow fell on my eyes and looked at the grey piece of paper through the Twilight. I imagined the book – a thick volume bound in human skin, the journal of a witch cursed by humans and Others alike . . .

Gradually the image began taking shape. The book was almost exactly as I had visualised it, except that the corners of the binding were protected by triangles of metal. Evidently a later addition – one of the *Fuarans*' owners had taken care to preserve it.

'So that's what it's like,' Gesar said with lively interest. 'Well, there it is . . .'

The magicians rose from their seats and examined the image of the book – which only Others could see. The note was quivering gently on the table, as if there was a draught in the room.

'Can we open it?' asked Kostya.

'No, it's only an image, it doesn't contain the essential nature of the object . . .' Gesar said. 'Go on, Anton. Stabilise it . . . and invent some kind of tracking mechanism.'

It was hard enough for me to stabilise the image of the book. And I was definitely not prepared to come up with a tracking mechanism. Eventually I settled on a grotesque simulacrum of a compass – it was huge, the size of a dinner plate, with a pointer swinging on a pin. One end of the pointer glowed more brightly – the end that was supposed to point towards the *Fuaran*.

'Add more energy,' Gesar said. 'Keep it working for at least a week . . . you never know.'

I added more energy.

And then, completely exhausted, but pleased with myself, I relaxed.

We looked at the compass floating in the Twilight. The pointer was pointing directly at Zabulon.

'Is this a joke, Gorodetsky?' he enquired, getting up and moving to one side.

The pointer didn't waver.

'Good,' Gesar said, sounding pleased. 'Edgar, get your agents back in here.'

Edgar walked to the door and called, then returned to the table.

One by one the Inquisitors came in.

The pointer didn't move. It still pointed at empty space.

'*Quod erat demonstrandum* – that's what we needed to prove,' Edgar said, relieved. 'Nobody here is involved in the theft of the book.'

'It's trembling,' said Zabulon, looking closely at the compass. 'The pointer's trembling. And since we didn't observe any legs on the book . . .'

He laughed a wicked, devilish laugh, clapped Edgar on the shoulder and asked.

'Well then, senior comrade? Do you require any assistance with the arrest?'

Edgar was also watching the compass carefully. Then he asked:

'Anton, how accurate is the device?'

'Not very, I'm afraid,' I admitted. 'The trace left by the book was very weak.'

'How accurate?' Edgar repeated.

'To within about a hundred metres,' I suggested. 'Maybe fifty. If I'm right, when the target's close, the pointer will start to swing about chaotically. I'm sorry.'

'Don't let it bother you, Anton, you did everything right,' Gesar said. 'No one could have done better with such a weak trace to work on. A hundred metres it is . . . can you determine the distance to the target?'

'Roughly, from how brightly the pointer glows . . . About a hundred and ten, a hundred and twenty kilometres.'

Gesar frowned.

'The book's already in Moscow. We're wasting time, gentlemen. Edgar!'

The Inquisitor put one hand in his pocket and took out a small yellowish-white sphere. It looked like a pool ball, only a little smaller, and it had incomprehensible pictograms engraved haphazardly on its surface. Edgar squeezed the sphere tightly in his hand and concentrated.

A moment later I felt something changing. As if there had been a shroud hanging in the air – invisible to the eye, but palpable nonetheless – and now it was disappearing, being sucked into the small sphere of ivory . . .

'I didn't know the Inquisition still had Minoan spheres,' said Gesar.

'No comment,' said Edgar. He smiled, pleased at the effect he had produced. 'That's it, the barrier has been removed. Put up a portal, Great Ones!'

Of course. A direct portal, without any reference points in place at 'the other end' was a riddle for Great Ones to solve. Edgar either couldn't do it, or he was saving his strength . . .

Gesar squinted at Zabulon and asked:

'Do you trust me to do it again?'

Zabulon made a pass with his hand without speaking – and a gap opened up in mid-air, oozing darkness. Zabulon stepped into it first, then Gesar, gesturing for us to follow. I picked up Arina's precious note, together with the invisible magical compass – and stepped in after Svetlana.

Despite the difference in external appearances, inside the portal was exactly the same. Milky-white mist, a sensation of rapid movement, total loss of any sense of time. I tried to concentrate – soon we would find ourselves near the criminal who had killed a Higher Vampire. Of course, we had Gesar and Zabulon leading us; Svetlana was just as powerful, if less experienced; Kostya was young, but he was still a Higher Vampire; and there was Edgar and his team with their pockets full of Inquisitors' artefacts. Even so, the fight could turn out to be deadly dangerous.

But a moment later I realised there wasn't going to be any fight.

At least, not straight away.

We were standing on a platform at Moscow's Kazan railway station. There was no one very close to us – people sense when a portal is opening nearby and spontaneously move out of the way. But we were surrounded by the kind of crush that even in Moscow you can only find at a railway station in summer. People walking to their suburban trains, people getting off trains and carting baggage along, people smoking in front of the mechanical noticeboards, waiting for their train to be announced, people drinking beer and lemonade, eating those monstrous railway station pies and bread wraps with suspicious fillings. There were probably at least two or three thousand people within a hundred-metre radius of us.

I looked at the spectral compass – the pointer was spinning lazily.

'We need Cinderella here,' said Zabulon, gazing around. 'We have to find a poppy seed in a sack of millet.'

One by one the Inquisitors appeared beside us. The expression of readiness for fierce battle on Edgar's face was suddenly replaced by confusion.

'He's trying to hide,' said Zabulon. 'Excellent, excellent . . .'

But he didn't look too happy either.

An agitated woman pushed a trolley full of striped canvas bags up to our group. Her red, sweating face was set in an expression of firm determination that could only be mustered by a Russian woman who works as a 'shuttle trader' importing goods by train to feed her idle, useless husband and three or four children.

'Haven't announced the Ulyanovsk train yet, have they?' she asked.

Svetlana closed her eyes for a moment and replied:

'It will arrive at platform one in six minutes and leave with a delay of three minutes.'

'Thank you,' the woman said, not surprised in the least by such a precise answer. She set off for platform one.

'That's all very nice, Svetlana,' Gesar muttered. 'But what suggestions do you have concerning the search for the book?'

Svetlana just shrugged.

The café was as cosy and clean as a railway station café could be. Maybe because it was in such a strange place – in the basement, beside the baggage rooms. The countless station bums obviously didn't show their faces here – the owners had cured them of that habit. There was a middle-aged Russian woman standing behind the counter, and the food was carried out from the kitchen by taciturn, polite Caucasian men.

A strange place.

I took two glasses of dry wine from a three-litre box for Svetlana and myself. It was surprisingly cheap and also – to my great amazement – pretty good. I went back to the table where we were sitting.

'It's still here,' said Svetlana, nodding at Arina's note. The pointer in the compass was spinning idly.

'Maybe the book's hidden in the baggage rooms?' I suggested.

Svetlana took a sip of her wine and nodded, either in agreement with my suggestion or in approval of the Krasnodar Merlot.

'Is something bothering you?' I asked cautiously.

'Why the station?' Svetlana asked in return.

'To make a getaway. To hide. The thief must have realised he'd be followed.'

'The airport. A plane. Any plane,' Svetlana replied laconically, taking small sips of her wine.

I shrugged.

It really was strange. Once he had the *Fuaran*, the renegade Other, whoever he might be, either could have tried either to hide or make a run for it. He'd chosen the second option. But why a train? A train as a means of escape – in the twenty-first century?

'Maybe he's afraid of flying?' Svetlana suggested.

I just snorted. Of course, even an Other didn't have much chance of surviving a plane crash. But even the very weakest Other was capable of examining the lines of probability for the next three or four hours and figuring out if there was any danger of a plane crashing.

And Witiezslav's killer was anything but weak.

'He needs to get somewhere the planes don't go,' I suggested.

'But he could at least have flown out of Moscow to shake off the pursuit.'

'No,' I said, enjoying the feeling of putting Svetlana right. 'That wouldn't be any good. We would have identified the thief's approximate location, worked out which plane he'd taken, questioned the passengers, taken information from the surveillance cameras at the airport and discovered his identity. Then Gesar or Zabulon would have opened a portal . . . they could open one to any place he happened to go. And we'd all be right back where we are now. Except that we'd know what our enemy looks like.'

Svetlana nodded. She looked at her watch and shook her head, then closed her eyes for an instant, and smiled calmly.

That meant Nadiushka was okay.

'Why does he have to try to get away at all?' Svetlana said thoughtfully. 'I doubt if the ritual described in the *Fuaran* requires much time. The witch turned a lot of her servants into Others when she was attacked. It would be much easier for the killer to use the book and become a Great One . . . the Greatest of all. And then either take us on or destroy the *Fuaran* and hide. If he becomes more powerful than us, we simply won't be able to unmask him.'

'Perhaps he has already become more powerful,' I remarked. 'Since Gesar raised the subject of initiating Nadya . . .'

Svetlana nodded in agreement:

'Not a very pleasant prospect. What if Edgar himself used the *Fuaran*? And now he's acting out a comedy, just pretending to search. He didn't get along too well with Witiezslav, and he's crafty . . . if he wanted to become the most powerful Other in the world . . .'

'But then what would he need the book for?' I exclaimed. 'He could just have left it where it was. We wouldn't even have known that Witiezslav had been killed. We'd have put it all down to protective spells that the vampire failed to notice.'

'That makes sense,' Svetlana agreed. 'I think you're right, the killer isn't after power. Or not only power. He wants the book as well.'

I suddenly remembered Semyon:

'There's someone the killer wants to make into an Other! He realised he wouldn't be allowed to use the book. That's why he killed Witiezslav . . . it doesn't matter now exactly how. He performed the ritual and became a hugely powerful Other, then hid the book . . . somewhere here, at the station. And now he's trying to get it away from Moscow.'

Svetlana reached out to me under the table and we shook hands triumphantly.

'Only how is he planning to get it out?' she queried. 'The two most powerful magicians in Moscow are here . . .'

'Three,' I corrected her.

Svetlana frowned and said:

'Then it's four. After all, Kostya's a Higher . . .'

'He's a snot-nosed kid, even if he is Higher . . .' I muttered. Somehow I just couldn't get my head round the fact that this boy had killed ten people in just a few years.

And the most despicable thing was that we gave out the licences . . .

Svetlana sensed what I was thinking. She stroked my hand and said softly:

'Don't get upset. He couldn't go against his own nature. What could you have done? Except kill him . . .'

I nodded.

Of course, he couldn't have acted differently.

But I didn't want to admit that, even to myself.

The café door opened and in came Gesar, Zabulon, Edgar, Kostya . . . and Olga. From the lively way they were talking, it was clear that Olga was already up to speed.

'Edgar agreed to call in reinforcements . . .' Svetlana said in a low voice. 'That's bad news.'

The magicians walked across to our table and I saw them glance in passing at the 'compass'. Kostya went over to the counter and ordered a glass of red wine. The woman behind the counter smiled – either he had used a little bit of vampire charm, or she just liked the look of him. Hey, lady . . . don't smile at that young man who rouses your maternal, or maybe even womanly, feelings. He could give you a kiss that will leave you smiling forever . . .

'Kostya and the Inquisitor have searched every inch of the baggage rooms,' said Gesar. 'Not a trace.'

'And we've combed the entire station,' said Zabulon with a good-natured laugh. 'Six Others, all clearly not involved.'

'And an uninitiated little girl,' Olga added, smiling. 'Yes, I was the one who spotted her. She'll be taken care of.'

Zabulon smiled even more broadly – we had a real smiling competition going on here.

'I'm sorry, Great One. She is *already* being taken care of.'

In an ordinary situation that would only have been the beginning of the conversation.

'That's enough, Great Ones!' Edgar barked. 'We're not concerned with just one potential Other here. This is a question of our very survival!'

'That's right,' Zabulon agreed. 'Will you give me a hand, Boris Ignatievich?'

He and Gesar moved another table over to ours. Kostya brought some chairs – and there we were, all sitting together. Nothing out of the ordinary – like people going off on holiday or a business trip, passing time in the station café . . .

'Either he's not here or he can conceal himself from us,' said Svetlana. 'In any case, I'd like to ask permission to leave. Call me if I'm needed.'

'Your daughter's perfectly all right,' Zabulon growled. 'I give you my word.'

'We might need you here,' said Gesar, backing him up.

Svetlana sighed.

'Gesar, please, why not let Svetlana go?' I asked. 'You can see it's not Power we need right now.'

'Then what do we need?' Gesar asked curiously.

'Cunning and patience. You and Zabulon have plenty of cunning. And you can't expect patience from a worried mother.'

Gesar shook his head. He glanced at Olga and she gave a barely perceptible nod.

'Go to your daughter, Sveta,' said Gesar. 'You're right. If you're needed, I'll call you and put up a portal.'

'Okay, I'm off,' said Svetlana. She leaned over to me for a moment and kissed me on the cheek – then vanished into thin air. The portal was so tiny I didn't even see it.

The people in the café didn't even notice Svetlana disappear. We were invisible to them, they simply couldn't see us.

'She's really powerful,' said Zabulon. He reached out to pick up Kostya's half-empty glass and took a sip. 'Well, you know best, Gesar . . . What next, Mr Inquisitor?'

'We wait,' Edgar said curtly. 'He'll come for the book.'

'He or she,' Zabulon added. 'He or she . . .'

We didn't set up an operational headquarters. Just sat there in the café, ate a bit, drank a bit. Kostya ordered steak tartare – the counter lady was astonished, but she went running into the kitchen and a moment later a young man came out and dashed off to get the meat.

Gesar ordered a chicken Kiev. The rest of us made do with wine, beer and various small snacks like dried squid and pistachio nuts.

I sat there watching Kostya wolf down the almost raw meat, wondering about the behaviour of our unidentified criminal. 'Look for the motive!' had been Sherlock Holmes's advice. If we found the motive, we'd find the criminal. He had already become the most powerful Other in the world – or he could do at any moment. But if that wasn't his goal, what was it? Blackmail. That would be stupid. He couldn't impose his will on all the Watches and the Inquisition, he'd end up like Fuaran . . . Maybe the criminal wanted to set up his own, alternative organisation of Others? An organisation of 'wild Others' had been crushed that spring in St Petersburg, hadn't it? But crushed with great difficulty. A bad example was infectious, someone might have been tempted. And the worst thing was that even a Light One could have been tempted. To create a new Night Watch. A Super-Watch. Wipe out the Dark Ones completely, break the Inquisition and lure some of the Light Ones over to his side . . .

If that was the way things were, it was bad, very bad. The Dark Ones wouldn't surrender without a fight. The modern world was bristling with weapons of mass destruction and nuclear power stations, and a strike at them could wipe out the entire planet. The time was long over when a violent solution could lead to victory. Perhaps that time had never even existed . . .

'The pointer,' said Edgar. 'Look!'

My compass had stopped pretending to be a fan. The pointer spun more slowly, then froze, quivered – and began turning slowly to indicate a direction.

'Yes!' Kostya exclaimed, leaping out of his chair. 'It worked!'

And for just a split second I saw again the vampire-boy who had still not tasted human blood and was certain he would never have to pay a price for his Power . . .

'Let's move, gentlemen.' Edgar jumped to his feet. He looked at the pointer, followed its direction and stared hard at the wall. 'To the trains!' he said, sounding very determined.

CHAPTER 3

IT'S A COMMON sight at a railway station – a group of people dashing along the platform, trying to work out where their train's leaving from, if it hasn't already left. For some reason the role of these late passengers is almost always played by female shuttle-traders loaded down with Chinese striped-canvas bags or, in contrast, cultured males whose only burden is a Samsonite briefcase.

We belonged to an exotic subspecies of the second category – we had no baggage at all. Our overall appearance was pretty strange, but it inspired respect.

On the platform the pointer started spinning again – we were already close to the book.

'He's trying to get away,' Zabulon declared grandly. 'All right . . . now let's see which trains are leaving . . .'

The Dark One's gaze clouded over – he was forecasting the future, looking to see which train would leave the platform first.

I looked up at the information board hanging in the air behind us. And said:

'The Moscow–Almaty train is about to leave. In five minutes, from platform two.'

Zabulon returned from his prophetic travels and announced:

'The train to Kazakhstan leaves from platform two. In five minutes.'

He looked very pleased with himself.

Kostya snickered quietly, and Gesar looked up ostentatiously at the information board and nodded.

'Yes, you're right, Zabulon . . . And the next one's not for half an hour.'

'We'll stop the train and comb all the carriages,' Edgar suggested quickly. 'Right?'

'Will your subordinates be able to find the Other?' Gesar asked. 'If he's disguised? If he's a magician beyond classification?'

Edgar wilted. He shook his head.

'That's the point,' Gesar said with a nod. 'The *Fuaran* was in the station. It was right here, and we couldn't find the book or the criminal. What makes you think it will be any easier on the train?'

'If he's on the train,' said Zabulon, 'the easiest thing to do is destroy the train. No more problem.'

There was silence.

Gesar shook his head.

'I know, I know, it's not an ideal solution,' Zabulon acknowledged. 'Even I don't like the idea of a thousand lives simply wasted . . . But what other choice do we have?'

'What do you suggest, Great One?' asked Edgar.

'*If*,' said Zabulon, emphasising the word, 'the *Fuaran* really is on the train, we have to wait for the moment when the train reaches an unpopulated area. The Kazakh steppes would be perfect. Then . . . we would follow the plans that the Inquisition has for such situations.'

Edgar gave a nervous jerk of his head and, as always happened when he was agitated, started speaking with a slight Baltic accent.

'That is not a good solution, Great One. And I myself cannot approve it – the sanction of the tribunal is required.'

Zabulon shrugged, his entire manner indicating that all he could do was make suggestions.

'In any case, we have to be certain that the book is on the train,' said Gesar. 'I suggest . . .' he looked at me and gave a barely perceptible nod. 'I suggest that Anton from the Night Watch, Konstantin from the Day Watch and someone from the Inquisition should get on the train. To check it out. We don't need a big group for that. We'll arrive in the morning. And then decide what to do next.'

'Off you go, Kostya,' Zabulon said affectionately, slapping the young vampire on the shoulder. 'Gesar's talking sense. Good company, a long journey, an interesting job – you'll enjoy it.'

The mocking glance in my direction was almost too fast to catch.

'That . . . buys us time,' Edgar agreed. 'I'll go myself. And I'll take my colleagues with me. All of them.'

'Only one minute left,' Olga said quietly. 'If you've made up your minds, better get moving.'

Edgar waved to his team and we ran towards the train. The Inquisitor said something to the conductor of the front carriage – a young Kazakh with a moustache – and the conductor's face suddenly went slack, assuming an expression of sleepy contentment. He moved aside to let us in, and we crowded into the little lobby at the end of the carriage. I looked out – Zabulon, Gesar and Olga were standing on the platform, watching us leave. Olga was saying something.

'In the situation that has arisen, I'll assume overall control,' Edgar declared. 'Any objections?'

I glanced at the six Inquisitors standing behind his back and said nothing. But Kostya couldn't restrain himself.

'That depends on what kind of orders you give. I only acknowledge the authority of the Day Watch.'

'I repeat – I am in charge of the operation,' Edgar said coolly. 'If you don't agree, then you can get out.'

Kostya hesitated for a second, and then lowered his head.

'My apologies, Inquisitor. It was a poor joke. Of course you are in charge. But if necessary I will have to contact my superior.'

'First you'll jump to attention and ask permission.' Edgar was determined to cross all the t's and dot all the i's.

'Very well,' Kostya said and nodded. 'My apologies, Inquisitor.'

That put an end to the incipient rebellion. Edgar nodded, stuck his head out of the lobby and called the conductor over.

'When are we off?'

'Right now!' the conductor replied, gazing at the Inquisitor with all the adoration of a devoted dog. 'Right away, I just have to get in.'

'Well, get in then,' said Edgar, moving out of the way.

The conductor climbed into the small space, still wearing that expression of joyful submission. The train began pulling away slowly. The conductor stood beside the open door, swaying slightly.

'What's your name?' asked Edgar.

'Askhat. Askhat Kurmangaliev.'

'Close the door. Do your job according to your instructions.' Edgar frowned. 'We are your best friends. We are your guests. You have to find places on the train for us. Do you understand?'

The door clattered shut, the conductor locked it with his key and stood to attention in front of Edgar again.

'I understand. We need to go to the chief conductor. I don't have enough free places. Only four.'

'Let's go and see him then,' Edgar agreed. 'Anton, what's the compass doing?'

I lifted up the note and looked at the Twilight compass.

The pointer was spinning idly.

'Looks like the book's on the train.'

'We'll wait a bit to make sure,' Edgar decided.

We travelled a good kilometre away from the station, but the pointer carried on spinning. Whoever the thief was, he was travelling with us.

'He's on the train, the son of a bitch,' said Edgar. 'Wait for me here. I'll go and see the chief conductor, we need to get ourselves seats somewhere.'

He went out into the corridor with the conductor, who was still smiling contentedly. A second conductor spotted his colleague and said something very quickly in Kazakh, waving his arms about indignantly, but then he caught Edgar's glance and fell silent.

'Might as well hang signs round our necks – "We're Others!",' said Kostya. 'What's he doing? If there really is a Higher Other in the train, he'll sense the magic . . .'

Kostya was right. It would have been far better to make do with money – it has a magic that works just as well with people. But Edgar was probably feeling too nervous . . .

'Can you sense any magic?' one of the junior Inquisitors asked unexpectedly.

Kostya turned towards him, perplexed. He shook his head.

'Neither will anybody else. Edgar has an amulet of subjection – it only works at close range.'

'Inquisitors' tricks . . .' Kostya muttered, clearly nettled. 'Even so, it would be better to keep our heads down. Right, Anton?'

I nodded reluctantly.

Edgar came back after about twenty minutes. I didn't bother to ask how he'd dealt with the chief conductor, by giving him money or – more likely – using his mysterious 'amulet of subjection' again. He had a calm, contented expression on his face.

'We'll divide into two groups,' he said, moving straight into command mode. 'You' – he nodded in the direction of the Inquisitors – 'are staying in this carriage. Take the conductors' compartment and compartment one, that's six places. Askhat will settle you in . . . ask him for anything you need, don't be shy. And don't take any positive action on your own, don't play the amateur detective. Behave like . . . like people. Report on the situation to me every three hours . . . or as necessary. We'll be in carriage number seven.'

The Inquisitors filed silently out of the lobby, following the smiling conductor. Edgar turned to Kostya and me and said:

'We'll take compartment four in carriage number seven. We can regard it as our temporary base. Let's go.'

'Have you come up with a plan yet, chief?' Kostya enquired. I couldn't tell if he was being ironic or sincere.

Edgar looked at him for a second, clearly also wondering whether it was a genuine question or a jibe. He answered anyway:

'If I have a plan, you'll hear about it. In good time. Meanwhile I want to get a cup of coffee and two or three hours' sleep. In that order.'

Kostya and I set off after Edgar. The vampire grinned and I couldn't help winking back at him. After all, we were united now by our position as subordinates . . . despite all my reservations about Kostya.

The carriage that the chief conductor rides in is the top spot in the whole train. The air conditioning always works. The boiler is always full of hot water, and there's always a fresh brew of tea ready. And finally, it's clean, even in the Central Asian trains, and they give out the sheets in sealed packs – they really have been laundered after the previous run. The toilets work, and you can boldly go into them without rubber boots.

To complete the passengers' comforts, the restaurant car is hitched to one end of the chief conductor's car. And the sleeper car – if there is one in the train – is at the other end.

The Moscow–Almaty train had a sleeper carriage. We walked through it, glancing curiously at the passengers. They were mostly solemn, well-fed Kazakhs, almost all with briefcases that they kept with them, even in the corridor. Some of them were drinking tea from bright-coloured bowls, others were setting out sliced meat and bottles on the little table and breaking boiled chickens into pieces with their hands. But most of them were still standing in the corridor, watching the Moscow suburbs slide past.

I wondered what they were feeling, these citizens of a newly independent country, as they gazed at their former capital. Were they content with their independence? Or could they possibly be feeling nostalgic?

I didn't know. You couldn't ask them, and if you did, you couldn't be sure they'd answer honestly. And breaking into their minds to make them answer honestly wasn't our style.

It would be better anyway if they *were* happy and proud – of their own independence, their own statehood, their own corruption. Especially since not so long before, at the three hundredth anniversary of St Petersburg, people had been saying: 'Let them steal everything, at least it's our own thieves doing it, not the ones from Moscow.' So why shouldn't the Kazakhs and Uzbekis, Ukrainians and Tajiks feel the same way? If our single country was demarcated along republican and municipal lines, then how could we complain about the neighbours from the old communal apartments? The little rooms with the view of the Baltic had gone, so had the proud Georgians, and the Kirghizhians. Everyone had been happy to go. The only room we had left was the big kitchen – Russia, where the different nations all used to stew in the imperial pot. So okay. No problem. Our kitchen's got gas! How about yours?

Let them be happy. Let everyone feel good. The Petersburgians, delighted with their anniversary celebrations – everyone knows you can dine off one good anniversary for a century. And the Kazakhs and Kirghizhians, who had founded their own states for the first time . . . although they, of course, could put forward heaps of evidence to prove their ancient statehood. Then there were our brother Slavs who had felt so oppressed by co-existence with their big brother. And we Russians, who despised Moscow so passionately from the provinces, and in turn despised the provinces from Moscow.

Just for a moment, quite unexpectedly, I felt disgusted. Not with the Kazakh passengers, and not with my fellow Russians. Just with people. With all the people in the world. What did we in the Night Watch think we were doing? Divide and protect? Nonsense! Not a single Dark One, not a single Day Watch, caused people as much harm as they caused themselves. What was one hungry vampire compared to the average maniac who raped and murdered little girls in lifts? What was one hardhearted witch who put a hex on someone for money, compared with a supposedly humane president who launched his high-accuracy rockets for the sake of oil?

A plague on both your houses . . .

I stopped and let Kostya go ahead. Then I froze, staring at the filthy floor, already littered with the first dozen stinking cigarette butts.

What was wrong with me?

Were these my thoughts?

I couldn't pretend they weren't. They were mine, no one else's. No one had sneaked into my mind, not even a Higher Other could have done that without me noticing.

It was me, the way I really was.

A former human being.

A Light Other who was burned out, disillusioned with everything in the world.

This was how you wound up in the Inquisition. When you stopped being able to see any difference between Light Ones and Dark Ones. When for you people weren't even a flock of sheep, but just a handful of spiders in a glass jar. When you stopped believing in the future, and all you wanted to do was preserve the status quo. For yourself. For those few individuals who were still dear to you.

'No, I refuse,' I said, as if I was pronouncing an oath, as if I was holding up a shield against the invisible enemy – against myself. 'I refuse! You have . . . no power . . . over me . . . Anton Gorodetsky!'

On the other side of two doors and four thick panes of glass, Kostya turned and gave me a puzzled look. Had he heard? Or was he simply wondering why I'd stopped?

I forced a smile, opened the door and stepped into the rumbling concertina of the short bridge connecting the two carriages.

The chief conductor's carriage really was a classy place. Clean rugs on the floor; a carpet runner in the corridor; white curtains; and soft mattresses that didn't remind you of the one stuffed with corncobs in *Uncle Tom's Cabin*.

'Who's sleeping up top, and who's down below?' Edgar asked briskly.

'It's all the same to me,' Kostya replied.

'I'd rather be up top,' I said.

'Me too,' said Edgar with a nod. 'That's agreed then.'

There was a polite knock at the door.

'Yes!' The Inquisitor didn't even turn his head.

It was the chief conductor, carrying a tray with a nickel-plated kettle full of hot water, a pot with strongly brewed tea, a coffee pot, cups, some wafer biscuits and even a carton of cream. He was a big, strapping, serious-looking man, with a bushy moustache and a uniform that was a perfect fit.

But the expression on his face was as dull and stupid as a newborn puppy's.

'Enjoy your tea, dear guests.'

Clear enough. He was under the influence of the amulet as well. The fact that Edgar was a Dark One did have some effect on his methods, after all.

'Thank you. Inform us of everyone who got on in Moscow and gets off along the way, my dear man,' said Edgar, taking the tray. 'Especially those who get off before they reach their stop.'

'It will be done, Your Honour!' The chief conductor nodded.

Kostya giggled.

I waited until the poor man had gone out, and asked:

'Why "Your Honour"?'

'How should I know?' Edgar said with a shrug. 'The amulet induces people to accept instructions. But who they see me as – an auditor, the girl they love, a well-known actor or Generalissimus Stalin – that's their problem. This guy must have been reading too much Akunin. Or watching old movies.'

Kostya chortled again.

'There's nothing funny about it,' Edgar said angrily. 'And nothing terrible either. It's the least harmful way of manipulating the human psyche. Half the stories about how someone gave Yakubovich a lift in his car or let Gorbachev through to the front of the queue are the result of suggestions just like this.'

'That's not what I was laughing at,' Kostya explained. 'I imagined you in a white army officer's uniform . . . chief. You looked impressive.'

'You go ahead and laugh . . .' said Edgar, pouring himself some coffee. 'How's the compass doing?'

I put the note on the table without speaking. A Twilight image appeared in the air above it – the round casing of a compass, a lazily spinning pointer.

I poured myself some tea and took a sip. It tasted good. Brewed to perfection, just as it should be for 'His Honour'.

'He's on the train, the scum . . .' Edgar sighed. 'Gentlemen, I'm not going to conceal the alternatives from you. Either we catch the perpetrator, or the train will be destroyed. Together with all the passengers.'

'How?' Kostya asked laconically.

'There are various possibilities. A gas main explodes beside the train, a fighter plane accidentally launches an air-to-ground missile . . . if absolutely necessary, the rocket will have a nuclear warhead.'

'Edgar!' I really wanted to believe he was overdramatising. 'There are at least five hundred passengers on this train!'

'Rather more than that,' the Inquisitor corrected me.

'We can't do that!'

'We can't let the book go. We can't allow an unprincipled Other to create his own private guard and start restyling the world to suit himself.'

'But we don't know what he wants!'

'We know he killed an Inquisitor without hesitation. We know he is immensely powerful and is pursuing some goal unknown to us. What's he after in Central Asia, Gorodetsky?'

I shrugged.

'There are several ancient centres of power there,' Edgar muttered. 'A certain number of artefacts that disappeared without trace, a certain number of regions with weak political control . . . And what else?'

'A billion Chinese,' Kostya suddenly put in.

The Dark Ones stared at each other.

'You're out of your mind . . .' Edgar said hesitantly.

'More than a billion,' Kostya replied derisively. 'What if he's planning to make a dash through Kazakhstan to China? Now that would be an army! A billion Others! And then there's India . . .'

'Don't be ridiculous,' Edgar said dismissively. 'Not even an idiot would try that. Where are we going to get Power from, when a third of the population is turned into Others?'

'But maybe he is an idiot,' Kostya persisted.

'That's why we're prepared to take extreme measures,' Edgar snapped.

He was serious. Without the slightest doubt that we really could kill these spell-bound conductors, chubby-cheeked businessmen and poor people travelling in the carriages with open seating. If we had to, we had to. Farmers who destroyed animals with foot-and-mouth disease suffered too.

I didn't feel like drinking tea any more. I got up and walked out of the compartment. Edgar watched me go with an understanding but by no means sympathetic glance.

The carriage was settling down as the passengers prepared for sleep. The doors of some compartments were still open, there were people still loitering in the corridor, waiting for the washroom to be free. I heard glasses clinking somewhere, but most of the passengers were too exhausted after Moscow.

I thought languidly that what the laws of melodrama required now was for little children with the innocent faces of angels to come dashing along the corridor. Just to drive home the true monstrosity of Edgar's plan . . .

There weren't any little children. Instead a fat man in faded tracksuit bottoms and a baggy T-shirt stuck his head out of one of the compartments. He had a red, steaming face that was already comfortably bloated by strong drink. The man looked listlessly straight through me, hiccupped and disappeared again.

My hands automatically reached for my minidisc player. I stuck in the earphones, put in a disc at random and pressed my face against the window. I see nothing, I hear nothing. And obviously I'm not going to say anything.

I heard a gentle, lyrical melody, and a voice started singing delicately:

> You'll have no time to dash for the bushes
> When the sawn-off mows you down
> There is no beauty more beautiful
> Than the visions of morphine withdrawal . . .

Yes, it was Las, my acquaintance from the Assol complex. The disc he'd given me as a present. I laughed and turned the volume up. It was exactly what I needed.

> The devil-kids will return to the stars,
> And they'll smelt our blood into iron,
> There is no beauty more beautiful
> Than the visions of morphine withdrawal . . .

My God! . . . It was more punk than any of the punks. Not even Shnur with his obscenities . . .

A hand slapped me on the shoulder.

'Edgar, everyone has his own way of relaxing,' I muttered.

Someone poked me lightly under the ribs.

I turned round.

And froze.

There, standing in front of me, was Las. Smiling happily, jigging in time to the music – I must have turned the volume up too high.

'Hey, but that's great!' he exclaimed enthusiastically the moment I pulled out the earphones. 'You're walking through the carriage, not bothering anyone, and there's someone listening to your songs! What are you doing here, Anton?'

'Travelling . . .' It was the only word I could get out as I switched off the player.

'Oh, really?' Las commented in delight. 'I'd never have guessed! Where are you travelling to?'

'Alma-Ata.'

'You ought to call it "Almaty".' Las admonished me. 'Okay, let's continue the conversation. Why aren't you flying?'

'Why aren't you?' I asked, finally realising that all this was rather like an interrogation.

'Because I'm *aerophobic*,' Las said proudly. 'If I really have to fly, a litre of whisky gives me some faith in the laws of aerodynamics. But that's for emergencies only, for getting to Japan, or the States . . . the trains don't go there, you know.'

'You travelling on business?'

'On holiday,' Las said with a grin. 'Couldn't go to Turkey or the Canaries, now, could I? Are you on a business trip?'

'Uhuh.' I nodded. 'I'm planning to start selling kumis and shubat in Moscow.'

'What's shubat?' Las asked.

'You know . . . kefir made from camel's milk.'

'Great,' Las said approvingly. 'You travelling alone?'

'With friends.'

'Let's go to my compartment. It's empty. I haven't got any shubat, but I can offer you kumis.'

Was it a trap?

I looked at Las through the Twilight. Stared as hard as I could.

Not the slightest indication of an Other.

He was either a human being . . . or an Other of absolutely unimaginable Power. Capable of disguising himself at every level of the Twilight.

Could this be a stroke of luck? Was this really him, standing there in front of me, the mysterious thief of the *Fuaran*?

'Okay, I'll just go and get something,' I said and smiled.

'I've got everything we need!' Las protested. 'Bring your friends along too. I'm in the next car down, compartment two.'

'They've already gone to bed,' I lied clumsily. 'Hang on, just a moment . . .'

It was a good thing Las was standing on one side and couldn't see who was in the compartment. I opened the door slightly and slipped in there – no doubt giving him the idea that there was a half-naked girl inside.

'What's happened?' Edgar asked, looking at me intently.

'There's a guy from Assol here on the train,' I said quickly. 'You remember, the musician, he was a suspect, but he didn't seem like an Other . . . He's inviting us to his compartment for a drink.'

An excited expression appeared on Edgar's face. Kostya even jumped to his feet and exclaimed:

'Let's take him now. While he's here . . .'

'Wait.' Edgar shook his head. 'Let's not be in such a hurry . . . you never know, it might not be him. Anton, take this.'

I took the small glass flask, which was bound with copper or bronze wire. It looked terribly old. There was a dark-brown liquid splashing around inside it.

'What's that?'

'Perfectly ordinary twenty-year-old armagnac. But the flask is trickier. Only an Other can open it.' Edgar laughed. 'It's just a trinket really. Some ancient magician put the same spell on all his bottles, so the servants couldn't steal anything. If your friend can open it, then he's an Other.'

'I can't sense any magic . . .' I said, turning the flask over in my hands.

'That's the point,' Edgar said smugly. 'A simple and reliable test.'

I nodded.

'And here's a simple snack to go with it.' Edgar reached into the inside pocket of his raincoat and took out a triangular bar of Toblerone. 'Right, get on with it. Wait. Which compartment is it?'

'The sleeper car, compartment two.'

'We'll keep an eye on it,' Edgar promised. He got halfway to his feet and switched off the light in the compartment. 'Kostya, get under the blanket, we're already asleep.'

So a couple of seconds later, when I went out into the corridor with the flask and the chocolate, my companions really were lying peacefully under their blankets.

But in any case, Las was considerate enough not to try to peep in through the open door – he must have genuinely got the wrong idea.

'Cognac?' Las asked, with a glance at the flask I was holding.

'Better. Twenty-year-old armagnac.'

'Good stuff,' Las agreed. 'There are lots of folk who don't even know that word.'

'Maybe,' I agreed, following Las into the next carriage.

'Uhuh. Serious types, wheeler-dealers, they handle millions, but apart from White Horse whisky and Napoleon brandy they haven't got a clue about civilised drinking. I've always found the narrow cultural outlook of the political and economic elite astonishing. Tell me, why did the Mercedes six hundred become our symbol of affluence? You're talking to this serious, intelligent guy and he suddenly comes out with: "They dented my Merc, I had to drive a five hundred for a week!" And he has this expression in his eyes, the submission of the ascetic who's been reduced to a five hundred, and the pride of the big-shot who owns a six hundred! I used to think that until the New Russians switched to the Bentleys and Jaguars that they ought to drive, the country would never come to anything. But then they did change, and it made no difference. You can still see the red club jackets under the Versace shirts . . . And there's another example . . . A fine designer they chose to turn into a cult . . .'

I followed Las into the cosy compartment. There were only two bunk beds, plus a little corner table with its top covering a triangular washbasin, and a little fold-down seat.

'There's actually less space than in a normal compartment,' I observed.

'Yes, but then the air conditioning works. And there's a washbasin . . . which comes in handy in many circumstances . . .'

Las pulled an aluminium suitcase out from under one bunk and started rummaging in it. A moment later a one-litre plastic bottle appeared on the table. I picked it up and looked at the label. It really was kumis.

'Did you think I was joking?' my 'neighbour' chuckled. 'It's a really great drink. Is that the kind you were thinking of selling?'

'Yes, that's the stuff,' I blurted out without thinking.

'Then you won't be able to, that's from Kirghizstan. The place you ought to have gone to is Ufa. It's nearer, and there's less trouble with the customs. They make kumis there, and buza. Have you ever tried buza? It's a mixture of kumis and oat jelly. Horrible stuff but it completely sorts you out if you've got a hangover.'

Meanwhile, other items had appeared on the table: salami, braised meat, sliced bread and a litre bottle of Polignac French cognac, a brand I didn't know.

I gulped and added my modest offering to the provisions, then I said:

'Let's try the armagnac first.'

'Okay,' Las agreed, taking out two plastic cups for water and two cupro-nickel shot-glasses for the armagnac.

'Open it.'

'It's your armagnac, you open it,' Las countered casually.

There was definitely something fishy here.

'No, you do it,' I blurted out. 'I can never pour the drinks evenly.'

Las looked at me as if I was a total idiot. He said:

'I can see you must be a serious drinker. Do you often share a bottle of vodka three ways out in the street?'

But he picked up the flask and started twisting the top.

I waited.

Las huffed and puffed, then frowned. He stopped trying to unscrew the top and took a close look at it. He muttered:

'Looks like it's stuck . . .'

Surely he had to be a disguised Other . . .

He lifted up the edge of his T-shirt, took a tight grip on the top and turned it sharply with all his strength. He exclaimed excitedly:

'It's moving, it's moving!'

There was a crunching sound.

'That's got it . . .' Las said tentatively. 'Oh . . .'

He held his hands out to me, embarrassed. One was holding the glass flask, the other was holding its broken-off neck, with the lid still firmly screwed onto it.

'Sorry . . . oh shit . . .'

But a moment later a glint of pride appeared in Las's eyes.

'That's some strength I've got! I'd never have thought . . .'

I didn't say a word, just pictured Edgar's face when he realised he'd lost his useful artefact.

'Valuable, was it?' Las asked guiltily. 'An antique flask, right?'

'It's nothing,' I muttered. 'It's the armagnac I'm upset about. Some glass got into it.'

'That's no problem,' Las said cheerfully. He went looking in the suitcase again, leaving the mutilated flask on the table. Taking out a handkerchief, he demonstratively stripped the label off it: 'Clean. Never even washed. And not Chinese, but Czech, so you don't need to worry about pneumonia.'

He folded the handkerchief in two, wound it round the broken neck of the flask and calmly poured the armagnac through it into the two shot-glasses. He raised his own:

'To our journey!'

'To our journey,' I repeated.

The armagnac was soft, fragrant and sweetish, like warm grape juice. It went down easily, without even inspiring the idea of some kind of snack to go with it, and then somewhere deep inside it exploded – humanely and precisely enough to make any American missile jealous.

'Wonderful stuff,' Las commented, breathing out. 'But very high in sugar, I'm telling you! That's why I like the Armenian cognacs – the sugar content right down at the minimum, but the full flavour's all still there . . . Let's have another.'

The glasses were filled a second time. Las looked at me expectantly.

'Here's to health?' I suggested uncertainly.

'To health,' Las agreed. He drank and then sniffed at the handkerchief. He looked out the window, shuddered and muttered: 'That's some stuff . . . it doesn't mess around.'

'What's wrong?'

'You'll never believe it, but I thought I just saw a bat fly past the train!' Las exclaimed. 'Huge, the size of a sheepdog. Br-rr-rr . . .'

I realised I'd have to give Kostya a couple of words of friendly advice. Out loud I just joked:

'It probably wasn't a bat, more likely a squirrel.'

'A flying squirrel,' Las said mournfully. 'God help us all . . . No, honestly, a huge bat!'

'Maybe it was just flying very close to the glass?' I suggested. 'And you only caught a glimpse of it, so you couldn't judge how far away it was – so you thought it was bigger than it really was.'

'Maybe so . . .' Las said thoughtfully. 'But what was it doing here? Why would it want to fly alongside the train?'

'That's elementary,' I said, taking the broken flask and pouring us a third glass. 'A train moves at such great speed that it creates a shield of air in front of it. The shield stuns mosquitoes and butterflies and all sorts of other flying creatures and tosses them into turbulent streams of air running along both sides of the train. So at night bats like to fly alongside a moving train and eat the stunned flies.'

Las thought about it. He asked:

'Then why don't birds fly around moving trains in the daytime?'

'Well, that's elementary too!' I said, handing him his glass. 'Birds are much more stupid than mammals. Bats have already guessed how to use trains to get food, but birds haven't figured it out yet. In a hundred or two hundred years the birds will discover how to exploit trains too.'

'How come I didn't realise all that for myself?' Las asked in amazement. 'It's really all so simple. Okay, then . . . here's to common sense!'

We drank.

'Animals are amazing,' Las said profoundly. 'Cleverer than Darwin thought. I used to have . . .'

I never got to hear what it was Las used to have – a dog, a hamster or a fish in an aquarium. He glanced out of the window again and turned green.

'It's there again . . . the bat!'

'Catching the mosquitoes,' I reminded him.

'What mosquitoes? It swerved round a lamp-post like it wasn't even there! The size of a sheepdog, I tell you!'

Las stood up and resolutely pulled the blind down. He said in a determined voice:

'To hell with it . . . I knew I shouldn't be reading Stephen King just before bed . . . The size of that bat! Like a pterodactyl. It could catch owls and eagles, not mosquitoes!'

That freak Kostya! I realised that in his animal form a vampire, like a werewolf, became completely brainless and had little control over his own actions. He was probably getting a kick out of hurtling along beside the train in the night, glancing into the windows, taking a breather on the lamp-posts. But he should at least take basic precautions.

'It's a mutation,' Las mused. 'Nuclear tests, leaks from reactors, electromagnetic waves, mobile phones . . . and we just carry on laughing at it all, think it's all science fiction. And the gutter press keeps feeding us lies. So who can I tell – they'll just think I was drunk or I'm lying!'

He opened his bottle of cognac with a determined expression and asked:

'What do you think of the supernatural?'

'I respect it,' I said with dignity.

'Me too,' Las admitted. 'Now I do. I never even thought about it before . . .' He cast a wary glance at the blind over the window. 'You live all those years, and then somewhere out in the Pskov peat bogs you suddenly meet a live yeti – and you go right off your rocker! Or you see a rat a metre long Or . . .' He waved his hand and poured brandy into the glasses. 'What if it turns out there really are witches and vampires and werewolves living right here alongside us? After all, what better disguise could there be than to get your image enshrined in the culture of the mass media? Anything that's described in artistic terms and shown in the movies stops being frightening and mysterious. For real horror you need the spoken word, you need an old grandpa sitting on a bench, scaring his grandkids in the evening: "And then the master of the house came to him and said: I won't let you go, I'll tie you up and bind you tight and you'll rot under the fallen branches!" That's the way to make people wary of strange happenings. Kids sense that, you know, it's no wonder they love telling stories about the Black Hand and the Coffin on Wheels. But modern literature, and especially the movies, it all just dilutes that instinctive horror. How can you feel afraid of Dracula if he's been killed a hundred times? How can you be afraid of aliens if our guys always squelch them? Hollywood is the great suppressor of human vigilance. A toast – to the death of Hollywood, for depriving us of a healthy fear of the unknown!'

'I'll always drink to that,' I said warmly. 'Tell me, Las, what made you decide to go to Kazakhstan? Is it really a good place for a holiday?'

Las shrugged and said:

'I don't even know. I suddenly got a yen for something exotic – kumis in milking pails, camel races, ram-fights, beautiful girls with unfamiliar kinds of faces, arboraceous cannabis in the town squares . . .'

'What kind of cannabis?' I asked, puzzled.

'Arboraceous. It's a tree, only it never gets a chance to grow,' Las explained, with the same kind of serious expression I'd used for my stories about bats and swallows. 'But what do I care, I'm ruining my health with tobacco. I just fancy something exotic . . .'

He took out a pack of Belomor and lit up.

'The conductor will be here in a minute,' I remarked.

'No he won't, I put a condom over the smoke detector.' Las nodded upwards. There was a half-inflated condom stretched over the smoke detector projecting from the wall. Delicate pink, with plastic studs.

'I think you probably have the wrong idea about the exotic fun that Kazakhstan has to offer,' I said.

'Too late to worry about that – I'm on my way now,' Las muttered. 'The idea just came to me out of nowhere this morning: Why don't I go to Kazakhstan? I just dropped everything, gave my assistant his instructions, and went to catch the train.'

I pricked my ears up at that.

'Just upped and left? Are you always so footloose and fancy-free?'

Las thought about it and shook his head.

'Not really. But this was like something just clicked . . . It's no big deal. Let's have one more for the road . . .'

He started pouring – and I took another look at him through the Twilight.

Even though I knew what to look for, I could barely even sense the vestigial trace, the unknown Other's touch had been so light and elegant. It was already fading, almost cold already.

Simple suggestion, the kind that even the weakest Other could manage. But how neatly it had been done!

'One more for the road,' I agreed. 'I can't keep my eyes open either . . . we'll have plenty of time to talk.'

But I wasn't going to get any sleep in the next hour. I had a conversation with Edgar coming up – and possibly one with Gesar too.

CHAPTER 4

EDGAR LOOKED SADLY at the broken pieces of the flask. Unfortunately he wasn't dressed appropriately for expressing profound sorrow – loose shorts with a jolly pattern and a baggy undershirt, with his paunch oozing out between the two of them. Inquisitors obviously didn't take great care to keep in good shape; they relied more on the power of their magic.

'This isn't Prague,' I said, trying to comfort him. 'This is Russia. When bottles don't surrender here, they're exterminated.'

'I'll have to write an explanatory note,' Edgar said gloomily. 'Czech bureaucracy is a match for the Russian version any day.'

'At least we know now that Las isn't an Other.'

'We still don't know anything,' the Inquisitor muttered irritably. 'A positive result would have been unambiguous. With a negative one, there's still a chance he's such a powerful Other that he sensed the trap. And decided to have a little joke with us.'

I didn't try to object. It was a possibility that we really couldn't exclude.

'He doesn't seem like an Other to me,' Kostya said in a low voice. He was sitting on his bunk in just his shorts, streaming with sweat and breathing heavily. It looked like he'd spent too long flitting about as a bat. 'I checked him out back at the Assol. Every way I could. And just now too . . . Doesn't look it.'

'I have something else to say to you,' Edgar snapped. 'Why did you have to fly right outside the window?'

'I was observing.'

'Couldn't you just sit on the roof and lean down?'

'At a hundred kilometres an hour? I might be an Other, but the laws of physics still apply. I'd have been blown off!'

'So the laws of physics don't prevent you from flying at a hundred kilometres an hour, but you can't stay on the roof of the carriage?'

Kostya frowned. He reached into his jacket and took out a small flask full of some thick, dark crimson liquid. He took a mouthful.

Edgar frowned:

'How soon will you require . . . food?'

'If I don't have to transform again, tomorrow evening,' Kostya waved the flask through the air, and it made a heavy slashing sound, 'I've got enough left for breakfast.'

'I could . . . in view of the special circumstances . . .' Edgar paused and cast a sideways glance at me. 'I could issue you a licence.'

'No,' I said quickly. 'That's a breach of established procedure.'

'Konstantin is on active service with the Inquisition at present,' Edgar reminded me. 'The Light Ones would receive compensation.'

'No,' I repeated.

'He has to nourish himself somehow. And the people in the train are probably doomed anyway. Every last one of them.'

Kostya said nothing, looking at me. Without smiling, a serious, intent kind of look . . .

'Then I'll get off the train,' I said. 'And you can do whatever you like.'

'That's the Night Watch style,' Kostya said in a quiet voice. 'Washing your hands of the whole business. That's the way you always behave, giving us the people yourselves, and then turning your noses up in contempt.'

'Quiet!' Edgar barked, getting up and standing between us. 'Quiet, both of you! This is no time for squabbling. Kostya, do you need a licence? Or can you hold out?'

Kostya shook his head.

'I don't need a licence. While we're stopped somewhere in Tambov I'll get out and catch a couple of cats.'

'Why cats?' Edgar asked curiously. 'Why . . . er . . . not dogs, for instance?'

'I feel sorry for dogs,' Kostya explained. 'Cats too . . . but where am I going to find a cow or a sheep in Tambov? And the train doesn't stop for long at the small stations.'

'We'll get you a ram in Tambov,' Edgar promised. 'There's no point in helping spread mystical rumours. That's how it all begins – they find the bodies of animals drained of blood, write their articles for the gutter press . . .'

He took out his phone and selected a number from its address book. He had to wait a long time before someone who had been sleeping peacefully answered his call.

'Dmitry? Stop whining, this is no time for sleeping, the motherland calls . . .' Edgar squinted at us and said in a clear voice: 'Greetings from Solomon, with all the signatures and seals.'

Edgar stopped talking for a while, either allowing the man to gather his wits or listening to his reply.

'Yes. Edgar. Remember now? Precisely so,' said Edgar. 'We haven't forgotten about you. And we need your help. In four hours the Moscow–Almaty train will stop in Tambov. We need a ram. What?'

Taking the phone away from his face and covering the speaker with his hand, Edgar said angrily:

'What stupid asses they are, these human personnel.'

'An ass would suit me fine too,' Kostya chuckled.

Edgar spoke into the phone again:

'No, not you. It has to be a ram. You know, the animal. Or an ordinary sheep. Or a cow. That doesn't bother me. In four hours, be standing near the station with the animal. No, a dog's no good. Because it's no good! No, no one's going to eat it. You can keep the meat and the skin. Right, I'll call you when we get there.'

Edgar put his mobile away and explained:

'We have a very limited . . . contingent . . . in Tambov. There aren't any Others there at the moment, only a human member of staff.'

'Ah.' That was my only comment. There had never been any humans in the Watches.

'Sometimes it's unavoidable,' Edgar explained vaguely. 'Never mind, he'll manage it. He's paid for it. You'll get your ram, Kostya.'

'Thanks,' Kostya replied amicably. 'A sheep would be better, of course. But a ram will do the job too.'

'Is the gastronomical discussion over now?' I asked sarcastically.

Edgar turned to me and spoke in a didactic tone:

'Our battle-readiness is a matter of great importance . . . So, you're telling us that this . . . Las . . . has been influenced by magic?'

'That's right. This morning. The desire to travel to Alma-Ata by train was implanted in his mind.'

'It makes sense,' Edgar agreed. 'If you hadn't discovered the trace, we'd have put serious effort into this guy. And wasted a bundle of time and energy. But that means . . .'

'That the perpetrator is intimately familiar with the affairs of the Watches,' I said with a nod. 'He knows about the investigation at the Assol complex, and who was under suspicion. In other words . . .'

'Someone from the very top,' Edgar agreed. 'Five or six Others in the Night Watch, the same number in the Day Watch. Let's say twenty altogether, at most . . . Even so, it's not many, not many at all.'

'Or someone from the Inquisition,' said Kostya.

'Okay. A name, brother, a name.' Edgar laughed. 'Who?'

'Witiezslav.' Kostya paused for a second and then added: 'For instance.'

For a few seconds I thought the Dark Magician, usually so unflappable, was about to let rip with a string of obscenities. And definitely in a Baltic accent. But Edgar restrained himself:

'Perhaps you're feeling a bit tired after the transformation, Konstantin? Maybe it's time to go bye-byes?'

'Edgar, I'm younger than you, but we're both babies compared to Witiezslav,' Kostya replied calmly. 'What did we see? Clothes filled with dust. Did we personally analyse that dust?'

Edgar didn't answer.

'I'm not sure you can tell anything from the remains of a vampire . . .' I put in.

'Why would Witiezslav . . .' Edgar began.

'Power,' Kostya answered laconically.

'What's power got to do with it? If he had decided to steal the book, why report that he'd found it? He could have just taken it and slipped away. He was alone when he found it. Do you understand that? Alone.'

'He might not have realised immediately what he was dealing with,' Kostya parried. 'Or not decided to steal it straight away. But to fake his own death and bolt with the book while we're trying to catch his killer – that would be a brilliant move.'

Edgar started breathing faster. He nodded:

'All right. I'll ask them to check it. I'll get in touch with . . . with the Higher Ones in Moscow and ask them to check the remains.'

'Just to be sure, ask Gesar and Zabulon both to check the remains,' Kostya advised him. 'We can't be sure one of them isn't involved.'

'Don't teach your grandmother how to suck eggs . . .' Edgar growled. He settled down more comfortably on the bunk, and switched off the light.

Gesar and Zabulon weren't going to get a good night's rest either . . .

I yawned and said:

'Gentlemen, I don't know about you, but I'm going to sleep.'

Edgar didn't answer – he was engaged in mental conversation with one of the Great Ones. Kostya climbed under his own blanket.

I climbed up onto the top bunk, undressed and shoved my jeans and shirt onto the shelf. I took off my watch and put it beside me – I don't like sleeping with it on. Below me, Kostya clicked the switch of the night light, and it went dark.

Edgar sat there without moving. The wheels of the train hammered on reassuringly. They say that in America, where they use incredibly long rails cast in single pieces, they put special notches in them to imitate the joints and recreate that comforting rhythm . . .

I couldn't sleep.

Someone had killed a Higher Vampire. Or the vampire himself had faked his own death. It didn't matter which. In either case, someone was in possession of unimaginable Power.

Why would he run? Why hide on a train – with the risk that the entire train would be destroyed or perhaps surrounded by hundreds of Others and subjected to an exhaustive search? It was stupid, unnecessary, risky. He had become the most powerful Other of all – sooner or later power would come to him. In a hundred years, or two hundred – when everybody would have forgotten about the witch Arina and the mythical book. If anybody should have understood all that, Witiezslav would have.

It was . . . too human, somehow. Messy and illogical. Nothing like the way a wise and powerful Other would have acted.

But only an Other like that could possibly have killed Witiezslav.

Again it didn't add up.

Down below, Edgar began to stir. He sighed and his clothes rustled as he climbed up onto his bunk.

I closed my eyes and tried to relax.

I imagined the rails stretching out behind the train . . . through the stations and the small stops, past the cities and the little towns, all the way back to Moscow, and the roads running away from the station until out beyond the ring road they were pocked by potholes and after the hundredth kilometre, transformed into strips of pulverised tarmac that crept towards the sleepy little village and up to the old log house . . .

'Svetlana?'

'I was waiting, Anton. How are you getting on?'

'Still travelling. But there's something strange going on . . .'

I tried to open myself up to her as much as possible . . . or almost. To unroll my memory like a bolt of cloth on the cutter's table. The train, the Inquisitors, the conversation with Las, the conversation with Edgar and Kostya . . .

'It's strange,' Svetlana said after a short pause. 'Very strange. I get the feeling someone's playing games with you all. I don't like it, Anton.'

'Me neither. How's Nadya?'

'She's been asleep for ages.'

In this kind of conversation that only Others can have, there is no real inflection of the voice. But there is something that replaces it – I could sense Svetlana's slight indecision.

'Are you at home?'

'No. I'm . . . visiting a certain old lady.'

'Svetlana!'

'I'm just visiting, don't worry. I decided to talk the situation over with her . . . and learn a bit about the book.'

I should have realised straight away that it wasn't just concern for our daughter that had made Svetlana leave.

'And what have you found out?'

'It was the *Fuaran*. The real one. And . . . we were right about Gesar's son. The old woman thought the good turn she'd done for Gesar was hilarious . . . and she re-established some useful contacts at the same time.'

'And then she sacrificed the book?'

'Yes. She left it behind, absolutely certain that the secret room would soon be found, and the search would be called off.'

'What does she think about what's happened?' I carefully avoided using any names, as if a conversation like this could be tapped.

'I think she's panicking. Although she's putting a brave face on it.'

'Svetlana, how quickly can the *Fuaran* turn a human being into an Other?'

'Almost instantly. It takes ten minutes to pronounce the spells, and you need a few ingredients . . . or rather, one . . . blood from twelve people. Maybe only a drop, but from twelve different people.'

'What for?'

'You'd have to ask Fuaran that. I'm sure any other liquid would have done instead of blood, but the witch bound the spell to blood . . . Anyway, ten minutes' preparation, twelve drops of blood, and you can turn a human being into an Other. Or a whole group of people, just as long as they're all within your field of vision.'

'And what grade of power will they be on?'

'It varies, but you can raise the grade of the weak ones with the next spell. In theory you can turn any human into a Higher Magician.'

There was something in what she'd just said. Something important. But I just couldn't grasp the thread yet . . .

'Sveta, what is the . . . old woman afraid of?'

'The transformation of people into Others on a massive scale.'

'Is she planning to come in and confess?'

'No. She's planning to run for it. And I can understand that.'

I sighed. We should have brought Arina to justice . . . if only the Inquisition hadn't charged her with sabotage. But then there was Gesar too . . .

'Sveta, ask her . . . ask her if the *Fuaran* will acquire great power at the place where it was written?'

A pause. What a pity this wasn't a mobile phone so that I could talk to the witch directly. But alas, direct conversation is only possible between soul-mates and people who have other close connections.

'No . . . She's surprised at the question. She says the *Fuaran* isn't tied to any particular place. The book will work in the Himalayas or Antarctica, or in the Ivory Coast if you want it to.'

'Then . . . then find out if Witiezslav could have used it. After all, he was a vampire, a lower Other . . .'

Another pause.

'He could have. Any vampire or werewolf could. Dark Ones or

Light Ones. There are no limitations. Except for one – the book couldn't have been used by a human being.'

'That's clear enough . . . Anything else?'

'Nothing, Anton. I was hoping she might be able to give us a clue . . . but I was wrong.'

'Okay. Thanks. I love you.'

'And I love you. Get some rest. I'm sure everything will be clearer in the morning . . .'

The subtle thread stretching between us snapped. I shifted around on the bunk, settling down more comfortably. Then I couldn't help myself, and I looked at the table.

The pointer of the compass was still rotating. The *Fuaran* was still on the train.

I woke up twice during the night. First when one of the Inquisitors came to Edgar to report that some reports or other were missing. The second when the train stopped in Tambov, and Kostya quietly left the compartment.

It was after ten when I got up.

Edgar was drinking tea. Kostya, looking pink and fresh, was chewing a salami sandwich. The pointer was rotating. No change at all.

I got dressed on the bunk and jumped down. I'd found a tiny piece of soap in the bundle of bedclothes, and that was the only personal hygiene product I had.

'Here,' Kostya muttered, moving a plastic bag over towards me. 'I picked up a few things in Tambov . . .'

The bag contained a pack of disposable razors, an aerosol can of Gillette shaving cream, a toothbrush and a tube of New Pearl toothpaste.

'I forgot the aftershave,' said Kostya. 'I didn't think of it.'

It wasn't surprising he'd forgotten – vampires and werewolves aren't too fond of strong smells. Maybe the supposed effect of garlic – which is actually quite harmless to vampires – is linked with the fact that it's smell makes it harder for them to find their prey?

'Thanks,' I said. 'How much do I owe you?'

Kostya shrugged.

'I've already given him the money,' Edgar told me. 'You're entitled to expenses too, by the way. Fifty dollars a day, plus food, on submission of receipts.'

'It's a good life in the Inquisition,' I quipped. 'Any news?'

'Gesar and Zabulon are trying to make sense of Witiezslav's remains.' He said 'remains' in a solemn, official voice. 'But it's hard to get much out of them. You know yourself – the older a vampire is, the less there is left when he dies . . .'

Kostya chewed intently on his sandwich.

'Sure,' I agreed. 'I'll go and have a wash.'

Almost everyone in the carriage was awake already, only a couple of compartments where the merrymaking had been a bit too intense were still closed. I waited in the short queue and then squeezed into the barracks-like comfort of the carriage's washroom. Warm water oozed sluggishly out of the iron tap. The sheet of polished steel that took the place of a mirror was useless, spattered all over with soap suds. As I brushed my teeth with the hard Chinese brush, I recalled my night-time conversation with Sveta.

There was something important in what she had said. Yet it had gone unrecognised by both of us.

I had to understand it.

When I got back to the compartment I was still no closer to the truth, but I did have an idea that I thought might lead somewhere. My travelling companions had already finished their breakfast and, when I closed the door, I got straight to the point.

'Edgar, I've got an idea. On a long stretch between stops your men unhitch the carriages. One by one. To make sure the train doesn't stop, one of them monitors the driver. We watch the compass. As soon as the carriage with the book is unhitched, the pointer will turn towards it.'

'And?' Edgar asked sourly.

'We get a fix on the book. We know which carriage it's in. Then we can surround that carriage and take the passengers aside with their luggage, one by one. As soon as we find the killer, the pointer will tell us. And that's it! No more need to destroy the train!'

'I thought about that,' Edgar said reluctantly. 'There's only one argument against it, but it's decisive. The perpetrator will realise what's happening. He'll be able to strike first.'

'Get Gesar, Zabulon, Svetlana and Olga here . . . Do the Dark Ones have any other powerful magicians?' I looked at Kostya.

'We can find a few,' Kostya answered evasively. 'But will we have enough Power?'

'To deal with one Other?'

'Not just an Other,' Edgar reminded me. 'According to the legend, several hundred magicians were assembled to destroy Fuaran.'

'Then we'll assemble them too. The Night Watch has almost two hundred members of staff, the Day Watch has just as many. There are hundreds of reservists. Each side can easily muster a thousand Others.'

'Mostly weak, sixth- or seventh-grade. We can't get more than a hundred real magicians together, third-grade and up.' Edgar spoke so confidently there seemed no doubt that he really had thought through the option of direct confrontation. 'That might be enough – if we back up the Dark and Light Magicians with Inquisitors, use amulets and combine the two powers. But it might not be.

Then the strongest fighters would be killed and the perpetrator left with a free hand. Haven't you considered that he might be counting on us taking this very approach?'

I shook my head.

'And another thing I've been thinking about,' Edgar said with gloomy resignation. 'The perpetrator might see the train as a trap that will draw together all the powerful magicians in Russia. He could have hung the train from end to end with spells that we can't sense.'

'Then what's the point of our efforts?' I asked. 'What are we doing here? One nuclear bomb – and the problem's solved.'

Edgar nodded:

'Yes. And it would have to be nuclear, to penetrate all the levels of the Twilight. But first we have to make sure the target won't slip away at the last moment.'

'Have you accepted Zabulon's viewpoint then?' I asked.

Edgar sighed.

'I've accepted the viewpoint of common sense. An exhaustive search of the train and the use of massive force is fraught with the danger of magical carnage. People would be killed anyway. Destroy the train . . . of course, I feel sorry for the people. But at least we'd avoid any global convulsions.'

'But if there's still a chance . . .' I began.

'There is. That's why I propose to continue with the search,' Edgar agreed. 'Kostya and I take my young guys and we comb the whole train – from the back and the front at the same time. We'll use amulets, and in suspicious cases, we'll try to check the suspect through the Twilight. And you have another word with Las. He's still under suspicion, after all.'

I shrugged. It all sounded too much like playing at searching. In his heart of hearts Edgar had already given up.

'So when's zero hour?' I asked.

'Tomorrow evening,' Edgar replied. 'When we're passing through the uninhabited area around Semipalatinsk. They exploded nuclear bombs in that area anyway . . . one more tactical weapon's no great disaster round there.'

'Happy hunting,' I said, walking out of the compartment.

It was all obscene. No more than a few lines in the report that Edgar was already preparing to write: 'Despite the efforts made to isolate the perpetrator and locate the *Fuaran* . . .'

There had been a time when I used to find myself thinking the Inquisition was a genuine alternative to the Watches. After all, what was it we did? We divided people from Others. We made sure that the actions of Others had as little impact as possible on people. Yes, it was practically impossible – some of the Others were parasites by their very nature. Yes, the contradictions between Light Ones and Dark Ones were so great that conflicts were inevitable.

But there was still the Inquisition, standing above the Watches. It maintained the balance, a third power and a dividing structure of a higher level, it corrected the mistakes made by the Watches . . .

But it turned out that things weren't as simple as that.

There wasn't any third power. There wasn't and there never had been.

The Inquisition was an instrument for keeping the Dark Ones and the Light Ones apart. It supervised the observance of the Treaty, but not in the interests of people, only in the Others' own interests. The Inquisition was made up of those Others who knew that we were all parasites and a Light Magician was no better than a vampire.

Going to work in the Inquisition was an act of resignation. It meant finally growing up, abandoning the naïve idealism of youth for healthy adult cynicism. Accepting that there were people and there were Others, and they had nothing in common.

Was I ready to accept that?

Yes, I probably was.

But somehow I didn't want to go over to the Inquisition.

It was better to keep toiling away in the Night Watch. To go on doing the work no one needed, protecting the people no one needed.

So why shouldn't I check out our only suspect? While there was still time . . .

Las was already awake. Sitting in his compartment and dully contemplating the bleak view through the window. The tabletop was raised and the bottle of kumis was cooling in the washbasin under a thin trickle of water.

'There's no fridge,' he said mournfully. 'Even in the best compartment you don't get a fridge. Want some kumis?'

'I've already had breakfast.'

'So?'

'Well, maybe just a little bit . . .' I agreed.

Las poured us literally a drop of cognac each, just enough to moisten our lips. As we drank it, Las said thoughtfully:

'Just what came over me yesterday, eh? Please, tell me, why the hell would any rational man go to Kazakhstan for a holiday? Spain maybe. Or Turkey. Or Beijing, for the Festival of Kisses, if you're looking for extreme tourism. But what is there to do in Kazakhstan?'

I shrugged.

'It was a strange mental aberration,' Las said. 'I was just thinking . . .'

'And you decided to get off the train,' I prompted.

'Right. And get on a train going the other way.'

'A sound decision,' I said, quite sincerely. In the first place, we'd have one suspect less. And in the second, a good man would be saved.

'In a couple of hours we'll reach Saratov,' Las said out loud. 'That's where I'll get off. I'll phone one of my business partners and ask him to meet me there. Saratov's a good town.'

'What makes it so good?' I enquired.

'Well . . .' Las poured another two glasses, a bit more generously this time. 'There have been people living around Saratov since time immemorial. That gives it an advantage over the regions of the Far North and suchlike. During Tsarist times it was the capital of a province, but a backward one. No wonder Griboedov's Chatsky said "into the wilderness, to Saratov!" But nowadays it's the industrial and cultural centre of the region, a major railroad junction.'

'Okay,' I said cautiously. I couldn't tell if he was being serious or just talking nonsense, and Saratov could easily be replaced by Kostroma, Rostov or any other city.

'The main reason to stop there is the major railway junction,' Las explained. 'I'll get a bite to eat in some McDonald's and then set off back home. There's an old cathedral too, I'll definitely have a look at that. So my journey's not been completely wasted, has it?'

Our unknown opponent had definitely been overcautious. The suggestion had been too weak and it had dissipated in only twenty-four hours.

'Tell me, what was it that made you suddenly go dashing off to Kazakhstan?' I asked cautiously.

'I told you, I just felt like it,' Las sighed.

'You just felt like it, and that's all?'

'Well . . . I'm sitting there, not bothering anyone, changing the strings on my guitar. Somebody got a wrong number, they were looking for some Kazakh . . . I can't even remember the name. I hung up and started wondering how many Kazakhs there were living in Moscow. And although I had only two strings on my guitar just then, like a dombra, I tightened them up and started strumming. It was strange. There was even a kind of melody . . . sort of haunting, alluring. And I just thought – why don't I go to Kazakhstan?'

'A melody?' I asked.

'Uhuh. Sort of alluring, calling to me. The steppes, kumis, all that stuff . . .'

Could it really have been Witiezslav? Magic is usually imperceptible to an ordinary person. But vampires' magic is something halfway between genuine magic and very powerful hypnosis. It requires a glance, a sound, a touch – some kind of contact, even the very tiniest, between vampire and human being. And it leaves a trace – the sensation of a glance, a sound, a touch . . .

Had the old vampire duped us all?

'Anton,' Las said thoughtfully. 'You don't really trade in milk products.'

I didn't answer.

'If I'd done anything that would interest the security forces, I'd be pissing myself,' Las went on. 'Only I get the feeling this is something that would frighten even them.'

'Let's not get into that, okay?' I suggested. 'It would be best that way.'

'Okay,' Las agreed promptly. 'Right. So what should I do, get off at Saratov?'

'Get off and make straight for home,' I said, nodding as I stood up. 'Thanks for the cognac.'

'Yes sir,' said Las. 'Always glad to be of help.'

I couldn't tell if he was clowning about or not. Evidently that way of speaking just comes naturally to some people.

After a fairly solemn handshake with Las, I went out into the corridor and set off back towards our carriage.

So it was Witiezslav then? What a devious trickster . . . A tried and tested agent of the Inquisition!

I was bursting with excitement. Obviously, having become unimaginably powerful, Witiezslav was capable of disguising himself as absolutely anyone. As that two-year-old boy peeping cautiously out of his compartment. Or that fat girl with the huge, vulgar gold earrings. Even that chief conductor who fawned on Edgar – and why not?

Even Edgar or Kostya . . .

I stopped and gazed at the Inquisitor and the vampire standing in the corridor outside the door to our compartment. What if . . .

No, wait, this is insanity. Everything is possible, but not everything happens. I'm me, Edgar's Edgar, Witiezslav's Witiezslav. Otherwise it's just not possible to do anything.

'I have some information,' I said, standing between Kostya and Edgar.

'Well?' Edgar asked with a nod.

'Las was influenced by a vampire. He remembers . . . something like music luring him into the journey.'

'How poetic,' Edgar snorted. But he wasn't smiling, and nodded approvingly. 'Music? That certainly sounds like bloodsu . . . Sorry, Kostya. Like vampires.'

'You could use the correct term: "Like haemoglobin-dependent Others".' Kostya said with a half-smile.

'Haemoglobin's got nothing to do with it, as you well know,' Edgar snapped. 'Well, it's a lead.' He smiled suddenly and clapped me on the shoulder. 'You never give up. Now the train has a chance. Wait for me here.'

Edgar moved off quickly down the corridor. I assumed he was

on the way to his men, but then I saw him go into the chief conductor's compartment and close the door.

'What scheme has he come up with now?' asked Kostya.

'How should I know?' I glanced sideways at him. 'Maybe there are some special spells for detecting vampires?'

'No,' Kostya snapped. 'It's exactly the same as for all the Others. If Witiezslav's hiding among the humans you won't weed him out with spells. It's all so stupid . . .'

He was clearly nervous now – and I could understand that. After all, it's tough being a member of the most despised minority in the world of Others – and to have to hunt down one of your own kind. He once told me when I was a young, stupid, bold vampire hunter: 'There aren't many of us. When someone departs, we sense it immediately'.

'Kostya, did you sense Witiezslav's death?'

'How do you mean?'

'You once told me you can sense the death of . . . your own kind.'

'We sense it if the vampire's registered. When it's the registration seal that kills him, the recoil is agony for everyone for miles around. Witiezslav didn't have any seal.'

'But Edgar's obviously come up with something,' I muttered. 'Some special kind of Inquisitor's trick, maybe?'

'Probably.' Kostya frowned. 'Why is it like that, Anton? Why are we the ones who are always persecuted . . . even by our own side? The Dark Magicians kill us too!'

Suddenly he was speaking to me the way he used to, when he was still an innocent vampire-boy . . . but then, what kind of innocence could a vampire have? It was terrible, it used to tear me apart – those damned questions and that cursed predestination: and now I was hearing it from someone who had already crossed the line. Who had started to hunt and kill . . .

'You kill . . . for food,' I said.

'And killing for power, for money, for amusement – is that more noble?' Kostya asked bitterly. He turned towards me and looked into my eyes. 'Why do you talk to me so . . . squeamishly? We used to be friends. What happened?'

'You became a Higher Vampire.'

'So what?'

'I know how your kind become Higher Vampires, Kostya.'

He looked into my eyes for a few seconds. And then he started to smile. With that special vampire smile, as though there are no fangs in his mouth yet, but you can already feel them on your throat.

'Ah yes . . . Drink the blood of young virgins and children, kill them . . . The old, classical recipe. That's how dear old Witiezslav became a Higher One . . . Do you mean to say that you never once looked in my file?'

'No,' I replied.

He actually went limp, and his smile became pitiful and confused.

'Not once?'

'No,' I said, already beginning to realise I'd made a mistake somewhere along the line.

Kostya made a clumsy gesture with his hands and began talking in nothing but conjunctions, interjections and pronouns:

'Why that . . . it's . . . look . . . but you . . . and I . . . yes . . . and you . . .'

'I don't like looking in a friend's file,' I said, and added awkwardly: 'Not even a former friend's.'

'And I thought you'd looked at it,' said Kostya. 'Right. This is the twenty-first century, Anton. Look . . .' He reached into his jacket pocket and took out his flask. 'A concentrate of donor's blood. Twelve people give blood – and there's no need to kill anyone. Of course, haemoglobin has nothing to do with it! The emotions a person feels when he gives blood are far more important. You can't imagine how many people are mortally afraid, yet they still go to the doctor and give blood for members of their family. My own personal formula . . . "Saushkins's prescription". Only it's usually called "Saushkin's cocktail". That must be in the file.'

He looked at me triumphantly . . . and probably couldn't understand why I wasn't smiling. Why I didn't mumble guiltily: 'Kostya, forgive me, I thought you were a low son of a bitch and a murderer . . . but you're an honourable vampire, a good vampire, a modern vampire . . .'

Yes, that's what he was. Honourable, good and modern. He hadn't wasted his time in the Haematological Research Institute.

But why had he told me about the formula? About the blood from twelve people?

I knew why. As far as he was concerned, I couldn't have known what was in the *Fuaran*! There was no way I could have known that the spell required precisely the blood of twelve people!

Witiezslav didn't have the blood of twelve people with him. He couldn't have worked the spell in the *Fuaran* and increased his powers.

But Kostya had his flask.

'Anton, what's wrong with you?' Kostya asked. 'Say something!'

Edgar came out of the conductor's compartment still talking, shook the chief conductor's hand and came towards us with a satisfied smile on his face.

I looked at Kostya. And read everything in his eyes.

He knew that I knew.

'Where are you hiding the book?' I asked. 'Quick. This is your last chance. Your only chance. Don't destroy yourself.'

At that moment he struck. Without any magic – unless you can call a vampire's inhuman strength magic. The world exploded in a white flash, the teeth in my mouth crunched and my jaw suddenly went numb. I was sent flying down the corridor and crashed into a passenger who'd come out at the wrong moment for a breath of air. I probably had him to thank for the fact that I didn't lose consciousness – in fact, it was the passenger who flaked out instead of me.

Kostya stood there, rubbing his fist, and his body flickered, moving rapidly into the Twilight and back out again, slipping between the worlds. That ability the vampires have that had once so astounded me . . . I remembered Gennady, Kostya's father, walking towards me across the courtyard, Kostya's mother Polina, with her arm round the shoulders of the vampire who was still a little kid . . . we're law-abiding . . . we don't kill anyone . . . what a surprise – to have a Light Magician as a neighbour . . .

'Kostya!' Edgar exclaimed, coming to a halt.

Kostya slowly turned his head towards Edgar. I couldn't see, but I sensed him bare his fangs.

Edgar flung his hands out in front of him – and the corridor was blocked off by a dull, translucent wall that looked like a layer of rock crystal. Maybe the Inquisitor still hadn't realised what was going on, but his instincts were in good order.

Kostya made a low, howling sound and pressed his hands against the wall. The wall held. The carriage lurched and swayed over the points and behind my back a woman launched into a slow, measured wail. Kostya lurched backwards and forwards, trying to break through Edgar's line of defence.

I raised my hand and directed a 'grey prayer' at Kostya – an ancient spell against non-life. The 'grey prayer' tears to shreds any organic matter raised from the grave that possesses no consciousness of its own and lives only through the will of a sorcerer. It slows vampires down and weakens them.

Kostya swung round when the fine grey threads wrapped themselves around him in the Twilight. He took a step towards me, shook himself – and the spell was torn apart before my eyes. I'd never seen such crude but effective work before.

'Don't get in my way!' he bellowed. Kostya's features had lengthened and sharpened, his fangs were all the way out now. 'I don't want . . . I don't want to kill you . . .'

I managed to get up and crawl over the felled passenger into a compartment. On the top bunks, two men of impressive dimensions started squealing, outdoing the woman who was yelling outside by the door of the washroom. There were glasses and bottles rolling around on the floor underneath me.

In a single bound Kostya appeared in the doorway. He cast a glance at the men – and they fell silent.

'Surrender . . .' I whispered, sitting up on the floor beside the table. The way my jaw moved felt strange – it didn't seem to be dislocated, but every movement was agony.

Kostya laughed:

'I can finish you all off . . . if I want to. Come with me, Anton. Come! I don't want to hurt anyone! What's this Inquisition to you? Or these Watches? We'll change everything!'

He was speaking utterly sincerely. Actually pleading.

Why do you always have to become stronger than anyone else before you can permit yourself weakness?

'Come to your senses . . .' I whispered.

'You fool! You fool!' Kostya growled, taking a step towards me. He reached out his hand – the fingers already ended in claws. 'You . . .'

A half-full bottle of Posolskaya vodka, with its contents draining out lazily, rolled right into my hand.

'It's time we drank to *Brüderschaft*,' I said.

Kostya managed to dodge, but a few splashes still got him in the face. He howled and threw his head back. Even for the Highest Vampire of them all, alcohol is still poison.

I stood up, grabbed a full glass off the little table and drew my hand back. I shouted:

'Night Watch! You're under arrest! Put your hands above your head! Withdraw your fangs!'

At precisely that moment three Inquisitors appeared in the doorway. Either Edgar had summoned them, or they'd sensed something was wrong. They grabbed hold of Kostya, who was still wiping his bloody face. One of them tried to press a grey metal disk against his neck – something charged up to the hilt with magic . . .

Then Kostya showed what he was really capable of.

A kick sent the glass flying out of my hand and flattened my back against the window. The frame gave a loud crack. And then where Kostya had been standing there was nothing but a grey blur – the punches and kicks followed each other faster than any movie hero could have thrown them. There were splashes of blood and scraps of flesh flying in all directions, as if someone was grinding up a piece of fresh meat in a blender. Then Kostya jumped into the corridor, glanced around – and dived through the window as if he hadn't even noticed the twin panes of thick glass.

The glass didn't notice him either.

I caught one last glimpse of Kostya outside, tumbling down the embankment – and then the train hurtled on.

I'd heard about that vampire trick, but I'd always thought it was pure fantasy. Even in the textbooks the phrase 'walking through walls and panes of glass in the real world' was marked with a prudish 'n.p.' – for 'not proven'.

Two of the Inquisitors were lying in a shapeless heap in the compartment, so badly mutilated there was no point in trying to find any kind of pulse.

The third one had been lucky: he was sitting on a bunk, squeezing shut a wound in his stomach.

There was blood slopping down over his feet.

The passengers on the upper bunks weren't yelling any more – one had covered his head with a pillow, the other was staring down with glassy eyes and giggling to himself.

I picked my way across the compartment and staggered out into the corridor.

CHAPTER 5

As THE HERO of a certain hoary old joke put it: 'Now life is returning to normal!'

The passengers in the chief conductor's car were sitting in their compartments, and staring vacantly out of the windows. For some reason people walking through the carriage lengthened their stride and only looked straight ahead. In one closed compartment there were two bodies packed in black plastic sacks and the wounded Inquisitor, who was lying down after a colleague had treated him with healing spells for about fifteen minutes. Another two Inquisitors were standing on guard at the door of our compartment.

'How did you guess?' Edgar asked.

He'd fixed my jaw in about three minutes, after helping his wounded comrade. I hadn't asked what the problem was – simple bruising, a crack or a break. He'd fixed it, that was all I cared about. But my two front teeth were still missing, and it was weird to feel the gap with my tongue.

'I remembered something about the *Fuaran* . . .' I said. In the commotion of the first few minutes after Kostya bolted, I'd had time to think of what to tell the inquisitor. 'The witch . . . you know, Arina . . . said that according to the legends, for the spells in the *Fuaran* to work, you had to have the blood of twelve people. Just a drop from each one would do.'

'Why didn't you tell me earlier?' Edgar asked sharply.

'I didn't think it was important. At the time I thought the whole story of the *Fuaran* was pure fantasy . . . And then Kostya mentioned that his cocktail was made from the blood of twelve people, and it clicked.'

'I see. Witiezslav didn't have twelve people handy,' Edgar said with a nod. 'If only you'd told me straight away . . . if only you'd told me . . .'

'You knew about the formula of the cocktail?'

'Yes, of course. The Inquisition has discussed "Saushkin's cocktail". The stuff doesn't work any miracles, it won't increase a vampire's strength beyond the natural limits. But it does allow a vampire to rise to his maximum potential without killing anyone . . .'

'Rise or sink?' I asked.

'If there's no killing involved, then rise,' Edgar replied coolly. 'And you didn't know . . . would you believe it . . .'

I said nothing.

Yes, I hadn't known. I hadn't wanted to know. What a hero. And now two Inquisitors were wearing black polythene and no one could do anything to help them . . .

'Let's drop it,' Edgar decided. 'What point is there now . . . He's flying after us.'

I glanced at the compass, and had to agree it looked that way. The distance between us and Kostya, or rather, the book, hadn't changed, although the train was travelling at seventy or eighty kilometres an hour. He had to be flying after us. He wasn't making a run for it after all.

'There has to be something he wants in Central Asia . . .' said Edgar, perplexed. 'The only thing is . . .'

'We should summon the Great Ones,' I said.

'They'll come,' Edgar said casually. 'I've informed them of everything, put up a portal . . . they're deciding what to do.'

'I know what they're deciding,' I muttered. 'Zabulon's demanding that Kostya be handed over to him. Together with the *Fuaran*, of course.'

'No one's going to get their hands on the book, don't you worry.'

'Apart from the Inquisition?'

Edgar ignored that.

I made myself more comfortable. Felt my jaw.

It didn't hurt.

But I was upset about the teeth. I'd have to go to a dentist or a healer. The trouble was that even the very best Light healers couldn't fix your teeth without any pain. They simply couldn't do it . . .

The pointer of the compass quivered, but maintained its direction. The distance hadn't changed – ten to twelve kilometres. So Kostya must have undressed and transformed into a bat . . . or maybe some other creature? A gigantic rat, a wolf . . . That wasn't important. He'd transformed, probably into a bat, and was flying after the train, clutching a bundle containing his clothes and the book in his claws. Where had he been hiding it, the bastard? On his body? In a secret pocket in his clothes?

He was a real bastard all right . . . but he had some nerve! The sheer insolence of it – to join in the hunt for himself, to come up with theories, give advice . . .

He'd duped everyone.

But in the name of what? The desire for absolute power? The chances of victory weren't all that good, and Kostya had never been particularly ambitious. He had ambition, of course, but without any crazy ideas about ruling the world.

Why wasn't he making a run for it now? He had the blood of three Inquisitors on his hands. That was something that would never be forgiven, even if he gave himself up and confessed, even if he gave back the book. He ought to run, after first destroying the book that the tracking spell was linked to. But no, he was still carrying the book and following the train. That was just plain stupid . . . Or was he hoping for negotiations?

'How were you expecting to identify Witiezslav among the passengers?' I asked Edgar.

'What?' he answered after a pause, lost in thought. 'A simple trick, the same thing you used: alcohol intolerance. We were going to get dressed up in white coats and carry out a medical inspection of the entire train. Supposedly looking for people with atypical pneumonia. We would have given everyone a thermometer well soaked in medical spirit. Anyone who couldn't take it in his hands or was burned would have been a suspect.'

I nodded. It might have worked. Of course, we'd have been taking a risk, but taking risks was our job. And the Great Ones would have been somewhere close at hand, on call, ready to strike with all their might if necessary.

'The portal's opening . . .' Edgar grabbed hold of my hand and pulled me down onto the bunk. We sat beside each other, with our legs pulled in. A trembling white radiance filled the compartment. There was a low exclamation – Gesar had banged his head against a bunk as he emerged from the portal.

Then Zabulon appeared. In contrast with my boss, he had a mellow smile on his face.

Gesar rubbed the top of his head, looked at me dourly and barked:

'You might as well have put up a portal in a Zaporozhets automobile . . . What's the situation?'

'The passengers have been pacified, we've washed away the

blood, the wounded agent is receiving treatment,' Edgar reported. 'The suspect Konstantin Saushkin is moving parallel with the train at a speed of seventy kilometres an hour.'

'No point calling him a suspect any more . . .' Zabulon said caustically. 'Ah, what a talented boy he was . . . what promise he had.'

'You don't seem to have much luck with promising young colleagues, Zabulon,' Edgar said in a quiet voice. 'Somehow they don't stay around for very long.'

The two Dark Magicians glared at each other with hostility. Edgar had old scores to settle with Zabulon, ever since that business with Fafnir and the Finnish sect. No one likes to be used as a pawn.*

'Please refrain from sarcasm, gentlemen,' said Gesar. 'I could say a few things on my own account . . . to you, Zabulon, and to you, Edgar . . . How powerful is he?'

'Very powerful,' said Edgar, still looking at Zabulon. 'The guy was already a Higher . . .'

'Vampire,' Zabulon said with a contemptuous laugh.

'Higher Vampire. Without much experience, of course . . . far less than you. But then he used the book, and became stronger than Witiezslav. That's already serious. I'm inclined to believe that Witiezslav was at the same grade as you, Great Ones.'

'How did he finish Witiezslav off?' Zabulon asked. 'Do you have any theories?'

'I do now,' Edgar said. 'Vampires have a hierarchy of their own. The boy challenged him to a duel for pre-eminence. It's not very . . . spectacular. A battle of minds, a duel of wills. Rather like a crude stare-out. After a few seconds one backs down and submits totally to the other's will. Whenever the Inquisition came up against vampires, Witiezslav always subdued them easily. But this time he lost.'

* See *The Day Watch*, Story Three

'And was killed,' said Zabulon, nodding.

'That's not necessarily the outcome,' Edgar observed. 'Kostya could have made him his slave. But either he was afraid of losing control or he decided to see it through to the end. Basically he ordered Witiezslav to dematerialise. And Witiezslav had no choice but to obey.'

'A talented boy,' Gesar said ironically. 'I won't lie, Witiezslav's final destruction doesn't exactly upset me . . . Okay, so Konstantin has become more powerful than Witiezslav. Just how powerful, what's your assessment?'

Edgar shrugged.

'How can I assess that? He's more powerful than I am. I assume he's more powerful than either of you. Maybe more powerful than all of us put together.'

'Don't start panicking,' Zabulon muttered. 'He's inexperienced. Magic isn't arm-wrestling, magic's an art When you have a sword in your hand, the important thing is to strike a precise blow, not just swing wildly with all your might . . .'

'I'm not panicking,' Edgar said in a soft voice. 'It's just hard to assess his level of power. It's very high. I used the "crystal shield" – Kostya very nearly broke through it.'

The Great Ones exchanged glances

'The "crystal shield" can't be broken,' Gesar observed. 'And anyway, how could you . . . all right, I understand. More artefacts from the special vault.'

'He very nearly broke through the shield,' Edgar repeated.

'And how did you manage to survive?' Gesar asked me. Maybe I imagined it, but I thought I heard a note of sympathy in his voice.

'Kostya didn't want to kill me,' I said simply. 'He went for Edgar . . . at first I hit him with the "grey prayer"' – Gesar nodded in approval – 'and then I found some vodka and I splashed it in his face. Kostya went wild. But he still didn't want to kill me. Then the Inquisitors distracted him, he tore them to shreds, and left.'

'A purely Russian approach – solving a problem with a glass of vodka,' Gesar said morosely. 'What for? Why did you provoke him? He's not a novice. It must have been obvious you couldn't handle him. Was I supposed to present Svetlana with your remains afterwards?'

'I got carried away myself,' I admitted. 'It was all just so unexpected. Then Kostya started saying "Come with me, I don't want to hurt anyone . . ."'

'He doesn't want to hurt anyone,' Gesar said bitterly. 'A vampire reformer. A progressive lord of the world . . .'

'Gesar, we have to decide what to do,' Zabulon said quietly. 'I can have the fighters from the military airport scrambled.'

Neither magician spoke for a while.

I imagined jet fighters screeching through the sky in pursuit of a bat, blazing away at it with their rockets . . .

A phantasmagorical vision.

'Helicopters then . . .' Gesar said thoughtfully. 'No. That's nonsense, Zabulon. He'll just brush any humans aside.'

'A bomb after all then?' Zabulon asked curiously.

'No!' Gesar shook his head. 'No. Not here. And it's too late for that . . . he's on the alert. We have to strike at him with magic.'

Zabulon nodded. Then suddenly he started giggling.

'What's this?' Gesar asked.

'All my life . . .' said Zabulon. 'Would you believe it, my old enemy? All my life I've dreamed of working in harness with you! Well, now I really am . . . from hatred to love . . .'

'You really are an absolute goon,' Gesar said in a quiet voice.

'We're all a little touched,' Zabulon chuckled. 'Well then? You and me? Or shall we bring in *our* colleagues? They can pump in power, and we can be the spearhead, striking the blow.'

Gesar shook his head.

'No, Zabulon. We shouldn't go near Konstantin. I have a different suggestion . . .'

He looked at me.

I felt at the broken stump of a tooth with my tongue. That was a real drag.

'I'm ready, Gesar.'

'Yes, there's a chance,' Zabulon said, with a nod of approval. 'Since Kostya still allows sentimental considerations to influence him . . . the only thing is, will you be able to strike at him, Anton?'

I paused. I had to think about it seriously.

There was no question of an arrest. I'd have to strike swiftly and surely and kill him. Become the spearhead, the focus of the power that would be pumped into me by Gesar, Zabulon, Edgar . . . maybe other magicians as well. Sure, I was less experienced than the Great Ones. But there was a chance I could get close to Kostya without a fight.

On account of those 'sentimental considerations'.

The alternative was simple – the Great Ones would gather all their power into a single fist. Even Nadya's power would be required – and Gesar would demand that Svetlana initiate our daughter . . .

There was no alternative.

'I'll kill Kostya,' I said.

'Wrong,' Gesar said in a low voice. 'Say it right, watchman!'

'I'll subdue the vampire,' I whispered.

Gesar nodded.

'And don't get all introspective about it, Gorodetsky,' Zabulon added. 'None of your intellectual snivelling. That nice boy Kostya doesn't exist any more. He never did. Maybe he hasn't killed anybody for blood, but he's still a vampire. Non-life.'

Gesar nodded in agreement.

I closed my eyes for a moment.

Non-life.

He was lacking that thing that we call a soul.

A certain vital component that even we Others can't define. From early in his childhood – thanks to his parents. As the boy grew up, the doctor in the local clinic had listened to his heart and admired his robust health. He had turned from a boy into a man, and no girl had ever said his lips were cold when she kissed them. He could have had children – perfectly ordinary children with a perfectly ordinary woman.

But it was all non-life. It was all borrowed and stolen, and when Kostya died, his body would instantly crumble to dust . . . because it had already been dead for a long, long time.

We're all condemned to death from the moment we're born.

But at least we can live until we die.

'Leave me alone with Anton,' Gesar said. 'I'll try to prepare him.'

I heard Zabulon and Edgar stand up. They went out into the corridor. There was a rustling sound – Gesar had evidently shielded us against observation. And then he asked:

'Are you suffering?'

'No.' I shook my head without opening my eyes. 'I'm thinking. Kostya tried not to behave like a vampire, after all . . .'

'And what conclusions have you reached?'

'He won't be able to hold on.' I opened my eyes and looked at Gesar. 'He won't be able to hold on, he'll lose control. He's managed to subdue the physiological need for living blood, but as for all the rest . . . he's non-life among the living and that's a torment to him. Sooner or later Kostya will lose control.'

Gesar waited.

'He's already lost control,' I said. 'When he killed Witiezslav and the Inquisitors . . . one of the Inquisitors was a Light One, right?'

Gesar nodded.

'I'll do the right thing,' I promised. 'I feel sorry for Kostya, but there's nothing to be done.'

'I have faith in you, Anton,' Gesar said. 'Now tell me what you really wanted to ask.'

'What keeps you in the Night Watch, boss?'

Gesar smiled.

'When you get right down to it, we're all tarred with the same brush,' I said. 'We don't fight the Dark Ones, we fight the ones that even the Dark Ones reject – the psychopaths, the maniacs, the lawless ones. For obvious reasons there are more of them among the vampires and the werewolves. The Dark Ones do the same . . . the Day Watch hunts the Light Ones who want to do good to everyone all at once . . . in other words, the ones who might reveal our existence to human beings. The Inquisitors supposedly stand above the fray, but what they actually do is make sure the Watches don't take their functions too seriously. Make sure the Dark Ones don't attempt to gain formal control over the human world and the Light Ones don't try to wipe out the Dark Ones completely . . . Gesar, the Night Watch and the Day Watch are just two halves of a single whole!'

Gesar just looked at me for a while without saying anything.

'Were things . . . deliberately arranged that way?' I asked. Then I answered my own question. 'I guess they were. The young ones, the newly initiated Others, might not have accepted a single Watch for Light Ones and Dark Ones: I can't do that – go out on patrol with a vampire! I would have been outraged by that myself . . . And so two Watches were set up, the lower ranks hunt each other fervently, the leaders plot and intrigue – out of sheer boredom – just to keep up appearances. But it's a joint leadership.'

Gesar sighed and took out a cigar. He cut its tip and lit it.

'And like a fool,' I muttered, still looking at Gesar, 'I always used to wonder how we managed to survive at all. The watches of Samara, of Novogorod Veliky, of little Kireevsky village in the Tomsk region. All supposedly independent. But basically, when there's any kind of problem, they come running to us, to Moscow . . . Okay, the arrangement's not de jure, it's all de facto – but the Moscow Watch runs all the Watches in Russia.'

'And in three of the newly independent states . . .' Gesar added. He blew out a stream of smoke, which gathered into a dense cloud in mid-air, rather than dispersing throughout the compartment.

'So what comes next?' I asked. 'How do the independent Watches of Russia and, say, Lithuania, interact? Or Russia, Lithuania, the USA and Uganda? In the human world what happens is clear enough, whoever has the biggest stick and the thickest wallet calls the tune. But the Russian Watches are stronger than the American ones. I even think . . .'

'The strongest is the French Watch,' Gesar said, sounding bored. 'Strong, but extremely lazy. An amazing phenomenon. We can't understand what the reason is – it can't just be a matter of consuming massive quantities of dry wine and oysters . . .'

'The Watches are run by the Inquisition,' I said. 'It doesn't settle disputes, it doesn't punish renegades, it runs things. It gives permission for one social experiment or another, it appoints and removes the leaders . . . it transfers them from Uzbekistan to Moscow . . . There's one Inquisition, with two operational agencies. The Night Watch and the Day Watch. The Inquisition's only goal is to maintain the existing status quo, because victory for the Dark Ones or the Light Ones means defeat for the Others in general.'

'And what else, Anton?' Gesar asked.

I shrugged.

'What else? Nothing else. People get on with their little human lives and enjoy their little human joys. They feed us with their bodies . . . and provide new Others. The Others who are less ambitious live almost ordinary lives. Only their lives are more prosperous, healthier and longer than ordinary people's. Those who just can't live without excitement, who long for battles and adventures, and struggle for ideals – they join the Watches. The ones who are disillusioned with the Watches join the Inquisition.'

'And? . . .' Gesar asked, encouraging me to continue.

'What are you doing in the Night Watch, boss?' I asked. 'Aren't you sick of it yet . . . after thousands of years?'

'Let's just say that after all this time I still enjoy battles and adventures,' Gesar said.

I shook my head.

'Boris Ignatievich, I don't believe you. I've seen you when you're . . . different. Too weary. Too disillusioned.'

'Then let's assume that I'd really like to finish off Zabulon,' Gesar said calmly.

I thought for a second.

'That's not it either. In hundreds of years one of you would have finished off the other already. Zabulon said that fighting with magic is like swordplay. Well, you're not fighting with swords, you're fencing with blunt rapiers. You claim a hit, but you don't really wound your opponent.'

Gesar nodded and paused before speaking. Another dense stream of tobacco smoke joined the blue-grey cloud.

'What do you think, Anton, is it possible to live for thousands of years and still feel the same pity for people?'

'Pity?'

Gesar nodded.

'Precisely pity. Not love – it's beyond our power to love the entire world. And not admiration – we know only too well what human beings are like'

'It probably is possible to pity them,' I said. 'But what good is your pity, boss? It's pointless, barren. Others don't make the human world any better.'

'We do, Anton. No matter how bad things still are. Trust an old man who's seen a lot.'

'But even so . . .'

'I'm waiting for a miracle, Anton.'

I looked at Gesar quizzically.

'I don't know exactly what kind of miracle. For all people to acquire the abilities of Others. For all Others to become human again. For a day when the dividing line won't run between Other and human being, but between good and evil.' Gesar smiled gently. 'I have absolutely no idea how anything of the sort could ever happen, or if it ever will. But if it ever does . . . I prefer to be on the side of the Night Watch. And not the Inquisition – the mighty, ingenious, righteous, all-powerful Inquisition.'

'Maybe Zabulon's waiting for the same thing?'

Gesar nodded.

'Perhaps. I don't know. But better an old enemy you know than a young, unpredictable freak. You can call me a conservative, but I prefer rapiers with Zabulon to baseball bats with a progressive Dark Magician.'

'And what would you advise me to do?'

Gesar shrugged and spread his hands.

'What advice would I give you? Make up your own mind. You can get out and have an ordinary life. You can join the Inquisition . . . I wouldn't object if you did. Or you can stay in the Night Watch.'

'And wait?'

'And wait. Preserve the part of you that's still human. Avoid falling into ecstatic raptures and trying to impose the Light on people when they don't want it. Avoid relapsing into contemptuous cynicism, imagining that you are pure and perfect. That's the hardest thing of all – never to become cynical, never to lose faith, never to become indifferent.'

'Not a huge choice . . .' I said.

'Ha!' Gesar said, smiling. 'Just be glad that there's any choice at all.'

The suburbs of Saratov sped by outside the windows. The train was slowing down.

I was sitting in an empty compartment, watching the pointer.

Kostya was still following us.

What was he expecting?

Arbenin's voice sang in my earphones:

From deception to deception
Only manna pours down from the sky.
From siesta to siesta
They feed us only manifestos.
Some have gone, some have left.
I have only made a choice.
And I sense it with my back:
We are different, we are other.

I shook my head. It should be 'We are Others'. But even if we were to disappear, everyone would still be divided into ordinary people and Others. No matter how those Others were different.

People can't get by without Others. Put two people on an uninhabited island, and you'll have a human being and an Other. And the difference is that an Other is always tormented by his Otherness. It's easier for ordinary people. They know they're human, and that's what they ought to be. They have no choice but to be that way. All of them, forever.

We stand in the centre,
We blaze like a fire on an ice floe
And try to warm ourselves,
Disguising the means with the goal.
Burning through to our souls
In meditative solitude.

The door opened and Gesar came into the compartment. I pulled the earphones out of my ears.

'Look.' Gesar put his palm-held computer on the table. There was a dot crawling across the map on the screen – our train. Gesar glanced at the compass, nodded and confidently marked a thick line on the screen with his stylus.

'What's that?' I asked, looking at the point that Kostya's trajectory was heading for. I guessed the answer myself: 'An airport?'

'Exactly. He's not hoping for negotiations.' Gesar laughed. 'He's making a dash straight for the airport.'

'Is it military?'

'No, civilian. But what's the difference? He has the piloting templates.'

I nodded. For 'backup' all operational agents carried a collection of useful skills – the ability to drive a car, fly a plane or a helicopter, emergency medical knowledge, martial arts . . . Of course the template didn't provide perfect skills, an experienced driver would overtake an Other with a driving template, a good doctor would operate far more skilfully. But Kostya could get any kind of aircraft into the air.

'Surely that's a good thing,' I said. 'We'll send up the jet fighters and . . .'

'What if there are passengers?' Gesar asked sharply.

'It's still better than the train,' I said quietly. 'Fewer casualties.'

That very moment I felt an odd twinge of pain somewhere

deep inside. It was the first time I'd ever weighed human casualties on the invisible scales of expediency and decided one side was lighter than the other.

'That's no good . . .' said Gesar, and then added: 'Fortunately. What does he care if the plane's destroyed? He'll just transform into a bat and fly down.'

The station platform appeared outside the window. The train blew its whistle as it slowed to a halt.

'Ground-to-air nuclear missiles,' I said stubbornly.

Gesar looked at me in amazement.

'Where from? The nuclear warheads were all removed years ago. Except for the air defence units around Moscow . . . but he won't go to Moscow.'

'Where will he go?' I asked expectantly.

'How should I know? It's your job to make sure he doesn't get anywhere,' Gesar snapped. 'That's it! He's stopped!'

I looked at the compass. The distance between us and Kostya had started to increase. He'd been flying as a bat, or running along as the Grey Wolf from the fairy tale, but now he'd stopped.

The interesting thing was that Gesar hadn't even looked at the compass.

'The airport,' Gesar said, sounding pleased. 'Okay, no more talk. Go. Requisition someone with a good car and get to that airport fast.'

'But . . .' I began.

'No artefacts, he'll sense them,' Gesar retorted calmly. 'And no one else goes with you. He can sense all of us now, you understand? All of us. So get a move on!'

The brakes hissed and the train came to a halt. I paused for a moment in the doorway and heard him say:

'Yes, stick to the "grey prayer". Don't make things complicated. We'll pump you so full of Power he'll be splattered across the airport.'

That was it. Apparently the boss was so fired up I didn't even have to say anything to him – he could hear my thoughts before they were formulated in words.

In the corridor I walked past Zabulon, and couldn't help shuddering when he gave me an encouraging slap on the shoulder.

Zabulon didn't take offence. He just said:

'Good luck, Anton! We're counting on you!'

The passengers were sitting quietly in their compartments. The chief conductor was the only one who watched me go, with a glassy stare, as he made an announcement into a microphone.

I opened the door into the lobby at the end of the carriage, lowered the step and jumped down onto the platform. Everything was moving fast somehow. Too fast . . .

There was the usual bustle in the station. A noisy group tumbled out of the next carriage, and one of them bellowed: 'Now, where are all those grannies with our favourite stuff?'

The 'grannies' – aged from twenty to seventy – were already hurrying to answer the call. Now there'd be vodka, beer, roast chicken legs and pies with dubious fillings.

'Anton!'

I swung round. Las was standing beside me with his bag thrown over his shoulder. He had an unlit cigarette in his mouth and an expression of blissful relief on his face.

'Are you getting off too?' he asked. 'Maybe I can give you a lift somewhere? I've got a car waiting.'

'A good car?' I asked.

'I think it's a Volkswagen.' Las frowned. 'Is that good enough? Or do you insist on a Cadillac?'

I turned my head to look at the windows of the chief conductor's carriage. Gesar, Zabulon and Edgar were watching me.

'That's fine,' I said glumly. 'Right . . . I'm sorry. I'm in a serious hurry and I need a car. I turn you towards . . .'

'Well, let's get going, why are we standing here, if you're in such a hurry?' Las asked, interrupting the standard formula for recruiting volunteers.

He slipped into the crowd so smartly that I had no choice but to follow.

We forced our way through the mindless, jostling throng in the station and out to the square. I caught up with Las and tapped him on the shoulder:

'I turn you . . .'

'I see it, I see it!' Las said, ignoring me. 'Hi, Roman!'

The man who came up to us was quite tall, with a well-fed look, almost like a plump baby. He had a small mouth with thin lips and narrow, inexpressive eyes that looked bored behind his spectacles.

'Hello, Alexander,' the gentleman said formally, holding his hand out smoothly to Las.

'This is Anton, my friend, can we give him a lift?'

'Why shouldn't we give him a lift?' Roman agreed sadly. 'The wheels go round, it's a smooth road.' Then he turned and walked towards a brand-new Volkswagen Bora.

We followed him and got into the car. I impudently slipped into the front passenger seat. Las cleared his throat loudly, but climbed meekly into the back. Roman switched on the ignition and asked:

'Where do you want to go, Anton?'

His speech was as smooth and streamlined as if he wasn't speaking, but writing the words in the air.

'The airport, it's urgent,' I said sombrely.

'Where?' Roman asked in genuine amazement. He looked at Las: 'Perhaps your friend ought to find a taxi?'

Las gave me an embarrassed look. Then he gave Roman an equally embarrassed one.

'All right,' I said. 'I turn you towards the Light. Reject the Dark, defend the Light. I grant you the vision to distinguish Good from Evil. I grant you the faith to follow the Light. I grant you the courage to battle the Dark.'

Las giggled. And then immediately fell silent.

It's not a matter of words, of course. Words can't change anything, not even if you emphasise every last one of them as if they were spelt with a capital letter. It's like the witches' spells – a mnemonic formula, a template implanted in my memory. I can simply compel someone to obey me, but this way . . . this way's more correct. It brings an old, tried and tested mechanism into play.

Roman straightened up and his cheeks even seemed to lose some of their plumpness. A moment ago the person beside me had been an overgrown, capricious infant, but now he was a man. A warrior.

'The Light be with you!' I concluded.

'To the airport!' Roman declared in delight.

The engine roared and we tore off, squeezing every last ounce of power out of the small German car. I'm sure that sports sedan had never really shown what it could do before.

I closed my eyes and looked through the Twilight – at a pattern of branching coloured lines against a background of darkness. Like a crumpled bundle of optical fibres – some green, some yellow, some red. I'm not the best at reading the lines of probability, but this time I found it surprisingly easy. I was feeling in better shape than I ever had before.

That meant there was already power flowing into me. Power from Gesar and Zabulon, Edgar and the Inquisitors. And maybe at that moment Others were entranced right across Moscow, Light Ones and Dark Ones – the ones Gesar and Zabulon had the right to draw Power from.

I'd only ever felt anything like this once before. That time when I drew Power directly out of people.

'We go left at the third turn, there's a traffic jam ahead,' I said. 'Then we turn right into the yard and out through the archway . . . into the side street there . . .'

I'd never been in Saratov before. But that didn't make any difference right now.

'Yes sir!' Roman replied briskly.

'Faster!'

'Very well!'

I looked at Las. He took out a pack of cigarettes and lit up. The car hurtled through the crowded streets. Roman drove with the wild fury of a tram driver who's been given a chance to lap Schumacher in a Grand Prix.

Las sighed and asked:

'Now what's going to happen to me? Are you going to take a little torch out of your pocket and tell me "it was a marsh gas explosion"?'

'You can see for yourself – no torch required,' I said.

'But will I survive?' Las persisted.

'Yes,' I reassured him. 'But you won't remember anything. I'm sorry, but that's standard procedure.'

'I get it,' Las said sadly. 'Shit . . . Why is that always the way? . . . Tell me, since it makes no difference . . .'

The car tore along a side street, bouncing over the potholes. Las stubbed his cigarette out and went on:

'Tell me, who are you?'

'An Other.'

'What sort of other exactly?'

'A magician. Don't worry – I'm a Light Magician.'

'My, but you've grown, Harry Potter . . .' Las said. 'What a crazy business. Maybe I've just lost my mind?'

'No chance . . .' I said, pushing my hands hard against the roof. Roman was really going for it, driving straight across some flowerbeds to cut a corner. 'Careful, Roman! We need to move fast, but safely!'

'Then tell me,' Las carried on. 'Does this car race have anything to do with that abnormally large bat we saw yesterday night?'

'Believe it or not, it does,' I confirmed. The Power was seething inside me, as intoxicating as champagne. It made me feel like clowning. 'Are you afraid of vampires?'

Las took a flat bottle of whisky out of his bag, tore the top off and took a long swig. Then he said cheerfully:

'Not a bit!'

CHAPTER 6

HALFWAY TO THE airport a militia patrol car pulled out and sat on our tail. I put a spell on the Bora that diverts attention and the patrolmen immediately fell back and disappeared. Others normally use that spell to protect their cars against being stolen, so I was delighted to have found a new use for it. But I quickly removed it when a truck nearly flattened us a minute later.

'We'll be there in fifteen or twenty minutes,' Roman reported. 'What will our instructions be, boss?'

Out of the corner of my eye I saw Las shake his head and take another swig. We were already out of town and hurtling along the road to the airport. A fairly decent road by Central Russian standards.

'Turn the radio on,' I said. 'This journey's getting a bit dreary.'

Roman turned it on. He just caught the end of the news:

'. . . to the delight of millions of readers, whose three-year wait has finally come to an end,' the presenter declared. 'And to conclude – an announcement from the cosmodrome at Baikonur, where a joint Russian-American crew is already preparing for lift-off. The launch is planned for six-thirty this evening, Moscow time. And now we continue with our musical . . .'

'Like some whisky?' Las asked.

'No, I've got work to do.'

'Alexander, pull yourself together, this is no time to be drinking!' Roman declared briskly. 'We've got work to do!'

This extremely amiable man, who probably couldn't even have slit a chicken's throat in real life, seemed to think that he was James Bond – or at least his assistant.

We all have something we never got out of our systems when we were children.

'You will guard the car,' I told him. 'This is a very responsible assignment. We are relying on you.'

'I serve the Light!' Roman barked.

'I'd never have believed it . . .' Las groaned on the back seat. 'Shall I guard the car too?'

'Yes.' I nodded. 'Only . . . please, please . . . don't try to run away.'

I heard more gurgling from the back seat. Maybe I ought to turn Las to the Light too? It would be more humane . . . the poor man was suffering unnecessary torment.

But I had no time left to think about it – the car flew out onto the square in front of the terminal building and pulled up at the entrance with a squeal of brakes. Nobody took any notice – someone was late for their flight, it happened all the time . . .

I took out Arina's note and looked at the compass.

The pointer was swaying, but it still indicated a definite direction.

Had Kostya sensed my approach? Gesar had been sure he would.

What lay in store for me?

Strangely enough, up until that moment, I hadn't felt any fear. In my heart of hearts I hadn't been prepared to see Kostya as an enemy – and especially not the kind of enemy who might kill me. I was a second-grade magician – that was already something not to be taken lightly. I had the entire might of the Night Watch behind me and now – something quite unheard of – the might of the Day Watch as well. What could one solitary vampire possibly do to me, even if he was a Higher Vampire?

But just at that moment I recalled Witiezslav's face with his fangs bared.

Kostya had killed him. Overwhelmed him.

'Las,' I said curtly. 'One small request . . . Walk behind me. At a distance. If anything happens . . . they'll find you afterwards, tell them about it.'

Las gulped, dropped the empty bottle on the seat and said soberly:

'I'll do it, why not? Forward, my pale-faced Blade!'

It seemed like he was past the point of worrying about anything. Getting drunk is a good way to give yourself partial protection against a vampire. They find the blood of someone who's drunk unpleasant – and if he's really drunk it's toxic to them. Maybe that was why vampires had always preferred Europe to Russia?

But a vampire doesn't have to drink the blood of someone he's killed. Nourishment is one thing, but business is business.

'Don't come close,' I repeated. 'Keep your distance.'

'Watch your back, boss!' Roman told me. 'Good luck! We're counting on you!'

I looked at him and remembered Zabulon's parting words.

How alike we are.

How alike all of us are – Others and people, Dark Ones and Light Ones.

'Keep it cool, no rush, no aggression,' I said to myself, glancing at the men smoking by the entrance to the terminal building. Most of them were respectable types, wearing ties. The cleaning woman in an orange work jacket standing beside them and puffing away on a Prima looked absurd.

'Calmly and quietly . . .'

I walked towards the building. The smokers moved aside to make way – there was so much Power in me now that even ordinary people could sense it.

Sense it, and do the sensible thing – move aside.

I looked round as I went in. Las was shambling after me, smiling benignly.

Where are you, Kostya?

Where are you, Higher Vampire who has never killed for the sake of Power?

Where are you, boy who dreams of becoming Lord of the World, like in some Hollywood action movie?

In the same place as the vampire trying to cheat his own destiny . . .

I will kill you.

Not 'I must kill you', not 'I can kill you', not 'I want to kill you'. No more auxiliary verbs. I've already been through 'I must' – in tearful soul-searching and self-justification. I've already been through 'I can' – struggling with the complexes of a third-grade magician who has reached his ceiling. I've already been through 'I want to' – with all those turbulent emotions: the passion, the fury, the pity.

Now I'm simply doing what I have to do.

I couldn't give a hoot for false ideals and fake goals, hypocritical slogans and two-faced principles. I don't believe in the Light or the Dark any longer. Light is just a stream of photons. Dark is just the absence of Light. People are our young brothers and sisters. The Others are the salt of the earth.

Where are you, Kostya Saushkin?

Whatever your goal is – ancient eastern artefacts or a million-strong army of Chinese magicians – I won't let you win.

Where are you?

I stopped in the middle of the hall – the rather small hall of a provincial airport. I thought I could sense him . . .

A heavily perspiring man carrying suitcases bumped into me, apologised and walked on. I noted his aura in passing – an uninitiated Other, a Light One. He was afraid of flying but he'd arrived safely and now he'd relaxed, which was what had made him noticeable.

I wasn't interested in that right now.

Kostya?

I swung round as if someone had called my name and stared at the door with a sign that said 'Service Entrance' and a coded lock.

A melody that no one else could hear threaded itself through the hubbub of the airport.

He was calling me.

The buttons on the keypad lit up helpfully when I reached my hand out towards them. Four, three, two, one. A very cunning code . . .

I opened the door, looked round and nodded to Las, then closed the door behind me carefully, so that it wouldn't latch shut.

Empty corridors, painted a depressing green. I moved along one of them.

The melody grew stronger, swirling in the air, soaring upwards and gliding back down. Like an intricate passage on a classical guitar, supported by the subtle notes of a violin.

This was it – a genuine vampire's call, directed at me . . .

'I'm coming as fast as I can,' I muttered, turning off towards another door with a code lock. A door banged behind me – that was Las following me in.

A new lock, a new code. Six, three, eight, one.

I opened the door, and found myself on the apron of the airport.

A round-bellied Airbus was creeping slowly across the concrete. Further away a Tupolev was taxiing out to the runway, its turbines roaring.

Kostya was standing about five metres away from the door, holding a neat little plastic briefcase – I guessed that was where the *Fuaran* must be. Kostya's shirt was ripped, as if at some moment it had suddenly become too small.

When he jumped off the train he must have started to transform straight away, without taking all his clothes off.

'Hi,' said Kostya.

The music stopped, breaking off in mid-note.

I nodded.

'Hi. You flew here very quickly.'

'Flew?' Kostya shook his head. 'No . . . flying that kind of distance as a bat is too hard.'

'Then what did you turn into? A wolf?'

This rather farcical conversation was wound up by an especially ridiculous remark from Kostya:

'A hare. A huge grey hare. I hopped all the way . . .'

I couldn't help smiling as I pictured the giant hare running through the market gardens, forging streams in massive leaps and hopping over fences. Kostya shrugged:

'Well . . . it was quite funny. How are you feeling? I didn't hit you too hard, did I? Have you still got all your teeth?'

I tried to smile as broadly as I could.

'I'm sorry about that,' said Kostya. He seemed genuinely distressed. 'That's because it was all so sudden. How did you realise I had the book? Because of the cocktail?'

'Yes. The spell requires the blood of twelve people.'

'How did you know that?' Kostya mused. 'There isn't any information available on the *Fuaran* . . . but that's not important. I have something to say to you, Anton.'

'And I've got something to say to you,' I said. 'Turn yourself in. You can still save your own life.'

'I haven't been alive for a long time,' Kostya said with a smile. 'I'm undead. Or had you forgotten?'

'You know what I mean.'

'Don't lie to me, Anton. You don't believe it yourself. I killed four Inquisitors!'

'Three,' I corrected him. 'Witiezslav and two on the train. The third survived.'

'Big difference.' Kostya frowned. 'They've never forgiven anybody even for one.'

'This is a special case,' I said. 'I'll give it to you straight. The Higher Ones are frightened. They can destroy you, but the victory will be too costly. So they will negotiate.'

Kostya just stared at me hard without saying a word.

'If you give back the *Fuaran* and turn yourself in voluntarily, they won't touch you,' I continued. 'You're a law abiding vampire. It's the book that's to blame. The balance of your mind was affected . . .'

Kostya shook his head:

'There was nothing wrong with my mind. Edgar didn't take what Witiezslav said seriously. But I believed him. I transformed and flew to the hut. Witiezslav didn't suspect a trick . . . he started showing me the book and explaining. When I heard about the blood of twelve people, I realised this was my chance. He didn't even object to an experiment. He probably wanted to make sure the book was genuine as quickly as possible. It was only when he realised I'd become stronger than him that he dug his heels in. But by then it was too late.'

'What's all this about?' I asked. 'Kostya, this is insanity! Why do you want the power to rule the world?'

Kostya raised his eyebrows. He looked at me like that for a moment and then laughed.

'What are you talking about, Anton? What power? You don't understand a thing!'

'I understand everything,' I insisted. 'You're trying to get to China, right? A million magicians under your control?'

'You idiots,' Kostya said, almost whispering. 'You're all idiots. There's only one thing you ever think about . . . Power . . . I don't want that kind of power! I'm a vampire! Do you understand? I'm an outcast! Worse than any of the Others! I don't want to be the most powerful outcast. I want to be ordinary! I want to be like everybody else!'

'But the *Fuaran* won't allow you to turn an Other into a human being . . .' I objected.

Kostya laughed. He shook his head:

'Hello! Anton, switch on! They've pumped you full of Power and sent you here to kill me, I know that. But think first, Anton. Understand what it is I want.'

The door squeaked behind me and Las came out. He gaped at me in embarrassment, then squinted at Kostya.

Kostya shook his head.

'Not a good time?' Las asked, taking in the situation. 'Sorry. I'll be going . . .'

'Stop,' Kostya said in a flat voice. 'This is a very good time.'

Las froze. I hadn't caught the note of command in Kostya's voice, but it must have been there.

'A natural experiment,' said Kostya. 'Watch how it's done . . .'

He shook the briefcase. The locks clicked, the briefcase opened and out flew a book, moving ponderously through the air.

The *Fuaran*.

The book really was bound in skin – it was a greyish-yellow colour. The corners were encased in triangles of copper, and there was a lock to prevent the book being opened.

Kostya caught the book in one hand and opened it with incredible agility, as if simply opening a newspaper, rather than manipulating a volume that weighed about two kilos. He let go of the briefcase and it clattered on the concrete.

'Most of the stuff in here is just padding,' Kostya laughed. 'A record of unsuccessful experiments. The formula's at the end . . . it's really very simple.'

With his free hand Kostya took a metal flask out of the back pocket of his jeans. He twisted off the top and poured a drop of liquid straight on to the open page.

What am I waiting for?

What is he going to do?

Everything inside me was crying out – attack! While he's distracted, strike with all your power!

But I waited, spellbound by the spectacle.

The drop of blood was disappearing from the page. Melting away, evaporating in a brown mist. And the book . . . the book began to sing. A strangled sound, like throat music – it sounded like a human voice, but there was nothing intelligible in it.

'By the Dark and the Light . . .' said Kostya, looking into the open pages. He could see something there that I couldn't. 'Om . . . Mrigankandata gauri . . .Auchitya dkhvani . . .By my will . . .Moksha gauri . . .'

The voice of the book – I had no doubt that it was the book that was making that sound – became louder. It drowned out Kostya's voice and the words of the spell – both the Russian ones and the other, ancient ones in which the *Fuaran* was written.

Kostya raised his voice, as if he was trying to shout down the book.

I could only make out his last word – 'om' again.

The singing broke off on a sharp, dissonant note.

Behind me Las swore and asked:

'What was that?'

'The sound of the ocean,' Kostya laughed. He bent down, picked up the briefcase and put the book and the flask in it. 'An entire ocean of new possibilities.'

I swung round, already knowing what I would see. I half closed my eyes, catching the shadow of my own eyelashes with my pupils.

I looked at Las through the Twilight.

The aura of an uninitiated Other was quite distinct. Welcome to our happy family . . .

'That's how it works on people,' said Kostya. There were beads of sweat clinging to his forehead, but he looked pleased. 'So there you go.'

'Then what is it you *do* want?' I asked.

'I want to be an Other among Others,' said Kostya. 'I want all this division to stop . . . Light Ones and Dark Ones, Others and people, magicians and vampires. They're all going to be Others, get it? Everyone in the world.'

I laughed.

'Kostya . . . you spent two or three minutes on just one person. How's your maths?'

'There could have been two hundred people standing here,' said Kostya, 'and they would all have become Others. There could have been ten thousand. The spell works on everybody in my field of vision.'

'Even so . . .'

'In an hour and a half the next crew of the International Space Station takes off from the Baikonur cosmodrome,' said Kostya. 'I think the space tourist from Germany is going to let me take his place.'

I was silent for a second, trying to make sense of what he had said.

'I'll sit quietly by the window and gaze at the Earth,' said Kostya. 'The way a space tourist is supposed to do. I'll look at the Earth, spread the blood from the flask on the paper and whisper the spells. And way down below the people will become Others. All the people – do you understand? From the infants in their cradles to the old folks in their rocking chairs.'

He looked genuinely alive now, and absolutely sincere. His eyes were blazing – not with vampire Power, but with undiluted human passion.

'You used to dream about that yourself, didn't you, Anton? That there wouldn't be any more ordinary people. That everyone would be equal.'

'I used to dream that all the people would be Others,' I said. 'Not that there wouldn't be any more people.'

Kostya frowned.

'Drop that! That's nothing but verbal gymnastics . . . Anton, we have a chance to make the world a better place. Fuaran couldn't have done it – in her time there were no space ships. Gesar and Zabulon can't do it – they haven't got the book. But we can – we can! I don't want any power, understand that! I want equality! Freedom!'

'Happiness for everyone, a free handout?' I asked. 'With no one left short-changed and resentful?'

He didn't understand.

'Yes, happiness for everyone. The Earth for Others. And no more grievances and resentment. Anton, I want you with me. Join me.'

'What a wonderful idea!' I exclaimed, looking into his eyes. 'Brilliant, Kostya!'

I'd never been good at lying. And deceiving a vampire is almost impossible. But Kostya evidently very much wanted me to agree.

He smiled. And relaxed.

And at that instant I raised my hands and struck out at him with the 'grey prayer'.

It was nothing like the blow I had struck in the train. The Power was seething inside me, streaming from the tips of my fingers – and it kept coming, on and on. How can you tell if you're a good conductor of electricity until they switch on the current?

The spell was visible even in the human world. Looping grey

coils sprang from my fingers, twining themselves round Kostya, clutching and wrenching at him, enveloping him in a writhing cocoon. What happened in the Twilight was incredible – the world was filled with a seething blizzard of grey that made the usual mist seem colourful. The thought came to me that if there were any ordinary registered vampires within a radius of several kilometres, they wouldn't be feeling too great either. They'd be swept away and dematerialised by the ricochet from the spells . . .

Kostya went down on one knee. He shuddered, trying to break free, but the 'grey prayer' was sucking Power out of him faster than he could work his spells.

'Hell's bells!' Las exclaimed in delight behind me.

Never had so much Power passed through me.

Something strange was happening to the world around me. The plane on the runway faded and became a colourless stone monolith. The sky faded to a dull white shroud hanging low above the ground. My ears seemed to be blocked with cotton wool.

The Twilight seemed to be breaking through into our world . . .

But I couldn't stop. I could sense that if I eased up on the pressure for even a second, Kostya would break free and strike back. Strike so hard, there'd be no pieces left to pick up . . . it would be me, not Kostya, smeared across the concrete apron . . .

He raised his head and looked at me. Not in fury, more in melancholic bewilderment. He parted his hands very, very slowly . . .

Could he really have any reserves of power left?

A transparent, bluish triangular prism took shape in the air around Kostya. It severed the grey threads of the spell, spun round and shrank to a tiny point. Then disappeared.

Taking the vampire with it.

Kostya had got away, through a portal.

The Power was still raging inside me. The Power of a thousand Others, transmitted to me by Gesar and Zabulon, a boundless flood of Power, seeking a use, a point of application. Human Power that came to me at third hand . . .

Enough . . .

I brought my palms together, crumpling the grey threads into a heavy ball.

Enough . . .

There was no enemy here any more.

Enough . . .

Magicians duel by fencing, not by flailing with clumsy clubs.

Enough.

Kostya had proved more skilful.

I was trembling violently, but I stopped myself. The sky took on a blue colour again, the plane on the runway picked up speed.

Kostya had gone.

Had he turned and run?

No, simply gone. I'd never heard of vampires capable of creating a direct portal. And it looked like the Higher Ones hadn't expected Kostya to pull an incredible stunt like that either.

He'd come to the airport, knowing that everyone would start thinking about planes and helicopters and relax, sure that there was still some time left. A vampire could be intercepted in mid-air, you could send up the jet fighters, you could hit him with a missile.

But he'd had the direct portal ready in advance. An hour and a half before the launch – he wouldn't have had time to get there by plane! And they wouldn't have let a plane anywhere near Baikonur – whatever they might be like now, the air defence forces still existed. That was why he'd been able to make the jump, even under pressure from the 'grey prayer' – the spell for the portal had been hanging there, ready for use, like the combat spells of a field operations magician.

That meant he hadn't believed I would go over to his side. Or at least he'd had serious doubts. But it had been important to him, very important, to defeat me, not by pure Power – what could Power prove, when he was a Higher Vampire, and I was a second-grade magician, even if pumped full of borrowed Power? The most complete and convincing victory is when your opponent admits that you're right. And surrenders without a fight. Accepts your banner as his own.

I'd been really stupid. I'd thought of him as being either a friend or an enemy. But he was neither. All he'd wanted to do was prove that he was right. I just happened to be the target he'd chosen for that. No longer a friend, not yet an enemy. Simply the bearer of a different truth.

'Did he teleport?' Las asked.

'What?' I swung round and looked at him. 'Well . . . something of the sort. He opened a portal. How did you know?'

'I saw something that looked like that in a computer game . . .' Las said uncertainly. Then he added indignantly: 'A lot like that, in fact!'

'People aren't the only ones who can design games . . .' I explained. 'Yes, he got away. He's gone to Baikonur. He wants to take the German space tourist's place . . .'

'I heard,' said Las. 'What an idiot.'

'Do you know why he's an idiot?' I asked.

Las snorted.

'If all people become magicians . . . Today they insult you on the trolley bus, tomorrow they'll incinerate you on the spot. Today they scratch their neighbour's door with a nail if they don't like him, or write an anonymous letter to the tax office, but tomorrow they'll hex him or suck all his blood out. A monkey on a motorbike is only good in a circus, not on the city streets . . . Especially if the monkey's got a machine gun.'

'You think the monkeys are in the majority?' I asked.

'We're all monkeys.'

'You're headed for the Watch,' I muttered. 'Hang on, I'll ask for advice.'

'What Watch?' Las asked cautiously. 'Thanks, but I'm no magician, thank God!'

I closed my eyes and listened. Silence.

'Gesar!'

Silence.

'Gesar! Teacher!'

'We were in conference, Anton.'

In mind conversations, there are no inflections of the voice. But even so . . . even so I thought I could detect a hint of weariness in Gesar's words.

'He went to Baikonur. The *Fuaran* really works. He wants to turn everybody on the planet into Others.'

I stopped, because I realised Gesar already knew. He'd seen and heard everything that happened – through my eyes and ears, or by using some other magical method, it wasn't important how.

'You have to stop him, Anton. Go after him and stop him.'

'And you?'

'We're keeping the channel open, Anton. Supplying you with Power. Do you know how many Others provided Power for the "grey prayer"?'

'I can imagine.'

'Anton, I can't handle him. Zabulon can't handle him. Or Svetlana. The only thing we can do now is feed Power to you. We're drawing it from all the Others in Moscow. If necessary, we'll start taking it directly from people. There's no time to regroup and use different magicians as channels. You have to stop Kostya . . . with our help. The alternative is a nuclear strike at Baikonur.'

'I won't be able to open a direct portal, Gesar.'

'Yes you will. The portal still hasn't closed completely, you need to find the opening and reactivate it.'

'Gesar, don't overestimate me. Even with your Power, I'm still a second-grade magician!'

'Anton, use your head. You were standing in front of Saushkin when he recited the spell. You're not second-grade any more.'

'Then what am I?'

'There's only one grade above first – Higher Magician. Enough talking, get after him!'

'But how am I going to defeat him?'

'Any way you like.'

I opened my eyes.

Las was standing before me and waving his hand in front of my face.

'Oh! Still alive!' he said, delighted. 'So what is this Watch? And do you mean to say I'm a magician too now?'

'Almost.' I took a step forward.

This was where Kostya had been standing . . . he fell . . . parted his hands . . . the portal appeared.

In the human world – nothing.

Just the wind blowing, the crumpled cellophane cover from a pack of cigarettes rustling over the concrete . . .

In the Twilight – nothing.

Grey gloom, stone monoliths instead of buildings, the rustling tendrils of the blue moss . . .

In the second level of the Twilight.

Dense, leaden mist . . . a dead, spectral light from behind heavy clouds . . . a small blue spark where the portal had been . . .

I reached out my hand –
in the human world,
in the first level of the Twilight,
in the second level of the Twilight . . .

I caught the fading blue spark in my fingers.

Wait. Don't go out. Here's Power for you – a raging torrent of energy, rupturing the boundary between worlds. Streaming from my fingers in drops of fire – onto the fading embers . . .

Grow, unfold, creep out into the bright light of day – there's work for you to do! I sense the trace left by the one who opened the portal. I see how he did it. I can follow his path.

And I don't need any incantations – all those formulae in obscure ancient languages – just as the witch Arina didn't need them when she brewed her potions, just as Gesar and Svetlana don't need them.

So this is what it's like to be a Higher Magician

Not to learn formulae off by heart, but to feel the movement of Power.

How incredible . . . and simple.

It wasn't a matter of new abilities, of a fireball with increased casualty capability or a more powerful 'freeze'. If he's pumped full of Power from outside or has accumulated a large reserve of his own, an ordinary magician can lash out hard enough to make a Higher Magician feel it. It was a matter of freedom. Like the difference between even the most talented swimmer and the laziest dolphin.

How difficult it must have been for Svetlana to live with me, forgetting about her Power, her freedom. This wasn't just the difference between strength and weakness – it was the difference between a healthy person and an invalid.

But ordinary people managed to live, didn't they? And they lived with the blind and the paralysed. Because, after all, freedom was not the most important thing. Freedom was the excuse used by scoundrels and fools. When they said 'freedom', they weren't thinking about other people's freedom, only about their own limitations.

And even Kostya, who was neither a fool nor a scoundrel, had been torn on the same hook that had caught the lips of revolutionaries of every breed – from Spartacus to Trotsky, from Robespierre to Che Guevara, from Emelyan Pugachev to the nameless suicide bomber.

Surely I would have been caught on it myself? Ten or even five years earlier?

If someone had told me: 'You can change everything at a single stroke – and for the better'?

Perhaps I'd been lucky.

At least with the people around me, who always shook their heads doubtfully at the words 'freedom and equality'.

The portal opened up in front of me – a blue prism with glowing filaments, a glittering, faceted membrane . . .

I parted the filaments with my hands and entered.

CHAPTER 7

THE PROBLEM WITH portals is that there's no way to prepare yourself for what's at the other end. In this sense a train is ideal. You go into your compartment, change your trousers for track-suit bottoms and your shoes for rubber sandals, take out your food and drink and get to know your travelling companions – if you happen to be travelling on your own, that is. The wheels drum on the rails, the platform slips past. And that's it, you're on your way. You're a different person. You share intimate experiences with strangers, you argue about politics, although you swore you never would again, you drink the dubious vodka bought at one of the stops. You're neither here nor there. You're on your way. You're on your own little quest, and there's a little of Frodo Baggins in you, and a bit of Paganel, a tiny drop of Robinson Crusoe and a smidgeon of Radishchev. Maybe your journey will last a few hours, or a few days. It's a big country slipping past the windows of your compartment. You're not there. You're not here. You're a traveller.

A plane is different. Still, you prepare yourself for the journey. You buy a ticket, get up at dawn, jump into a taxi and drive to the airport. The wheels measure out the kilometres, but you're already looking up at the sky, in your mind you're already there, in the plane. The nervous hassle of the airport lounge, instant coffee in the buffet, the baggage check, the security check and – if you're leaving the country – the customs and the duty free shop, all the small joys of travel before the narrow seats in the plane, the roar of the turbines and the optimistic gabble of the air hostess: 'The emergency exits are located . . .' And then the ground has already fallen away, the seatbelt signs have been switched off, the smokers have sneaked off guiltily to the toilets and the hostesses have considerately ignored them, the meal in the plastic trays is handed out – for some reason in planes everyone stuffs themselves. It's not exactly a journey. It's a relocation. But you still see the cities and rivers drifting past and leaf through a guidebook or check the bookings for your business trip, wondering about the best way to handle the negotiations, or the best way to enjoy a ten-day tourist trip to hospitable Turkey or Spain or Croatia. And you're on your way.

But a portal is a shock. A portal is a sudden change of scenery, a revolving stage in a theatre. You're here, then you're there. No journey.

And no time to think about anything either.

I tumbled out of the portal. One foot struck a tiled floor, the other went straight into a toilet.

At least it was a perfectly clean toilet. I pulled my foot back out, wincing with pain as I did so.

I was in a tiny cubicle with a little lamp, a grille on the ceiling and a roll of toilet paper on a holder. A fine portal this was! Somehow I'd been expecting Kostya to run his portal straight to the launch pad, close to the foot of the rocket.

I opened the door, still in pain, and peeped cautiously through the crack. The washroom seemed to be empty. Not a sound, apart from a tap running in one of the basins . . .

Then I was struck hard in the back and thrown bodily out of

the cubicle, pushing the door open with my head on the way. I rolled over onto my back and flung my hand up, ready to strike.

Las was standing in the cubicle with his arms out to the sides, holding onto the walls, and gazing around with a crazy expression on his face.

'What are you doing?' I growled. 'Why did you follow me?'

'You told me to follow you,' said Las, offended. 'Big-shot magician!'

I got up. It was pointless arguing.

'I need to stop a crazed vampire,' I said. 'The most powerful magician in the world at the present time. It's . . . it's going to get pretty dangerous around here . . .'

'Are we at Baikonur then?' Las asked, not frightened in the least. 'Now that's what I call magic, that's great! But did we really have to teleport through the drains?'

I just waved a hand at him despairingly. Then I focused intently on what I could hear inside me. Yes, Gesar was somewhere close by, and Zabulon . . . and Svetlana . . . and hundreds, thousands of Others. They were waiting.

They were counting on me.

'How can I help?' Las asked. 'Maybe I could look for some aspen stakes? By the way, they make matches out of genuine aspen, did you know that? I always wondered why it had to be aspen, does it really burn better than anything else? But now I realise it's for fighting vampires. Sharpen a dozen matches . . .'

I looked at Las.

He spread his arms apologetically.

'All right, all right . . . I'm only trying to be helpful.'

I walked across to the door of the washroom and looked out. A long corridor, daylight lamps, no windows. At the end was a man in uniform with a pistol on his belt. A guard? Yes, there had to be security guards here. Even these days.

Only why was the guard frozen in such a stiff, awkward pose?

I went out into the corridor and moved towards the soldier. I called quietly:

'Excuse me, do you mind if I ask you something?'

The guard didn't mind. He was staring into space – and smiling. A young man, not yet thirty. Absolutely rigid. And very pale.

I pressed my fingers against his carotid artery – I could just barely feel the pulse. The bite marks were almost invisible, there were just a few small drops of blood on the collar. Kostya must have been drained after that exit he'd made. He'd been in need of refreshment, and there hadn't been any cats around . . .

But if the soldier was still alive, there was a chance he would make it.

I took his pistol out of the holster – it looked like he must have been reaching for it when the vampire's command made him freeze – and carefully laid him out on the floor. Let him rest. Then I turned round.

Of course, Las had followed me. And now he was gazing at the motionless soldier.

'Can you use a gun?' I asked.

'I'll give it a try.'

'If you have to, aim for the head and the heart. If you hit him, it might just slow him down.'

Naturally, I was under no illusions. Even if Las emptied the entire clip into Kostya, which was unlikely enough, bullets wouldn't stop a Higher Vampire. But at least it gave Las something to do.

I just hoped he wouldn't get the jitters and shoot me in the back.

Finding Kostya wasn't hard, even without using magic. We came across another three men – a guard and two civilians – who were in a trance and had been bitten. Kostya must have been moving in that vampire style that becomes too fast for the eye to follow, when feeding takes no more than ten seconds.

'Will they become vampires now?' Las asked me.

'Only if he wanted them to. And they agreed.'

'I didn't think there was any choice.'

'There's always a choice,' I said, opening yet another door.

I realised we'd arrived.

It was a spacious, brightly lit hall, full of people. At least twenty men. The cosmonauts were here – our captain, and the American, and the space tourist, a German chocolate manufacturer.

They were all in a state of blissful trance. Apart from two technicians in white coats, that is, whose eyes were vacant, but whose hands were moving with their customary skill as they helped Kostya put on a spacesuit. It wasn't an easy job – flight suits are made to measure, and Kostya was a bit taller than the German.

The unfortunate tourist, stripped naked – Kostya hadn't even been worried about putting on his underwear – was sitting at one side, sucking on his index finger.

'I've only got two or three minutes,' Kostya said cheerfully. 'So don't try to stop me, Anton. Get in my way and I'll kill you.'

My appearance was no surprise to him, of course.

'They won't let the rocket take off,' I said. 'What were you expecting? The Higher Ones know what you're planning.'

'They'll let it go, they have no choice,' Kostya replied calmly. 'The air defence cover here is pretty good, you can take my word for it. And the cosmodrome's head of security has just given all the necessary instructions. Are you trying to tell me they'll launch a ballistic missile strike?'

'Yes.'

'You're bluffing,' Kostya replied coolly. 'A strike by the Chinese or the Americans is out of the question. That would start a world war. Our rockets aren't targeted on Baikonur. They won't let planes with tactical warheads get close. You've no way out. Lie back, relax and enjoy.'

Maybe he was right.

Or perhaps the Great Ones did have a plan to incinerate Baikonur with a nuclear strike – and not start a world war.

That wasn't important.

The important thing was that Kostya had made up his own mind that he wouldn't be stopped. That now they would take him out and put him in the rocket . . . and what then?

What would he be able to do, sitting in a metal barrel, when the portals of a dozen Higher Magicians opened on the launch pad? When they instantly purged the brains of the head of security and those who had to press the start button and destroyed him with a portable nuclear missile or by activating some secret satellite with an x-ray laser?

He wouldn't be able to do a thing!

A space ship isn't a car – you can't just steal it and drive it away. A space launch is the co-ordinated effort of a thousand people, and at every stage all it needs is for one little button to be pressed to make sure the ship never reaches orbit.

Even if Kostya was a stupid fool, he was a Higher One now, he should be reading the probability lines to foresee what would happen – he must realise that he'd be stopped.

That meant . . .

That meant all of it – the cosmodrome, the rocket, the people whose minds he'd taken over or put to sleep – all of it was a blind, a bluff. Saratov airport all over again.

He didn't need a rocket! Just as he hadn't needed a plane!

He was going to open a portal straight into space.

So why had he come dashing to Baikonur? For the spacesuit? Nonsense. Zvyozdny would have been much nearer, and somehow or other he could have found a functional spacesuit the right size there.

So it wasn't just for the spacesuit . . .

'I need to read the incantations,' Kostya said. 'To smear the blood on the page. You can't do that in a vacuum.'

He got up and pushed the technicians aside. They stood obediently to attention.

'I'll have to open a portal to the space station. For that I need to know its precise position. And even so mistakes are possible . . . maybe even inevitable.'

I couldn't sense him reading my thoughts, but he clearly was.

'You got everything right, Anton. I'm ready to depart for the station at any second. Before all of you can do anything about it. And even if Gesar and Zabulon turn themselves inside out, you won't have enough Power. I'm as powerful as it's possible to be, get it? Absolute Power! There is nowhere higher to go! Gesar dreamed that your daughter would be the first enchantress to do that . . .' Kostya laughed. 'But look – I'm the first!'

'Enchantress?' I asked, allowing myself a smile.

'Absolute Magician,' Kostya snapped. 'And that's why you can't beat me. You can't gather enough Power, do you understand? I am absolute!'

'You're an absolute zero,' I said. 'You're an absolute vampire.'

'Vampire, magician . . . what's the difference? I'm an absolute Other.'

'You're right, there is no difference. We all live off human Power. And you're not the most powerful of all – you're the weakest. You're an absolute vacuum, sucking in Power that isn't yours.'

'So be it.' Kostya wasn't going to argue. 'That doesn't change a thing, Anton. You can't stop me, and I'm going to carry out my plan.'

He paused for a second, then said:

'And still you won't join me . . . What's going on in your head?'

I didn't answer. I drew in Power.

From Gesar and Zabulon, from Dark Ones and Light Ones, from the Good and the Evil. Somewhere far away those I loved and those I hated were all giving me their Power. And right then it made no difference to me if that Power was Light or Dark. We were all in the same boat now – in the same small boat out in space, adrift in the absolute void . . .

'Go on, strike,' Kostya said contemptuously. 'You won't take me by surprise again.'

'Strike,' Gesar whispered. 'Strike with the "white mist".'

The knowledge of what the 'white mist' was came creeping into me together with the Light power. The knowledge was terrible, frightening – even Gesar himself had only ever used the spell once, and afterwards he'd sworn never to use it again . . .

'Strike!' Zabulon advised me. 'Better use "shades of the rulers".'

The knowledge of 'shades of the rulers' slid into me together with the Dark power. The knowledge was even more horrifying – not even Zabulon had ever dared raise those shadows from the fifth level of the Twilight . . .

'Strike!' said Edgar. 'Use the "sarcophagus of the ages". Only the "sarcophagus of the ages"!'

The knowledge of what the 'sarcophagus of the ages' was flooded into me with the Power of the Inquisitors. The knowledge was utterly spine-chilling – the one who used the spell remained in the sarcophagus with his victim forever, until the universe came to an end.

'What if I put a hole in his spacesuit?' asked Las, standing in the doorway with his pistol.

An absolute Other.

An absolute zero.

The most powerful of all, the weakest of all . . .

I gathered together all the power I had been given – and put it into a seventh-degree spell, one of the very simplest, one every Other can manage.

The 'magician's shield'.

So much power had probably never been wasted so senselessly.

Now not a single magician in the world was so reliably protected.

Against everything.

A white reticulated cocoon appeared around me. The threads of the cocoon crackled with the energy streaming through them. It was rooted way down in the deepest depths of the universe, beyond the countless levels of the Twilight, where there is no matter, or space, or time – nothing that a human being or Other can comprehend.

'What are you doing?' Kostya asked, with an expression of childish resentment on his face. 'What are you doing, Anton?'

I didn't answer, just stood there, looking at him. I didn't want even the shadow of a thought to show on my face. I wanted him to think whatever he wanted to think.

Let him.

'Are you frightened?' Kostya asked. 'You . . . why you . . . you're a coward, Anton!'

I didn't answer.

And the Higher Ones were silent too. Or, more likely, they were shouting, swearing, cursing me – because I'd squandered all the power they'd collected on absolute protection for myself.

If they hit Baikonur with a thermonuclear warhead now, I'd be left safe and unharmed. Floating in a cloud of plasma, encased in boiling stone, but completely safe.

'I don't even know what to say . . .' Kostya shrugged. 'I wasn't going to kill you anyway. I haven't forgotten that you were my friend.'

I didn't answer.

Forgive me, but I can't call you my friend any more. That's why you must not realise what I have realised. You must not read my thoughts.

'Goodbye, Anton,' Kostya said.

The technicians came over to him and lowered the glass shield of his helmet. He cast a final glance at me through the glass – a glance of incomprehension and resentment. And then turned away.

I was expecting him to open the portal into space there and then. But Kostya had made his preparations for the leap thoroughly. What did I know? I'd never even heard of anyone attempting to transport themselves on board an aeroplane in flight, let alone a space station in orbit.

Abandoning the cosmonauts and the personnel in their state of trance, Kostya walked out of the hall. Las moved aside and squinted at me, holding up the pistol.

I shook my head, and he didn't shoot.

We simply followed him into the flight control room, where the technicians and programmers were all sitting at their computers like zombies.

When had he found the time to subject them all to his will?

Could he really have done it all the moment he reached Baikonur?

An ordinary vampire can easily keep one or two people under his control. A Higher Vampire can manage about twenty.

But Kostya really had become an absolute Other – he had the entire fine-tuned mechanism of the huge cosmodrome dancing to his music.

They brought Kostya some kind of print-outs, and pointed out something to him on the screens. He listened and nodded but didn't look in our direction once.

A clever boy. Well educated. He studied in the physics faculty, and then moved to biology, but it looked like he'd maintained his enthusiasm for physics and maths. Those diagrams and graphs wouldn't have meant a thing to me, but he was preparing to put up a magical portal directly into orbit. To go out into space using magical means – one small step for an Other, one huge leap forward for all mankind . . .

Just don't let him drag it out too long.

Just don't let Gesar panic.

Just don't let them make that nuclear strike – it won't do any good, and there's no need, there's no need!

Kostya didn't look at me until after he'd opened the prism of the portal. He stared at me with that contemptuous resentment in his eyes. The lips behind the glass moved and I realised what they'd said: 'Goodbye'.

'Goodbye,' I agreed.

With his life-support pack in one hand and the briefcase containing the *Fuaran* in the other, Kostya stepped into the portal.

And then I allowed myself to remove the shield – and all that Power that wasn't mine zoomed away from me, spreading out in all directions.

'Just how do you propose to explain all that?' Gesar asked.

'What exactly?' I sat down on the nearest chair, shaking. How long would the air supply last in a light spacesuit never intended for spacewalking? A couple of hours? It was unlikely to be more.

Kostya Saushkin didn't have long left to live.

'What makes you so sure . . .' Gesar began. Then he stopped. I even thought I heard him exchange a few words with Zabulon. No doubt something about orders that had to be rescinded, about bombers that had to be returned to base. About the team of magicians that would start covering up the traces left by the outrageous events that had taken place at Baikonur. About the official cover story for the failed launch.

'What happened?' Las asked, sitting down beside me. The technician he had unceremoniously shoved off the chair gazed around, perplexed. People were gradually recovering their wits.

'That's it,' I said. 'It's all over. Or almost all over.'

But I knew it wasn't really over yet. Because somewhere high in the sky, up above the clouds, in the cold starlight, the Absolute Other was tumbling over and over in his stolen spacesuit. Kostya Saushkin. He was trying to open a portal – but he couldn't. He was trying to get to the space station drifting past him – but he couldn't. He was trying to get back to Earth – but he couldn't.

Because he was an Absolute Zero.

Because we were all vampires.

And up there, beyond the bounds of the warm, living Earth, far from the people and animals, the plants and microbes, far from everything that breathes and moves and lives, we all become absolute zeroes. Without the free supply of power that allows us to fling bright ball lightning at each other so elegantly and heal sicknesses and cast hexes and turn maple leaves into banknotes or sour milk into vintage whisky.

All our Power was not ours.

All our Power was weakness.

That was what the fine young man Kostya Saushkin had failed to understand and refused to accept.

I heard Zabulon laugh – far, far away in the city of Saratov, standing under an awning in an open-air café with a glass of beer in his hand. Zabulon was gazing up at the darkening evening sky, looking for a swift new star whose flight would be brilliant but brief.

'You look like you're crying,' said Las. 'Only there aren't any tears.'

'You're right,' I said. 'No tears, and no strength either. I won't be able to open a portal to get us back. We'll have to take a plane. Or wait for the clean-up team, maybe they'll help.'

'Who are you?' a technician asked. 'Eh? What's going on?'

'We're inspectors from the Ministry of Health,' said Las. 'So why don't you tell us what you thought you were doing, burning cut cannabis plants by the air intake of the ventilation system?'

'What cannabis?' the technician asked, starting to stammer.

'Arboraceous!' I snapped. 'Come on, Las, I still have to explain officially.'

As we walked out of the hall, several technical personnel and soldiers with automatic weapons came running towards us. But the chaos was so total that no one took any notice of us – or perhaps we were still protected by the remains of the magical shield. At the end of the corridor I caught a glimpse of the German tourist's rosy backside – he was hopping and skipping along, with his finger still stuck in his mouth. There were two men in white coats chasing after him.

'Okay, listen to me,' I told Las. 'Apart from the ordinary human world that is visible to the eye, there is also a Twilight world. The Twilight can only be entered by those . . .'

I gulped and faltered – I'd had another vision of Kostya. Kostya as he had been years ago, the vampire-boy who had no powers yet . . .

'Look, I'm transforming! I'm a terrible bat! I can fly! I can fly!'

Goodbye, Kostya. You made it.

You're flying now.

EPILOGUE

SEMYON CAME INTO the office, pushing Las in ahead of him, as if he was a low-grade Dark Sorcerer caught red-handed in some petty crime. Las was fiddling with a tightly rolled tube of paper, trying to hide it behind his back.

Semyon flopped down into an armchair and growled:

'Your protégé, Anton? You sort this out.'

'What's happened?' I asked cautiously.

Las's expression wasn't guilty at all. Just slightly embarrassed.

'His second day in training,' said Semyon. 'Absolutely basic, elementary assignments. Not even anything to do with magic . . .'

'And?'

'I asked him to meet Mr Sisuke Sasaki from the Tokyo Watch . . .'

I chortled. Semyon turned scarlet.

'It's a normal Japanese name! No funnier than yours – Anton Sergeevich Gorodetsky.'

'I realise that,' I agreed. 'Is he the same Sasaki who handled the case of the girl werewolves in '94?'

'The same.' Semyon squirmed in his chair. Las carried on standing by the door. 'He stopped off on his way to Europe, and wanted to discuss something with Gesar.'

'And what happened?'

Semyon looked at Las indignantly, then cleared his throat and said:

'Our trainee here enquired if the highly respected Mr Sasaki knew Russian. I explained that he didn't. Then our trainee printed out a notice and went off to Sheremetievo to meet the Japanese gentleman . . . Show him the notice.'

Las sighed and unrolled the tube of paper.

The Japanese name was written in very large hieroglyphs. Las had made an effort and loaded a Japanese font into the computer.

But at the top, in slightly smaller Russian characters, it said:

'Second Moscow Congress for Victims of Forcible Infection with Cholera.'

It took an immense effort for me to keep a straight face.

'Why did you write that?' I asked.

'I always meet foreigners like that,' Las said, sounding offended. 'My business partners, and my relatives – I've got family abroad . . . If they don't know any Russian, I print their names in big letters in their own language and something funny in Russian in smaller letters. For instance: "Conference of Non-Traditionally Oriented Transsexuals", "European Festival of Deaf-Mute Musicians and Performers", "Forum of Activists of the International Movement for Total Sexual Abstinence" . . . And I hold the notice up like this . . . turning in all directions, so that everybody who's waiting for someone can see it . . .'

'I get the idea,' I said. 'What I want to know is what do you do it for?'

'When the person I'm meeting comes out of customs, everyone in the place wants to see who he is,' Las explained, unmoved. 'When he appears, everybody smiles, some even applaud and whistle and wave. He doesn't know why they're reacting like that. All he can tell is that everyone's glad to see him, then he spots his name and comes over to me. I promptly roll up the notice and take him to the car. And afterwards he tells everyone what wonderful, friendly people the Russians are. Everyone greeted him with a smile.'

'Blockhead,' I said emphatically. 'That's fine with an ordinary person. But Sasaki's an Other. A Higher Other, as it happens. He doesn't know Russian, but he perceives the meaning of written words on the conceptual level.'

Las sighed and lowered his head:

'I realise that now . . . Well, if I've screwed up, chuck me out.'

'Was Mr Sasaki offended?' I asked.

'When I explained everything, Mr Sasaki was kind enough to laugh long and loud,' Las replied.

'Please,' I said, 'don't do it again.'

'Never?'

'Definitely not with Others.'

'Of course I won't.' Las promised. 'It spoils the whole point of the joke.'

I shrugged and looked at Semyon.

'Wait for me in the corridor,' Semyon told Las. 'Leave the notice here.'

'Actually I collect . . .' Las began, but he put the notice down and went out.

When the door closed Semyon laughed, picked up the notice, rolled it back into a tube and said to me:

'I'll go round the departments with it and give everyone a laugh . . . How are you getting on?'

'Not too bad.' I leaned back in my chair. 'Settling in.'

'A Higher One . . .' Semyon drawled. 'Ha . . . and they used to say everyone has his limits. A Higher Magician . . . you've made a great career for yourself, Gorodetsky.'

'Semyon . . . It was nothing to do with me. It just turned out that way.'

'I know, I know . . .' Semyon stood up and started walking round the office. It was a small office, of course, but even so . . . 'Assistant director for personnel . . . Ha. The Dark Ones will start stirring things up now. With you and Svetlana that makes four Higher Magicians we have. And without Kostya Saushkin, the Day Watch only has Zabulon . . .'

'They can recruit someone from the provinces,' I said. 'I wouldn't object. Or we can expect another visit from a Mirror.'*

'We're wiser now,' Semyon said with a nod. 'We always learn from our mistakes.'

He moved towards the door, scratching his stomach through his linen T-shirt – a wise, benign, tired Light Magician. We all become wise and benign when we get tired. He stopped at the door and looked at me thoughtfully:

'It's a shame about young Saushkin. He was a decent guy, as far as that's possible for a Dark One. Is it getting to you?'

'I had no choice,' I said. 'He had no choice, and I didn't either.'

Semyon nodded.

'And it's a shame about the *Fuaran* . . .'

Kostya had burned up in the atmosphere twenty-four hours after his leap into space. He hadn't calculated his orbit all that precisely after all.

The briefcase had burned up with him. They'd kept a radar fix on them to the very last moment. The Inquisition had demanded a space shuttle launch to collect the book, but there hadn't been enough time.

As far as I'm concerned, it's just fine that there wasn't enough time.

Maybe he was still alive when the fiery kisses of the atmosphere started burning up his spacesuit hundreds of kilometres

* See *The Night Watch*.

above the Earth. After all, he was a vampire, and lack of oxygen might not have affected him as badly as an ordinary Other – like the overheating and overcooling and other delights of outer space that lie in wait for a cosmonaut in a light flight suit. I don't know, and I'm not going to go searching through the reference books to find out. If only because no one can say which is more terrible – death by suffocation or death by fire. After all, nobody dies twice – not even vampires.

'Look,' he used to say, 'I'm a terrible immortal vampire! I can turn into a wolf and a bat! I can fly!'

Semyon went out without saying another word, and I sat there for a long time, looking out of the window.

The sky's not for us.

We weren't meant to fly.

All we can do is try not to fall.

July 2002 – July 2003

This text contains extracts from songs by the following groups: The Hibernation of Beasts (Zimovie zverei), Belomor, The White Guard (Belaya gvardiya) and Picnic; and also by Alexander Ulyanov ('Las'), Zoya Yashchenko and Kirill Komarov.